THE ORC CHIEF'S BAKER

ORC MATES OF FAEDA

BOOK FOUR

AURORA WINTERS

Cover Art By Aurora Winters

Formatting by Weaver Way Author Sevices

ISBN: 978-1-963552-16-4

CONTENT WARNINGS

All content warnings can be viewed on Aurora Winters' website at www.AuroraWintersRomance.com/ books/content-warnings.

PRONUNCIATION GUIDE

I want to preface by saying that however you want to pronounce the characters and locations in my novels is absolutely fine by me. But if you would like to know how I read them in my own head, I have a pronunciation guide on my website here:

https://www.aurorawintersromance.com/books/pronunciation-guide

CHAPTER ONE

TRINIA

This was, without a hint of doubt, the *worst* day Trinia had endured in a *very* long time.

The list of misfortunes was endless. Burned bread, overproofed dough, even *more* missing pans, stolen by none other than her own obnoxious, selfish, rotten—

A pleasant autumn breeze filtered through the trees and Trinia began to sway, spinning slowly. The forest around her was dizzying. The golden leaves were breathtaking as the midday sunlight filtered through to cast dappled shade on her rigid form.

Even though they were upside down.

Blast the Oakwall Village trappers back to the depths. *How* they had managed to create a snare trap strong enough to scoop her right off her feet and fling her upside down was beyond her. Last she checked, they could barely catch a squirrel, let alone any large game.

And yet, here she was, swinging by her feet from a tree like a sack of soiled grain. When she'd first gotten stuck, she'd panicked her way into straining every muscle in her stomach and back before logic caught up with her. There was no *way* she'd ever be able to reach up and untie herself. Her arms might have been strong from hours of kneading dough every day, but the rest of her was more plump than burly. She had no tools with her, only a bag that was barely within reach filled to the brim with rosemary and a few vanilla cookies she'd packed as a little treat.

Now her stomach was all churned up, and the thought of eating made her grit her teeth.

Her ankles smarted almost as much as her pride as she desperately tried to keep her skirt from falling around her face and giving all the woodland creatures a show. She could almost hear the trees snickering as she wriggled against her plight.

She hadn't been hanging long, but it already felt like *ages*. Her head pounded and her mouth tasted a bit metallic. When the trappers finally showed up to get her, she was going to strangle them.

Or never trade her baked goods with them again. Whichever one hurt more.

She let out a long sigh and shut her eyes, grateful for the darkness to soothe her throbbing head. The clean, crisp smell of wet leaves and frost helped to calm her down as she tested the binding around her legs.

Maybe if she shifted her leg back a bit, just to take the pressure off her foot slightly, she could—*ouch!*

She went limp and allowed her hands to drop as well. Her skirt fell around her face and blocked out the view of the forest. She could feel the cold air curling around her thick thighs as her underwear was on full display.

She mused darkly that if *she* didn't kill the trappers for this, they'd likely die laughing at her.

With another long exhale, she looked toward the ground. She could touch the sodden dirt just enough to draw and her eyes drifted over the sketch she'd made.

She *should* be thinking about the work she still had to do. The dozens of rosemary loaves she still needed to make for the trade the next day. *Why* the orcs had ordered so many was beyond her. That, combined with her stupid, selfish sister stealing the pans she needed to bake them in batches, had resulted in the bread taking twice as long as it usually did.

She'd been almost relieved when she'd run out of rosemary and had an excuse to finally get outside. Her mother's bakery held a lifetime of wonderful memories, but it was also small and stuffy and hot, and she just needed a few moments to *breathe.*

She had not, however, expected those few moments to be spent upside down.

Another breeze caught her and the Fades themselves must have had a hand in it because it was *just* strong enough to make her start spinning again. Honestly, she was no dainty flower. She couldn't believe that the wind alone could move her.

But move her it did, and she quickly put her fingers down in the dirt to stop herself before she grew nauseous. She was careful not to touch the drawing she'd done. She retraced the outline with the tip of her index finger to make it clearer.

"I need to *stop* bothering with this," she muttered to herself. But she didn't. Instead, her mind sprung with a new idea, and she quickly moved a few lines around. Adjusting. Redrawing. Until . . .

"There." Satisfaction warmed her chest as she memorized the image. "That will do."

The little floor plan was done, and with it, she'd cut Petr's living room into three small bedrooms for his growing family. If her numbers were correct, the rooms would be just big enough for a bed and a trunk to store their clothes and each would have their own door leading out.

And making this was a complete waste of time.

She swiped the drawing away, muddying her hand and losing her grip on the ground. Her body swung, and she let out a groan of frustration.

A snap from the woods instantly caught her attention.

The trappers!

Suddenly, all irritation evaporated into relief, and she hastily pushed her skirts back up around her thighs. There was nothing she could do to cover her butt, but that didn't matter because she was about to be *free*. Finally!

Free to go back to work baking rosemary loaves in her mother's bakery.

She sighed heavily before calling out. "Here! I'm over here!"

There was no verbal response, but the cracking of twigs continued to her left, getting closer. She tried to swing herself in that direction so she could see who was coming. Would it be Willford or Victir? Fades, she hoped it wouldn't be one of their kids. They both had teenage sons, and she would *never* live this down if one of them saw her like this.

And then her savior burst through the tree line.

But it wasn't a savior at all.

Her skin broke into goosebumps and her hair stood on end. Her gaze narrowed on the animal at the edge of the tree line as her limbs began to shiver with electric energy. Matted fur. Yellow eyes. Long dripping teeth. A sour rotting stench that could only be caused by one thing.

CHAPTER ONE

Blight.

The saber cat skewered her right through with too-wide eyes. It wavered slightly as it advanced on her, stalking its prey. Lips pulled back to display its rotten teeth and drooling pus hung from its mouth. The low growl rumbled right through her gut.

How had a blighted saber cat even come to be in the Rove Woods? This place was supposed to be safe from such travesties!

It took a step forward, and she jerked her leg hard, desperate to flee as terror poured shivering heat down her spine. The knot held her tight. She couldn't run. Couldn't fight!

"Y-you don't want me," she said stupidly as her eyes fixed on the creature's huge claws. They were longer than her hand! "You don't want to eat me! I'm far more fat than meat!"

The cat leaped toward her, swiping with one of its massive claws.

Trinia shrieked and yanked her body away. She felt the swish of the blighted predator hit her skirts as they fell back down. Terror seized her as the fabric cut out her vision, but she could hear the cat scrambling to turn around, snarling and hissing and furious it had missed.

She managed to get her skirt back up when she saw the cat leap toward her again. Claws out. Teeth bared.

Her life flashed before her eyes in a quick, shuddering burst. Fighting with Yerina, even though it was pointless. Lecturing her father before he'd drunk himself into an early grave.

Her mother's smile as she taught her endless recipes. How to knead bread, how to stoke the fire, how to properly haggle an honest trade.

She had that same smile the night she died. Even after being sick for three seasons, she still smiled.

Trinia was going to join her now.

A green blur shot out of the woods and slammed into the saber cat while it was in midair.

Her heart jumped up into her throat and choked her. Her whole body froze in realization.

A whole new kind of predator had arrived—the deadliest predator of all.

An orc.

The snarling of the huge green male cut through her like a hook blade through overproofed dough.

The orc was enormous, and he only wore a tattered pair of leather shorts and some roughly made shoes. Muscles rippled across his back. His dark green skin was riddled with jagged scars. His nearly black hair was cropped short in blunt chunks.

She didn't recognize him.

The cat had recovered from the blow. Its matted tan hide was coated with muck from the ground and the pupils within its yellow eyes were tiny pricks. It snarled at the orc and took a step forward, preparing to pounce again.

The orc let out another harsh snarl, so electrifying that all the hair on her body stood up and the blood in her veins went cold.

Oh Fades, she could hardly move.

The saber cat froze too. Its pupils rapidly dilated. She could see something flicker in its eyes. Some kind of recognition that was usually lost on blighted creatures.

She held her breath, fists clenched in her skirts to keep them from falling back down.

And the cat turned and bolted back into the woods.

CHAPTER ONE

Had she not been strung up in a tree, she would have collapsed in relief.

But her relief was short-lived. Now it was her and the huge, powerful orc.

She scrambled to keep her skirt up, and it only made her spin again. She yipped in horror as her body helplessly swayed around to display her ass to the stranger who'd just saved her.

She was *never* going to recover from this. She may as well stay strung up and let the next predator eat her.

Warmth encircled her legs, and she let out a yip of surprise. She'd not even heard the orc approaching.

Suddenly the tension around her ankles loosened and her body dropped like a ton of bricks.

She squeezed her eyes shut, prepared for a stinging impact against the cold, hard ground.

Instead, she was swung up into *warmth.*

Mercy help her, it was *so* warm! She hadn't realized just how icy cold she was until now. Now that she was . . . she was . . .

Her eyes widened as she looked up at the orc, who held her in a tight embrace.

The male looked just as tense as she did. His dark green eyes were glittering in the dappled autumn light. They were pretty really, a deep green hue that contrasted with the red and yellow leaves reflected in them.

His *teeth*, on the other hand . . . she gulped hard.

His tusks were enormous. Almost as long as the saber cats. They went all the way up past the bridge of his nose. His fangs poking into his bottom lip were so sharp it was a wonder they didn't cut him. His face was riddled with as many scars as the rest of him, old light green lines that marred his features along his cheek, brow, his nose. There was even one on his full bottom lip.

Orcs of Rove Wood Clan didn't display their teeth like that. They tucked their jaws up to hide them away. Kept them concealed so the villagers of Oakwall didn't become frightened. She'd spent her whole life trading with those orcs every fifteen days. She knew each and every one of them personally.

She didn't know who *this* orc was.

He was a *complete* stranger.

The male quickly put her down on her feet and her legs collapsed beneath her.

Pins and needles crawled up her calves and her muscles refused to obey. She'd been hung upside down for far too long.

And then something landed at her feet.

A knife.

And not just any knife. A good quality one. The kind of metal workmanship that the blacksmiths in her village could only dream of producing. It was twice as long as her hand, perfectly sharp, with no rust or divots in sight.

She snatched it up quickly even as the orc began to back off, his hands raised, his body hunched.

He looked about as threatening as a puppy and the oddity of that struck her a little dumb.

"W-what are you doing?" she asked breathlessly, as he continued to move away. He was *littered* with scars. The white lines and pock marks were stark against his dark skin.

She tried to find her voice, but her head was still foggy and scrambling to decide what to ask first.

Who was he?

Why had he given her a knife?

Had *he* been the one to set this snare trap?

Didn't he know this area of the woods was off limits to the orcs of Rove Wood?

She didn't have time to ask a single one because in the next breath, he turned on his heel and bolted into the woods.

And despite all logic, Trinia found her legs, got to her feet, and rushed after him.

CHAPTER TWO

BROVDIR

Brovdir had been with many women in the woods but never once had he ever been *chased* by one.

Fades blast it, the woman was quick. It was like she'd grown up scampering through this forest and knew each tree and bush by heart. She was keeping pace with him.

And he was . . . hesitant to leave.

Not because she smelled good. Certainly not that. He'd smelled plenty of human women and *yes*, she smelled the best of them. Like something sweet and rich he'd not encountered before. It drifted into his nose and made a quiet, comfortable bed in his mind, settling around him like a thick fur on a chilly night.

The feel of her, all full and heavy in his arms, made him long for another touch. He'd held a few women like that, but they'd always felt too light. Like there was nothing on their bones but skin. This woman felt *lush*.

And she hadn't immediately tried to squirm out of his hold.

And now she was *running after him.*

Perhaps . . . he could stop just for a moment.

Brovdir shook the crazed thought right out of his head and kept going.

Blast, he had no time for this. Karthoc would *skin him alive* if he found out he'd spoken to a woman from Oakwall Village. The village Brovdir wasn't even supposed to *know* about. The one he'd sworn to keep secret from the rest of his brethren and go absolutely nowhere *near.*

"Wait! Please come back! I just have a few questions!"

Curiosity seized him so tight he could feel it in his throat. Questions about what? About the saber cat he'd just sent packing? About the knife he'd given her? About why she smelled so good . . .?

Would it really be so bad to just . . .

No. *No!* He would not disobey his Warlord's orders. Absolutely *not.*

"I have cookies!"

As she brought out a cloth package, a delicious aroma flooded everything else. It was sweet and soft and rich. He'd smelled something like it when traveling past a human town before. One of the big ones with elaborate stone walls surrounding the perimeter. The wooden gates had been open as he'd snuck by, so the stench of human bodies was strong, but through that, he'd caught a whiff of surgery bliss. Just one.

He'd dreamed about what the taste might be like . . .

Ah, blast it. He was in *so* much trouble.

"Please? Just for a moment?"

He squeezed his eyes shut and leaned against the trunk of one of the huge fir trees. His head hit the trunk hard, and he wished it would jar some sense back into his miserable skull.

CHAPTER TWO

He never should have gone walking through the woods. No matter *how* badly his throat hurt.

And it did hurt. The only thing more potent than the delicious aroma of this woman and her baked goods was the searing agony gripping his vocal cords. It burned like the foul depths of the goblin's deepest mines and blistered like he was swallowing down magma.

She wanted to ask him questions, but with how much he'd been forced to speak this day, there was no way he'd be able to utter a single word in response to her.

"At least take these as a thank you for saving me!"

Her call made him flinch because it was *right* next to him. Right around the tree. If he tipped his head a little . . .

There she was. With her curly dark hair and her plump cheeks and her bright brown eyes. She was short and curvy, and his fingers itched to touch her again. She was so *soft.*

Her eyes slid his direction.

He jerked back into hiding, but not fast enough.

"There you—oh!"

She tripped over a root right in front of him and—*blast* his warrior reflexes back to the Fades who'd given them to him—he caught her.

And she felt just as good as she had before. His hand curled around her forearm, and he was pleased with how firm her muscles were. She was nowhere near fragile. His other hand rested around her back. The soft cotton of her dark gown was tight around her curves and the image of her mostly bare lower half flashed in his mind. His blood heated up against his will.

The woman sucked in a breath as he tightened his grip on her.

She looked up at him with huge doe eyes through thick dark lashes, and his rational thoughts evaporated right out of his skull. His chest tugged tight as warmth bloomed high. Fades have *mercy*.

She blinked in surprise, but there was not a hint of fear in her beautiful gaze.

"Goodness, thank you." She didn't struggle to escape him even slightly, and he held his breath. "Sorry. I swear I'm not this klutzy on a normal day."

Her voice sounded like a dream, husky and smooth. A little lower than typical for a human female. He wanted to hear more.

"And thank you for saving me too, from that saber cat. I would have . . ." Her face paled, and her throat worked in a gulp. Then she narrowed her eyes at him. "Were you the one who set that snare?"

Ah boarshit. He forced himself to nod.

"So, I suppose I wouldn't have been attacked by a saber cat at all if not for you." She shifted against his grip and his heart squeezed. "Are you going to let me go?"

He did so in an instant, even as his whole body prickled with the urge to resist.

She brushed at her skirts before stepping back. Her arms crossed over her chest and her eyes narrowed in a glare and her gaze did not avert from his face even once.

She was not afraid of him.

Were all the humans from Oakwall this brave?

"I'm guessing you didn't know that orcs aren't supposed to trap in this area of the woods. This is where the trappers from Oakwall hunt."

Blast it! No, he *hadn't* known that. But he wasn't supposed to be anywhere near the village in the first place.

Her brows shot up and she let out a little chuckle that made his whole world brighten. Fades be praised. *That* was the loveliest thing he'd ever heard. Like the melody of his *soul*. It danced through him, energizing and exquisite.

"Don't worry. We aren't going to string you up over it," she said so casually. As if it wasn't a complete revolution to meet a human who didn't want to slaughter him on sight. "In fact . . . I'll let it be our little secret."

She . . . would?

"Here." She dug into a bag slung around her shoulder. The heady scent of sugar and rosemary wafted from it and his mouth began to water as she withdrew a beeswax-covered drawstring sack. "One might think vanilla cookies aren't a good enough reward for saving my life, but, like I said, my life wouldn't have been threatened had you not set that trap so . . ."

She grabbed his hand and he quickly sheathed his claws. As a warrior, he typically would never sheath them. He needed to be ready for an attack at any moment. Soldiers of the Waking Order could appear at any time.

But . . . there were no such attacks like that in the Rove Woods. No human's ready to slice him clean through. No war or strife or even much blight. The saber cat had been the first blighted animal he'd seen since they'd arrived a few days prior.

This place was at peace. Serene. Tranquil.

With women willing to give out food in thanks for saving them instead of . . . he unconsciously reached up to rub the scar at his throat.

The generous woman turned over his hand and plopped the bag into his palm. The weight of it shocked him almost as much as her willingness to touch him without fear.

"Now we're even, I say." She gave a quick nod that bounced her curls. Her nose was adorably round, lips red and plump, and her dark eyes sparkled in the dappled midday light.

Fades help him.

Her brows rose again, and she shifted her gaze from the bag to his face. "You don't have to be so timid. I'm not going to hurt you. Never thought I'd have to assure a *warrior* orc of that. You are a warrior, right? Visiting Rove Wood Clan?"

He nodded slowly.

"I've heard that you warriors come to collect the healing potions every moon or so." She released his hand, and it felt like the sun had set on him. "Really good timing with that cat. You saved my life. Truly. Thank you for saving me."

He could only nod again. His eyes were so wide he could feel the chilly breeze on them.

"You don't have to be worried. My village, Oakwall, we're friendly with orcs. We trade with you twice a moon. I personally have been trading with the orcs of Rove Wood since I was about yay-high." She tapped her skirt where he supposed her knee would be.

Wide-eyed realization brightened her beautiful face.

"Speaking of"—she held up the dagger by the blade to show the handle—"did you make this?"

Her fingers were *far* too close to the sharp edge and his eyes fixed to them as he nodded in response.

"You did make it? I assume . . . that means you have access to metal?"

Access to metal? His brows furrowed, but he nodded.

"Wonderful! That makes things much less complicated."

What . . . was less complicated? This was so difficult to follow.

A smile spread across her face, and Brovdir was captivated by her once again as she gushed, "It's really beautiful work. Great quality. The skill is . . . how often do you visit Rove Wood? I hear the couriers for the tinctures come once a moon or so. Are you here that often?"

His brows pinched.

"Sorry. I suppose I'm muddling things up a bit." She adjusted the knife to hold the handle again, and he breathed a sigh of relief that she was no longer in danger of cutting herself.

And then she extended her hand out to him.

"I'm Trinia, the baker at Oakwall Village, and I'd like to make a trade with you."

CHAPTER THREE

TRINIA

The orc looked at her like she'd just sprouted wings and offered to teach him to fly.

"I swear that honest trade is all I'm looking for." Trinia held up her hands to look non-threatening, only to realize that she still held the knife. She dropped it back down again. The orc still looked about as uncomfortable as a fish on a line, but *Fades help her*, she really needed this!

"I know humans don't trade with orcs much outside the Rove Woods," she continued. "With the war going on, I'm sure it's dangerous even to try. But Oakwall has been friendly with the orcs of Rove Wood Clan for centuries. We really depend on each other since we're so cut off from the outside world. Trading between us isn't just normal, it's *expected*."

Unfortunately, her diatribe had only resulted in making the orc grow stiff and his feet shifted, as if readying to leave.

She supposed she shouldn't have been surprised. The poor

orc was literally covered in scars. Face, neck, chest . . . rippling abs . . .

Her cheeks heated, and she quickly averted her gaze. Most of the orcs in Rove Wood Clan didn't have muscles like this guy and she really needed to *stop* ogling at him before she scared him off.

She could *not* scare him off. She needed him.

She gestured to the bag of cookies he still had held aloft in his palm. "Why don't you try those first?" Maybe a little food would get him to calm down and give her something to concentrate on that *wasn't* his half naked body.

He hesitated a moment before opening the bag. His brows screwed up, and for a moment, she worried he might be upset with the offering. The vanilla cookies inside hadn't cooked very well. Divots in the bottom of the pans she was forced to use caused them to overheat too quickly. They still tasted good, but not *as* good as they could have, and because of that, they wouldn't trade well.

But with this orc's help, her future batches would!

Then he plucked one out—it looked so tiny in his hand—and popped the whole thing in his mouth. He chewed once, twice.

And then his eyes shuttered closed, and he made a strangled noise in the back of his throat. The first sound he'd made so far. She searched his face for any hint of upset, only to find him looking . . .

Looking absolutely adorable.

Her cheeks heated at the stupidity of her reaction. She'd never met someone who looked as much like a *puppy* as this male did. With big pleading eyes and shaggy messy hair and a hesitant posture. She wanted to coo at him and give him a little belly rub.

There was something wrong with her.

She waited a moment. “So, you like them?”

He nodded, his shaggy green hair fell over his forehead and almost covered his eyes. She was sorely tempted to push it away.

Instead, she clasped her fingers together and asked, “How long are you going to be visiting here?” She assumed not long. She knew the orcs who came to fetch the healing tinctures only stayed long enough to pack them up. She’d never met one before now.

The male didn’t respond, only glanced behind himself, as if looking for an escape.

“I assume your forge is at your home clan. How far is it from here?”

He opened his mouth as if to answer, and then . . . grimaced. His hand came up to rub his neck briefly before dropping away.

Her eyes focused on a deep jagged pale green scar that sliced all the way across his neck. Really taking a good look for the first time, pock marks lined each side from where it had been stitched back together. Judging by the size of it . . .

It looked like he’d nearly been *decapitated.*

“You . . . can’t talk?”

He shook his head.

Fades blast her back to the depths. Of *course* they couldn’t make this easier on her. It was one thing to have been born into a village completely isolated from the outside world with only one forge and an extremely limited supply of metal. But now, to inexplicably find someone who *could* only to have them be mute?

This really was the absolute worst day.

As she tried to come up with another plan, she looked back

up at the orc. He was gobbling down another cookie. His eyes fluttered shut, his shoulders slumped, and his face went slack in a way that could only be described as sheer *bliss.*

Trinia blinked as heat tingled from the top of her head all the way down to the tips of her toes. Her stomach knotted up as unfamiliar emotions swirled around her rational thoughts until she had none at all. She could only watch the burly orc stranger melt with pleasure as he ate the food she'd made.

She made treats for literally everyone she knew, and not one of their reactions had made her body quake like this. *What was wrong with her?*

The orc swallowed hard and then looked down at the bag, his expression telling.

"Go ahead and eat them. I can make more and give them to you . . ." Her breath caught as the idea sprang into her mind. "I can give them to you at the trade tomorrow."

His brows screwed up in adorable confusion and her cheeks heated as she cleared her throat. "Like I said, my village trades with the Rove Wood orcs. We come together every fifteen days or so. Tomorrow is that day. Why don't you come?"

He hesitated, face going stricken.

"Is something wrong?" Her stomach twisted up. "Do . . . you have to leave before tomorrow?"

He took a tentative step back, eyes averted.

Desperation gripped her. This was her *only* chance. Her chance to *finally* have more to her life than slaving over an oven day in and day out!

She came right up to him and placed her hand over his arm.

His eyes shot wide at her touch, but she didn't let him go. Instead, she met his gaze firmly, pleading with him with every fiber of her being. "*Please*. I know I'm a stranger, but I swear to you I will make this trade worth it. Just . . . come to the trade tomorrow, even for a few moments."

He was frozen, looking down at her with huge eyes. They flitted from her face downward and her back straightened.

But his eyes didn't linger for long. Instead, they continued to where her hand was still resting on his arm. His skin was surprisingly soft under her fingertips and incredibly warm. He smelled good—heady and spicy, almost like cinnamon, but deeper.

His arm twitched under her touch. There was a thick, raised scar right to the left of her pinky. The white was stark against his pine-needle-colored skin. She moved her finger slightly to stroke it and found that it was almost perfectly smooth.

A hard, hot exhale rustled her hair.

She let out a yip and pulled her hand away. "Sorry! I didn't mean to take liberties."

The smolder in his eyes indicated he absolutely did not mind. It was so hot she lost her breath all over again.

"S-so"—she cleared her throat, cheeks heating up at the intensity of his gaze—"the . . . the trade?"

His eyes flickered down her body again and she wished to the Fades and back she'd been built like Yerina—bright eyes, beautiful golden hair, and curves in the right spots with grace to match. Her sister had been blessed and Trinia had grown up seeing just how many benefits that got her. Had Yerina been here, this orc would have said yes to attending the trade in a *heartbeat*.

Instead, he sized her up for far too long and she could do nothing but hold her breath.

Then *finally*, the orc nodded. And she knew that everything was going to turn out right.

She would ensure it!

CHAPTER FOUR

BROVDIR

Winter wreck him, he was in *huge* trouble.

"Thank you for walking me back. I really appreciate it."

He looked down at her as disbelief swelled in his chest. She was walking next to him without hesitation, keeping an easy pace, unaffected when he drew near enough to reach out and touch her. Though he was very careful not to do so.

"These woods are usually safe. I take walks in them all the time, and I've never seen a blighted animal like that cat around here before. Thank you again for saving me."

He mentally counted how many times he'd walked women through the forest back to their homes like this, keeping close watch for predators, ensuring they didn't lose their way . . .

"And about the trade tomorrow, it's fairly simple and organized. Like I said, we trade every half-moon, so it's *very* routine. There's an open-air structure, and the humans use tables."

Twenty-seven. He'd walked twenty-seven women back to their families like this.

"My table is always set up to the very far right when you're facing it from the orc side. I primarily trade bread and baked goods. I'll bring a good selection tomorrow, but if there's something you want that I *don't* have, do let me know."

And not one of them had ever genuinely thanked him for the task the way this woman had. In fact, most of the time he was *attacked* for his efforts. A thick swallow caused his throat to burn and throb.

"I'll bring paper as well, so you can write things down, er —" She glanced up at him through her thick, dark lashes, and it took every scrap of his willpower not to gaze at her cleavage. "You *can* write, can't you? I realize I never actually asked."

He nodded, resisting the urge to gulp. She smelled so *good*, warm and rich. Just like the cookies she'd given him. Endlessly sweet and comforting . . .

Vanilla. She'd called them vanilla cookies.

"Great." She cast an easy smile that made his heart thunder rapidly in his chest.

Blast, this woman was so *nice*. Far too nice. It was giving him hope.

"You should stop here," she said, and he blinked in surprise that the walk had taken so little time. A quick draw into his lungs revealed the scent of humans was strong. "Orcs are welcome in town, but only with an invitation from the headman."

He'd never heard of an orc being welcomed in a human town under *any* circumstances. Outside these woods, there were some human settlements that were so small they'd been overlooked by the Waking Order. Those very few sometimes allowed trade with orcs, but his kind certainly wasn't *welcome*.

She grinned at him, and it made his heart squeeze. "Don't worry. You won't get in trouble for lingering about. Like I said, we're friendly with orcs."

A tension in his chest eased. How is it that this little human he'd only just met could read his expressions so easily?

"I'll draw up some sketches of the things I want made as well. It's all fairly basic. I'm certain you can accomplish it."

He nodded slowly, especially because she sounded so *chipper*. So easygoing. As if trading with an orc was commonplace. He supposed in these woods it was. He wondered, after he and the warriors left the Rove Woods, how long he would look back on these few moments with awe.

Probably forever.

"Are you all right?"

He snapped his gaze to the woman and found her brows pinched together in mild concern. Concern for *him*. His stomach flipped over, and pleasure zinged through his veins.

Fuck, he was lost. One kind look from her was all it took for him to lose his head.

"You're a little pale. You aren't getting sick, are you? I hope you don't become unwell before the trade."

He could be on his deathbed, and he'd still find a way to drag himself to the trade. He held up his hands and adamantly shook his head.

"Good. Well . . . then . . ." She took a deep breath and then held out her hand to him. "I'll see you tomorrow."

He looked down at her hand in surprise for long enough that she laughed and grabbed him of her own accord.

Now he was *really* stunned. He could do nothing but freeze in place as she gave his clawed, calloused, and scarred hand a gentle squeeze. She let him go far too soon and his hand tingled at the loss.

With that, she turned away from him and was . . . well not *gone*, but going. It felt like the sun was setting on him again and it was barely past midday.

Looking beyond her, he was suddenly struck by the sight of a long line of oaks so tightly compacted they created an intricately woven barrier. It was at least five times his height and so large that he could not see the end of either side.

He was no stranger to barriers around human settlements. The Waking Order liked to build the monstrous structures of brick and mortar around their larger towns. They often had walkways and turrets on which soldiers could shoot their arrows, allowing them to easily cut down any who approached.

But . . . a wall made entirely of *trees*?

It must have been made with magic. Orc magic. By the conjurers of the Rove Wood Clan. Males who were distinct among his kind. Their regal and poised demeanor contrasted his gruff, muscular exterior in every way.

That was the kind of orc this woman was accustomed to. And yet she still had not flinched away from him.

Fades blast him back to the depths. *How* was he going to convince his brother to let him attend the trade with Oakwall? Karthoc had ordered him to stay as far away from Oakwall Village as possible. To not even *breathe* its name.

Trinia paused at the wooden plank gates of the village and turned back. Her rich brown eyes scanned for him, beautiful dark hair caught in a breeze. Her cheeks were flushed deep red, and her lips matched.

She met his eyes, and he could not look away. His fingers twitched with the want to touch her. To trace his hand over the curve of her hip, the roundness of her stomach, her full breasts . . .

A smile touched her lips, and she gave a final wave.

And then she was gone.

He turned on his heel and journeyed back through the woods under a canopy of gold and red leaves that glowed in the afternoon sunlight. The crisp scent in the air was so perfect it almost stung his nose. The whistling of the wind kept him cool as he walked.

This place was so pure and whole. He'd never seen anything like it in all his days. He wondered how he would convince himself to leave when Karthoc finally gave the order to move out and return to Baelrok Forge. He was already dreading the half-moon of travel through dangerous war-torn lands only to return to a fortress that was overcrowded and on the verge of crumbling.

His hand clenched hard around the baked treats, mind working as he returned to the warrior camp on the western side of Rove Wood Clan. The agony of his throat was all but forgotten as he made a plan.

A stupid, foolhardy plan.

And he'd carry it out regardless.

His absence had not been noticed but his return certainly was.

Most of the orcs were seated around the main bonfire for the midday meal. It was stoked high, because there was no threat of attack here. They'd carried in large logs for seating though a few relaxed on the moss and leaf covered ground instead. They chatted amicably, chewed messily, threw large branches over the blaze and let the embers dance upward and disappear against the bright blue sky.

Ogvick, the youngest male in their band, sniffed the air just as Brovdir got within earshot. His eyes snapped to the bag in Brovdir's hand.

Brovdir knew this was a very dangerous game he was about

to play, that it could backfire, but he had to take the risk. He'd thought through every course he could take, and this was truly the only option with any real chance of success. The Rove Wood orcs would stop him if he tried to go to the trade without their permission. They'd catch him using their keen sense of smell and magic if he tried to sneak over.

But they couldn't stop fifty orc warriors all at once.

With that in mind, he unwrapped the cookies and let the full force of the delectable scent waft toward the orcs seated at the fire. They all turned in an instant.

Ogvick got to his feet first. "Brovdir, what is that?"

"Where did you get that?" Caivid was next to reach him. The bright green male was one of his closest friends and did not hide his confusion.

Brovdir swallowed hard, tensed. His throat felt like it was being stabbed by a thousand poison-soaked knives, but he worked out the words. "Woman. Oakwall Village."

"From a woman? What is Oakwall?"

Brovdir hesitated only slightly before he waved his brethren to follow him, tying the bag of treats to his empty knife sheath as he went.

He led them to his brother, Warlord Karthoc, a male who was as powerful as his temper was fiery. Brovdir would be lucky if Karthoc didn't string him up and lash him for this.

But it would be worth it to see the woman again.

The woods concealed the camp well. Rough leather tents blended with the foliage. Each structure was only large enough for an orc to sleep and crouch and was held up using branches they found on sight. The flaps were worn, and some even had holes where arrows had pierced or were stitched up from blades. Every one of them had seen battle or attack by soldiers. They were as tattered and tired as the orcs who lived in them.

As they passed, any orc who'd been relaxing within their tent came out to follow the crowd, curiosity pulling them from their privacy.

The clamoring of orcs as the word spread of this mysterious "Oakwall Village" surrounded Brovdir, and in an instant, nearly all fifty of the warriors who lived within these woods were in tow.

The tent that his brother owned was significantly larger than the rest, big enough to sleep ten grown warriors. As the warlord, it wasn't outlandish for Karthoc to have a more comfortable dwelling, but this was the first time Brovdir had ever seen Karthoc actually *stay* inside his own tent. Typically, his brother reserved the space as a healing house.

But no healing was needed here. Not a single warrior had gotten more than a stubbed toe since they'd arrived in these woods.

Upon hearing nearly his entire camp approaching, the warlord threw back the flap and exited into the fray.

Karthoc was a burly male, taller and larger than the rest of his clan, with just as many scars as the rest of them. His square jaw and cropped short hair made him seem ruthless and unrelenting but there were bags under his dark eyes. Despite being in the Rove Woods, Brovdir's brother was more exhausted than he would be in the heat of battle.

Karthoc's brows shot up as he saw his entire camp of warriors clamoring with questions.

"Fucking calm down. *Calm down!*" Karthoc threw up his hands and walked into the center of the circle of males before narrowing his gaze on Brovdir. "What is the meaning of this?"

Brovdir moved into the center of the circle as well and tapped his throat.

Karthoc scowled. "Your voice is still gone? How much did you speak today?"

The incredulous tone forced Brovdir to give his brother a flat, unamused look. Karthoc had been in a meeting with Chief Ergoth of Rove Wood Clan since before dawn. The discussion of his cousin Govek's ascension to the role of chief was *not* going well, and while Brovdir didn't fault his brother for needing to default the leadership of the warriors onto his shoulders for the time being, it *did* mean he was forced to talk more often than his damaged vocal cords could withstand.

Ogvick spoke up. "Warlord, he says he got this food from a village called Oakwall."

"He smells of a woman!" another proclaimed. "One without the stench of her Rove Wood mate. You told us the only women here were mated to the males."

Karthoc shot Brovdir a withering look that made him feel like a daisy baking in a roasting pit.

"You said the orcs here got their women from outside Rove! So, what did Brovdir mean when he said there was a village?"

"A village with *women* in it?"

"Men too, I'd guess."

"Yes, but no men of the Waking Order."

"Just regular men. And women friendly enough to give Brovdir *food*."

"It's not poisoned, is it?" Hendr, a surly, gruff male with a mossy green hide, moved toward Brovdir as if he were going to inspect the bag. Brovdir's snarl had the bright green male backing off in an instant.

"Don't smell poisoned."

"How could the conjurer orcs not tell us of this?"

"Did you know of this, Warlord?"

"Shut it!" Karthoc roared with such volume it shook the soil beneath their feet. "The lot of you."

The orcs fell into a somewhat tense silence.

Karthoc let out a low, fury laced growl before slowly saying, "Are you defying my *direct* orders?"

Brovdir could feel the shift of energy under his skin. A command from their warlord, especially among these males who were his most elite warriors, took precedence over nearly *everything.*

Nearly.

"*Brovdir.*"

A slither of prickling fear ran down the column of his spine as Warlord Karthoc turned his violent gaze on him. The venom exuding from every one of his brothers' muscles had Brovdir briefly regretting his choice to defy the powerful male's command.

And then Trinia's face flashed in his mind's eye. Her smile. The low sound of her laughter was so clear in his memory it made him feel light.

As if he could sense the defiance in him, Karthoc's claws extended with a *shlink.* The ice dripping down his spine crystallized, and he froze, eyes wide on those claws.

"You have defied me, Brovdir. You will fight in a challenge. *Now.*"

Fuck.

He barely had time to catch a breath before Karthoc struck. He crashed into Brovdir's chest and took him down.

On instinct alone, Brovdir fought, though his mind quailed. There was no winning this fight. But it was win or *die*.

And he did not want to die. Not yet.

Not with Trinia waiting.

He swung his legs out for leverage and thrusted Karthoc's weight off his chest and to the left.

His brother was too quick and strong. He regained his footing before Brovdir had even gotten to his feet and shot forward again. Brovdir barely dodged the male's wrath. The wind whistled next to his ear as Karthoc struck at his face.

The other males scrambled back as Brovdir leaped to dodge the warlord's next attack. He evaded the claws, but Karthoc's foot connected to his gut with a searing crunch.

Brovdir kept his footing, though his vision blurred, and his skin grew clammy. Each breath felt like clanging rocks were in his lungs and his head grew hazy from the lack of air.

Karthoc swung again. This time with a balled fist to the side of Brovdir's head and his vision blackened. The hit to the ground jerked his mind back to the present just as Karthoc swung him onto his stomach. His head burned as the warlord grabbed his hair, yanked him back until he thought his spine would break, and displayed his neck.

The prickle of Karthoc's claw against the scar on his neck brought true terror. The line was perfect and stark against his dark skin, a path for any to trace with their weapon. To slice open the wound and finish the job that sneaky human had started so long ago.

But Brovdir did not feel the slice of his skin. Instead, his brother hesitated. Pain bloomed as the panic died out. His body shivered and convulsed for air. Blackness bled around the corners of his eyes.

He could feel the eyes of his brethren on him. None would help him. None would want to defy their warlord, knowing their fate would be to die in the muck, gasping for air with tears streaming from their blackening eyes.

"*Give me her sweets.*"

Brovdir's ears prickled with every word, and he grappled with his own instincts.

"*Give them*." Karthoc snarled into his ear. Each word shivered through him like the slice of a blade. He may as well have cut his neck then.

And then Trinia's face flashed again. Her red lips. Her round cheeks. Her eager words.

She wanted to trade with him.

He couldn't do that if he was *dead.*

As if sensing his submission, Karthoc dropped his head and got up from his back. Brovdir fell flat onto his stomach, hissing with agony. Pain radiated up his spine with even the most minor twitch.

But he struggled past the pain. Orcs were not so easily broken, and he'd been through horrors far worse than this.

He got to his knees, assessing the damage in a swift instant. Both lungs were punctured by his own ribs. His legs were partially numb from the crack in his spine. His arm hung limp and was drenched in blood.

He sliced the beeswax pouch away from where he'd tied it to his sheath and with his good arm, held it toward Karthoc, though his whole body buzzed with the desperate need to keep it.

Karthoc snatched it from his grip and Brovdir watched in muted devastation as he threw back his head and upturned the bag over his unhinged gaping maw. Not a single crumb was spared from his brother's jaws.

He swallowed thickly as the memory of the taste of them coated the back of his tongue and made his mouth water.

Then Karthoc took the bag and brought it over his face. The Warlord's deep inhale brought agony slicing though Brovdir anew. He was taking in Trinia's *essence.* Pulling her vanilla and sunshine deep into himself and learning it in a way that Brovdir could only dream of.

His brother's ruthless and relentless strength was nothing compared to the powers he kept hidden. Powers Brovdir sensed but had never spoken of. Secrets that had never been vocalized even when they were alone.

His blood skittered in horror as Karthoc's green eyes dilated until they were nothing but black and his muscles fought to rise. To meet the challenge. He would *not* let his brother take this woman from him! He'd rather be dead than—

"Fuck, Brovdir." Karthoc's voice was a low whisper on the wind. So quiet that had Brovdir's ears not been so keen, he would never have heard it. "How'd you find her like *this* . . .?"

The tension drained out of him with a pop and shock took its place. Warm, tingling shot down his every limb. Vanilla curled up in his mind and sunlight baked his broken flesh.

"Give him a fucking tincture before he dies," Karthoc snapped, throwing the beeswax bag onto the ground. "I've won this challenge."

Brovdir collapsed, unwilling to expend any further energy as he waited for someone to give him a magical potion. Relief had sapped his strength. Challenges between orcs were the main way warriors resolved their conflicts and most did not end in death, but the warlord was not typically one to be merciful.

Ogvick appeared at his side and pushed him onto his back. The pain was nearly enough to make him blackout but then the tincture was thrust between his lips and the familiar taste of bitter swill thundered into his muscles like the spike of an electric shock. His bones knitted back together with agonizing snaps and his lungs refilled. The blackness of his eyes faded. His arm stitched itself, leaving only a coating of sticky cold blood to remind him it had nearly been slashed off.

The moment it could function, Brovdir snatched up the discarded bag out of the muck and hid it in his fist. It still smelled sweet despite being covered in mud.

"I'll challenge you, Warlord."

The silence that descended was so chill it was like winter had come early. Brovdir managed to his knees, though his healing was only half done, and stared at the foolhardy male that had just challenged their warlord *moments* after Brovdir had been cut down so easily.

Toj stepped forward, looking only half as burly and not nearly as swift as his warlord counterpart. But still he repeated strongly, "I challenge you!"

"*What*?" Karthoc's single word was a breathy, shocked hiss. He had not a single mark on his hide to heal. Brovdir hadn't even gotten a chance to strike.

Toj rose his square chin. "I will fight you for the right to meet these humans of Rove Wood."

"No," Karthoc said, more in disbelief than anger.

"I challenge as well." Hendr spat thickly upon the ground and Brovdir was not surprised in the least that the obstinate male had stepped forward. "You know how dire our numbers are. How can you, as our leader, not give us a single fucking chance to woo these humans? How can you deny us the opportunity to find a conquest? To have *sons*?"

There was a hum from the other warriors. Murmurs of agreement.

And Brovdir exhaled low and slow, releasing tension as his plan was set in motion.

"This is *my command*," Karthoc growled low in his throat. "It is the agreement that Ergoth and I came to."

"Since when do you follow that whiney Chief Ergoth's whims?" Hendr demanded.

Brovdir went cold as he watched as Karthoc's face flattened. His brother's jaw clenched, his eyes narrowed. His long, sharp claws slunk out from between his fingers. They still dripped with Brovdir's blood.

"I have *never* followed Chief Ergoth's whims." Karthoc's words were low and clipped. "And in this, I only based my decision on *his logic*. The only way the Rove Wood orcs can sustain their numbers is through the peace with Oakwall. We cannot risk threatening that peace by thrusting you warriors into their midst. You know how different you are from them."

"We wouldn't scare them off!" Ogvick argued.

"It is not worth even *risking* it. Without the human women playing conquest, the conjurers of Rove Wood would die out in just a few generations, and their healing tinctures will die out *with* them."

"But we have magic wielding warriors now," Ogvick said.

Karthoc scowled. "Yes, and you *all* know that those warriors don't know how to do a blasted thing with their magic, let alone produce enough healing tinctures to sustain our legions."

Another tense silence descended as the warriors considered their warlord's words. Brovdir could see their thoughts on their faces. The will to obey their leader's commands fighting against the desire for a son.

The crowd of orcs grew restless. Their muscles bunched and flexed. Their feet took steps forward. Their murmuring hardened into mutters of indignation.

Karthoc's eyes widened just slightly in shock that his incredibly loyal subordinates would argue, but Brovdir wasn't surprised. Deep in his guts, he'd known which one would win.

He knew which *he* would choose if he were in their place. Which one he *had* chosen.

"I challenge you, Warlord Karthoc. For the right to at least meet these humans," Toj said again.

"I will not—"

"I am done with talk!" Toj stepped forward as the others stepped back. "Fight me or concede."

Karthoc swung back his fist without preamble and slammed it hard into the stomach of the male. The orc crumbled instantly, gasping and writhing.

And then another male stepped forward.

And another.

And more still.

Every male in the circle stepped forth, ready to challenge the moment Karthoc cut another down.

Brovdir felt a hard pang of remorse in his chest.

He'd preyed upon their kinds' primal urge to bear sons. To find conquests. The drive to protect and woo and win was instinctual. As ancient and strong as the Fades themselves.

Every male in the clan would fight Karthoc, one by one, despite odds and logic. They would follow Karthoc into certain doom under any other circumstances, but the need to breed was a force the warlord could not fight against.

His brother would have to fight every male in his party to stop this now.

It was no wonder he'd wanted to keep Oakwall a secret from the males.

Karthoc growled low under his breath, fury lacing his every muscle.

"*Fine*," he snarled so harshly dread skittered through Brovdir's veins. "I will find a way for you to meet with the humans of Oakwall Village. But you will obey every one of my orders while we do so."

Brovdir felt his still stitching body tingling hot with *relief*.

His plan had worked.

His brother had conceded to the will of the warriors.

"Yes, Warlord." A chorus of low voices sounded as the males stepped back.

"And if any one of you steps out of place, I *will* challenge you. You may be my best warriors, but I will not have insubordination among my males. I'll cull you the very moment you step out of line." Karthoc's tone left no room for denial or hesitation. He meant what he said.

The males all nodded silently and returned to their duties. But there was a distinct energy to them. A kind of unsteady relief and brightness.

Hope.

There was not one of them in this party who had not tried to have a son before. And very few of them had succeeded.

But now, with these humans who did not fear or hate them, they might stand a better chance.

Trinia's bright face flashed behind Brovdir's eyes and his breath caught in his newly healed lungs.

"Brovdir." Karthoc's voice was a deadly low rumble that quaked in Brovdir's gut. "Follow me. *Now*."

Brovdir didn't hesitate and he finally clambered back to his feet, though his body danced with the anxiety that he was about to be challenged again. And this time, Karthoc would not hold back.

He followed his brother into the tree line and deep into the forest, past deep springs that were bubbling with healing waters, over fallen logs that were springing with life even in death, around huge trees so thick all fifty of the Warlord's orcs could fit inside the mighty trunk.

Karthoc finally paused in a clearing and Brovdir stood tense under his brother's furious gaze.

"*What happened*?"

Brovdir tried to speak, but all that came out of his throat was a painful garbled growl. The old wound in his neck might have been physically healed but only rest would allow his voice to return. No magic could bring it back.

"I *told* you to avoid Oakwall. It was my *highest* order. How dare you defy me?"

Brovdir swallowed hard, willing his voice to come so he could explain about the blighted cat that had forced his hand.

"Did she even *see* you, or are you just caught up in your own blasted urges?"

Brovdir stood tall and tapped next to his eye.

"She really saw your ugly mug and didn't run screaming?" Karthoc snapped. "Fuck, I guess the warriors might have a *blasted* chance."

Brovdir's gut twisted at the slight.

"I'm already run to the bone trying to get Ergoth and his half-crazed conjurers to see a little *reason* and now I must also add this task as well! How the *fuck* am I going to manage to introduce fifty orcs to the people of Oakwall? It's not like I can just show up at their gates! They'll think we're there to fucking *invade*."

Brovdir swallowed hard, worked for the last scrape of volume he had and managed a single word.

"Trade."

"Trade." Karthoc searched his face, but Brovdir's eyes were already watering from the pain that single word caused and he was unable to force another. "What do you mean *trade*?"

Brovdir held up the beeswax bag and pointed toward Oakwall.

Karthoc searched his face a moment, putting together the parts. "Do you mean the trade Ergoth mentioned? The one they all do with Oakwall twice a moon?"

Brovdir nodded, tapped his chest, the bag, and then pointed toward Oakwall again.

"You saying she *invited* you to the trade?"

He gave another swift nod.

"Fuck, Brovdir." Karthoc threw back his head in exasperation. "Why didn't you just sneak over there and leave the rest of the males out of it? Why did you have to make this whole thing a fucking blasted *mess*?"

Brovdir gave his brother a dry, unamused look and jerked his head toward the Rove Wood Clan.

"Don't give me that. You could have managed to get there somehow . . ." Karthoc paused, swiped a hand over his face, and cursed under his breath. "Fuck. Fine, you're right. They would have spotted you. You really met a woman from Oakwall? One whose never met a warrior outside *Govek*, with your teeth looking like *that* and all your battle-hardened scars, and instead of running like the rest of them do, she fucking gave you sweets and invited you to see her again?"

That pretty much summed it up.

Karthoc groaned and Brovdir held his breath.

And then the tension finally left his brother's frame, and he thought he might collapse with relief.

"Brovdir, I can't decide if I want to slap your back or punch your nose clean off your face."

Brovdir huffed a laugh and was pleased to find that his ribs had fully healed.

"You really have made my work here so much more complicated. I was hoping we could *leave* in a few days' time. I'll never be able to tear my males away from the women if they start getting their attention."

Brovdir brought arms up and rocked them as if he was cradling a babe.

Karthoc sighed heavily. "Yes, I know it would be worth it. I know better than all of you."

His brother's expression turned haunted and Brovdir lowered his arms back down. Karthoc hadn't had a son, but he'd gotten incredibly close. The woman he'd taken for his own had lived with them for nearly a year and none could deny how dearly their warlord had cared for her.

Brovdir did not know what had transpired between Karthoc and Ovinia in those final days before she had gone, but whatever it was still haunted his brother even now.

"Fine." Karthoc's voice was flat. "I will find a way. Perhaps Govek knows of a path we could take that would conceal our sight and scent and prevent Ergoth from stopping us. But you are going to owe me quite a weighty boon. I hope you realize that."

All the pain was instantly forgotten, and he gripped the bag tight in his hand. Pleasure and contentment burst through him at the warm, sweet scent.

He'd pay any price to see his woman again.

CHAPTER FIVE

TRINIA

"Ulia, it's *really* fine. You don't need to apologize again."

Trinia's stomach was already in knots and the sun had only just started to rise above the horizon. The bakery was too hot from hours of endless baking. Many of the loaves had overbaked or underproofed. There just hadn't been enough time.

But somehow, she'd managed to get all the rosemary bread done *and* finish three batches of cream buns. She was sure the orc would like them. He'd liked the vanilla cookies, and the buns were just a larger, more flavorful version of them.

She'd made the vanilla cookies too just in case.

Fades, she hoped this would work. She really didn't have any other options.

"I still feel bad. I know your cart is stuffed to the brim this week," Ulia said from where she was perched on the edge of the counter. Her golden hair looked particularly shiny and soft, and her bright blue eyes were outlined with a dark charcoal line. She wore her best yellow cotton gown which accentuated her slender figure and brought out the peachy color of her creamy skin.

Trinia was the *exact* opposite of her friend, but with a lifetime of being compared to her sister, she had plenty of practice stopping herself from making harsh comparisons. She'd never minded being a larger woman, and her body had always been able to carry out every task she needed it too, from long walks in the woods gathering herbs to carrying stacks of trays full of bread loaves.

Except for, of course, pulling her massively overwhelmed hand cart. But she doubted she ever would have been able to accomplish that, even if she were slender.

"My father feels terrible he can't help you as well." Ulia's face was a mask of contrition and her red lips were downcast in a pretty frown. "I swear I'll find someone to pull your cart for you."

"There's no need, Ulia, really," Trinia said with a wave of her hand. "I'll just ask Victir to do it."

"I suppose," Ulia conceded quietly. Trinia crossed the room and put on her thick gloves and pulled open the front of her huge cast iron oven.

The loaves were placed directly on the baking rack which left dark lines etched into the bottoms as they burned. She could only fit half the number she usually would inside because the oven was too hot at the back without the barrier of a pan and would scorch them even worse.

She carefully pulled one of the loaves near the hottest part of the oven and let out a ragged sigh as she examined the burned bottom and still doughy top. They weren't done, but any longer and the bottom would be completely inedible.

Trinia took out the loaves and tossed them onto the counter with the rest of the burned ones.

"*All* those are bad?" Ulia hopped down from her spot and came over to look.

"Yes," Trinia muttered. "I hope the Fades ruin Yerina for stealing all my good pans. She took the round ones last night while I was collecting herbs! Can you believe it?"

"Yes?" Ulia said with a little shrug. "Your sister is as selfish as they come, and the witch—er, I mean, *Leanna* has been stricter about her trades recently. Especially for her face colors and lotions."

Trinia blinked. "Stricter with her trades? Why?"

"I can't get her to tell me." Ulia pushed back her hair and edged away from the oven's heat. "Something about the ground being too wet and preparing for disaster? You know how she is."

Trinia did. The woman's mind was addled half the time. Leanna was one of the people she gave free bread to a few times a moon. The young woman's family had been exiled from Oakwall during her great-grandmother's generation and often struggled in the winter.

There were many residents who struggled to get enough food during the harsher season. And it was coming in fast this year. The trees had lost their leaves so much sooner and the air had a particularly icy bite to it.

Trinia picked up a couple of the loaves from the pile that weren't too bad off. "You're going to get more rouge from Leanna, right? Could you take this to her? Take this one to Rebekia too. Her arthritis has been acting up, and she wasn't able to knit anything for today's trade."

"Of course." Ulia took the loaves from Trinia and went to wrap them in one of the cotton cloths. "You know, you probably wouldn't be so overworked if you didn't give away so much bread for free."

Trinia shot her friend a hard look. "I wouldn't be overworked if I could get new pans commissioned. But *someone's* father has horded all the metal to make nails and tools."

"It's not his fault he's gotten so many commissions for beds lately," Ulia countered with a shake of her golden head. "It seems like everyone and their brother has outgrown sharing beds with their siblings all at once. Outgrown their houses too." She tapped her fingers and asked hesitantly, "You . . . didn't happen to find time to think about Petr's house plan, did you?"

Trinia snorted in amusement as she recalled just *how* she'd managed to carve out time for it. "You know what? I actually did. The diagram is on mother's desk."

Ulia hurried over and picked it up. "This is perfect! Father will be thrilled. Thank you for helping. We really do appreciate it."

Trinia cast her a teasing grin as she reloaded the oven. "So appreciative that you can't pull my cart today."

"I'm sorry!" Ulia said, looking far too contrite.

"I'm teasing, Ulia." Trinia finished off in the oven and quickly closed the door. Blazing biscuits. It was *hot*. She moved around toward the window to get some fresh air. "I like doing room designs, you know that."

"Yes, and my father wouldn't be able to make half the furniture he does without your measurements."

"I'm sure he'd be able to figure it out." Trinia threw open the window. The crisp morning air filtered into the hot bakery and cooled her overheated skin. It smelled incredible. Like clean frost and decomposing leaves. There was a light layer of fog around the tops of the red and yellow trees. The sun was starting to peak through, casting the neighboring cottages and dirt paths in a golden glow.

"I doubt he would," Ulia said. "He poured over that living space for days trying to make everything fit before he came to you."

"He didn't have to do that." Trinia turned her back to the window. "He can come to me anytime. I really do like doing that kind of work."

Ulia gave her a smile that was laced with pity, and Trinia's stomach twisted. "I know. He would take you on as an apprentice if you weren't already the town baker."

Trinia forced the thoughts of what could be out of her mind and went back to readying the loaves. Ulia was right. This bakery was more important than anything else. It had been in Trinia's family for four generations. Every tool, every piece of furniture, every floorboard held precious memories of her mother, grandmother, and great-grandmother. She could still feel them here, surrounding her while she worked.

"Perhaps you could do both if you hired help?" Ulia ventured.

Trinia shook her head. "It's not about help. It's the lack of tools. It takes five times as long to make my loaves without the pans. And the blacksmiths just don't have the metal to spare to make new ones."

They didn't . . . but that orc might. Hope swelled in her chest again.

"What do you think Yerina did with them?"

"I don't know. I've asked more times than I care to admit." *Begged* more like. "But she's not talking, and you know how she gets when she wants to keep a secret." Gloaty and smug and infuriating.

"She must have traded them to someone in town. Have you asked around?"

"I have, and not a single person I've asked could tell me what she did with them either."

There was a pause as the mystery settled heavily on them both.

"It's your own stubbornness that's holding you back, Trinia." Ulia broke the silence. "You could easily get the metal for your pans if you would just play conquest for an orc like a normal woman."

Trinia's stomach twisted up harshly at her friend's words. "No."

"But metal for an orc son is a perfectly reasonable agreement!" Ulia countered. "Rowena played conquest because she wanted cherries through the winter. *Cherries*. Metal is far more difficult to come by, especially since the goblins aren't around anymore."

"Exactly. It's likely none of the orcs even *have* enough metal to make my baking pans."

Unless they had access to metal *outside* of the Rove Woods like the orc potion courier did.

Her eyes drifted to the cookies and cream buns, which were stacked on the end of the counter. Underneath was a stack of paper and a drawing of the pans she wanted made with all the specifications he would need to get it done.

This would work. *It had to.*

"I have it on good authority that Sofidin has a collection of harvesting tools his grandfather invented."

Trinia scowled at her friend. "And how would you know that?"

Ulia blinked innocently. "Oh, you know, word gets around."

"You better not have been asking *for* me," Trinia said darkly.

"Why not?"

"Because I'm not going to be playing conquest and I don't want to get their hopes up!" Trinia said sharply. "Are you really saying I should convince Sofidin to give me his family heirlooms just so I can make baking pans?"

Ulia scratched the back of her neck. "What good are heirlooms if you have no one to pass them on to?"

Anger made Trinia's jaw tight. "I'm not doing it, Ulia."

Ulia threw back her head in frustration. "Come *on*, Trinia! You're as bad as my sister was, but even she got there in the end."

"She didn't get there, Ulia. Savili is *mated* to Iytier. She wasn't a conquest. She didn't carry an orc son in exchange for boons. She had a babe with her *life partner* because she *loves him*."

"You make it sound like playing conquest is something dirty," Ulia said flatly. "It's completely normal. Far more normal than taking one as a mate. We have *three* conquests carrying orc sons in Oakwall right now."

"I'm not saying it's dirty," Trinia said quickly. Playing conquest for an orc was one of the primary ways women in her village made their own way. "I'm just saying it's not for me."

"Are you just worrying about being able to work while you're pregnant?" Ulia asked. "Because I could help you!"

"It's not that," Trinia assured. She already had a big belly. She doubted that being pregnant would make too much difference.

No. Instead, what flashed in her mind was the sight of the little orc boys coming to the trade moon after moon. They'd play and laugh and barely even notice the human women, let alone bother with which one might have carried and birthed them. And the women didn't care much either. None of the women who played conquest regularly were married.

None of them had ever wanted children of their own.

Trinia touched her rounded stomach and worried her lip.

"Are you worried you'd get too attached to the orc baby like my sister was?" Ulia asked. "Because there are options. Jenida and the others who play conquest all the time have loads of tips. Like finding someone else to breastfeed the baby for you and finding things to keep busy."

Trinia narrowed her eyes. "You've talked to the other conquests about this before?"

"I mean . . ." Ulia averted her eyes and then spouted, "or you could be like my sister and just get mated to the one you're playing conquest for."

"It wouldn't work, Ulia," Trinia said dryly. "I cannot be mated to an orc."

"But why not? Savili has been so happy with Iytier. Why not allow yourself the *chance* to be happy too?"

Trinia cast her friend a hard look. "Even if by some strange chance one of the orcs I've known my entire life suddenly fell in love with me out of nowhere, he wouldn't be allowed to live in Oakwall Village and I have to be here every day, from dawn till dusk, to run the bakery. How can I be mated to an orc and only see him once every fifteen days to trade?"

"You . . . could set up a bakery at Rove Wood?"

"My great-grandmother *built* this bakery, Ulia. My grandmother and mother worked together to furnish it. Even the creation of the oven was overseen by them personally. I can't leave it behind."

Ulia let out a long, ragged sigh. "You're too loyal for your own good, Trinia."

It wasn't just loyalty; it was tradition. But that wasn't something that Trinia felt she could explain to Ulia or anyone. Trinia spent almost every moment in this bakery. She even *lived* here, sleeping on a cot made of old flour sacks near the back behind the oven. Her devotion to this place wasn't just out of a love for her family, this bakery was her entire *world.*

Despite this determination, Trinia found her eyes lingering on the paper in Ulia's hand. The little floor plan she'd made. The delight she'd felt in the task even as she was swinging upside down . . .

She pushed it out of her mind and went back to concentrating on finishing the rosemary rolls.

The door to her bakery swung open and Trinia barely managed to withstand a groan as her sister walked through the door.

Yerina was dressed to impress. The tight red wool gown she wore accentuated every one of her sister's best features. Wide hips, large breasts, golden shimmering hair. *Where* she had gotten such a gown was a mystery Trinia didn't want to know the answer to, though she suspected the missing pans had something to do with it.

"Govek is coming to the trade today!" Yerina announced without preamble.

Trinia felt her eyebrows arch despite herself, and Yerina, unfortunately, latched right onto her surprise.

"It's true, sister! The headman *just* spoke to me about it! And he's going to be named *chief* too. Can you *believe*?" Yerina came over and clutched Trinia on the shoulders so tightly it stung. "Now I need your help. I need you to make your *best* bread for me to give to him so I can win him back."

Trinia's mouth dropped open, and she sputtered. "I don't have time for that. The trade is in an hour!"

"Of course you'll make time for it!" Yerina demanded. "I'm going to become *matriarch* of Rove Wood Clan. Just think of what that means for *you*."

Almost nothing from what Trinia could figure. She tried to move out of Yerina's grasp. "Even if I did have time, you've stolen all of my good pans. I *couldn't* make extra bread for him even if I wanted to."

Yerina pursed her perfect red lips. Her cheeks had rouge on them and her eyes were darkly outlined with coal. She must have visited Leanna and gotten the woman to fancy her up. "Did you not hear me, sister? Govek is going to be *chief* and I'm going to be *matriarch.* It would be rather stupid of you to defy me in my time of need, wouldn't it?"

Trinia's breath caught as Yerina's expression turned hard and calculating.

"Maybe if you helped instead of stealing, things would have moved in your favor."

Yerina moved her attention to Ulia, and Trinia shifted out of her sister's grasp.

"This has nothing to do with you, little girl," Yerina said as Ulia rose her brows. Trinia also thought it was a stretch to call the nineteen-year-old a little girl. "Don't you have some wood to whittle?"

That quip got Ulia to scowl. But instead of backing down, she said, "I'm shocked you would even believe the rumors that Govek would become chief. We all know that's never going to happen."

"Headman Gerald told me *himself,*" Yerina said with far too much confidence. "You would know if you'd gone to the meeting this morning."

Trinia's back straightened and Ulia gave her a quick look

before saying, "My parents were there. I can find out the truth from them. I'll come back and let you know, Trinia."

Trinia nodded, but no relief came when none of Yerina's haughty arrogance diminished.

She was telling the truth.

"I'll ask Victir to come pull your cart for you too," Ulia said quickly before giving a little wave and hurrying out the door into the chilly autumn morning. A tiny breeze cooled Trinia's overheated skin and then it shut tight, and she was trapped in the stifling heat.

With her sister.

Who was now curling up her nose at the sight of the blackened mess. "What is *this*? I can't give this to Govek! When did you become such a horrible baker? Mother would be ashamed."

Trinia took a deep breath and ignored her bait. "Headman Gerald is really going to *let* you come to the trade, Yerina?"

"Of course he is!" Yerina tossed the burned bread she'd been examining back into the pile causing a handful of loaves to roll off onto the floor. "After you almost got attacked by that blighted cat yesterday, he knows how important it is to get Rove Wood's best hunter back in our good graces!"

That was true. Govek had been the one to cull most of the blighted animals. But still, after everything Yerina had done and all the lies she'd spread, it seemed more prudent to keep her *away* from Govek.

Trinia wasn't going to argue. She knew from experience that if her sister was involved, it was best to stay out of it.

"So, hurry up! I need Govek's favorite bread. What's his favorite bread?"

She'd been with the surly orc for the better part of three seasons and she didn't know what he liked to eat? Gathering her courage, Trinia tried again. "Perhaps if you gave me back the pans you've taken, I'd be able to bake better and would have something good enough to turn Govek's head."

"We aren't *bargaining* here, Trinia." Yerina's voice was so cold it sent a little shiver down Trinia's spine. "And I didn't steal anything. Half of everything in this bakery is *mine*, or did you forget?"

Of course she hadn't forgotten. Yerina would never *let* her forget that their drunkard of a father, in all his great wisdom, had made sure to leave the *entirety* of their family home to Yerina but mentioned nothing about the bakery. As such, by village law, it was owned by both of them equally.

Yerina snapped her fingers. "So, the bread. Hurry up!"

"He doesn't like my bread, Yerina. He makes his own," Trinia said with a heavy sigh. "He makes his own *everything*."

Yerina chuckled and rose her nose into the air. "That's only because he's so loyal to me that he doesn't even want to *glance* in another woman's direction. Not even to broker trades."

Trinia could not believe how delusional her sister was, but she wasn't about to comment. She'd learned long ago that even a sliver of snark Yerina's way would result in an onslaught of petty, manipulative, and cruel retribution that would last for days, sometimes moons.

It was far better to swallow her tongue and pride, even though it took every scrap of will she had to do so.

"What about these?" Yerina picked up one of the cream buns, and Trinia's breath caught.

"Not those. He wouldn't like those," she said too quickly.

"And why not? You think he's not good enough for them?" Yerina took a big bite and then scowled before picking up a cotton cloth and spitting it out. "How much *sugar* did you put in these? It's no wonder you're so fat."

Trinia's throat tightened, but getting angry would only give Yerina more ammunition, so she hid the fury as best she could behind a mask of indifference.

It must have worked because Yerina's eyes scanned the room instead, looking around in a way that was far too scrutinizing before her attention landed on a stack of cutting boards.

She needed to get her sister out of here *now*.

Trinia hurried over to one of the cheese breads that were still cooling and hurriedly wrapped it up. They were technically part of another orc's order, and she hoped he wouldn't mind too much she was missing one. "Here. Take this."

"What is it?"

"My best cheese roll. Govek will love it," Trinia lied through her teeth. Govek would probably *hate* it. Or at least she hoped he would. She hoped he wouldn't take Yerina back. No good had come from their relationship, only chaos.

Yerina snatched it out of her hand with a haughty smirk. "There. Was that really so hard?" She moved off toward the door and Trinia breathed a sigh of relief. "Maybe if you wagged your tongue around someone's cock as often as you wagged it at me, you'd have a man by now."

Trinia's anger rose in the back of her throat and made her eyes sting, but she kept the hurt off her face as her sister turned back and looked her up and down.

"Though I suppose he would also have to be *blind*." With that, Yerina burst into cackles and slammed the door behind her.

Trinia clenched her fists hard enough that the bite of her nails distracted her from her anger. Yerina might have been the *pretty* sister, but her vindictive personality hadn't won her any friends. Only men who were desperate to win her favor. Men who often tripped over themselves to give her *anything* and all because she was beautiful.

Would . . . looking nice help win over the orc?

On a hard exhale, she moved off toward her clothes trunk and began digging toward the bottom to find her best dress. The one she saved for weddings and funerals.

It was tighter than she remembered, hugging her curves and stretching around the buttons. She wasn't the least bit surprised she'd gained some weight. She hadn't been able to trade for anything but bread supplies since her pans had been stolen. She was *always* in the bakery, constantly kneading and mixing and baking.

The moment she felt like she had time to herself, she'd look over and see dishes that needed scrubbing or a counter that needed to be wiped or bread that needed to be shaped and scored. She opened her eyes in the morning and her *work* was the first thing that greeted her.

She couldn't escape.

Her throat felt tight. She shouldn't want to escape. This was her legacy. Her mother and grandmother and great-grandmother's life's work. It was an honor to carry out that tradition.

She got up and brushed off her skirts, going back to work.

Readying for the trade was always a hassle. There was so much to *do*. So many orders to arrange and pack, to say nothing of the goods she'd use to decorate her table. Today was especially difficult because she had the added task of evaluating each loaf and deciding whether the black at the edges was too bad to be traded.

But she got it done, and soon enough, Victir was loping up the dirt path to her bakery. She gave the usually quiet and calm older man a smile and found the white bread she'd made him.

"Here you are, Victir. Thank you for pulling my cart again today. The family isn't coming with you?" His wife and four children almost always attended the trade with him.

Her brow creased as she looked at his empty arms. He didn't reach out to take his bread. Her hand lowered slowly. "Where are your fabric samples? Are you not going to take any commissions today?"

His eyes grew wide a moment and then understanding flooded his warn features. "You weren't at the town meeting this morning."

"No, I wasn't. What's going on?"

Fades, what if the trade had been called off for today?

"The warlord is visiting with an entire troop of warriors."

Trinia felt suddenly very cold. Her eyes grew so wide she could feel the breeze on them.

Victir continued as if he didn't see Trinia had been struck dumb. "Viravia sent word late last night and asked if they *all* could attend today. Nearly fifty of them."

"How . . . er . . . I mean, *when* did they get here?"

"Couple days ago now."

It all clicked rapidly into place then. The scars, the way he'd easily scared off the cat, the good quality knife and blacksmithing skills . . .

The orc wasn't a courier, he was a *warrior*.

A warrior for the dreaded Warlord of Baelrok Forge.

She went so dizzy with shock that for a moment she thought she might be sick.

"I don't feel right going."

She rapidly came back to present and stared at Victir in muted shock.

"I appreciate you making the bread, but I'll not bring my kids into a fray of orcs worse than Govek. No matter what the headman says." Victir stepped away, shaking his head. His graying hair was messy, as if he'd been raking his hands through it in worry. "Sorry, Trinia, I won't be able to pull your cart today."

Her breath caught in her throat and her stomach clenched so hard she felt nauseous. "But . . . Victir, I can't pull it on my own." It was stacked full this time. There was just no way.

And it didn't matter who the orc was. Warrior or courier, she *needed* to get these pans commissioned. She just had to!

"Terribly sorry," Victir stepped back. "I've got to get back. My kids are in a right state."

With that, he turned on his heel and began a rapid pace down the path into town.

"Victir!" Trinia called, stepping forward to follow him, but the set of his shoulders told her it was no use. His mind was made up.

She watched him disappear into the trees. Smoke from the other homes curled above the oaks and firs. A few of the log cabin houses peeped between the foliage. Just a short way up the path stood the gates of Oakwall. All those who were attending the trade today would already be gathering there.

There was no time. The trade group would be leaving in a few moments. Anyone who was attending the trade would be gone. She'd not be able to find another person to pull for her.

She left her wares and her cart and bolted toward the gates.

CHAPTER SIX

BROVDIR

"Just look at how pissed our dear uncle is," Karthoc chortled as he led the group of warriors along the woodland path. The scent of the deep forest was soothing despite the predicament they had gotten themselves into. The chill of the morning was harsh against Brovdir's naked upper half but that wasn't the reason he regretted not finding a shirt to wear.

Would the woman be put off by his scars?

His stomach twisted with the thought. It wasn't logical to think she might, considering she hadn't been put off the night before. But when he looked back at his brethren, some of whom had far fewer scars and much more attractive frames, Brovdir couldn't help but wonder.

Would he be compared to them? Would she change her mind about him?

"He's up there griping. I just know it," Karthoc said with a grin, bringing Brovdir's attention back to the matter at hand.

He looked toward where Chief Ergoth was sitting in a cart at the front of the line. His white hair was braided intricately, and his posture was high and regal.

His voice was low, calculating, and too quiet for Brovdir to make out, but the tone was clear.

"He's plotting," Brovdir said quietly. He was trying to save his voice.

"He can't do a fucking thing." Karthoc's grin was so wide Brovdir could see all his teeth. "The headman invited us personally. No getting around that."

Behind him, Brovdir sensed all the other warriors were equally thrilled as they followed the dozen or so wagons that the orcs of Rove Wood were pulling to the trade. The carts were full of fruits and vegetables that should never have been able to grow in this late season. Sweet strawberries. Hearty potatoes. Corn and carrots and barrels of fish.

Brovdir's mouth watered. The males of Rove Wood ate so *well*. He was lucky to find an edible root in the outer forest. And half the time he was attacked while he was trying to dig it up.

"That woman—Viravia—must have a keen sense of negotiation." Karthoc didn't look even the least bit frustrated by the slow gait. At the rate the Rove Wood orcs were going, a dung worm would arrive faster than them.

"I wonder what she said. She wouldn't even answer the door last night when I went to ask for aid. I was certain she was ignoring me on purpose. Almost burned my nose to *bits* waiting. Just my luck the woman would be obsessed with sage." Karthoc sniffed loudly and scrubbed at his nose with the back of his hand.

Of course the woman wouldn't open the door. She was

likely terrified. Warlord Karthoc was so surly he'd scrap with the air if it rustled his hair too hard.

Karthoc glanced at the warriors behind them, some of whom were getting rowdy in their excitement. Brovdir wished he was back there getting distracted by this talk.

But he had to follow the Warlord's orders. That was his duty.

"Keep in line!" Karthoc barked, and the warriors quieted back down.

Brovdir gritted his teeth against the anticipation gnawing in his gut. What if the woman wasn't there? What if she'd decided not to attend after all?

"She must not trust Ergoth either, or she would have questioned why I was trying to go around him." Karthoc's brow furrowed up. "Blasted odd, that. She was Tavggol's wife after all. You'd think she'd trust her mate's sire."

It was an oddity that Brovdir's tired mind did not have the desire to puzzle over.

Karthoc chuckled. "Though I suppose I can't blame her. Ergoth is about as trustworthy as a snake."

That was the truth. There was something odd in his uncle's voice, a strange tension Brovdir couldn't place. It made his hair stand on end.

He was so tired of worrying about it. The Rove Woods may have been peaceful, but Brovdir would have taken a hard battle over calculating manipulation any day.

His woman's beautiful rounded face flooded his memory, and his tension quieted for a moment. Her sunshine scent flitted into his mind. The memory of her curves under his touch made his fingers twitch.

It had felt like the world had dimmed when she'd walked away.

But now, at this very moment, she was walking back to him.

He had far too much blasted hope. He begged the Fades not to destroy it.

Beside him, Karthoc snorted and Brovdir tensed up, glancing at his brother, wondering if he'd missed something.

The warlord scrutinized him with a hard look that made Brovdir resist shivering. He could feel Karthoc's eyes burrowing deep into his mind, like he was reading it.

"Go join the ranks."

Brovdir blinked in surprise at the sudden order.

"I can *feel* you tensing up. That's not like you. Go calm down. Now."

He couldn't fight a direct order from his warlord so he stepped out of his place at Karthoc's side and slowed his steps until he was walking among his brethren and their easy chatter.

Fades, it felt different here than up there. The tension was almost gone as the boisterous nature of the warriors surrounded him.

"I don't fucking know what I'm going to eat while I'm there. Why are you asking stupid questions?"

It was Hendr's voice who cut through the fray. He sounded more irritated than usual.

"Fuck off, Hendr. You don't want to talk to me then go fucking walk somewhere else." Ogvick's voice was tense and low, and Brovdir could hear the hurt in it.

"I can walk where I Fades blasted please," Hendr growled.

"I know *one* thing that's certainly going to be there to eat." Caivid's voice was light as he broke the tension between the two. "*Women.*"

Brovdir sucked in a breath as his clothes suddenly felt too tight. The very thought made his mouth water.

His woman had smelled so *good.*

Would she let him taste her?

"What the fuck are you even talking about? Karthoc would have your hide if you tried to eat one of the humans," Hendr snapped.

Brovdir looked back toward them, drifting closer to try to see if Hendr was jesting or if he was a complete idiot.

Caivid was looking at him in disbelief before he muttered, "I feel sorry for any woman who ends up lying with you, Hendr."

The burly males face contorted with anger. "Say that again, you wretch."

Brovdir's fists balled as he readied to break up the inevitable brawl.

"You think a woman would actually want *our* mouths on 'em? Teeth and all?" Ogvick's question instantly painted a delicious picture in Brovdir's mind and his attention swiftly turned away from the fight.

He imagined her sweet taste as her thick hips rolled under him. What sounds would she make? What motions? Would she try to squirm away or edge in for more . . .

"Are you thinking about the woman you met?"

Brovdir snapped out of his little daydream at Caivid's question. The male was grinning and Brovdir couldn't deny the truth. The woman was all curled up in his mind like a red squirrel in its burrow. Getting cozy and warm and ready to stay there all winter.

"What did she look like?" Ogvick asked from behind them.

Brovdir scowled at the male but Caivid said, "Must have been a beauty to capture your attention so well."

Hendr snorted. "You must be jesting, Caivid. Brovdir would fuck a boulder if the shape was right."

Brovdir honestly couldn't decide if he wanted to laugh or slug the male in the face.

"You're one to talk, Hendr. You're so ugly, I doubt even a boulder would let you fuck it," Caivid remarked dryly.

"Shut your fucking mouth."

"Hey!" Karthoc snapped from the front of the line. "No brawling or I'll send you back to camp."

That shut the whole group down. Usually at least one or two would make a quip at such an odd order. Brawling was as common as breathing for the warriors. But no one wanted to risk losing the chance to see the women.

Brovdir knew the silence would be short-lived, and he welcomed the start of the banter again, even if he was on the butt end of the joke.

"Wonder if they'll be any with dark hair," Ogvick said, and Brovdir blinked in surprise. Not that the chatty, young male had spoken first but that he had preferences when it came to females.

"Getting picky, huh?" Caivid asked with a grin.

"You ain't got room to be picky either," Hendr muttered. "Your mug's as ugly as Brovdir's. You couldn't pull an elk in heat."

That was a low blow. Ogvick could at least pull a desperate buck if he wore the right pelt.

"Why the fuck you acting like you got an angry weasel up your ass, Hendr?" Caivid growled.

Angry? More like a horny and jealous weasel.

"Just trying to be fucking rational," Hendr snapped. "These women have seen nothin' but rosy-assed Rove Wood conjurers. Look yourself straight and tell me you think they'd choose *you.*"

At least Caivid looked like he could protect a woman. Most

of the conjurers were so scrawny a stiff breeze could blow them into next week.

"Why wouldn't one pick me?" Ogvick narrowed his eyes. "One chose Brovdir!"

"She wants to *trade* with him. Doesn't mean she wants to fuck him."

Brovdir felt his chest tighten at the truth of that. What she wanted was his blacksmithing skills. She likely did not want his company.

"Doesn't mean she *doesn't* either. What if what she wants to trade is for pleasure?" Caivid asked.

His mouth went dry at the thought.

"She won't be finding it in Brovdir," Hendr muttered.

"How would you know?" Caivid asked with a sly grin. "You lay with him before?"

Brovdir snorted with laughter as Hendr sputtered with indignation.

Before the male could think of something logical to say, Caivid butt in. "Brovdir's been with more women than the both of us combined. If anyone's gonna pleasure a human, it's him."

His good humor cooled quickly. Because although he'd technically been with many women, he'd never actually *lain* with any of them.

He was just as inexperienced as the rest of them.

"All that and nothing to show for it," Hendr said darkly, shooting Brovdir a hard look. "Should have a dozen sons being raised at Baelrok by now, but you haven't even *one*."

Brovdir let out a low growl, and the male looked away. It was no question that the first priority for most of these warriors was to produce sons. Their kind were being steadily eradicated by the Waking Order.

Despite this, Brovdir could not bring himself to do it.

He was always with Karthoc. On the move. Seeing battle almost daily. The few sons that the Warlord's elite had produced were fiercely trained in combat and would one day know just as much hardship and war as Brovdir did himself.

How could he in good conscience bring a child into such chaos?

"We all know how difficult it is to get a woman to lie with us let alone carry a pregnancy to term," Caivid said. "You really going to blame Brovdir for *their* deception?"

"All's I'm saying is that if it was me, if it was *my* son at stake, I'd never let the woman want for *nothing*. She'd be so satisfied and hale she'd never want to leave my side, let alone condemn my son."

Brovdir wasn't going to argue with that. But a woman willing to open herself up to an orc and accept his care was as rare as blooming roses in a dark cave.

But perhaps . . . his brave little woman who survived a wild cat and chased down a warrior orc was the kind of beauty who thrived in adversity.

"That's enough!" Karthoc's order punctuated over the talk. "We're almost there. Fall in line! Brovdir, get back up here now!"

Brovdir's chest tightened with anticipation as he followed his warlord's order and went to stand behind him on the left.

"Ergoth did something."

Brovdir went tense. Karthoc's eyes were trained toward the front cart where Ergoth was sitting. The male looked so regal in his bright robes. Cloth that shimmered in the dappled sunlight and revealed how privileged he was. It looked almost slippery.

"I think Ergoth just released a bird," Karthoc muttered. "I

saw it swoop low and then dart into the trees. And why are we moving so Fades blasted slow?"

Brovdir rose his brows.

"You were right. He is plotting something." Karthoc hummed a low growl under his breath. "Don't think questioning him now would do much good. He'd just stonewall us. Just stay alert for anything unusual."

He nodded.

"I wish Tavggol were still with us."

He blinked in surprise as he looked at his brother. Karthoc wasn't one for sentimentality and rarely spent any time mourning, but there was a sorrow in his eyes that unsettled Brovdir. It reminded him of how Karthoc looked after Ovinia had fled.

Hopeless.

But the warlord quickly shook the grief away and said, "Can't change the past. Can only move forward. And mark my words, I *will* be moving forward with this, no matter what Ergoth does. His time in that seat of power is coming to an end."

Brovdir said nothing. There was nothing *to* say. Karthoc was his superior, and he was a warrior. He was born to follow orders and had never strayed from that Fades-given duty.

No matter how badly he may want to.

He took a deep breath in through his nose. It was a long way off yet, but on the wind, his keen sense of smell picked up the heady scent of dozens of humans.

One of whom was his woman.

He would be with her soon.

CHAPTER SEVEN

TRINIA

Trinia was out of breath, half panicked, and completely illogical by the time she'd made it to the group waiting to walk over to the trade.

She had to find someone to help her. She just *had too.*

The open area in front of the village gates was large enough to fit every craftsman in the village and their wares comfortably. On a typical day, it would be nearly filled with fifty or more families bustling around. Children would be dashing through the yard and causing mayhem. Elderly folk usually sat beneath the only tree, which was barren of leaves now. The chatter would be loud and the laughter even louder.

But not today. Today Trinia walked onto the packed dirt meeting place to find near silence and less than twenty craftsmen. The ones who had shown up looked somber and nervous. Even Hermest, who was usually bellowing greetings and booming with laughter, was silent as he waited next to his cart of cheese and milk. Those who did speak, did so in hushed tones as they strapped their goods down tightly. Some of the folk who typically had cows or donkeys to pull hadn't brought them today.

Trinia's stomach twisted as she looked around for anyone who might be willing to pull her cart for her.

She gave up after a few moments and made a beeline for the headman, who, as usual, was at the head of the line with his ledger book, checking in folks attending and writing down their inventory. Even if he hadn't been in his usual spot, Headman Gerald would have been easy to find. He was the tallest man in Oakwall and one of the burliest, though that didn't make him any less spry. He had a boisterous laugh and a kind smile and had done right by their village since he'd been made headman nearly twenty years prior. He always went out of his way to help and such altruism is what got him voted into the position year after year.

She hoped that would extend to her today.

Headman Gerald saw her rapid approach and looked up. In his eyes, she could see how exhausted he was.

"Trinia, hello, you're here to check in?" The eager tone of his voice had her both nervous and relieved.

"I want to, it's just . . ." She glanced around, still searching for someone, *anyone* who could pull her cart.

"I swear to you that the warriors mean no harm. They only want to trade. And, as promised, every family who participates is guaranteed one full elk processed and dried by the warriors themselves. *Just* for participating. Additional trades with them can still be bartered."

Trinia snapped her gaze back to Headman Gerald, eyes wide. One full elk *each*. It was a wonder more families hadn't chosen to attend.

But then . . . she could also understand their reservations.

They were probably picturing the burly and quick-tempered Govek. His reputation for being unpredictable and dangerous was so prominent, it nearly drowned out all the good his hunting skills had done for them over the years.

"It's true," Headman Gerald said with a quick nod. "I just received the bird from Chief Ergoth a few moments ago with this offer. They are bringing the elk to the trade as we speak. Before they only made assurances of our safety, but they must have realized that some of our members might be put off and well . . ." He looked out over the group readying to trade with a long sigh. "Hopefully, this means that more will participate. I am thankful that you are here, at least. Your goods will be well received."

"I want to participate, but Victir decided not to come. He can't pull my cart for me."

The headman blinked his gray eyes wide. "Ah. That is a problem. Let's see . . ." He glanced around, obviously seeing what she did. A complete lack of anyone who could help.

"Tobbis can pull for you, Trinia."

Trinia turned around to find Ronhold, the best and most profitable cobbler in Oakwall, approaching with his teenage son. The young Tobbis looked about as grumpy as a sheep on sheering day, but his father's burly hand was so tight on his shoulder there was no way to escape.

Ronhold and his family were well-known in the village, both for their outgoing personalities *and* their extremely successful footwear business. They were the only cobblers in Oakwall with the skill of making boots large enough for the orcs' feet.

And it earned them *many* successful trades.

"Tobbis would be happy to pull for you today, wouldn't you, Tobbis?" Ronhold looked to his young son, daring him to argue. The boy looked at the ground and grumbled something Trinia couldn't hear.

"Are you sure, Tobbis?" Headman Gerald obviously saw the same hesitation that Trinia did.

"Course he's sure!" Ronhold slapped his son's back. "Now go on son. Follow Trinia back to her cart."

Trinia wanted to argue, but she didn't have any room to do so. The only other option was to have the headman himself pull for her. So, she waved Tobbis toward the path to her bakery and examined his scrawny arms. She wondered if he even had the strength to pull all her goods.

"It's just this way," she told him.

"I know where the bakery is," he grumbled indignantly.

She rose her brows.

"Tobbis. Get along," Ronhold said sternly.

The way it was worded had Trinia wondering if he meant get along *on your way* or get along *with her.*

Didn't matter regardless. He was just pulling the cart for her. If she did a good enough trade, the load would be lightened, and she'd be able to pull it back on her own. The awkward walk would only last for a small portion of the morning.

She glanced at Tobbis from the corner of her eye. The boy was about as gangly as a wet noodle with stringy brown hair to match. His mother and father had lush waves of auburn hair and she wondered how their son had gotten the color but lost the texture. Or perhaps it was just unwashed?

The silence was deadly uncomfortable, and she ventured to break it.

"You . . . just turned nineteen, didn't you? A few days ago at that," Trinia asked casually. She only remembered because his mother had commissioned a cake. "Congratulations on becoming an adult."

He blinked at her and then scratched the back of his neck. There was a noticeable sweat stain under his arm. One that was dry. There were old oil and food stains marring the cream-colored cotton too. How many days in a row had he worn this shirt? Trinia edged away, grateful she wasn't downwind.

"It was. You and your sister didn't show." His voice was rather flat and Trinia's brow pinched with confusion. Being the only child of the best cobbler in town, the man who made *all* the orcs' shoes, Tobbis was well renowned. Their meeting hall had been used to host his coming of age party and the entire village had been invited.

But he'd noticed *her* lack of attendance?

"I'm sorry. I was too busy with the bakery." A pang of guilt twinged in her chest.

The boy just shrugged.

"Figured. Baking's about all you ever do."

The flat disinterest in the boy's tone made her feel a little slighted. "People do like bread," she remarked with narrowed eyes. Her goods were considered more of a luxury than a staple in their village, but she still had regular customers.

"I guess." He started to pick at his teeth with his pinky finger. "The cake was dry."

Trinia's mouth fell open, but before she could quell her urge to trip him, he said, "How come Yerina didn't attend, then?"

That question had a mite more emotion behind it. Emotion akin to a toddler whining about a toy. "I don't know. I'm not my sister's keeper."

"I thought her and Govek were broken up."

"They are."

"I'll give him a what for if he tries to touch her again."

Trinia barely managed to prevent a snort. Govek could flatten this little boy with his big toe.

"She's going to the trade today. I saw her looking all prettied up. She going to meet someone?"

Trinia rolled her eyes. Of course, Tobbis would have a crush on her sister. Just about every teenage boy in town did. "She wants Govek back."

"What?" the boy shrieked so loud his voice cracked.

"He's going to be the next chief of Rove Wood Clan," Trinia remarked carefully. "Or have you not heard?"

"I heard. I thought they were bad jokes!"

"Well, according to my sister, it's not. And she wants to be matriarch of Rove Wood, so . . ."

"What the blast does she even see in that beast anyway? All he's got is a raging, dangerous temper and a hideous crooked nose."

"It's probably the muscle. Most women like a man who's fit." Trinia mused over how fit the orc from the woods was. He was a little leaner than Govek, a little less intimidating.

And he was probably one of the warlord's fighters. Her stomach twisted up again.

"You've got no room to be arrogant."

Trinia snapped from her thoughts. "Excuse me?"

"You think you could get someone with muscles looking like you do? You could stand to skip a few meals."

White hot anger flashed down Trinia's spine and her palm itched with want to slap the mouth right off this wretch's face. Her voice took on a deadly low tone. "*Excuse me*."

"N-nothing." The boy actually shrank away a bit and Trinia gritted her teeth. Slapping him would do no good in the long run. Even if it would feel mighty fine right now.

Tobbis hurried over to her cart and lifted the handles. He wouldn't even meet her eyes as he adjusted the weight of it. She walked to the back to load up the last few bags.

"You aren't thinking of riding, are you?"

"And what if I did?" she said low and slow. "You saying you're so weak you can't even pull a full cart? No wonder Yerina doesn't give you the time of day."

The boy went so red she almost felt bad, but he just turned his head away and muttered something under his breath that he was lucky she didn't catch. Then he began to pull.

Trinia's mood was dark as she picked up her basket of cookies and creams.

This would be a very long walk.

By the time they returned to the meeting place, the village gates were open and the group was heading out. They both hurried to catch up.

The Rove Woods were lovely this time of year with bright orange and red leaves streaming down from a crystal blue sky. The sunshine dappled the world in color and the bright green moss growing on all the rocks was covered in dewdrops as the warmth melted away the hard freeze from the night before.

And beauty was completely ruined by her walking partner. Between shooting her scornful looks and muttering slights she couldn't quite hear under his breath, Trinia was starting to wonder if it was even worth it to bring her cart at all. She could have bundled everything for the warrior orc and carried it herself.

But what was done was done and she certainly wasn't going to waste any time. She set a grueling clip, wanting the walk to be over as soon as possible.

She couldn't stop thinking about how to convince the warrior to make the pans for her. The sketches were tucked safely away in her skirt pocket. The sweet buns and cookies were carefully placed on her cart. Would he like them? Should she have made something else?

Would one of the prettier girls in the village turn his head instead?

What if he decided he didn't want to trade with her after all and instead wanted to pursue a conquest? She bunched up her skirts.

"Slow down!"

She blinked in surprise and glanced to find Tobbis laboring beside her, gasping for breath with his forehead beaded with sweat and his underarms drenched despite the chill of the morning.

"Sorry." She slowed her gait.

"I'll just go walk in back." Tobbis gasped.

And then Ronhold showed up right next to him, pulling their own cart of shoes. "Keep pace. It's shameful to leave a woman walking alone."

Trinia wasn't fond of Tobbis but she felt a little bad as he paled. His labored breathing continued as they walked on.

"So, Trinia, what new wares do you have?"

Trinia blinked at Ronhold's question and was especially shocked that his eyes were alight with eager anticipation. "Just the usual things today."

"Oh?" His disappointment was obvious.

"Did you want something specific?"

"No. I was just thinking that you might try to experiment with more profitable wares more often. Your mother used to come up with new recipes every moon."

She had. Trinia's mother had adored baking and was naturally gifted. Trinia was good, but she more often than not followed the recipe exactly.

"Your bakery could be far more lucrative if you found recipes that were irresistible," Ronhold continued.

"I didn't think my profitability would be much interest to you." Trinia tried to keep the tension out of her voice. Ronhold was a shrewd and calculating businessman. He had an innate ability to find town laws that worked in his favor and did not hesitate to run competitors out of business.

She'd never worried though, because baked goods were the absolute furthest thing from shoes.

Ronhold's expression shifted then. His eyes narrowed and his lips quirked into a grin, and Trinia suddenly felt incredibly small next to his large, burly frame.

"We'll talk of this another day."

Talk of what?

"Have a good trade, Trinia," Ronhold said as he moved off toward his usual spot.

The trade took place in a location set an equal distance between Oakwall Village and Rove Wood Clan. The flanking birch trees on either side of the makeshift pavilion spiraled up and twined their branches into a roof to keep the weather out. The mossy ground was soft underfoot. The lower branches of the trees had been adjusted to make tables for each of the craftsman to display their goods upon. It smelled of clean soil and crisp frost. Birds sang in the trees above. There was an overwhelming sense of peace here. Serenity.

It had been built by the orcs using magic centuries prior and she wasn't sure if the tranquility was their doing or if it was simply a byproduct of their communities' continued harmony. Hundreds of years of calm that allowed their two communities to survive in these woods. They were the only ones here. The nearest human town and orc clan was a full two-day walk out of the Rove Woods completely. Too far to even trade with.

But there was security in that. Outside these woods, there was *war*. A war that Trinia never even thought much about. A war that the orc she was going to trade with today had seen firsthand.

Tobbis dropped her hand cart hard enough that it *thunked* to the ground and a few loaves fell out. She would have censured him for dropping them, but the boy was red faced, covered in sweat, and shaking from the exertion. His shoulders were hunched as he took a moment to catch his breath.

Despite her irritation, she was grateful he'd pulled her cart. She grabbed one of the rosemary loaves from the pile and held it out. "Here. Thank you for helping me."

The winded boy screwed up his nose. "I don't like rosemary."

Trinia let out a long sigh and looked back at her wares. Despite her reservations, she plucked one of the vanilla cookies out of the basket and held it out.

His face brightened, and he snatched it. He returned to his father's side without a word, stuffing his face as he went.

Trinia rolled her eyes. Despite having just come of age, he still acted like a child.

She spent a few long moments organizing her goods and watching for the orcs to arrive at their end of the trade. They usually arrived soon after the humans did.

Had something held them up?

What if the male wasn't coming?

Would he—

A rumble sounded in the trees beyond the trade pavilion and her heart jumped into her throat as the first orcs broke through the foliage.

The faces were too familiar.

There was an almost audible sigh of relief from the folks

around her as their green neighbors gathered in their usual way. They parked their handheld carts at the edge of the tree line and organized their crates of produce, barrels of fish, and a few furs.

Not much meat.

That lack didn't go unnoticed by the men around her. Hermest, who was setting up his cheese and milk with narrowed eyes, went so far as to mutter under his breath about the orcs being liars.

"I don't see the warriors either though," Jock, his adult son, replied. "Perhaps they changed their minds?"

The relief and frustration that resulted from that statement was palpable in the air. For the last season, there had been constant complaints about the lack of meat. Govek was the lead hunter and since his break with Yerina he hadn't attended any trades.

"There they are!"

Her heart jumped into her throat as the burly orc warriors appeared at the tree line.

Fades, were they *different*!

The Rove Wood orcs were slender, regal looking with wispy hair, thin tusks, and graceful movements. These orc warriors were the exact opposite of grace. They were burly, with heavy brows and even heavier steps. Trinia swore she could feel their footfalls vibrating the ground beneath her.

The hush that fell over the villagers was punctuated by Headman Gerald's exuberant welcome. He marched right up to one of the orcs without preamble. One whose hide was littered with scars and whose thick leather belt was lined with empty loops where weapons once hung.

Forged weapons.

Trinia's hand clutched at her chest, and she went up on her

toes as if that would help her see through the sea of green bodies.

She needn't have bothered. Movement caught her eye, and there he was. The orc from the woods.

Headed right for her.

He still had no shirt on and his rippling abs looked like they'd been sculpted by the Fades own hand. The raised, puckered lines of his scars distracted her. He had so many.

She swallowed thickly and jerked her gaze back up to his face. His expression was unreadable, dark eyes shadowed by thick, flat brows. They hooked her right in the gut and stirred up her heart until it was fluttering. The scar on his neck looked even more ghastly in the shadowed lighting of the canopy.

This was it. He was here. She just needed to be confident and find the right words to convince him to trade with her.

She prayed that she could.

CHAPTER
EIGHT

BROVDIR

Fades help him. She was a beauty.

The vanilla scent of her was tinged with something warm and sweet. It wafted across the open space and curled in his nose like a vice, yanking him toward her unbidden. He knew he was moving too fast, the storming of his feet was too hard, but he couldn't stop himself.

And the woman's expression didn't flicker at his rapid approach. In fact, she seemed eager. An actual *smile* played at her lips.

When was the last time a woman had smiled at him?

Had one *ever* done so?

He was nearly at her cart when a man loudly proclaimed to his left. A human man with beady eyes, a scruffy chin, and a table of milk-based goods that smelled nearly sour.

"What are you doing?"

Brovdir paused, examining the human male. His muscles

tensed under the scrutiny of the man's gaze. What did it look like he was doing?

"Hermest, he's obviously here to trade. As they all are. I suggest you calm your nerves, or do you want to be on bad terms with these males?"

Fades breath, her voice was lovely. His eyes slid back to the woman, with her soft, round body and crossed arms. Her eyes were shooting daggers at the man who had spoken, and they were far sharper than any one of Brovdir's claws.

"An apology for Hermest. He's not so bad, just stubborn and opinionated." She shot the human a harsh look as she said this and he bowed his head, appearing almost sheepish. The other men who had started to walk over also turned away.

Such power wielded with such ease.

"Here." She waved him over with one hand and picked up a round ball of dough with another. It was a little larger than her fist and was so soft it gave slightly around her fingertips.

Brovdir would have snatched it and gobbled down the offering in an instant had Trinia not leaned over the table just so. Her breasts were pushed up and together and threatened to burst from her bodice. Her neck elongated as she tipped her head and her curly dark hair fell down to drape over her cleavage.

Were they as soft as the food she was offering him? Maybe if he was quick, he could touch and no one would notice.

Save Trinia, of course.

"Trinia."

His woman snapped to attention and looked toward the woman who'd called her.

The blonde woman who approached was younger and had somewhat pointed features. She glanced between him and the woman, eyes lingering on his bare chest.

"Trinia, I've come to help with your table," the woman said, eyes still on him but not in a malicious or antagonistic way like the man's had been. This young woman was more curious than anything.

"I don't really need any help, Ulia," his woman said with a light frown marring her perfect features. "But thank you."

"Who's your friend?" the blonde asked and Trinia's scowl deepened.

"He's an orc I'm going to trade with."

"But you've met him before? How? When?" The girl was almost bouncing with eager interest.

"We can talk about that later."

Yes, after I am done with her. Will I ever be done with her?

"I want you to talk about it now," said Hermest, who was back to listening in. His beady eyes were narrowed into a suspicious squint and his fists were balled.

Brovdir rose an eyebrow in amusement. The male was about as threatening as a mace made of wool.

"Go back to your trading, Hermest."

"How come you knew about the warriors, but we didn't until this morning? Have you been keeping secrets?"

"No," Trinia said flatly.

"Then explain how you know him?"

Trinia crossed her arms over her chest and it pushed up her breasts delightfully. He needed to look away. *Look away!* "I've told Headman Gerald everything already. He's the only one who needs details on this matter."

"I think you've got a duty to your community as well. You should be telling us if there's a band of dangerous—"

"Hermest." Trinia's cold tone made Brovdir's spine straighten. "Do you think Headman Gerald would be pleased to hear you speak this way?"

The man shut his mouth so quick it all but disappeared off his face. Apparently, keeping the peace was very important to the villagers.

Such an oddity.

"I don't owe you an explanation for anything, Hermest, but I will tell you this, the warrior orc standing before you saved my life yesterday. For that, he has earned my respect and trust. I will not allow you to insult him without cause."

Brovdir's eyes were so wide he could feel the morning chill on them.

Was she defending him? Truly? He felt weightless.

"How about we take this somewhere more private?"

The question Trinia asked was directed at Brovdir specifically. She met his eyes with a quiet determination that warmed his chest and made a smile curl at his lips.

She took his smile as agreement. "Good, I just need to grab something from my cart." She hurried over to the wooden hand cart packed with every kind of delicious looking bread one could fathom. There were things he didn't even recognize. Items that smelled so divine it was unreal.

"Oh, and here."

She approached so rapidly he had no chance to back off. She reached for him and gentle fingers clasped around his hand, bringing it palm up.

She plopped the round ball of bread into his hand. The weight of it surprised him. He'd thought it would be light as a feather with how soft it was. His fingers melted into its perfectly tan surface.

"Go ahead and eat. Let me know if you like it." She turned away and suddenly it felt like every being at this trade was looking at him, watching him.

He wasn't going to let that stop him. He brought the bread

to his lips. It smelled so sweet it made his mouth water. He unhinged his jaw a little so he could pop the whole fist-sized bread roll into his mouth.

The flavor exploded on his tongue. The bread itself was light and fluffy like a cloud and melted with barely any chewing. And the center had been filled with some sort of thick sweet milk. His tastebuds danced with delight at this new experience.

He hadn't realized he'd closed his eyes to relish it until he opened them and found that the young woman manning Trinia's table was staring at him, aghast. A few other humans were also regarding him with wide eyes and nervous expressions.

Blast it, he'd forgotten that the Rove Wood orcs hid their teeth from the humans.

There was no going back now. He finished chewing and swallowed quickly, too unnerved by their abject discomfort to even lick his lips.

Trinia came about then, a woven basket over her arm. She blinked at him. "Did you eat it already?"

He nodded slowly, still relishing the taste even as some of the male humans at a nearby table began to whisper and point at him. One of them was the male who'd confronted him.

Trinia didn't notice and went back to her table, picking up two more of the dough balls. "I'll be right back, Ulia. Will you watch my cart while I'm gone?"

The blonde girl nodded. She was the only one near who didn't seem completely aghast by his teeth. "Good luck."

Trinia shot her a quizzical look, but didn't take the time to question her. Instead, she turned and gestured into the woods. "Shall we?"

He nodded eagerly.

He'd follow her anywhere.

CHAPTER NINE

TRINIA

She pushed down her irritation and embarrassment by guiding the warrior orc deep into the woods, far enough away that she couldn't hear the clamoring of gossip anymore. She stopped them right next to a fallen log underneath the canopy of a bright red oak tree. The gentle autumn breeze rustled the leaves, raining them down and dappling the bright sunlight through them. The dazzling blue of the sky peeped through, and the smell of crisp, clean air and decaying foliage flooded her senses.

The beautiful scenery did little to improve her nerves.

Her breath exhaled hard to push out her frustration as the orc regarded her with a calm, almost passive, expression. "I'm sorry about that."

He nodded, clearly unaffected by the mistrust. She didn't know what things were like outside the Rove Woods. It was probably far worse than how he was treated here. But it didn't matter. She still wasn't keen on him feeling unwelcome.

Especially when she wanted so much from him. She needed him to be willing to come back.

"Uh, do you want to sit down?" She gestured to the fallen log, and he rose a brow questioningly. "I guess it's too wet, isn't it?"

He nodded.

"Oh, here." She held out the cream bun to him. "Another apology."

He took them, expression going slack before a wide grin stretched his face. His eyes twinkled with delight. Almost *reverence*.

Her heart fluttered. Fades, that felt good. Folks usually enjoyed her baking, but not *this* much. Watching him fall all over himself with glee made her whole body tingle.

His mouth opened wide to place the *whole bun* on his tongue, and she suddenly knew exactly why Ulia had wished her luck.

The tusks were one thing, as long as her palm and as thick as three fingers at the base, but at least those had been filed to a blunted end, so they didn't skewer him in the cheek when he was chewing.

His fangs were a whole other story. They were nearly as long as her pinky finger and *deadly* sharp. It was a wonder his green tongue hadn't been skewered.

She'd seen the Rove Wood orc's teeth when they ate her pastries, but they were *nothing* like these teeth. She swallowed hard.

Then he closed his mouth and began to chew.

And his eyes fluttered shut with delight, his lips curled, his whole body went a little limp as he savored the treat.

Her blood heated up in a way that was far too telling.

She needed to get control of herself, or she was going to be too flustered to trade with him!

"Thank you."

Her heart plunged with shock.

He quirked a smile. "Thank you, Trinia."

She clenched her thighs together as a zing of pleasure shot down her spine. Oh Fades, his voice sounded like the blissful combination of a thunderclap and the crunch of footsteps on icy snow.

"Y-you can talk," she said stupidly, and his amusement was clear from the grin on his face. "S-sorry, I just really didn't think you could. You didn't talk at all yesterday . . ."

"I am Brovdir. Sorry, talked too much yesterday. Ran out of words." He tapped the jagged scar at his neck with two of his thick fingers.

Trinia swallowed though her mouth had gone dry. His blasted voice was so low and rough and yet it suited him perfectly.

She wanted him to keep talking, but his statement finally processed in her mind. "Does it hurt to talk?"

He nodded.

Her stomach twisted. "Oh, I'm sorry. I shouldn't have . . ."

"I am fine." He used a tone that was so firm it was almost tangible. "Been saving for you."

Her cheeks heated despite herself. "You've been saving your words for me?"

He nodded.

A flush of pleasure shivered from the top of her head all the way down to her toes and she was certain she was blushing as bright as the sun right now. The male's expression softened into something so tender it only made the sensation worse.

She had to stop looking at him or she was going to turn into a bumbling ninny. Her tongue already felt tied.

But she managed to get back to the matter at hand anyway.

"I'm not really one for small talk, so I'll get right to it. I really just wanted to talk to you about creating these." She pulled the parchment out of her basket of sweets and passed over the first one. It was a simple diagram. Just a flat pan with slightly raised edges with measurements. It would be easy for any blacksmith worth his salt to make.

But the amount of metal needed was a whole other story.

Her heart clenched as Brovdir took the book from her hand. He examined it inquisitively and her anxiety forced her into unusual babble. "My sister . . . well . . . let's just say I don't have my baking pans anymore. It's made getting the loaves done almost impossible. I've been basically cooking all night in order to get them done. Which is fine since that's where I live anyway but . . ."

The male rose a brow at her.

"It's far better to live there than my former home. Believe me. My sister can be a nightmare." And her childhood home was basically in shambles anyway. After years of being neglected by her drunkard of a father who traded every extra scrap he had on mead, it was a wonder the whole thing hadn't caved in.

He rose both brows now and blinked with surprise.

"I know what you're thinking, but trust me, sleeping behind the oven is preferable to sleeping in the same room as Yerina. She can be . . ."

Conniving. Manipulative. Petty . . . how she'd convinced their father to write a will specifically saying *she* inherited their childhood home was beyond her. Their father may have been fallen over drunk half the time, but he was usually somewhat fair.

It didn't matter now and judging from the orc's shocked expression, she'd been rambling about this far too long.

"I just need to get my pans replaced. And since the goblins abandoned the surface world two decades ago, there hasn't been any metal trade. The supply we've got here in the Rove Woods is so limited. That's why . . . well . . . I was hoping you had some extra where you are from?"

"Much."

The single word sent a cascade of relief and delight through her. "Really?" She breathed. "So, you have enough to make that pan? Perhaps a few of them? And maybe these too?" She pulled the other sketches out of her basket and passed them over.

He purposefully brushed her hand with the pads of his fingers as he took them, and a little shiver raced down her spine. Fades, his hands were *huge*.

"Those"—he pointed to the basket she still had on her arm —"for these?"

A zing of delight burst through her. She'd done it! This was actually going to work!

She pulled a bun back out of her basket and handed it to him. He took it carefully. "You mean these, right? Because I can actually make you anything. If you tell me what flavors you prefer, I can bake goods specifically for you."

The male tipped his head in thought as he considered this. It made his shaggy hair flop over his forehead and her fingers twitched with the want to brush it back.

"W-we should discuss quantity too." She hoped the flush of her cheeks wasn't noticeable. "How many do you think is fair?"

His brows furrowed as he considered before he ventured carefully. "Three?"

Trinia tried to stop her laughter. She really did, but it came anyway, and before long, she was wiping her eyes and trying to get words out. "I'm sorry. I'm *so* sorry. I just thought you meant you only wanted *three* buns in exchange for a pan."

"Three pans, three buns."

Her laughter died out.

He was serious? "That is not a fair trade."

His brows came together and disappointment flashed on his face. He carefully tapped the bun as if testing its softness. "Two pans for one?"

"By Fades, *no*. Brovdir, you cannot be serious." She searched his face and found no humor there. "You are serious. Brovdir, have you traded with someone before?"

"Yes."

"Really? And that trade still seems fair?" He nodded his head, and she was instantly flummoxed. How bad *were* things outside of Rove Wood?

Now was not the time to ask.

"Brovdir, look here." His eyes snapped right to her face and held so powerfully she felt a zing of warmth shoot through her entire body. His full attention gave her confidence. "Brovdir, three of my cream buns are *not* worth metal working like this. Metal is incredibly valuable these days, and the skill to bend it to your will is so much more difficult than baking."

His expression shifted, mouth quirked, brows gentled. His posture loosened as his eyes mirrored disbelief.

Her stomach erupted into butterflies all over again.

"Not to me," he rumbled in such a low, exquisite tone she felt it all the way down in the balls of her feet. It made her want to shift from side to side. "For me, these sweets are worth a lifetime."

A . . . lifetime?

She didn't understand his meaning, and she was afraid to ask. Nor could she find her voice. The earnest praise for her baking combined with the heated gaze Brovdir was giving her made her almost giddy.

"W-we should still make it *fair*, Brovdir," she said, pointing to the drawing. "Can you tell me what you think this pan would be worth in . . . let's say . . . dried meat?"

He nodded and looked down at the drawing for a moment before his brow screwed up and he rose his hand to look at it in confusion.

"You want . . . seven hand widths?"

She burst into embarrassed laughter. "Oh, no, no! Why didn't I think of that? I used my own hand as a measurement! I didn't mean *any* hand." She looked down at his massive hands. "Fades, if you built it off yours it wouldn't even fit in my oven."

A grin flitted across his face and her stomach flipped over. "H-here. Hold out your hand for me." He did so, and she sat her own hand flush over his.

Biscuits and jam, his hand was *huge.* Almost twice the size of her own! Her middle finger barely made it up to his first knuckle.

And his palm was so deliciously *warm.* It was a lighter color than the rest of his dark skin, more of a bright green. There were white calluses and scars all over it.

She traced a particularly awful scar that ran from the top of his index finger to the bottom of his thumb. He was so lucky he hadn't lost it.

The hand under her shivered, and she was reminded that he was a *person* as she jerked away. "Sorry! Very sorry. I don't know why I keep forgetting myself around you."

She could barely look him in the eye as she took the parchment back. "Let me change the numbers on this so you can use your own hand to measure."

"Trinia."

His voice felt like fire in her veins, and she helplessly looked up into his dark green eyes. "Yes?"

His light smile made her stomach flip-flop. "I like it when you forget yourself."

She forced herself to focus all her attention back on the diagram even as her heart was hammering and her mind was quailing and her eyes kept flitting to where he stood, tall and strong and focused *directly* on her.

Her breath caught. This male was a *warrior*. He couldn't possibly be flirting with her.

Could he?

"I'll just fix these up over . . . uh . . ." She pointed to a nearby boulder with a semi flat top and settled down with her charcoal pencil.

She busied herself with the calculations, determined to take a moment to catch her breath and let her mind stop reeling. She moved from one diagram to the next, steadily working through the stack until she was on the final one.

"This one would be almost five of your hand widths long." Trinia tapped her charcoal pencil on the boulder. Was that going to be too big? He didn't seem worried about the amount of metal, but—

A broken hiss of pain yanked her right out of her thoughts, and she straightened up to find that Brovdir was holding *willow spike* of all things!

"Fades! Uh—" She fished into the pocket of her skirt to find her handkerchief as the orc's face screwed up with pain. He dropped the deceptively lovely red flowers as his hand swelled up. His dark green skin was mottled with pock marks where the dozens of barbs had dug into his flesh.

He sucked more air between his clenched teeth and went to wipe his hand on his pants.

"Don't!" She rushed over and grabbed his forearm above the wrist which had started to swell. "Those barbs are so sticky! You'll get them all over your pants and they'll be harder to get out than a raspberry jam stain."

Biscuits, what possessed him to touch a willow spike root? She looked down at the plant in confusion. It was rather pretty. The bright red petals cascaded into yellow at the stem. It carried this gradient pattern all the way down to its barbs, which began at the roots. She used her foot to cover them up with dirt.

This plant was totally harmless unless you pulled it up. Why had he pulled it up?

The orc let out a loud huff, and she looked up to find that he appeared a little less pained than before. She stroked his warm arm gently. She knew how bad those barbs stung. "Do you have any healing tinctures on you? The stinging can last for more than a day without treatment."

Brovdir shifted his weight. "Goes away on its own?"

Her brows pinched. "Well, yes, eventually. If you get the barbs out."

He shrugged then, and she blinked in shock. "No need to waste a tincture."

"But it must hurt terribly! And you won't be able to use your hand at all until it's healed."

"How do we remove them?" Brovdir used his free hand to

point to one of the black spiked barbs that were stuck deep into his palm.

"Don't pull them, they have hooks on the end. You should probably go back to the clan and get Hovget." The orc healer would have a better idea of what to do.

Brovdir shook his head so hard it made his shaggy hair flop. "No need. Don't mind pulling."

"No wait! That really will only make it worse." She continued to stroke his arm gently, hoping the touch would distract him from the pain. She was rewarded with a little huff from him as he released some tension. "Just let me think . . ."

She glanced around the forest, trying to come up with something to help . . . and then it dawned on her.

"Oh! The spring! Come to the Fade spring. It will heal you."

Brovdir's face lit with relief. "One is near?"

"Yes, I think right through there, actually." She pointed toward some thick underbrush. "We'll have to find a way around . . ."

Brovdir placed a hand to the small of her back and her skin instantly warmed beneath her dress. "What is it?"

Seeing her surprise, he let her go. "Follow."

"Follow," she repeated dumbly as he moved toward the thicket. "Follow you into the brambles? I don't understand."

But she should have, because a moment later, Brovdir was bashing right through the middle of the bushes, making a path so wide she could walk through without her skirts getting snagged.

Trinia could do nothing but hurry after him and marvel at the brute efficiency of the male. "I suppose this is one way to get there."

He shot her a wide grin over his shoulder and her heart jumped in her chest.

When they finally broke through the brush, Trinia let out a sigh of relief. The spring before them looked crisp and clear and a little higher than usual. Which was odd because, although it was near winter, they hadn't had much rain. It was bubbling up from beneath more too.

Despite those few oddities, it was beautiful. The gold and red trees swayed in the breeze above them and reflected on the blue pool below. The surface was dappled with sunlight making the water seem to glitter. The rocky shore was made inviting by the thick layers of green moss that covered the hard surfaces.

Brovdir let out a hum of approval and moved up toward the left side where there was a flat boulder to perch on. Trinia quickly followed and had only just gotten up onto the rock when Brovdir dipped his hand in.

He let out a long sigh of relief as the water engulfed his hand. The swelling had already gone down and a few of the barbs popped free on their own.

The magic of the spring worked wonders for orcs. She wished it healed humans too.

She crouched back slightly, adjusting on the slippery rocks. "Why did you pull up that willow root?"

The poor orc's cheeks instantly darkened with embarrassment, and he darted his eyes away from her.

Adorable.

She cleared her throat and pushed down the odd thought even as her fingers itched to brush his shaggy hair away from his forehead. "It's such a common plant. I'm surprised you didn't recognize it before you picked it."

"Never seen it."

Shock struck her. "Really? *Never*?"

He shook his head. "None outside Rove. Things don't grow well."

Oh. She'd forgotten.

She shifted her weight slightly to try to get better traction on the moss and wondered just how bad things really were outside of these woods. Was it true the ground was ashen, and people were starving? Was it true most of the villages had moved behind huge stone walls as the wars raged on?

Brovdir's hand was looking better by the moment, but the crisp water accentuated the many white, puckered scars on his hands. He'd led such an incredibly hard life, and this forest was like a whole new world.

"Perhaps I should teach you about the plants, so something like this doesn't happen again," she said softly, looking around at what was growing here at the water's edge. "Then you would know what was poisonous or barbed. You'd know what was and wasn't good to eat too. Take that, for example." She pointed to the cattail hovering right near his face.

Brovdir's gaze shifted from her to the brown, sausage-shaped plant and before she could utter one more word, he'd plucked it and taken a bite.

"Wait!"

The plant's fuzz exploded in his mouth.

Brovdir coughed and sputtered as a massive plume of fuzzy hairs stuck to his lips and tongue. He spat them out, but the spittle only made them stick more. He scrubbed at his mouth with his free hand.

And Trinia couldn't help it. She burst into laughter.

"I'm sorry!" She barely managed between fits. "I'm so sorry! I didn't think—I didn't know you would—" She should have *guessed*, though! The plant did look like a sausage on a stick. Of course he'd try to eat it.

The mental picture of him biting down on the fluff, his eyes shooting wide, his brows rising, and his body going rigid with regret—she couldn't stop laughing. She gripped her stomach as tears streamed down her cheeks.

And then her foot slipped on the moss. Her body tipped toward the icy water as she scrambled to get a good hold.

She was scooped up, right out of the air, and cradled to a hard wall of muscle so warm it felt like jumping into a fire pit.

She could barely catch her breath as Brovdir carried her away from the spring. He held her under her back and knees and didn't look even the least bit troubled by her weight. His arms were thick with muscle and she had to clench her hands tight to keep from reaching out to see how firm they were.

"Y-you're really strong, aren't you?" The words slipped out before she could stop them.

Brovdir blinked wide, and biscuits bake her, he was so *cute*. Why was a warrior orc with all this rippling muscle and massive frame so *cute*?

Her cheeks went so hot she was shocked they didn't catch fire. "You can put me down. I'm not some dainty flower, you know?"

Brovdir's fingers brushed against her side, right under the swell of her breasts. Her skin went hot and tingly, and she had to stop herself from squirming.

"I like it."

She suddenly couldn't get enough air as she searched his face. Was he mocking her?

"You're sturdy." He followed with a nod of determination. "And . . . soft."

Sturdy and soft.

Her stomach fluttered and her mind reeled, and her thighs clenched together as if trying to fight her own reaction to such a delightful compliment.

Brovdir set her down on her feet and she continued to stare at him. She couldn't help herself. His eyes were soft, and his brows were unfurrowed and he wore a light smile that made her giddy.

There was a bit of fluff still sticking out of the corner right next to his tusk.

"You, uh . . . you've got a little . . ." She tapped her own mouth, and he quickly brushed his mouth on the wrong side. "Oh, no, not there. Here, let me . . ."

She reached up and brushed the fluff away. His skin was so much softer than she expected. And he was so blasted tall. She had to stretch all the way up to reach.

There was a little more fluff in his hair too. "Lean down a little."

In less than a flash of light, Brovdir had gone down onto his knees.

"Oh! No, you don't have to—you're going to get soaked!"

But he was already staring up at her with such an amused smile on his face that she couldn't help stuttering to a halt. He really *did* look like a puppy when he was looking up at her like this. Huge eyes and shaggy hair.

She reached down to brush the fluff out of his hair. It was so soft, and his scalp was so warm, and he leaned into her touch slightly. Her heart skipped right over itself.

"I'm sorry for laughing," she said, combing her fingers through his hair somewhat absently. He leaned into her touch further and his eyes softly shut.

He wasn't bad looking by any stretch. The scars gave him a

rugged charm and accentuated the dark green of his skin. His lashes were long and his jaw was square and . . . and . . .

What was she doing? She needed to stop ogling at him.

She released him and stepped back. His eyes opened somewhat lazily, and his smile widened when he looked at her.

"Thank you," he rumbled and her whole stomach burst with happy flutters.

"O-of course!" she said. "Sorry again for um . . ."

"I like your laughter."

Her cheeks went hot again.

"I'll make your pans as a gift."

As a . . . "What? Brovdir, no, you don't have to do that!"

"I want to."

"It's too much!" Trinia wrung her hands. Fades, this male was far too generous. He was going to get taken advantage of. "Trades need to be fair, Brovdir. Promise me you won't just give your skills away to anyone who asks."

"Not anyone," he said smoothly. "Just you."

Her breath caught in her throat.

"Only for you, Trinia." His voice was so warm and low and . . . and . . .

"I could just kiss you."

Biscuits bake her! She had *not* meant to say that out loud! She may as well just go jump into the spring and drown herself.

But then a broad grin spread across the warrior orc's face. All his teeth flashed and Trinia should *not* have been so thrilled at the sight of them. She should not have zinging anticipation coursing down her back and pooling between her legs.

"Yes." His voice rumbled so low she actually felt it in her gut. "You may, Trinia of Oakwall."

He sounded far too excited about it, and she couldn't bring herself to deny him.

It was just one little kiss. Just a quick thank you for everything he'd promised to do. That he'd *already* done. He'd saved her life.

Her thighs clenched tight together and her mind reeled with delighted excitement.

CHAPTER
TEN

BROVDIR

She leaned in and put her warm hands on his shoulders. It took everything in him not to shiver. His mind was reeling from shock at how quickly things had progressed and he turned his head slightly so she could have better access. He'd *expected* a quick peck on the cheek.

Instead, she kissed him *full on the lips.*

His heart thundered, and it felt like it would fall out of his chest.

Fades, he couldn't breathe. His mind scrambled to understand what was happening. His nose flooded with her sweet scent. His mouth felt like it'd caught fire as her soft, plump lips lingered on his own. Her body was so incredibly *warm*.

It was over long before he wanted it to be. He'd wanted to relish it. Memorize it. Instead, she pushed back from him, came back to her full height. He lost his balance and plopped down onto his ass in the muck and barely minded.

Her cheeks were bright, but she was *smiling*.

She was a beauty. He wanted to wrap his arms around the warmth of her body, press her curves into his frame and drown in her.

Instead, a cry sounded from the woods. One he could not ignore.

The warlord's call.

Fuck, he wasn't ready. He wanted more time. Why did Karthoc want him *now*?

Just when he was trying to war with his instinctual need to obey the authority of his leader, Karthoc yelled again. A giant *roar*. Loud enough that Trinia heard it and whipped her curly haired head toward the cry. The strands that had fallen loose from her queue tempted him. He wanted to clench it in his grip and tip her head back and—

"BROVDIR!"

Trinia jumped, hand over her mouth in shock. "W-who was *that*?"

"My brother," Brovdir said under his breath. There was no fighting the call. "I must go."

"Go just for a moment or . . ."

Judging from his brother's tone. "Go for today."

Her expression fell to one of disappointment, and that should not have made him so ecstatic. He wanted to keep her.

And then his brother's roar caused the birds to fly out of their perches in terror and Brovdir inhaled sharply as dismay tightened in his chest.

"You'll come back, right?"

He grinned. "Yes. I will."

"All right, then," she said with a nod. She'd recovered from her shock rather quickly.

She was a brave woman.

Fades, he wanted her.

"BROVDIR!"

Blast it. "I apologize. I must answer the warlord."

Her eyes went huge, and his stomach dropped as she said, "But you said it was . . . you're . . . the warlord's *brother*?"

Wrench him to the depths, he'd fumbled this. He should have taken the time to explain. "I am. I—"

"BROVDIR, NOW!"

Fuck, he couldn't fight it. And really, what more was there to say?

He bowed his head slightly. "I will see you again."

She swallowed so thickly he heard it, but she nodded. Tension left him in a rush.

After one last look, he turned away and followed the sound of his brother's angry yells back to the trade pavilion.

It would take at least a moon to travel back and forth from Baelrok, plus the time it would take to make the trays. He'd have to convince Karthoc to let him come back here . . .

He'd manage it somehow. There was no doubt in his mind that he would find a way. He'd visit her as often as he was able and eventually . . . maybe . . .

She might play conquest for him.

His hope at the thought was too stark to ignore. He'd lost count of the times he tried to find a conquest. So many women who'd shrunk from him in terror. Who he'd kept at a respectful distance and returned to their homes untouched.

Trinia was far different from them. They'd never wanted something from him, only wanted him to go away. Trinia wasn't like that. She'd kissed him.

His lips still tingled from the touch. Fades be praised. He almost couldn't believe this was reality.

"Brovdir!" Karthoc hollered as he made his way out of the

woods and back under the canopy of the birch trade pavilion. "Where the fuck have you been?"

"I apologize, Warlord," he said. "I was preoccupied."

Karthoc inhaled deeply and said, "I can smell that. She got awfully close."

Brovdir wasn't keen on giving his brother any of the details and, thankfully, Karthoc didn't ask for them.

"Ergoth—the bastard—told the village headman we would bring elk to every family here. Insinuated we'd gone back on our word because we showed without them. Now I've promised we'll all leave *now* and get them hunted before the end of tomorrow."

Fuck, *that* would certainly be a feat. He looked toward the line of tables, counting. There were almost thirty separate tradesmen. Thirty elk. He could hardly fathom it.

Though, he supposed it would be easier to find thirty or more unblighted elk in Rove Woods than it ever had been outside them.

His mouth was watering with want already. He'd smelled the roasted elk in the hall the night before but hadn't been invited for a meal. Perhaps he could bring down an extra and the warriors could feast tonight.

"And I told them *you* would get five, as a show of good faith."

Brovdir jerked with surprise. "Five?"

"Yes. I'm certain you can handle it."

He could, but it would still be a challenge. Would likely take him all day and perhaps into the night.

But if it was the warlord's order, then he would obey. He nodded.

The confusion must have still lingered on his face because Karthoc said, "You need to do this in order to leave a good impression on them. You need to be well liked by Oakwall, Brovdir. That is my order to you. To be friendly and outgoing toward them. Them *and* the orcs of Rove Wood."

Brovdir's brow furrowed and his stomach sunk with dismay. Being sociable and outgoing was difficult enough for him already to say nothing of how his voice faltered after a few sentences.

He would normally never question Karthoc, but his confusion got the better of him.

"Why?"

Karthoc took a deep breath, his expression flat, his eyes stern. They left no room for argument.

"Because I'm naming you the next chief of Rove Wood."

And with that, Brovdir's heart fell out of his chest for the second time that day.

CHAPTER
ELEVEN

TRINIA

Three trades later, Trinia had given up waiting for Brovdir to come back.

She pounded the dough on her counter with a kind of fever that could only be brought on from bone-deep embarrassment and suppressed disappointment. Her chest tightened more and more with each passing day and her patience for dealing with customers had dwindled to the size of a pinprick.

But she couldn't help it, her mind simply *refused* to relent.

Where had she gone wrong with him?

He'd liked her, right? He'd seemed delighted when she'd kissed him . . .

And now he was just . . . gone. The other warriors came to the trades, but Brovdir never did.

On a heavy sigh, she bowed her head and looked over the mangled lump of beige dough on her counter. The indents were slowly smoothing out as the yeast resisted her pummeling. She wished she could bounce back from embarrassment just as easily.

Now he was the new chief of Rove Wood Clan, and he avoided her like she had the blight.

The door to the bakery banged open.

Yerina stood in the dim light of it.

Trinia wanted to groan as the driving urge to hurl the dough at her sister's head overwhelmed her. "What do you want?"

"You aren't seriously still moping, are you?" Yerina flicked her hair back and neglected to close the door behind her as she walked inside.

"If anyone should be accused of moping around, it's *you*," Trinia said with too much force. She was still shocked Yerina hadn't gone insane trying to snatch Govek away from his new mate.

Her sister smirked. "*I* don't have to mope about anything. I don't need to win Govek back. Who would want him, anyway? Since he's fallen in with that strange woman, who's supposedly from another world, he's been a complete *disaster*. No hunting, no craftwork, refusing to become *chief* even."

Trinia kept quiet. The rumors surrounding Govek were rampant and no one from Rove Wood Clan would speak on it. Not even her friend Savili had been willing to pass on information.

But one thing was certain, the surly orc who'd once been regarded as dangerous was *happy*. And the new woman, Miranda, made him that way. No matter the circumstances of how she had come here or how they had found each other, Trinia couldn't see how Govek being calm and content was a bad thing.

"I have other, much more *powerful* orcs, who have their eyes set on me," Yerina continued.

"Orc eyes who can't even *see* you? You've been banned from the trade, remember?" Trinia continued to punch her dough on the counter.

She could feel Yerina's scowl burning the back of her neck. "The trade isn't the only place you can meet an orc, you know. Though I suppose you *wouldn't*, would you? You've never been invited by any orcs anywhere. In fact, Brovdir has been skipping the trade *just* to avoid you. Even though he is the new second-in-command."

"Co-chief," Trinia corrected Yerina even as her chest stung from the harsh truth of her words.

Her sister rolled her eyes. "Some co-chief. Poor Chief Sythcol has been doing all the work. Not that he *needs* help. That conjurer is the most powerful male in the clan now. They are all under his command."

The look in Yerina's eyes made Trinia's skin feel tight. "Yerina, don't you dare."

Yerina snorted. "We're not talking about me right now, dear sister. We're talking about you and how you have completely run out of options except to live as a spinster for the rest of your life."

Trinia clenched her teeth together. *Better a spinster than a manipulative bitch.*

"Now, with that said, I have a surprise for you."

"A *surprise* for me?" Trinia snorted and continued to knead, imagining it was her sister's face she was squishing.

"You need to come now if you want it."

"I don't want it."

"Trinia."

"Yerina, it's nearly time for *bed*." Though Trinia wouldn't sleep for a long while yet. She had too much work to do. "Can't this surprise of yours wait until morning?"

"No. It can't. You need to come *now*. And take off that disgusting apron."

An unusual amount of rage bubbled up in Trinia's throat and she shot Yerina the kind of look that made her sister's eyes widen. "I am *not* in the mood for this, Yerina."

There was a tense silence in which Trinia thought she could smell her sister's mind smoking. Or perhaps that was just the bread burning in the oven. Trinia went and took the slightly too dark rolls out and slid them onto a cooling rack.

"Trinia, I know things have been hard."

Trinia's back straightened, and she whipped around to find her sister looking *earnest*.

Yerina met her eyes. "I know I haven't been the easiest. But . . . this is important. Will you come with me? *Please*."

Fades, had her sister *ever* said please to her in a tone that wasn't sarcastic or demeaning? Trinia couldn't recall.

She knew her sister was trying to manipulate her. She *knew* that. But curiosity bubbled up within her and despite the warning blaring in her mind, Trinia couldn't fight the bone deep jittering to discover what *exactly* it was her sister had cooked up. She certainly wasn't going to drop her guard, not at all, but . . .

"All right." Trinia undid the tie of her apron. "Do I have time to freshen up?"

"Unfortunately, no," Yerina said with a hard exhale that took quite a bit of tension with it. Trinia was surprised that her sister was this tense over something and her curiosity doubled.

Trinia hung the apron and turned to face her sister. Yerina's nose wrinkled. She looked down at Trinia's dress with disgust and Trinia couldn't even blame her.

She hadn't bothered to change it since yesterday. She'd even slept in it. Her hair was coated with flour, her skin felt sticky, and her sister insisted that all she had time for was a quick wash of her hands and face before they headed out into the chilly evening. They walked toward their home near the far east of the village.

Oakwall was rather pretty at this time. The sun had nearly set and only a smear of orange remained behind the tree line. Winter had fallen steadily, but they'd only suffered one major snowstorm so far. The paths had been shoveled clear and fluffy white heaps lined them. Many bore the signs of children playing: footprints, snow balls, tiny snowmen.

The house windows glowed merrily, revealing residents whom she recognized, settling in and readying for bed. She glanced through one large window into the living room of Kavin and his family. His three children were all bundled up in blankets, listening to him tell a tale. His wife sat on the couch next to him, looking drowsy and content.

Trinia wondered what that would have been like. To have a family that actually *cared* for each other instead of a louse for a father and a selfish twat for a sister.

She followed Yerina closely all the way to their cabin. The log structure had been built by their great-grandfather, and from looking at it, one might assume that had been the last time anyone had bothered taking care of it.

It was a single-story home with two bedrooms and no bathroom. They used an outhouse accessible from the back door.

As they got close, her fingers itched to sketch. To plan. She'd spent many late nights outlining a way to split the house down the middle. Create a wall that would make the single dwelling into two spaces. One for her, the other for Yerina. So, they would each have a place to live, but would never have to see or speak to each other.

That was before her father had died and his will had been read. Back when Trinia had assumed she'd get half the house and not just half of the bakery.

Trinia looked at the outside of the tiny, bedraggled cabin and found that the two windows that had once had cracks were *mended.* "Who fixed those?"

"Rori. Who else?"

"Rori doesn't fix glass for free. What did you trade for it?" Trinia's mind flitted over which pans Rori might have taken in exchange.

Perhaps she could try to get them back. Rori did like sourdough . . .

"I gave him father's old hand wagon."

"You did . . . he wanted *that* old thing? It was half rotten."

"It's better than none at all," Yerina said with a sly smile.

"But why would he want one? He carries all his tools on his belt."

Yerina rose her brows. "Because he wants to *leave*, of course."

Trinia swallowed hard. "You're not serious."

"Why wouldn't I be? Plenty of folks are talking about leaving since the warrior orcs started to settle here."

Trinia's chest felt tight. "But it's only *rumors* that the warlord's warriors are going to come settle in these woods. And Rori is so practical. It's not like him to be pulled along."

"Guess you've had your nose so deep in the flour you hadn't heard," Yerina said with a scoff. "It's not rumors anymore. Headman Gerald confirmed that more are going to come back to stay."

"What? When?"

"Come inside and I'll tell you," Yerina said, and Trinia followed somewhat helplessly. They walked up the three narrow steps, which had also been mended, to the front door, which no longer squeaked, and Yerina made room for Trinia to walk past.

Inside, the house was *clean.* So clean. Cleaner than Trinia could ever remember it being, even before her mother had passed away. The floor was shining in the firelight. The hearth had been swept out and crackled brightly. The stonework around it had been patched. The cabinets in the kitchen had been fixed up and painted.

Trinia didn't have time to marvel because one look toward the kitchen table revealed they were not alone.

Ronhold and Tobbis were here.

The door clacked shut behind Yerina and Trinia's back straightened as she recalled the insults the obnoxious young adult had thrown her way. He looked just as filthy as he had the day of the trade a moon and a half ago, but honestly, she wasn't much better, with flour and grime stuck to her dress.

If Ronhold noticed her state, he didn't make it known. The powerful merchant rose to his feet with well-kept clothes of cotton and leather and a wide grin that engulfed his rounded face. Ronhold looked like he was about to cut a deal sharp enough to make her toes curl. Though, at this point, Trinia couldn't be certain if that was because he was about to don her feet in some of his best footwear or attempt to chop off her toes.

"Trinia"—Ronhold's grin somehow widened—"glad you could finally get here. We've been waiting a long time for you."

"I had no idea," Trinia said, casting Yerina a look out of the corner of her eye. Her sister refused to meet her gaze.

"You were at the bakery, weren't you?" Ronhold asked, and Trinia was surprised to see a gleam of pride in his eye.

"Yes." She glanced at Tobbis, who's head was down as he also avoided eye contact. The boy was all bunched in on himself, shoulders hunched, fists balled on the tabletop.

"You work hard, don't you, Trinia?"

"I believe that's subjective based on who you are asking."

"You supply bread to the village daily. I would say that is hard work."

"I suppose."

"You even moved into the bakery so you could complete tasks more easily. Bake more efficiently."

"Why are you asking me all this?" Trinia narrowed her eyes.

"Why don't you go sit down, Trinia?" Yerina said before Ronhold could answer. She pushed the small of Trinia's back.

Trinia stepped away from her sister's prodding. "I'd rather stand, thank you."

Ronhold slapped his son's arm. "Quite right, it's better to stand for these things."

"Father," Tobbis hissed, as his father tugged him to his feet. He cast a disgusted look Trinia's way before his gaze lingered on Yerina. "You said we would discuss first."

"What is there to discuss?" Ronhold swept his hand toward Trinia. "She's the best fit, clearly. Hard working. Dedicated. You would do well to learn from her."

Trinia blinked rapidly in shock. "You . . . want me to take your son on as an apprentice?"

The idea of having to spend so much time with Tobbis made her skin crawl.

Ronhold burst into robust laughter that flooded the house until she felt like she was drowning.

"Of course not!" Ronhold's voice was tinged with mirth. "No, no. Though I suppose you could consider him as such in some respects. He does have quite a bit of maturing to do, but I know with you at his side, he'll age into a fine man."

"What are you talking about?"

"You and Tobbis will be wed."

The statement hit her so hard she felt like she'd been slapped across the face.

"It's the perfect union. Tobbis needs to learn some discipline and working with you in the bakery will be just the thing to do it."

She was reeling, completely gobsmacked. Her whole body froze up to the point that she couldn't get air into her lungs, and the room spun a little.

"Tobbis, tell her how excited you are to be her new husband."

The boy had gone pale, and his nose curled like he'd smelled something foul.

"Tobbis has been waiting a long time to come of age. He's always wanted to have children. And won't they be lucky to be born into such a profitable family?"

He'd always wanted *what*? Trinia felt sick and she could tell from the color of Tobbis's complexion he felt much the same.

"With my business sense, I'm certain I can make significantly better trades and get the bakery running the way it was meant to. Both you and your children will sing my praises by the end."

The words punctuated through Trinia like a poker. They left her feeling raw, heated, and determined to escape this complete insanity.

She turned on her heel and stomped toward the exit.

"Where are you going?" Yerina snapped.

"Away from the lot of you. This is madness. I'm not marrying anyone."

"Trinia, Tobbis will make you a fine husband," Yerina said.

"I am *not* marrying the cobbler's son." Trinia punctuated each word so hard that she could feel them vibrating in the air around them.

"I think you will." Ronhold's confidence was something tangible, and Trinia could feel herself sinking even before he finished. "Because if you don't, you will lose the bakery entirely."

Trinia sputtered, undaunted by the man's ruthless tone. "The bakery has belonged to my family for generations. You can't do anything to change that."

"I'm sure this is all coming as quite a shock to you. Yerina tells me she never actually *told* you about the predicament you're in." Ronhold looked her square in the eye, and she couldn't break his stare as he shattered her world. "The bakery is *ours*, girl. And I've got the contracts here to prove it."

Trinia felt a zing of fear go down her spine. Ronhold picked up a scroll that she hadn't noticed on the table and displayed it to her view. "Take a look for yourself."

Trinia's hands shook as she snatched the yellowed and frayed paper from the man's hands. She unrolled it to find her late father's scrawling handwriting marring the surface.

A contract. A contract to get liquor on a regular basis from Ronhold.

In exchange for the bakery.

Her knees felt weak, her head spun, and the forest around her dimmed. "This . . . this cannot be."

"I'm sure you recognize your father's hand and signature. You see the bakery was officially owned by *me* the moment he died. It's out of the good of my own heart that I allowed you and your sister to continue working these last few years. Well . . . that and Yerina's prompting."

Trinia shot a look at her sister and her stomach dropped so hard she felt dizzy. Yerina's head was bowed, her eyes were misty, and her posture was *defeated.*

Trinia had never seen her sister look contrite before.

"She convinced me that the bakery means *nothing* without you at the helm to bake. And I very much agree. You have a keen talent, Trinia. Though you aren't so wise on the *business* side of things. You give far too much away and offer far more charity than I will allow. Giving away food to the needy and elderly . . . pah! What good does that do you other than to diminish your resources? Better to give scraps to the pigs. At least they get fattened up for our table."

Fury sparked in Trinia's veins and the itch to slap the horrible man was so strong her palm tingled.

"From this moment forward, you will obey my commands, and I'll hear no complaints. I could have left you destitute long ago, you know? Why, I've been *extremely* generous in allowing you to not only continue to take *all* the bakery's profit, but also *live* inside it."

"I'll . . . I'll go to Headman Gerald," Trinia said in desperation, but Ronhold only laughed. The chortling sound swirled around her.

"Go right ahead, Trinia. This contract is completely *valid.* Anyone can see that's your father's signature."

"Yes, and you took *advantage* of him. He was struggling, desperate, unable to give up the drink, and you took full advantage of that."

"He was well enough to understand what he was doing," Ronhold said. "I have three witnesses to contest if you try to say I forced his hand."

"You *did* force his hand. You found his weakness and exploited him!"

Ronhold shrugged his thick shoulders, as if taking advantage of a drunken man was nothing of his concern. "That's business."

Trinia felt like she would be sick.

"I highly suggest you marry Tobbis." Ronhold gestured to his son, who was standing behind him, looking pale and uncomfortable with his jaw clenched tight. His eyes shifted from Trinia to Yerina and the longing in his gaze when he looked at her sister was clear.

"If you don't marry him, you'll have no stake in the bakery whatsoever."

A sinking feeling pulled Trinia down, sucking her in until she felt like she was being swallowed up whole.

There was no way out of this.

She couldn't escape.

She was going to lose *everything.*

But she couldn't give in. *She just couldn't!*

She went to the front door and yanked hard.

It did not budge.

It was locked.

Her hand shot up to the bolt and found it had been replaced with one that required a key.

"Yerina! Let me out right now."

"I can't do that, Trinia. It's high time you marry."

"Excuse me?"

Yerina took her wrist. "Trinia, be reasonable—"

Trinia yanked her hand out of Yerina's grip so violently that her sister tripped. Then, without thought, Trinia marched over to one of the mended windows and threw it open with ease. It slid like a hot knife through butter. Didn't even creak.

"Trinia, what are you doing?"

Yerina's cry did nothing to stop her. Nothing could at this point.

"Stop this madness." Ronhold barreled toward her.

But he wasn't fast enough. In a blink, she swung up onto the sill and jumped out into the night.

"Trinia!" Her sister screeched on the wind. Trinia landed with a hard thud and broke into a run.

There was a lower bellow, likely from Ronhold, but she couldn't make it out with the sound of the wind roaring in her ears.

She had to get out of here.

She had to get away.

She rounded a bend in the path and came into the clearing before the village gates. Her eyes had adjusted to the darkness, but it still took her a moment to realize the gates were shut.

Of course they were. It was nearly the end of the day.

But she certainly wasn't going to let that stop her. Because the only other option was to face the end of her *life* as she knew it.

She turned on her heel to run down along the wall, to the crack in the base she used to slip through as a child. She found it by muscle memory and tried to shove her way inside without thinking.

The space was so much smaller than she'd realized, but she pushed on without care. Brittle branches tore at her clothes and cut into her arms. One slashed her cheek, and she swiped at it, cursing at the stinging the action caused. Her hand came back wet with blood.

Her body was zinging with fury, and her mind was desperate for escape. She clawed her way through, and the branches gave into her demands, breaking apart to make room.

She burst out on the other side. Out of the village and into the night.

She set a bruising clip into the woods, uncaring where she went. Undaunted by the dark and chill. The snow crunched under her feet and soaked into her leather shoes. Shoes that had not been made by Ronhold. She'd never once given him her business. She'd never wanted anything to do with him or his high prices or his ruthless ways.

And now he was going to take control of her mother's bakery.

Of her *life*.

And there was nothing she could do about it.

"Fuck you, Ronhold!" she screamed into the night as her steps slowed. Her lungs were giving out, but her fury had only just begun. "You and your worthless, whiny son! And fuck you Yerina! I hope you choke on that worthless selfishness of yours!"

If she hadn't stolen all those pans, if she had just *helped* around the bakery like she was supposed to, perhaps Trinia would have been able to make enough profit to trade back the bakery.

If only she hadn't given away so much free bread.

If only she hadn't spent so much time on worthless house plans.

If only she could work faster and better and . . .

And if only Brovdir, the new chief of Rove Wood, hadn't cut her off so completely, he might have been able to help her.

It wasn't rational. She knew that. But the anger gripped her nonetheless.

"Curse you too, Brovdir! None of this would have happened if you'd just traded with me!"

She screamed, as loud as she possibly could. So loud that

the Fades themselves would wake from their slumber. So loud that her rage bloomed into the woods and shook the ground under her feet.

No, the ground under her feet *actually* shook.

Trinia's scream broke off as she looked down. The snowy ground was *rippling*. There was an odd roaring sound.

And then the surface of the ground *ripped open.*

Her stomach plunged.

And her whole body plunged with it as she fell into the dark icy depths.

CHAPTER TWELVE

BROVDIR

"We can dig pits and line the bottom with spikes. We'll dig them all around the whole clan. I think two of your lengths deep will work fine."

Brovdir's skin went chill at the elderly orc's words. Jolin, who'd earned his place as one of the clan's wisest by outliving most of his generation, appeared passive and easygoing in his loose cotton clothing.

He never thought the harmless elder would want to bring such egregious harm to the warrior orcs who would soon settle in the Rove Woods.

"What do you think, Plog?" Jolin asked the equally serine orc on his left. "Do you think two body lengths would be far enough to skewer them through?"

"I think we'd better go with three, Jolin," Bolsan, an elderly orc with dark gray hair and a square jaw, interrupted with a voice as low as the goblin mines. At least it held some hard inflection when he so brutally began to describe their murderous intentions. "Three would ensure that they couldn't hoist themselves back up off the things and pounce out."

"True. But it will take much longer to dig," Jolin replied, lacing his long, wrinkled fingers together on the wood tabletop. A light evening breeze fluttered in to rustle the elderly man's thin greenish-gray hair. "Would be terribly hard work. Much conjuring would be needed."

"We could get the sons to do it," Plog said with a firm nod. He was the last of the three elders and his exuberant, boisterous nature would lead one to believe he was significantly younger than he was. "They need practice with their magic, anyway."

"They could even compete!" Jolin pronounced with a grin. "What fun they would have, seeing whose spear would best skewer through the beast's hard hide!"

Brovdir's stomach churned with nausea over the ghastly image these elderly orcs were painting. Were they really going to get the orc *children* to help *murder* orc warriors? Males who were coming here by order of the Fades themselves?

"What if we put poison on them, too?" Plog tapped his fingers on the tabletop. "Might help them die quicker."

Bolsan grumbled. "True, but then we wouldn't be able to eat them."

Eat them? His stomach churned threateningly. "*No.*"

All three of the elder orcs turned their full attention to Brovdir and his stomach lurched again at the thought of these males *cooking* and *eating* him.

He repeated vehemently. "*No.*"

Plog spoke up first. "No? No, what? Speak up warrior—er, I mean, Chief."

"No pits," Brovdir grated. He couldn't even believe he was having to tell them *not* to dig pit traps for the warriors to be skewered alive in.

There was a terse silence in which the elders narrowed their eyes and straightened their green and brown shirts, and Brovdir imagined them hoisting him up and throwing him into a pit of poisoned spikes.

"I don't see how else we're going to keep them out then," Plog finally said tersely.

"We *don't*." He'd been talking far too much this day, and his throat was blistering. "We *let them in*."

Now the elders stared at him aghast, their wrinkled eyes wide, their mouths agape. Brovdir, desperate for some reprieve to the madness, turned his head up to look at the canopy of the Great Rove Tree. The balcony they were all seated upon was large and spacious with an incredible view that overlooked the clan. They were protected from the winter wind by the huge tree's thick branches, covered in crystalline leaves which did not fall in the autumn. The glittering foliage above him was so perfect and reflective that he could see the dark blue of the dimming sky through it.

He wished Trinia was here to see it.

He jerked his gaze away from the view and pinched the bridge of his nose tight, but it did nothing to extinguish the sight of her in his mind's eye. Her easy smile. Her thick body. Her soft lips that tasted so sweet and divine.

Fades, what was *wrong* with him?

He needed to let her go. There was nothing he could do to win her now. He knew that.

And still the longing for her continued.

"You . . . *want* the boar to come in?" Jolin finally broke the silence.

Brovdir finally looked at the elders. "Boar?"

"Yes, the boar. The boar you said you wanted us to come up

with a plan for? The thousands of boars that are going to descend upon these woods in the next few seasons."

Sudden understanding slapped Brovdir right across the face and left him stinging. "Not *boar*. *Warriors*."

The three elderly males blinked. "Oh . . . what?"

"Warriors," Brovdir insisted again. "The warrior *orcs*. I told you to come up with a way to take care of the *warriors*."

"Oh, goodness gravy." Plog threw up his wrinkled hands. His two friends looked just as exasperated. "*That's* what you said. By Fades, I didn't hear you properly. My hearing is not what it used to be, you know. I thought you'd said you wanted us to come up with a way to take care of the *boar*."

Brovdir couldn't decide if he wanted to strangle the males or burst into laughter.

What would Trinia think of this? Would she laugh?

His mood lightened as he imagined it. "Yes, the *warriors*. Not boar."

"Well . . ." There was a short pause in which the three of them looked between each other. Plog pinched his lips with his long fingers. Bolsan's brow wrinkled as he thought. Jolin's eyes unfocused as he sat back.

"You want us to house the warriors?" Plog asked.

Brovdir nodded.

"And you said there are five *thousand*."

"Or more."

Another long silence.

Bolsan broke it with a bark. "Blast, *you're* our leader now. Shouldn't you be the one coming up with the ideas?"

Brovdir glowered, but the elderly male just shrugged him off.

"I don't have any idea how to take care of five thousand orc warriors." Bolsan waved his hand dismissively and the other two elders appeared just as resigned. "I don't even know how they're all going to *fit* in these woods. You're the chief. Housing them and ensuring their wellbeing is your responsibility."

Brovdir heaved a heavy sigh. He *knew* that. But he had hoped these elderly males, with much more life experience, might help him come up with an idea.

Because, as of right now, they had *nothing* prepared. Certainly, there were some warriors, like his own brethren, who were accustomed to camping over the winter, but most of them lived in clans. Most of them enjoyed thick walls to keep out the chill and warm beds to lie down in and only slept under the stars in the heat of summer.

To say nothing of the ones with human mates and children.

He couldn't just welcome them to these woods and then foist them out into the wilderness to brave the elements. The hardship they'd suffer was one thing, but without clear rules on when to hunt and forage, the Rove Woods would quickly be picked clean of resources.

He'd talked to every spear-fisherman and gardener orc within the boundary of this clan and not one of them could think of a way to feed and house so many males.

Asking the elders for advice had been a long shot, but Brovdir still felt a bit hollow that his last hope had been so thoroughly dashed.

He wished . . . he could speak to Trinia about it.

He rubbed his chest as an odd, pulsing sensation plagued him. One that had lingered often of late.

"So, what do we do about the boar, then?"

Brovdir let out a long sigh. "Warriors, no boar."

"Warriors . . . *know* the boar? How do the warriors know the boar?" Plog's brow screwed up.

Jolin leaned forward in his seat. "Are the warriors bringing the boar? I must say, that's rather convenient. That many boars will be mighty useful. Think of all the meat and leather!"

"I've already made plans on how to use the hide." Bolsan crossed his arms over his chest.

"Oh really?" Plog rose his brows eagerly. "What are you making, then?"

"Ronhold said he could tan the hide and turn them into thicker shoes that wouldn't slip on the rocks. And his whiny son said he had some glove and belt designs he wanted to try. Said they'd only keep two-thirds of what they made, and I could keep the rest."

"Two-thirds is robbery," Jolin said with a snort.

"Perhaps, but what am I to do with dozens of belts and shoes?"

"You could trade them to me. I've got some new herbs that might help with your joint pain."

The conversation continued on and on and *on* and Brovdir began to question everything about his decision to involve these males. To involve *any* of the males, honestly.

Karthoc made leadership seem so *easy.* His brother delegated tasks like he was passing around dried elk meat and the orcs leaped to do his bidding just as fast as they would gobble down the grub.

But every one of Brovdir's commands had led to nothing. Plans fizzled out before they even got started. Orders were forgotten by clan members within days of giving them. Any attempts to force compliance was treated with contempt and outrage, so Brovdir had no choice but to default to Sythcol.

It was easier that way. Sythcol knew this clan best and Brovdir had been Karthoc's second his entire life. That was where he was comfortable and where he would remain.

But he couldn't bring himself to follow all Sythcol's decisions. Which is what led him here, to this *lunacy.*

"All right, all right, it's time for you all to go."

Brovdir looked up to find Sythcol had come up the spiral staircase that led from the hall and was crossing the balcony to the huge ovular table where they sat. The four elders did not question or fight Sythcol for even a moment. They simply rose to their feet and continued to babble about the leather goods they were planning to make as they exited. Brovdir remained in his seat, too exhausted to rise.

"Chief Sythcol, is that . . . what they're fixing in the hall?" Plog said as he eyed the bowl of soup in Sythcol's hand.

"Yes," Sythcol muttered darkly. Both their eyes flickered to Brovdir and his back straightened as he prepared for a complaint.

But it didn't come. Instead, the elder male muttered something about not being hungry anyway and wandered off. Brovdir couldn't blame him. He could smell the steam from Sythcol's bowl, and the distinct scent of pine needles mixed with day old fish wafted in like the stench of a privy on a hot summer night.

Once the elders had disappeared, Sythcol came to the table and set down his soup bowl far too close for Brovdir's liking. "I thought I told you they weren't worth talking to."

Brovdir's stomach twisted. "Had to try."

"Waste of time," Sythcol muttered. There were dark bags under his eyes and his white hair was knotted up to the point that Brovdir was convinced he'd not brushed it in days. Why the male didn't just shave it off was beyond him.

Sythcol was his opposite in every way. He was slender and regal, with pale skin and even paler hair. His face was slender. His tusks were thin. His cheeks were hollow like he'd skipped too many meals and his gait was slow, like each step took effort.

He looked wrung out.

Sythcol scooped up the half empty jug of mead from the middle of the table. His hands were shaking, and black discoloration ran all the way up his arms, nearly to his shoulders. It had grown significantly of late from his overuse of magic.

Sythcol capped the mead jug and Brovdir wasn't surprised. He'd never seen his chief counterpart take even a sip of the mind addling drink. "I warned you about the elders, didn't I? They have as much knowledge as the trees themselves, but you're better off asking the trees when you need wisdom."

Brovdir snorted in amusement despite himself, then watched in mute horror as Sythcol put a spoonful of the stew into his mouth.

The male's brow screwed up in disgust and, by sheer force of will, swallowed the muck down. "Gegvi's really struggling to adapt, isn't he?"

That was an understatement. Gegvi had been in charge of the cooking within the Great Rove Tree for over a decade, and until now, not one male had ever complained about his cooking. Which was a feat, considering the orcs of Rove Wood Clan took all their meals in the Great Tree.

But until now, Gegvi had had one vital tool endlessly at his disposal.

Magic. Spells made by Sythcol's elite conjurors. Tinctures and potions that they no longer had time to make.

Because they had far greater catastrophes brewing than inedible soup.

"I'll think of someone else to cook." Sythcol pushed the bowl away.

"I can find someone," Brovdir offered.

But Sythcol waved him off. "You don't know the clan like I do. I'd rather not risk making it *worse.*"

Brovdir's fists balled, but he gritted his teeth. It wasn't worth the argument. Sythcol was right. He *did* know this clan best.

And besides, the only person he knew who could cook was . . .

He gulped hard and pushed the thought of the beautiful human out of his mind. Guilt and shame gnawed at his gut.

"I'll just add finding a cook to my ever-growing list of tasks." Sythcol pulled a metal container from his robe sleeve and popped off the cap. The scent of lavender and roses was a welcome change from the stew. Sythcol winced as he rubbed the salve into the blackened skin of his arms. It was nearly up to his shoulders now and would only grow worse as he continued to use his magic.

Creating the spell and tinctures for menial tasks would have to come to an end, or Sythcol was going to lose his arms.

Once done applying the salve, Sythcol put the container away and moved off toward the door near the trunk of the tree that led to the former chief's office. The elegant space was furnished with intricately carved and oiled furniture, the drapes were made of a soft material Brovdir had never even encountered during his travels. The carpet was so soft and lush it felt unsettling under his feet.

And it was completely littered with papers, vials, and crates as Sythcol attempted to investigate former Chief Ergoth's past atrocities.

"It was the housing for the warriors, wasn't it? That's why you brought the elders together?"

Brovdir nodded slowly.

Sythcol let out a long sigh as he began to organize the papers on the desk as if looking for something. "I told you, temporary shelters will be more than sufficient. Your warriors don't seem to be having trouble in their leather tents, why should any others?"

Yes, the warriors were doing fine in their tents, but it wasn't *comfortable* by any stretch. There was snow on the ground for Fades sake. "What of the women and children?"

The thought of Trinia sleeping in a tent in the snow made his throat burn and his skin crawl.

"There are really that many?"

Brovdir growled low. It was certainly more difficult for the clans outside the Rove Woods to find mates, but that didn't mean they had *none*.

Sythcol's face softened with contrition. "I apologize. That was snide. Of course, we'll give any empty dwellings to the orcs with mates and sons. Once those are full, we'll fashion something sturdier. I'm not sure *how*, but . . . we'll figure it out."

"I could," Brovdir said but the harsh look from Sythcol had his back straightening and a lifetime of conditioning as the warlord's second sealed his mouth shut.

"We'll do it together. Again, you don't know this clan like I do. You'd have no idea where to even put extra housing."

Brovdir wanted to argue. He knew he *should* argue.

But his throat throbbed and constricted around the words.

With that, Sythcol changed the subject. "Have you received any reports from your warriors?"

Brovdir sighed and fished into his trouser pocket for the messages he'd been sent throughout the day. Brovdir's only official task as chief was keeping track of the warriors. It was the main reason Karthoc wanted him to become a joint chief.

"I don't trust anyone in this clan to control my warriors or carry out my orders for them. That is why you must stay here and play chief."

So Brovdir had, although it went against his nature to do so. He was born to be a follower, not a leader. And he'd expected Karthoc to send more messages with orders. He'd half expected to get a bird two or three times a day.

Instead, his brother was far too busy gathering up the orc clans and hunting down his wayward mate to send more than one every half-moon.

Brovdir was on his own.

Sythcol took the small scraps of paper from Brovdir's grasp without hesitation and began to go through each one with a furrowed brow. Even communication with the warriors was met with intense scrutiny.

"They gave me all these already," he muttered as Brovdir crossed his arms. "There are no others?"

"No," Brovdir said darkly. "They would not withhold from you."

Sythcol's jaw tightened with remorse again, but it was gone quickly and Brovdir had to stop himself from heaving another great sigh of frustration. The male was so on edge. So suspicious. He double checked every scrap of information that was thrown his way against multiple sources and only trusted himself. Even his personal elite team of powerful conjurers had voiced complaints at his wary nature.

But Brovdir did not know how to combat it. The male had been greatly deceived by Ergoth and the wound ran deep.

Perhaps too deep.

"Odd . . . they're all moving closer to Oakwall," Sythcol said under his breath.

Brovdir's mind instantly flashed with the image of Trinia. "The . . . sinkholes are close to Oakwall?"

The urge to bolt to her side and drag his woman away from the danger was almost overwhelming.

But she wasn't *his* woman.

"*Closer*," Sythcol corrected quickly. "Not *close*. They aren't in danger."

"Yet," Brovdir said quietly and Sythcol glowered at him.

"We aren't telling them."

Brovdir leveled the chief with a dark look.

"We are *not* telling them," Sythcol repeated firmly. "You saw how they reacted when we mentioned more warriors were coming to stay. We didn't even mention how *many* and they still panicked. Just today, Headman Gerald sent a message that three more families were talking of leaving the woods. If they knew that sinkholes of churning, icy water were opening up randomly and swallowing up everything in their wake, the whole village might decide to leave. Which would be a *death* sentence—for both them *and* us."

Brovdir sagged. Sythcol was right. With the prophecy of the Fades looming, they simply couldn't take the risk.

Because when the reckoning came, everything outside of these woods would be . . .

He squeezed his eyes shut against the vision he'd seen of Miranda's world of the desolation and chaos and heat. He tried not to think about it.

"I cannot tell them about the sinkholes until I know how to stop them," Sythcol said. "And I've almost got it. I think I've found a pattern, at least." He rubbed at his blackened hands and his eyes took on a haunting glimmer. "I'm *so close.* Just a little more, and I'll . . ."

Sythcol's claws extended suddenly, and he gashed the back

of his hand. Brovdir straightened in shock as the male cursed and slapped his hand over the wound to stop the bleeding. Then he went to the shelves and plucked up a healing tincture.

"I'm fine," Sythcol snapped as Brovdir unsuccessfully tried to keep the worry from his expression. "I'm just tired." The powerful conjurer downed the tincture in a single gulp. "Stop looking at me like that."

Brovdir averted his eyes.

"Anyway." Sythcol finished and came back to sit at the desk. "I can't tell the village yet and cause a panic. You agree, right?"

Brovdir nodded. The villagers would panic. Because what was happening in these woods was *worth* panicking about.

The ground under their feet was being eaten away by a huge underground river. One they'd not even known was *there*.

It shouldn't be there at all.

"Tell your warriors to keep patrolling regularly and report often," Sythcol demanded. "Perhaps I should talk some of the Rove males into joining them. Fifteen isn't enough."

On that, Brovdir could agree. The fifteen warrior orcs Karthoc had left behind had been worked almost to the bone, searching for cracks in the forest floor. Brovdir had spent much of his time toiling right alongside them. Trinia's face flashed in his mind as motivation to keep searching. She liked to walk in these woods.

"We have to at *least* know how to stop them before we bring it up to Headman Gerald. This *and* the prophecy. Otherwise, it could very well be the driving force that would make them *leave*. And you know what would happen if they left, don't you? There would be no more conquests. No more *sons*. This clan would die out in a few generations."

Brovdir couldn't argue with that. This clan was so remote,

so cut off from the outside world, that it wouldn't be possible for them to stay here long term if the humans of Oakwall abandoned these woods.

But it was here they had to stay. *All* orc kind did. The Fades had willed it. The prophecy had been foretold. Their world would be remade. There was no escaping that fate.

And it was a fate Oakwall was blissfully unaware of. In less than two seasons, thousands of orc warriors would move into these woods. They'd outnumber the small village of humans five to one.

"We need answers first," Sythcol said firmly. "Once I know more, at least enough to ease their fears, I will go to Headman Gerald myself and tell him everything. I swear it. But right now, we can't. You know that, don't you, Brovdir?"

Brovdir sighed and rubbed at his aching throat.

"We are *not* going to get Oakwall involved, Brovdir." Sythcol's firm conviction had him straightening in steady agreement with the clear command.

Brovdir nodded despite the churning in his gut that told him that keeping their human neighbors in the dark was going to backfire—badly.

But Sythcol had lived in these woods all his life. He knew every human in Oakwall Village. He was better suited for the role of chief than Brovdir ever could be.

"Go fetch the soup for me," Sythcol said quietly, rubbing at his stomach. Brovdir completed the order without complaint or thought and settled the still steaming bowl of pine-needle fish down on the desk next to the conjurer.

The male wrinkled up his nose at the sight, but relented and took a quick bite.

It crunched.

Brovdir could not decide if he was more amused or

disgusted as Sythcol grimaced. He flinched as he swallowed down the mysteriously crunchy soup.

Then he looked back down at the messages the warriors had been sending and asked absently. “Any word from Karthoc?”

Brovdir shook his head.

Sythcol nodded, brows furrowed. “I have a bad feeling about it. We should be getting more updates from them.”

“Rendid sent one yesterday.”

“Yes, and all it told us was that he’d separate from Karthoc to fetch the western clans,” Sythcol muttered. “Six hundred warrior orcs delivered here by winter’s end . . . there’s just too much to do.”

“Orders for me?” Brovdir asked cautiously.

“Just stay on top of your warriors and keep hunting,” Sythcol demanded before sighing raggedly. “Last we heard, Karthoc still had Ergoth with him. If the male was capable of all this”—Sythcol stretched his hands out to indicate the stacks of scrolls and papers on the desk—“then he’s capable of anything. Even slithering into Karthoc’s ear.”

“No. Ergoth couldn’t,” Brovdir insisted. Karthoc had never trusted Ergoth. He wouldn’t fall for the male’s tricks.

“We should have kept Ergoth here.” Sythcol laced his fingers together as he thought. “We could have locked him beneath the Rove Tree. Then we could have questioned him.”

Brovdir opened his mouth to respond, only to have his stomach plunge.

“He has something to do with *all* of this. I just know it.”

Brovdir sucked in a hard breath as the odd sinking feeling intensified.

“Brovdir.” Sythcol rose to his feet. “What’s wrong?”

"Don't know." The sensation of falling made his hair stand on end. He clenched his jaw, flexed his muscles.

Sythcol looked up just as a bird swooped in and landed on his shoulder. The messenger robin tweeted brightly as Sythcol removed the note from his leg.

It was all Brovdir could do to keep standing. Why had he suddenly gone so *dizzy*?

And *cold*?

"This is . . ."

The shocked tone from Sythcol caught Brovdir's attention just as the male yanked a scroll out from the sleeve of his robes and spread it out on top of the messy desk. The map of Rove Wood was clear, and Sythcol used a charcoal pencil to mark down the location of the new crack that one of his warriors had just sent in.

Cracks that always led to new sinkholes.

"Fades," Sythcol gasped as he scribbled down calculations Brovdir couldn't understand. The map was littered with angles and numbers and dark blots where sinkholes had already formed. Where deep chasms were still dangerous and churning. Many grew larger by the moment. So far, no one had gotten hurt when the ground broke open and sucked everything above it into the depths beneath.

But it was only a matter of time.

Sythcol drew lines across the map from three different cracks to a single point.

A very large point.

Dangerously close to Oakwall Village.

And suddenly something deep inside his mind . . . *screamed.*

"That's . . . odd." Sythcol pulled out his notebook and

scribbled notes as his brow furrowed. "It's not following the usual pattern."

Brovdir could hardly spare a grunt in response. The sensation gripping his veins was growing *stronger.* Like pouring cold water over his flesh. The intensity increased with every passing moment. His skin prickled like he'd just been caught in a spider's web. A web that was *tugging* on him.

Tugging toward the depths of the Rove Woods.

"Perhaps it's aligning with these ones here? Though it's not perfect." Sythcol's voice barely broke through the fog clouding him.

The pull was so *vivid.* Almost like a compulsion. The web strummed around him, vibrating like sound waves he could feel against his flesh.

And then he felt his *name*.

Brovdir!

And he knew in an instant who it was.

He snatched up the map right out from under Sythcol and bolted for the stairs, ignoring the conjurer's confused demands. There was no time to explain or stop.

He had to get to Trinia before it was too late.

CHAPTER
THIRTEEN

TRINIA

Water raged around her, threatening to pull her down. She was submerged in water to her ankles as it sucked her toward a blackened tunnel. Waves crashed and ripped into it like a deadly funnel. She clung to a root desperately. Her grip on the slippery wood was so strong, it's a wonder she didn't break it.

The underground current was dark and frothing. She'd be sucked deep into the ground. Into a hole that was growing bigger with every gasp of breath she took. Chunks of grass and mud splashed into the raging current, soaking her with each plunge.

She screamed, but she was too deep in the woods. No one could hear her!

She should never have come out here.

She was going to die.

She was going to die and Ronhold the asshat and his sniveling son were going to get her bakery!

Her throat closed up and her tears streamed down her face. Her mouth opened in a wail and spilled a name.

"Brovdir!"

She didn't know why she called him. She'd met him *twice.* He was just as far from her as Headman Gerald, or her sister, or literally *anyone* else from Oakwall Village or Rove Wood Clan.

But if anyone would make it to her in time, if anyone *would hear* her way out here in the woods, it would be him.

And she had so much she wanted to say to him! She'd thought of little else for an entire moon.

Fades, she wasn't going to be thinking *anything* soon.

The root started to give way.

She looked up and saw that the dirt had been shaved away to the bush to which the root was attached. It shook at the precipice of the cliff, slipping downward. The water was up to her calves.

She didn't have the strength to pull herself up. Years of kneading dough for hours every day hadn't been enough. She was going to fall in. She was going to get sucked down into the underground cavern below her and drown in the murky, pitch black water. No one would ever know what happened to her.

The bush jerked and her stomach plunged. The water splashed all the way to her thighs. The current was so strong!

The root gripped her wrist so hard she felt like it might break. But then she was being yanked swiftly upward.

The bush barreled past her, caught in her hair and scraped her already gashed cheek. But where it went down, she went *up*.

Into a hard wall of naked green muscles.

Trinia gasped as the body holding her jerked away from the hole, ran backward past trees that were being sucked into the churning water. Over a massive, downed log covered in moss.

CHAPTER THIRTEEN

Oh Fades! I am alive!

She couldn't seem to get enough air into her lungs. Her eyes stung and tears coursed hot tracks down her icy cheeks.

She was plopped down on a boulder. Mud caked her body, and her dress was soaked.

"Trinia."

The deep growl warmed her up from the inside out and her eyes snapped to meet the gaze of her savior.

Brovdir.

Her vision blurred with tears. "Y-you really saved me," she managed on a gasping sob.

"Yes."

The confirmation hooked deep in her guts and stirred them up until they felt as tempestuous as the deadly water she'd just survived.

She couldn't believe it. He was *here*. Right now. Just in time.

Just like *last* time.

Gratitude and relief were palpable in her chest and she took a deep breath, ready to babble her thanks. "I can't believe you've been ignoring me all this time and *now* you show up."

Her mouth snapped shut as Brovdir's eyes widened to engulf his face. Fades, *that* hadn't been what she'd meant to say at *all*.

But it was too late now. Everything else in her life was already in chaos. Why wouldn't she ruin things with the male who had saved her life?

Saved her life . . .

The roaring of the sinkhole right behind her flooded her senses and her feet scrambled as she tried to get away.

Brovdir held her firm, keeping her from bolting blindly into the forest. "You're safe."

She'd almost died. *Died.*

"Hush . . . no harm will come to you."

The low sound was so soothing in her ears and her terror eased. Brovdir held her tightly, and she leaned into him. He was huge. And warm. And she felt like a half-drowned rat and probably didn't look much better, but there was nothing she could do about that now.

"Fades, have mercy."

Trinia yipped with surprise at this new voice and whipped around to find that Sythcol had appeared at the tree line. He was gasping for breath, his hair disheveled, and his robes soaked to the knee.

"This is . . ." Sythcol's eyes were stricken with horror as he walked through the brush toward the still raging sinkhole.

"D-don't go close!"

"This is three times the size of the others." Sythcol's words pummeled her in the chest and her mind lit up.

Others?

The powerful conjurer held out his hands toward the bubbling water. A tightness swirled through the air. A shuddering sensation tingled up her spine as the orc spun his magic. She could not see it, but she knew it was there.

And the water stopped its churning. It stopped ripping away at the land. The growth of it slowed to a halt, and the water level receded to the point that she could no longer see it. She wasn't sure what was more unnerving—churning destructive water or a seemingly bottomless pit.

Sythcol lowered his hands and stepped back, breathing a sigh of relief as he examined his handiwork. He'd stopped it so fast.

Like he knew exactly how to already.

She managed to keep the tremble from her voice. "There're more than one of these? You've seen them before?"

Sythcol's back straightened and Brovdir, who was still sitting directly in front of her, tensed noticeably.

"You have," Trinia gasped. "Is that how you found me? Have you been keeping track of them?"

Neither male spoke nor met her eyes.

Anger burned at her throat. "If you knew about them then why wasn't I warned? Why hasn't *anyone* been warned? I never would have run out here had I known!"

"This doesn't concern you," Sythcol said. "Brovdir, take her back to Oakwall."

"Doesn't concern me?" Trinia's voice was shrill as she got to her feet and pushed Brovdir out of her way. Her sopping wet gown was so heavy she almost couldn't rise. "I nearly *died* just now!"

Warmth caught right around her chin and her face was tipped slightly as Brovdir examined her. His eyes were intense and bright. They glowed green in the dim light so there was no confusing his brooding expression. She'd forgotten orcs' eyes glowed in the dark. She saw them at night so rarely.

Brovdir let out a low growl that shot tingling heat throughout her body and she could do nothing but suck in air as he said, "You're wounded."

She gulped as he gently stroked her cheek right below the stinging cut. She could feel the heat radiating off him. Just like before, he hadn't worn a shirt, just a pair of worn leather slacks. His dark complexion and rippling muscles threatened to undo all the thoughts from her mind.

He looked like he was sculpted by the Fades themselves.

But he'd also avoided her for over a moon. Hadn't even sent a *note*.

She pushed his hand away. "I'm fine. Let me go."

Brovdir flinched away and made a strangled noise in the back of his throat that made her heart twinge. Had she been too harsh? *He* was the one who'd ignored *her*. Why should she feel guilty about upholding the boundary he'd put up?

But then his head drooped, and his floppy hair covered his dejected eyes and she'd never seen an orc look more like a kicked puppy.

Why did that make her stupid heart flutter?

She went back to the matter at hand, desperate to cover up the fact that her cheeks were heating. "Sythcol, tell me *what* is going on. Right now. And don't you *dare* try to tell me it's not of my concern again."

"They're sinkholes."

She jerked her attention back to Brovdir.

"Brovdir!" Sythcol snapped. "I told you we can't—"

"Sinkholes," Brovdir confirmed again, ignoring Sythcol's anger. "Started opening a moon back."

She shook her head in disbelief. "That's so long ago! Why don't I know about them? Or anyone? Headman Gerald—"

"Your headman doesn't need to know *anything*," Sythcol said as he rubbed at his blackened hands.

"What do you mean he doesn't need to know? Of course, he needs to know. You have a moral obligation to—"

"I have this under control," Sythcol snapped. "This crisis will be over soon. There is no need to cause panic among the humans over a problem I've nearly solved."

"Nearly solved?" Trinia snapped with disbelief. "I *nearly died*. 'Nearly solved' isn't fast enough."

"But you didn't die because my methods are working. We're tracking them. Keeping them in check."

"If you really had them in check, I wouldn't have fallen in

one in the first place!" Trinia cried, "What if I'd been a child? Or an old woman out for a stroll? What if I hadn't been strong enough to hold on to that root?"

Brovdir made another choked noise, and she looked up to find him pale and stricken in the dimming light. She saw his hands twitch as he reached for her, but he didn't grab. Didn't force anything.

The cold of the night was penetrating her sodden gown, and the snow crunched as she shifted her feet. The urge to fall into his arms and let him warm her up was almost overwhelming.

She took a step away to combat the desire and Brovdir's face fell.

"They aren't opening up near the village," Sythcol's voice was hard and unyielding. "All of them have been on the opposite end of the clan."

"*This* one did!" She looked from Sythcol to Brovdir.

Was Brovdir not going to say anything? His expression was still downcast and stricken.

Whose side was he on in this?

"This one is an anomaly."

"Anomaly or not, I *insist* you tell Headman Gerald. He needs to know of the danger that—"

"*Enough!*" Sythcol's roar had Trinia's mouth falling open in shock. She'd *never* heard the male raise his voice. "*I* am chief and I will not be swayed by anyone! Especially not a woman who knows *nothing*."

Brovdir instantly barreled toward Sythcol. The only thing louder than the pounding of his feet was the ferocious snarl that left his lips.

Sythcol scrambled back, far too close to the sinkhole's edge.

"Stop!" Trinia demanded. "You're both acting like fools! Sythcol, get away from the sinkhole before you fall in."

The male scowled but did so, giving Brovdir a wide birth.

Brovdir instantly backed off and the deadliest, most uncomfortable silence she'd ever experienced in her life descended on the lot of them. And she'd experienced *many* uncomfortable moments in her life.

"Brovdir." Sythcol's smooth voice punctuated with every icy word. "Were you *threatening* me just now?"

It was dark now, but even in the dim, she could see Brovdir go stiff, his breathing labored, and his fists balled.

She should have wanted to bolt at this moment, get as far away from the furious male as she could.

Instead, she carefully approached and touched his arm.

He jolted and swung his head around to look at her. Rum cakes and raisins, his glowing eyes were both unsettling and . . . enchanting.

"Take a breath," she demanded. "No good will come from fighting with him."

He dutifully sucked in a hard gulp of air as his eyes searched hers. Finally, he turned his hard gaze back to Sythcol and said, "No threat. *Apologize*."

"Apologize?" Sythcol's brow furrowed in confusion. Trinia was just as confused until Sythcol said, "Fine. Yes. I was wrong to take all the authority in this. You do indeed hold half, Brovdir."

"No. To *her*."

Trinia blinked, wildly uncomfortable. Especially when Sythcol's lips parted in shock, and he sputtered. "You want me to apologize to her? For *what*, exactly?"

"Raising your voice."

He was mad because Sythcol had yelled at her?

Her cheeks heated and pleasure warred with her embarrassment.

Sythcol sputtered in disbelief, his glowing eyes widened, showing the bags under them more clearly. His hair was matted, and his clothes were rumpled. “All right. Trinia, I apologize for startling you. I should not have raised my voice and threatened the peace between our people.”

“It’s fine,” Trinia said quickly before Brovdir could get any angrier. “I . . . can see this is a matter of dire importance to *both* of our communities.”

“Yes,” he said gruffly. “I do concede to that, at least. But I ask you not to get involved in this matter. I am so close to solving this, just a few days’ time, and these sinkholes will no longer be a problem. Please. Allow me time to fix this before going to your headman about what transpired here tonight.”

“I can’t do that, and you know it,” Trinia said firmly. “I almost died. The peace between our communities will be shaken when they find out you’ve kept these dangers from us.”

“It is the *peace* that has forced me to hold my tongue.” Sythcol’s voice was clipped with determination. “Until now, the sinkholes have only formed within the borders of our clan. There was no threat to your village. I did not want to cause needless panic.”

“But now there *is* a threat.”

“Yes, and now I know how to stop them. I just need time.”

“But how much time? *How* are you going to stop them?”

“I can’t get into that now.” Sythcol waved her off and anger bloomed at the back of her throat. “But they will be stopped completely by the end of the season. Of that I can assure you. We are in winter. None from the village walk these woods at this time.”

“I do.”

"You are an anomaly, Trinia. Please, see it from my side. How would your people have reacted had they been told sinkholes were opening up? I know many are already talking of leaving the village and resettling outside these woods."

She sucked in a breath, wanting to refute him, wanting to tell him he was wrong. That they wouldn't have panicked, that they wouldn't have left. She wanted to insist that Headman Gerald would have handled it.

But then the memories of the first trade with the warriors flashed in her mind. Of the day more than half the villagers hadn't gone despite the boons. Some *still* refused to attend. Rumors about the warriors were constant. Negative gossip spread like wildfire.

Her sister's voice echoed in her mind. *"Plenty of folks are talking about leaving since the warrior orcs started to settle here."*

She didn't want to admit Sythcol was right, but he was. Her people would have panicked in the worst way.

"You . . . still need to at least tell Headman Gerald," Trinia insisted. "He would never do anything to threaten the peace. And I can't lie for you, Sythcol. I'm not going to keep your secrets for you."

"I understand. All I ask for is time. Can we speak on this tomorrow? When it's not so fresh and emotions are not so high? Please."

Trinia let out a long breath. She couldn't blame Sythcol for being cautious. Since Chief Ergoth's betrayal had come to light, everything had been tense. The cruelty and manipulation of the former chief had shocked the villagers into intense disquiet because no one had seen it coming. They had all liked Ergoth. They'd all thought he was a good leader who put peace first.

But they had been wrong.

And since that moment, Sythcol had done everything in his power to keep their communities banded together. He'd gone to every trade, chatted with every merchant, met with the villagers who were wary, and proved to them that the orcs wanted nothing but goodwill between their peoples.

"Trinia?" Sythcol pressed softly. "Tomorrow? Please?"

She exhaled hard. And nodded.

"Thank you." Sythcol's own breath left in a whoosh.

"Trinia."

She snapped her gaze to Brovdir. She'd been so caught up in the debate with Sythcol she'd nearly forgotten . . . he was chief too. What was his say in all this?

Did . . . he want to hide the sinkholes from her village?

But when she searched his face, all she saw was a mask of concern. His glowing eyes were stuck on her cheek, which stung from the cut. His fists were curled. His chest and arms were coated with mud . . .

And so was she. She was a right state, soaked to the bone and caked with grime. She was shivering so hard she felt like she might vibrate right out of her own skin.

"Here." She turned to find Sythcol digging in the sleeve of his robe. He produced a small green vial and tossed it over.

Brovdir caught it with ease. Then he paused, eyes narrowed at Sythcol for a long moment before he grated. "Robe too."

Sythcol's nose screwed up and Trinia might have laughed under other circumstances. "Excuse me?"

"The robe. For her."

Sythcol's scowl deepened, but, surprisingly, he conceded with a puff of irritation. "Fine. Here." He quickly emptied the pockets and sleeves of the dark brown cloak, piled up his belongings on a nearby rock, and shrugged it off.

Brovdir took it and brought it back to her, but he uncorked the vial first. A light minty scent flooded her nose, telling her this was a magical healing tincture.

She wasn't about to turn that down. She took it from Brovdir and was about to swallow it when he stepped *much* closer. The firm wall of his bare chest, rippling muscular perfection, was all she could see. Her breath caught as the desire to lean into him swarmed her. What was he doing? Was he going to kiss her again—

Brovdir swung Sythcol's cloak around her shoulders and heat flooded back into her bones. She let out a long exhale. So *that's* all he was doing.

She should be grateful for the generous act, but a silly tinge of disappointment edged at the corners of her mind. She was being stupid. He hadn't even sent a message by bird. Of course he wasn't interested in her.

Not that it mattered. It really shouldn't matter. She had far bigger things to worry about.

Like the fact that three generations of hard work had just been stolen away from her.

Her eyes stung and the world around her blurred.

"Drink."

Brovdir's sharp demand had her tipping the tincture into her mouth without question. The familiar prickling sensation began at her tongue but quickly spread through her whole body, warming her briefly before she was shivering cold again. The cuts along her arms and face stung for only a moment, and then they were gone completely. Only smears of blood remained to prove she'd been hurt at all.

"I do apologize for this."

Sythcol's words caught her attention. Brovdir stepped back so she could meet the conjurer's tired eyes. "It never should have happened. I've been relying on the warriors to warn us of the cracks in the ground so I can predict when and where the sinkholes will form." He looked toward the massive chasm again, his expression a mask of concern. "But I failed. I alone am at fault for this travesty."

Trinia's gut twisted at the heavy weight of guilt flickering behind the orc's green eyes. He had much to answer for, certainly, but she didn't see the benefit of wringing him out here. Especially now that the chill of the forest was getting to her. She tugged the cloak tighter.

As if he could read her mind, Brovdir said, "Taking her back."

"Good. Send a bird to my conjurers and your warriors to meet me here. I'll need their help tonight."

Brovdir nodded before turning to her. His eyes pierced her, from the top of her head all the way down her sodden frame, or what he could make of it since she was covered by the cloak.

She suddenly wished they didn't glow, so his intense expression could have been lost to the darkness.

"I'll carry you."

She jerked at that. "Oh. No. You don't need to."

"Too dark."

"I can see just fine, Brovdir."

"Too wet."

"Being wet doesn't inhibit my ability to walk."

"Too . . . small."

She almost laughed. "All right. Now you're just making things up. I don't need you to carry me. I'm just fine on my own." To prove it, she began walking in the direction she supposed the village to be.

And immediately tripped on a thick root.

She yelped as she went down, but the sodden ground

wasn't what she hit. Instead, she slammed up against a firm wall of muscle. Hot and hard and smelling of spice and woodsmoke.

She should have pushed away from him. Absolutely should have immediately.

But . . . he was so *warm*.

Her half moment of hesitation was her undoing because Brovdir took full advantage and swung her up into his arms without preamble.

Her breath caught in her throat as he tucked her into his chest. His arms were banded around her back and under her knees. Her head was right next to his. The shock of it gave her pause.

Maybe . . . she could let him carry her for just a little while. Just until they were back at the main path leading to Oakwall.

He began a quick clip through the tree line, which was now pitched into near blackness. Not even a glimmer of sunlight remained. Another reason to let him carry her. The snow crunched under his feet as he walked, and the icy wind raked over her chilly skin. The last of her anger and adrenaline wore off, and she began to shiver almost violently.

The orc carrying her tightened his grip, adjusting the cloak slightly so she was covered more thoroughly.

And then he finally spoke. "*Why*?"

His single grated word made her stomach flip. "Why . . . what?"

"Why are you out here?" He winced from the pain the words caused him and pity made her quick to answer.

"I—" Her throat constricted as new tears flooded her eyes. She couldn't get the words out. It hurt too much.

She'd lost her mother's bakery. *She'd lost it.*

"Trinia?" Brovdir's voice was awash with concern and his

hand curled around her waist, hot but gentle. She could feel the deadly prickle of his claws against her shoulder and leg before they flashed away, but his grip never loosened.

His warmth and strength distracted her from the pain and exhaustion flattened her. She went a little boneless in his arms and he didn't flinch. He only adjusted her so she could rest her head against his shoulder if she'd wanted. And Fades did she want to. She wanted to close her eyes and collapse against him. She wanted to soak up his warmth and strength and let him chase away all her anxieties while she slept peacefully.

"Sorry."

She blinked rapidly and adjusted so she could search his face. She could only see his expression by the light of his glowing eyes.

"I'm sorry," Brovdir repeated.

"Sorry for what?"

He swallowed thickly and turned away, but said, "For . . . not seeing you."

She couldn't see his expression now that he wasn't looking at her. "Why didn't you come to see me?"

A slightly strangled noise came from his throat. His voice was incredibly raspy, and she supposed it would be cruel of her to force him to speak. She was too exhausted to quiz him, anyway.

She leaned her head down against his shoulder and he let out a little huff, only for it to dawn on her. He was taking her back to Oakwall Village.

And she didn't have anywhere to go.

CHAPTER FOURTEEN

BROVDIR

Fades be praised! She felt good in his arms.

His blood was zinging with the contact. Her sweet scent was all curled up and content in his head. His chest felt light and thrummed with a deep-seated security that he recognized despite never having experienced it before.

An imprint.

"Healed?" he asked this despite the logic that he'd witnessed her injuries disappearing with his own eyes. The cuts were gone, but the scent of blood remained, and she was coated with mud.

He would take her to his bath.

"Yes, I'm healed." Her voice was a little lower and huskier than he'd remembered. He'd gone to sleep with the memory of her sweet voice playing in his mind, and now he finally got to hear it again. "I've taken those tinctures many times and they've never failed. Did you think it might?"

"No," he said with an exhale of relief.

"It was pretty lucky you got to the sinkhole in time. Your hearing must be pretty good to have heard me all the way out here, even for an orc."

He hadn't heard her. It was the imprint that had told him she was in peril. The connection allowed him to hear her call, even over great distances.

He tightened his grip slightly. That meant she'd called for him. It hadn't only been the imprint warning him she was in danger. In her time of greatest need, she'd wanted *him*. His throat tightened as the urge to nuzzle the top of her head with his cheek grew overwhelming.

"So . . . um . . . I have a favor to ask."

He nodded. He'd give her anything.

She let out a little puff of breath that warmed his shoulder before saying, "Instead of going back to Oakwall, could you take me to Savili and Iytier's home?"

He blinked rapidly as shock flattened him.

"I know it's not really allowed to have unmated women stay in the clan," she said carefully.

Was that not allowed?

"But Savili has been my friend since childhood. Her sister is one of my closest confidants."

His hands tightened around her slightly as his face went flush with . . . jealousy.

He wanted to be her closest confidant.

"And Iytier is mated, so it shouldn't be too big a thing to stay at his home for the night."

Oh, *fuck* no.

She would not be staying with *any* other male. Human or orc. He would not allow it.

"Uh . . . Brovdir your claws are out."

His breath caught in his throat as he realized he'd clutched her far too hard. The wet fabric of her dress was caught slightly around the sharp tips of his claws. He *slunk* them back into his hands so quickly it almost took the cloth with it.

"Hurt?" Fades help him, if he'd harmed her without thinking—

"No. I'm fine."

He exhaled a sigh of relief. Fuck, he'd never considered himself the jealous sort.

But he'd never imprinted on anyone before, either.

"Your claws are so much bigger than the orcs from Rove Wood. It was almost as long as my pinky."

Pleasure flushed him. "Thank you."

She sputtered and her cheeks reddened delightfully. "That wasn't—I . . . I mean I don't . . ."

He waited, wishing to hear more compliments from her.

"Never mind."

Disappointment made him sag.

"Anyway, I really need a place to stay. Just for tonight." She added that last part far too rapidly. "Just for now. And then I'll go back to the village in the morning."

"Stay with me."

The request came out before he even realized it was coming.

Trinia's beautiful eyes widened. "Uh . . . Brovdir, I don't think that's such a good idea."

Why not?

Her brows shot up and her eyes got big, and his heart felt like it would thunder right out of his chest.

Especially when she reached up to scratch at the back of his neck, right at the hairline.

That felt *good*. So fucking blasted *good*.

"Don't look at me like that." Trinia's voice was a little

tight, but she didn't stop scratching. His knees felt like they might go weak. "You know it's not a good idea for me to stay with you."

Why wasn't it?

She gave him a hard stare. "Brovdir, you are the unmated orc *chief,* and I am an unattached woman. You know what everyone will think."

They would all think that she was his woman and not go anywhere near her.

"Brovdir." Her tone was low with warning. It made his back straighten. "We do *not* want to give them that impression. Trust me."

But he did. He did *so badly*.

He'd give anything for that impression to be *reality.* The very idea of other males in the clan thinking that this woman, *his* woman, was still a prospect for them . . .

His blood heated all over again.

"Put those claws away, Brovdir, and take me to Savili." She shivered slightly, and he worried that his claws might have frightened her. "Biscuits and jam, it is *cold* out here."

He picked up the pace, and a moment later, they broke through the tree line onto one of the clan's lit paths.

Even after all this time, he couldn't get used to the sight of it. The huge oak and fir trees that lined the paths were so large it was almost intimidating, but the fact that they'd been carved into *houses*, with doors and windows and furniture, was still unbelievable to him.

Outside these woods, clans struggled to keep the elements from knocking down their homes. He spent most of his nights in a roughly made tent. He'd been told stories of the Rove Woods. They all had, but hearing about it and seeing it were two entirely different things.

"Oh, you brought me here *already*?"

His stomach dropped as she leveled him with a hard stare.

"You had no intention of taking me back to my home at all, did you?"

He couldn't quite meet her gaze. "To . . . to Hovget."

She put a finger under his chin and forced his face to turn back to her. He blinked in surprise at the warmth in her gaze. "Don't try to lie, Brovdir. You aren't very good at it."

He . . . wasn't? He'd been able to deceive thousands of humans in the past. It was part of the reason he was still *alive*.

"I can't imagine that you were taking me back to your home to take advantage of me."

Never. The idea of having any woman who was in any kind of duress repulsed him, but the thought of abusing Trinia in such a way made him feel physically ill.

"I can tell you aren't the type." She patted the middle of his chest and his whole body went flush with pleasure. "And I know you have a tough time speaking, but honestly, you need to tell me where we're going if you're going to cart me around. *And* you should take me to Savili. I insist."

He had no valid arguments to this.

"Put me down now, Brovdir. I'm a big girl. I can walk on my own."

Everything in him rebelled at the idea.

But she'd given him an order and he could not disobey.

He lowered her to her feet.

"Warrior—er, I mean Chief Brovdir! So glad to catch you."

His stomach dropped.

Barreling up the path toward him was Elder Plog and judging from his expression, he was extremely *eager* to catch Brovdir.

Fades help him.

CHAPTER FIFTEEN

TRINIA

The noise Brovdir made in the back of his throat was so thickly laced with exasperation that Trinia almost laughed.

Or at least she might have, had she not been covered head to toe in mud and grime, in a clan she wasn't supposed to be in, with an orc who'd been carting her around all night, after having almost been sucked underground and *drowned*.

Elder Plog approached with a natural spring in his step. Trinia had known him all her life, and although his face had wrinkled and his slender body had hunched, his eyes had never lost their twinkle.

His penchant for mischief was well-known and she *really* didn't need any more insanity tonight.

"Why Trinia, this is such a delight to see. You'll be a wonderful mate to our chief."

Her spine instantly straightened as the idea smacked right around inside her already scrambled brain. She didn't even have the wherewithal to step away from Brovdir's hands, which were warmly placed on her upper arms.

"Don't mind me. I don't want to meddle in your business. Being so late at night, I'm certain you have some glorious plans. Glad I'm half deaf."

Trinia was at a complete loss for words. This biscuit-blasted male was an absolute blabbermouth and if he left with the impression she and the orc chief were together *everyone* would know it before the sun came up.

And she'd have to tell every single being here that the elder was still insane, and that was *not* what was going on.

And her sister would be *fuming* that she was becoming the clan matriarch and not her.

And her patrons would gossip constantly, never giving her a moment's peace.

And she'd have to nail the bakery door shut to get anything done.

And . . . and . . .

And she didn't have patrons anymore.

She didn't work at the *bakery* anymore.

"Trinia?"

Brovdir's warm hands tightened on her shoulders, and she looked up to his face, illuminated by the torches lining the dirt path. He was awash with gentle concern. His grip felt steady and reminded her of how safe she'd felt when she was in his arms. How cared for. How comfortable . . .

Her eyes widened as a dangerous, stupid, *horrible* idea flashed in her mind.

One that would solve all her problems in an instant.

Even though it made her knees buckle.

Even though it would make all the gossip *true*.

"Chief, I'm here about those boars we were discussing."

Trinia blinked, so thrown off that she had nearly forgotten that the elder was there.

"You appear confused, Trinia," the elder said. "Did our good chief not mention to you that hundreds, perhaps even *thousands*, of boars will be entering the Rove Woods within the next few seasons?"

Trinia went cold very quickly despite the warmth of Brovdir's frame hovering right behind her. "*What*? Brovdir, how is that even possible? Does it have to do with the blight?"

First the bakery, then sinkholes, and now *this*?

Had the Fades abandoned them?

"No!" Brovdir snapped so forcefully that Trinia flinched and his brow knitted with regret. "No, there're none."

"None what? Boar or blight?"

"Chief, I apologize, but it's long past my nightly cap and my nose has already begun to tickle to say nothing of my hinter region." Trinia's mind spun itself into knots, trying to both decipher and *forget* whatever it was the elder had just said. "I just want to say a few quick things and then you can continue carrying her around to your heart's content. Or whatever it is you plan to do to each other."

She took a quick step away from Brovdir. "W-we're not doing—I mean, I wasn't planning on . . . er . . ." She actually *had* been planning that, hadn't she?

She needed a house . . . a new bakery.

And a conquest to the orc chief could request those things in exchange for their service.

Brovdir moved in a little closer to her, close enough it felt like the sunrise warming her back after a long, cold night. The idea that she could so easily have back what she'd lost after a few seasons of carrying a babe was a revelation.

A revelation that made her stomach knot up and her skin go

clammy and her mind quail at the thought of passing her tiny child over to the orc standing behind her and leaving the rearing of that child to him.

"I was thinking we could try to herd the boar toward one of these sinkholes that keep cropping up all around the clan," Elder Plog continued, and it took everything in her to concentrate on what he was saying. "The water rushing through them is quite deep and rapid, but the holes beneath the water surface that lead into the ground aren't too big. I bet you the boars' fat bottoms would be big enough to plug them up."

The mental image that the elder painted was so insane that it almost made her laugh.

"Then when we're ready to eat them, we could fish them out. Somehow . . . Bolsan had a rope and pulley idea that was quite intriguing. He'll be bringing it to you in various sketches tomorrow at breakfast."

Brovdir looked like he wanted to cry, and despite her turmoil, mirth danced around in her chest. "No."

"No? What do you mean?" The elder's eyes widened, and he smacked his forehead with his palm. "Ah, shitscoodle. I forgot we weren't supposed to tell the villagers about the sinkholes. This is why Sythcol won't let me go to the trades." His pleading eyes caught Trinia up. "Don't suppose you could forget everything you heard, could you? Or pretend you've gone raving! I do that all the time. Barrels of fun."

She blinked at him.

"She knows," Brovdir said. "She'll keep it secret."

Would she? She glanced back to look at Brovdir with narrowed eyes, and he instantly shrunk back.

He really was eager to please, wasn't he?

That . . . would make it much easier to bed him.

Was she really going to go through with this?

"Well, thank plumb for that," the elder exclaimed with a grin that fell just as quickly as it rose. "So, what's the problem with my boar-stopper plan, then? We can't just leave them in the sinkholes to rot, you know. Sythcol believes that these underground waterways connect to our drinking water. Good way to get everyone knocking on the Fades door, drinking rotting boar water. Blech!" The elder spat on the ground.

In a flash, she was being hauled away from the wayward spittle, which was, in truth, nowhere near her. Her back hit a hard wall of muscle and an instant shiver coursed down her spine. Her toes curled in her wet shoes.

Brovdir let out a low rumbling growl that vibrated from the top of her head all the way down into the pit of her stomach. It took everything in her not to squirm.

Fades help her! She was in *trouble*.

"Careful." Brovdir's voice was hard and unyielding, and her face heated up.

The elder didn't appear the least bit perturbed. "Sorry, young lady, forgot you were here. My eyesight's not what it used to be, and you're such a tiny thing."

Trinia blinked in shock at this male's lunacy. Of all the things she'd been described as in her life, tiny was not one of them.

"Anywho, I just thought you should know my idea. Just in case you wanted to bring it up with Sythcol, wasn't sure when those boars were set to arrive so—"

"There are no boars!" There was such desperation in Brovdir's tone that her shock and dismay faded and mirth threatened to burst from her lips. She pinched them to stop her laughter.

"Have a good night, then. I'll be sure to let the folks know to get their earplugs ready." The male was gone before Brovdir could throttle him, but it looked like he wanted to.

"Did you really ask the elders for advice?" Trinia asked as she tried to get all her emotions under control. "No one warned you about them?"

He let out a ragged sigh, squeezing his eyes shut, and pinched the bridge of his nose.

Trinia lost control of her laughter. Tonight had probably been the most horrible, terrifying, and devastating day of her entire life—save the day her mother had died—but this was the hardest she'd laughed in a very long time.

She wiped the wetness from her eyes as she finally got herself back in check. When she looked up, Brovdir was regarding her with a warm, soft expression that made her stomach do flips. Her heart hammered rapidly in her chest, her mouth went dry, and her mind reeled . . . and blasted burned biscuits . . .

She was actually going to do this.

She was going to try to bed this orc.

"I'll . . . I'll stay with you tonight, Brovdir. If you'll still have me."

He blinked, eyes going wide with surprise.

Then he nodded, far too eagerly. A huge grin spread across his face. He looked like he would have whooped for joy had his injured throat allowed it.

Her guilt mounted so high she was certain it would touch the stars, but this was her best chance to have a new place to live, wasn't it? A new bakery . . .

Her eyes prickled with unshed tears, and her skin went clammy. Her heart clenched so hard in her chest it hurt.

She had a storm of emotions brewing inside her and she

begged the Fades to help her keep them at bay long enough to become his conquest.

CHAPTER SIXTEEN

BROVDIR

Brovdir could not decide if he was elated or terrified.

Trinia walked quietly beside him, her form completely concealed under Sythcol's large cloak. It smelled of the conjurer. Salt and floral herbs. He wanted to rip the thing off her and toss it into the woods before it tainted her.

But the instinct to keep her warm and content was stronger than the basal need for her to smell like him.

"Does your throat hurt?"

He blinked at the question. His throat was in agony. Even taking a deep breath was painful, but that was nothing new. He hadn't expected her to notice.

"You keep rubbing it and grimacing." She tapped her smooth neck with her perfect finger, leaving a little splotch of mud behind.

He needed to get her into his tub.

"Do you have honey?"

Honey? He did . . . somewhere. He didn't much care for

sweets, so if he did, it had gotten shoved to the back of a cabinet.

"After I bathe, I can make you something. You do have a bath, right?"

She wanted to make him something? What? He couldn't wait.

"Please don't tell me you bathe in the iced springs or something crazy like that."

He grinned.

"You better be teasing me!"

He shrugged, and his sly smile widened.

"Brovdir, I'm not taking a bath in the cold. I'll walk right back home first."

Oh, he couldn't have that. He quickly shook his head. "Have one."

"Good." Her eyes narrowed but a small smile still played at her lips. Then she looked around. "This home of yours is on the outskirts, isn't it?"

He nodded and her brow furrowed as she asked, "But you're the chief. Shouldn't you have a home that's central to the clan?"

He didn't see why that would matter much. "Took what Sythcol gave."

She was quiet a moment before saying, "I noticed you default to Sythcol quite a bit. My sister mentioned you've let him take control almost completely."

He shrugged. "He knows Rove better."

"That doesn't mean you shouldn't have your own opinions. That you shouldn't get involved," she said firmly. "You're a chief too, Brovdir. Though I suppose its habit for you to take orders, isn't it? Does your brother give you a lot of orders too?"

"He is Warlord."

"Does it get annoying? Having to obey all the time?" She searched his face, and he was surprised at how good it felt for her to be giving him her full attention.

He shook his head.

"Really? My sister's demands always get on my last nerve." Her voice was tinged with wry mirth.

"Not demands. Orders."

"What's the difference?"

He paused to consider. "Consent."

"W-what?" Trinia blinked as his brows rose at the sight of her heated cheeks. Why was she embarrassed?

"Difference is consent."

"So . . . you think demands are nonconsensual but orders are?"

"Orders are given to willing followers," he said. "Demands are made of those who are not willing."

"Ah, I get it." She tapped her finger against her plump lips, drawing him to distraction. "That does make sense. Still, you don't have to follow *my* orders. It's not like you're *my* follower."

"Trinia."

She met his eyes and longing clenched in his gut.

"I'd follow you anywhere," he said.

He was rewarded by her cheeks heating up. She pushed back her hair and averted her eyes, but there was not a hint of displeasure on her face.

Then her eyes turned forward. "Is this it?"

The realization that he'd stopped them in front of his home jolted him, and now, Trinia was looking up at him with equal parts concern and confusion.

He quickly guided her up the rest of the path to the disheveled oak tree he lived within. Its leaves had already fallen by the time he'd moved in, so he'd never seen it looking anything but entirely dead. He hadn't bothered to shovel the snow, so the path was mushy and slick. The door was crooked and stuck, so he had to yank hard to get it open. The bottom step creaked so loudly when she stepped upon it, she flinched.

And then she entered his home. Her face was illuminated by the fire in the hearth and the three torches lining the walls. Her expression was flat as she looked around, and his guts twisted up with worry. What if she hated it and insisted he take her to Iytier instead?

He liked that male. He did not want to have to beat him to a bloody pulp.

"This is . . ." Trinia tapped her cheek as she looked around at the old furniture and gritty surfaces. His bed sat to the left under a window, his couch was a few steps away in front of the fire. There was a row of storage cabinets next to them that ended with a tiny two-person table.

He'd been satisfied with his tree dwelling so far, though it had taken a long time to get it fixed up. The trunk walls were incredibly thick, so it was quiet and warm within. It had all the amenities he needed. He was used to sleeping in a tent, for Fades' sake.

But Trinia wasn't. His stomach twisted as she crossed the room to the only door aside from the entry. "Is this a bathroom?"

He nodded, very grateful that it had been the first room he had renovated. She opened it and peered inside. A few candles that stayed lit by magic dimly illuminated the space, and her silence made his chest tighten.

"At least it's functional." She looked at the floor. "Could do with a sweep."

He nodded and went to the wall, where he kept a broom and dustpan.

“Oh, not now!” She held up her hands to ward him off. “That wasn’t a command. Just a remark. Sorry . . . I . . .”

Her eyes drifted toward the kitchen area. They lingered on the tiny stove sitting against the opposite wall. Her eyes grew misty and her throat worked in a gulp and Brovdir felt like he was drowning.

She was about to cry. Why was she crying? What had he done?

“I suppose that you orcs don’t have big stoves, do you? Since you take all your meals in the hall.”

Her voice warbled and *fuck*, what could he have done to cause this? Over the years, he’d gotten very good at figuring out what made women cry, but not this time.

“Brovdir, I—” She broke off and took a shuddering breath before she closed her eyes. When she opened them again, her expression was steadfast and confident, but he could still see the storm brewing. “I . . . want to broker a trade with you.”

Oh fuck, *fuck*.

This was about the pans she needed. About the *kiss*.

He dropped his head and looked down at the floor, shoulders slumped in defeat. “Can’t.” The single word felt like daggers.

“You . . . you can’t trade with me? But why? Did I do something wrong?”

Her voice was a bit high, and *fuck*, she was about to cry again. That fact made his muscles clench with agony. His mind reeled. What to do . . . what to *do*?

But he’d already gone through every possible avenue. Every scrap of metal in this clan was accounted for. Every piece had value to the one who held it. And Karthoc had taken all the weapons with him when he'd gone.

"There's no metal here." He forced himself to admit as his body drooped. "No scraps. Not even a forge. Cannot even pay you back for the kiss."

There was a stretch of silence in which he felt like he was sinking into the deepest, darkest hole.

"Don't deserve to be in your presence," he said mournfully. He'd taken advantage of her. Gotten her hopes up only to dash them. Stolen a kiss from her and now she'd never forgive him.

"Is that . . . really the only reason you've been avoiding me?"

He finally looked up and blinked in the face of her obvious confusion. No anger or disappointment, just . . .

He nodded slowly.

And then she began to laugh.

It wasn't a happy laugh. It was a little too high, a little too shrill. It made his skin feel clammy and his chest tightened to the point he couldn't get enough air.

"Oh, biscuits and jam, that *would* be the reason, wouldn't it? And you know what? If you'd told me before dinner this evening, I *would* have been upset." Her laughter turned hysterical as her eyes became misty. "I would have been devastated because you really were my last hope."

Her last hope.

He felt like a monster.

"But it doesn't matter anymore, Brovdir. The *pans* don't matter anymore. Because my mother's bakery is *gone*."

CHAPTER
SEVENTEEN

TRINIA

She'd said it. She'd gotten the words out. Her tongue burned and her stomach clenched and her heart felt like it was shattering into a million splintered shards in her chest. It was tearing her apart from the inside out.

This was real.

Her bakery was *gone*.

Everything had been taken from her.

Brovdir went still, eyes wide. She looked away, unable to meet them as she let out a little hiccuped sob. She tried to hold it back. She really did. She just *couldn't*.

"I've lost *everything*." She wasn't sure he could even make out what she was saying. It was so garbled by sobs. "I lost my mother's bakery. My family legacy. Almost a hundred years of hard work and it's *my* fault."

She covered her face more securely as the cries worked out of her chest. Her shoulders shook and her body trembled, and she couldn't get her tears to *stop*.

There was shuffling, movement, steps approaching. She tried to dash the tears away, but more replaced them.

There was a quiet thump, and she looked up to find Brovdir kneeling before her. His shaggy hair hung over his green eyes and his mouth was set firm and his brow was gentle.

There was no pity in his face. No judgment or discomfort. Only . . . support.

And Trinia lowered her head back into her hands and sobbed harder and longer than she had since her mother died. Since she'd buried the only person she ever loved and who had ever loved her. All her security and safety was stolen away from her when her mother had passed.

Now it was happening all over again.

It wasn't *fair*.

Brovdir shifted slightly, and she found herself reaching for his hand. His eyes went wide as she pulled it into her lap and clutched it tight, used him as an anchor. It wasn't logical. He was a stranger. She shouldn't even *be* here.

But she needed him.

And he didn't pull away.

He kneeled before her with his steadfast strength and waited. He rode out the storm of her emotions with her and finally her sobs turned to shuddering breaths and her tears stopped flowing and her mind cleared.

"What happened?" Brovdir asked quietly, obviously sensing she had gotten herself back under control.

She swallowed and took a few deep breaths. "My stupid, drunkard father traded the bakery away to Ronhold."

There was a moment's pause before Brovdir asked, "The cobbler?"

"Yes. It sounds strange, doesn't it?" A few more breaths, then she lifted her head and wiped at her cheeks again. "A man who works with *feet* wanting a bakery. But he's one of the meanest, shrewdest businessmen in Oakwall."

"Headman Gerald?"

Trinia shook her head. "There's nothing the headman can do. I saw the contract myself. After mama died, the bakery was my father's. His to keep or trade away. And he traded it." Her throat closed again, and she took a deep breath. "No. This is *my* fault. I should have known he'd trade it. He was so desperate for mead at the end, and he'd already traded literally everything he had except our rotting home, which no one wanted. *Blast it.*"

She felt a gentle brush to her fingers. Brovdir stroked her knuckles gently with the pad of his thumb. "Not your fault."

"It is. The bakery was *my* responsibility. It was my duty to keep it running. If I'd just done *more*, I would have had savings. I could have bought it back from Ronhold. But I didn't . . ."

Instead, she'd used all her spare time drawing up floor plans and daydreaming. She was a fool.

"You worked it. Should be yours."

"That isn't how it works." Her body felt heavy and cold despite the thick cloak that was still nestled around her. "And Ronhold is too *cunning*. He conned Rebekia out of her leather *the day after* his father dropped dead. Said the debt owed was his *father's* responsibility, so he didn't have to pay her back a cent and she should collect from the folk who'd bought the shoes the leather made. He worked all that out before his father had even been *buried*. There was nothing anyone could do, not even Headman Gerald, and Rebekia still struggles to this day."

Brovdir's brow furrowed, and she had to work hard not to avert her gaze.

"And now Ronhold has his sights set on *me*. Not just the

bakery. He knows he needs a baker to run it. He's trying to convince me to marry Tobbis, his worthless, sniveling son. But I will *never* do that. *Never.*"

The conviction in her tone was punctuated by Brovdir tightening his grip on her hand. His eyes turned dark as his brows came down. He was looking at her so intently she couldn't help but squirm. She knew she must be a dreadful sight. Covered in mud, puffy eyes, red cheeks, leaking nose.

"Fades," she said glumly. "Maybe it would have been better if that sinkhole had swallowed me up."

She watched the orc's face crumble, and suddenly, she was in his arms.

"Never say that again." His voice was harsh next to her ear. His breath hot. "*Never.*"

Trinia sat stiff and frozen as the huge male wrapped her up in his strength. His warmth. He felt so strong and solid and stable. The complete opposite of how she had felt when the ground had fallen out beneath her and the sinkhole had sucked her up.

It was like he was pulling her right back out of the depths all over again.

"*Never*, Trinia," he said again, right into the top of her scalp. Firm and confident and warm, and her body melted into him.

A hard, shuddering breath left her as she rested her cheek on his wide shoulder. Her hands came up to rest against his bare chest. The muscles contracted under her touch. So hard, but his skin was so soft. He smelled wonderful. Like warm woods. A shady walk in summertime. A gentle breeze and sweet, clean water. Familiar and soothing.

"I will do all I can to aid you, Trinia." His warm words rustled her hair. "I vow it."

How long had it been since she'd been given a hug? Since she'd felt so comfortable in someone's embrace?

Not since her mother had died.

And it felt so *good.*

Would it feel this good when he bedded her?

A jolt of embarrassment shot through her, and she scrambled out of his embrace.

"I apologize," he said rapidly. He backed away from her but stayed crouched, like she was an animal he was afraid to spook. "I forgot myself. I will not touch you again."

"What? No, that's not . . ." She'd messed this up. "It wasn't you. It— The hug was nice. Thank you. I feel better."

Brovdir's eyes went huge, and his fingers twitched like he wanted to pull her into his arms again. She wished he would. She wished she could fall into his embrace and close her eyes and forget this night had ever happened.

But she couldn't.

It was time to ask him. Time to set her plan in motion. She'd be his conquest, and he'd build her a new house. She just had to get the words out. Right now.

"Could I have a bath?"

Blast her worthless bread-based bones back to the Fades who'd made her.

He nodded instantly and got up from the floor. He crossed the room to the large trunk at the edge of the bed and pulled out a towel.

Why couldn't she get the words out? It wasn't a big thing. There were at least ten women at Oakwall who played conquest for orcs regularly and many more who had done it once.

Only once.

Because it was *hard.* Growing a child, feeding him at the

breast for a season, passing him off to his father to raise . . . it would be *so hard*.

But would it be as hard as being homeless? As hard as being forced to live with Yerina again? As hard as being pressured by Ronhold to slave away in a bakery that wasn't *hers*, day in and day out?

Brovdir waved her into the bathroom, and she followed, desperate for a distraction to her rounding thoughts. The room was small but clean and the bath was huge. It was lit by three torches and every fixture was made of wood, giving it a dim yet cozy feel.

"Thank you," she murmured as he placed the towel on the edge of the sink. Her hand grazed down her soaked and muddy bodice. "Do you have any clothes I could borrow?"

His eyes grew wide for a half moment and then he went back to the trunk. He was so tall he had to duck through the doorway.

Her mouth went a little dry as she considered what it might be like to lie with such a huge male. She'd been with men before, but they'd been human. And small humans at that. Their attention had always been quick and efficient.

Being with this particular orc would be different.

He placed a clean, white shirt on top of the towel and turned to regard her with a tip of his head.

"I think that's all I—oh, actually, can you pull that for me? I'm a bit too short." She pointed to the trapdoor above the tub. She knew from Savili's descriptions that it let heated water in from where it collected at the top of the tree. Savili's had a string attached, though, so she could easily pull to start it without Iytier's help.

Brovdir crossed the room and pulled down the slender door. A thin wooden pipe popped out from inside and a cascade of steaming water fell into the tub. It warmed the room up in an instant, and she breathed a sigh of relief.

"Thank you." She turned to the orc, who was edging toward the door.

"Take your time." And with that, he turned on his heel and shut the bathroom door behind him.

And then she was alone with her thoughts—again.

CHAPTER EIGHTEEN

BROVDIR

He was *really* out of his depth here.

He went over to the sink at the end of the storage cabinets near the woodstove, grabbing a thin towel from a wall hook as he went. He cleaned himself up with practiced efficiency, and changed into a clean pair of slacks, but every rustle and splash from behind the bathroom door drew his attention.

When would she come out? She was going to be dressed in *his* shirt. The vision of her dressed in it, her curves gently highlighted by the thin layers of cotton fabric, the short length that would give generous glimpses of her round thighs . . .

The lush vanilla smell of her would cover the shirt. He may never wash it again.

Fades help him. Was that her sigh just now?

He shook his head in frustration. He'd had plenty of women stay the night with him before. Almost twenty. He had a set procedure for every step. If they cowered, he'd sit down and keep still. If they threatened, he'd show his hands and stay out of striking distance. If they cried, he'd turn away to give them privacy. If they were quiet, he'd count himself lucky and go about his business until it was time to take them back to their home.

He didn't know what to do with *this* woman. A woman who wasn't afraid in the least. A woman who was used to the presence of orcs.

A woman who sought his comfort when she was in tears instead of scrambling for escape.

He was a wretch for wishing she would cry again just so he'd have an excuse to hold her. Next time, he wouldn't hold back. He'd take her in his arms and cradle her to his chest and . . . and . . .

He wanted her so badly. The imprint in his chest was blooming, and he wasn't sure he could stop it.

With a deep sigh and a rub to the center of his chest where the thrumming was beating a soothing rhythm, Brovdir went to his bed. It sat at the far corner of the room and was the newest thing in here, since he'd had to replace it before his first night. The mattress was plush, the blankets were warm, and the pillows were clean.

Though sometimes, when night crept in and his body sunk down into the wool-stuffed fabric, he missed being out in the woods with the laughter of his brethren a few feet away. Escape from his shelter was as quick as a slice of his claw. The sounds and smells around him were clear and unmuted by thick wood walls.

He took a deep breath and reminded himself that he was, in fact, perfectly safe here. Humans weren't trying to slaughter him in his sleep. Blighted animals weren't raging in the darkness beyond the windows. Deadly, spiraling wind storms weren't appearing from nowhere and swallowing up everything in their path.

But the sinkholes were.

Blast! He'd gotten so caught up with Trinia he'd forgotten Sythcol's order to call the warriors and conjurers to him. Brovdir went to his desk at the corner of the room and pulled up the top. The wooden slats rolled to the back. He'd marveled for a long time at the craftsmanship when he'd first seen it, especially when he'd been told magic wasn't at play.

Humans had made this wooden marvel.

It took no time for him to write the messages and call the birds to deliver them. Karthoc's warriors had no fewer than a hundred trained robins and sparrows that followed them during their travels. And the messenger birds in the Rove Woods were all enchanted, so all one had to do was murmur the name of the recipient and it was as good as delivered.

He'd just sent out the final bird and closed the window when a crash sounded from the bathroom. A tremendous splash as water gushed under the door.

Trinia let out a cry.

Panic seized him and he bolted for the door. Had a sinkhole opened under his tree? Was she drowning? He slammed his whole weight into the door.

He really should have anticipated how flimsy the wood was compared to his brute strength. It *shattered* on impact, splintering into a million tiny pieces and he landed on the sopping wet floor.

"Trinia!" He tried to rise as he searched for her, but the ground was slick from spilled soap bottles.

"W-what are you doing?"

Ah, fuck.

Trinia was huddled in the tub, perfectly fine.

And very naked.

His blood ran so hot he could feel it pulsing behind his eyes.

"B-Brovdir, what— Biscuits and jam! I'm sorry! I didn't mean to—I can't get the water to stop."

He shakily tried to rise to his feet. He reckoned that nearly all the soap tinctures he'd had lined up on the edge of the tub had fallen. The floor was as slick as ice.

The water was still spewing and flowing over the edge. He managed to his feet and went to the tub.

His eyes simply *would not* obey him and kept sliding over to catch a glimpse of Trinia. She was huddled in a little ball, bare legs crossed, knees to chest, arms covering as much of her as she could.

Fuck, he was an absolute *wretch* for peeping in on her. He went back and snatched up the towel from the counter and handed it to her, even as every part of him was longing for a better look.

"Th-thank you." Her voice was still warbly and panicked. He quickly reached up and snapped the spout closed. She began wrapping herself up and he wondered if she would think him odd for weeping at the loss.

"I'm so sorry!" Trinia said. "Savili said her spout stops on its own, and when yours didn't, I panicked. I thought I'd be able to reach if I got on the edge of the tub, but I lost my balance and fell and—"

"You fell?" He searched what little of her he could see. "Are you hurt?"

"No, I'm fine. I just fell into the water and made it slosh over the edge and it took the soap with it. I'm so sorry. I'll find a way to replace them!" She looked far too concerned for his liking.

"It's fine." He didn't give a shit about the soap. "They aren't mine."

"The . . . soap in your bathroom isn't *yours*?"

"Belongs to the warriors. Still in tents. I let them bathe here." He started to step back, but the floor was incredibly slick and he went still to keep from sliding.

She nodded. "Oh, that makes more sense then. I wondered why you had so many. For a moment, I thought you might have a very specific routine, but none of the soap smelled half as good as you do so—"

She stopped talking as his brows rose. She liked how he smelled?

Her cheeks went a delightful pink and her gaze fell away from him. "N-never mind. Thank you for helping. I'm so sorry about the floor. I'll get it cleaned up . . . somehow."

"I will." He turned to go to his trunk for another towel.

And his feet slipped right out from under him.

He hit the floor hard, but it paled in comparison to hearing Trinia yelp with shock.

"A-are you all right?" There was more splashing as she started to get out.

"Fine. Don't. The wood is slick!"

But it was too late. She was already hurrying over to him, and he tried to get up, only to slip forward again.

Just as she slipped.

His arm snapped out to catch her. He nearly pulled every muscle twisting around.

But it was worth it because she landed snuggly in his arms.

With her ass right on top of his groin.

Blast his miserable hide back to the depths. She felt so *good.* All curvy and soft and warm. His cock hardened in an instant and his heart thundered as Trinia's eyes grew wide.

She started to get off him.

"Wait!" He gripped her thigh to stop her and she hiccuped in response, so he quickly let her go. "You might—the wood, it—let me get you!"

"Get me *where*?" Her voice was a squeak of shock and she squirmed against him as if trying to get away, but it felt so *good*. He was an absolute beast.

"That isn't what I—fuck—" He scooped her up under her knees and started to get up off the floor.

Only to slip again and pitch forward.

She yelped, and he barely managed to cushion her fall.

But now he was caged directly over her, with a knee between her thighs and her wrist pinned in his hand and her *blasted* towel had fallen down and her perfect breasts were almost completely visible, and his wretched eyes would simply *not* obey his command to look away from her.

She was panting under him, cheeks red, lips parted, eyes so huge he felt like she was swallowing him up.

Her leg shifted as she bent her knee. He could feel it grazing along his thigh all the way up, up . . . what was she doing? Why was she—

Her knee grazed against his throbbing cock and his lungs constricted as primal *need* flooded through his veins.

"Let me up, please."

Her command was barely a whisper and never had he wanted to disobey an order so badly.

"I apologize." Fades, even his voice sounded disheartened. His cock was still throbbing and pulsing under his pants.

One accidental touch, just the barest hint of a graze, and he was absolutely *losing his mind.*

He scooted back off her.

"Wait. Don't go. I want you."

Every part of him froze. Even his heart.

Her cheeks were burning like fire, and she had her eyes averted. Her stammering sounded more like sounds of pure shock than anything resembling words.

What? She wanted what?

"I mean—I—er. That isn't what I—uh—" She closed her eyes as if steeling herself. Swallowed hard. He held his breath.

When she opened her eyes again, she looked determined, resolved. "I want to play conquest for you."

A zing of elation sparked through him like lightning. *"Yes."*

Fades be praised, *yes!* That was absolutely the best possible request she could have given. There was nothing he wanted more right now.

Her eyes blinked rapidly. "B-but you haven't heard what I want from you in return yet."

"Don't care," he said firmly, but when she flinched, he forced himself to swallow. Logic was so hard to find, and words were even more difficult. "What would you like?"

"A house. I want a house," she said this quickly, decisively.

Absolutely, yes. "This one?"

Her eyes went wide and then she quickly shook her head. "Oh no. No, not *this* one."

What was wrong with it? "Needs changing? What? I can fix."

"N-no, Brovdir, I don't want to take your house."

He shrugged. "Don't mind." He'd sleep in a half-frozen creek to have her right now. She was still half under him, with her full, soft body, all curvy and lovely. He wanted to trace every part of her with his tongue.

Would she let him taste her? What if he offered her more—

"I want a house in Oakwall."

His chest suddenly felt tight and his rational mind caught

back up with him. She wanted a house in her own village. Not here. Not anywhere near him.

"All I need is for you to supply the materials and build it. I can draw up the plans."

He balled his fists against the soapy floor. His throat clenched so hard he could feel the agony all the way down in his gut. It caged his heart and squeezed.

"It shouldn't take too long. I don't want anything fancy. Just a room and maybe some storage space. You'll be done long before I finish carrying the babe, I promise."

Why did that sound so wrong? Why did his throat constrict instead of bellowing with excited agreement?

After Karthoc demanded he be a chief of Rove Wood, all his reservations about raising a son vanished. This clan was *safe*. His child would grow happy and strong in a community where food was not scarce and comforts abounded.

And yet his heart twinged despite this logic. Both Hendr and Caivid had found women of their own. Women who were not their conquest but desired their company. Woman who they may soon call their *mates*.

"All right," he said past the lump in his throat. He was being foolish and ungrateful. He should take what he could get.

"Really?" She sounded so relieved, and she pulled the towel up to cover herself from him. It seemed like the color in the room dimmed. "We . . . we have a deal?"

He nodded even as his jaw clenched.

"Good!" she exclaimed as she exhaled in obvious relief. "That's really . . . that's good. Um . . . maybe you could step out while I change. I should probably clean this mess up too. Do you have another towel?"

"Don't." Fades, the image of her on her hands and knees,

scrubbing the ground, rhythmically rocking as she worked the cloth over the sopping floor . . .

"It's such a mess. I think it will take a while to clean it—"

"No." The word came out like a growl, and he rose to his feet, taking her with him. She let out a yip of surprise, followed by a trail of shocked laughter. The sound was so warm it made him light up like a beacon. The sweet, melodic tone had him grinning and all thoughts that he'd pushed her too far flew out of his mind. He vowed to make her laugh every day she was in his presence. He wanted to savor the sound, drown in it.

He carefully navigated the damp, slippery floor as he carried her to the bed. He set her down without preamble and only after she'd sunk into the cushy mattress did he realize he shouldn't have been so eager. He should have eased into this.

He searched Trinia's face, worry panging in his chest as he waited for her reaction.

But instead of noting her new placement, her eyes were fixed on him. His *face*.

He gulped hard, suddenly self-conscious in a way he hadn't been before. Even before he had scars, he'd been well aware he wasn't the prettiest among his kind. Scores of women had examined his countenance, and most of them looked upon him with revulsion. He'd grown accustomed to it.

But he hadn't been imprinted to those women. The idea of being rejected by Trinia made his flesh prickle with anxiety.

She met his eyes. "I think . . . this is going to be fun."

His apprehension fell away and his heart began a frantic, needy tempo that made him breathless.

Trinia's expression softened, as if she had no idea how high she'd queued him up. "I have so much to thank you for, Brovdir. You've saved my life twice now."

His chest tightened at the reminder.

"L-let me show you how thankful I am." Her voice was that wonderful husky timbre he loved so much. He didn't want her to stop talking.

But then she reached for him and stroked her fingers up his abs. The gentle caress made his knees weak and the last thing on his mind was speaking. He couldn't have gotten another word out if he tried.

Her fingers teased around his muscles and soothed the scars. His body shivered quite against his will.

This was really happening. The Fades truly smiled on him. The same way Trinia was smiling at him now.

From here on, he would do everything in his power to prove to her how grateful he was.

CHAPTER NINETEEN

TRINIA

Trinia's heart felt like it was about to thunder right out of her chest as Brovdir moved in over her, bracing himself on the bed with hands on either side of her hips. His weight sunk into the mattress and she was completely surrounded by him.

She was really going to do this, wasn't she? She hadn't meant to blurt out that she'd wanted him. Hadn't meant to actually offer. She'd spent most of her bath debating between her options and then the words just spilled out and now there was no going back. This was it. She'd made the offer and . . . and . . .

She was going to go through with playing conquest for him.

Brovdir's gaze lingered on her face and then flashed down her body. Her stomach flipped and her thighs clenched and the room felt too hot all of a sudden, even though she was still draped in a towel.

There was no turning back now. Even if she'd wanted to.

"I should get rid of this, or we'll soak the bed," she said, peeling the damp towel away from her body. The room was chilly, and she clenched her teeth to stop herself from shivering.

The male stopped breathing entirely and the slacked jawed, wide-eyed expression as he examined her breasts was exactly what she'd expected. They were her only universally admired feature and even some of the most pious men in her village took a glance when she wore more revealing tops.

Brovdir reached out but then hesitated, drawing back with a worried glance.

He really was cute. "You can touch me, Brovdir. I'll tell you if I want you to stop."

He nodded. His throat worked in a swallow as he reached out again.

His palm cupped her left breast. His hand was so *warm,* and his touch was incredibly gentle.

Her cheeks heated with embarrassment as she let him explore. He flicked her nipple slowly with the pad of his thumb until it budded against this touch. It felt a little tingly, but nothing more.

She was rather surprised when his hand pulled away. She looked up at his furrowed brow and confused expression.

"You don't like it?" he asked.

She blinked rapidly. "Oh, it's fine. You can touch me wherever you'd like."

"No." Brovdir moved back from her and kneeled at the foot of the bed. His expression was focused. "Do *you* like it?"

She blinked. What did it matter? Bed play wouldn't get her pregnant any faster. She should just tell him he could do whatever he liked so they could get to the main act.

But she couldn't. The words wouldn't come off her tongue.

Brovdir moved further away, nearly off the bed, and her stomach clenched with worry.

"Y-you don't have to stop." She shifted onto her knees so she could get closer. "I'm fine."

Should she fake it? She'd made a vow never to do so with any lover, but this wasn't about *pleasure*, was it?

Her chest ached.

Before she could worry more, he said, "Where . . . else do women like to be touched?"

Her brows flew up and her tension eased to make way for shock. "Where else do . . .? Brovdir, have you been with a woman before?"

He swallowed thickly and shook his head.

Biscuits and jam! *That* was unexpected. Why hadn't she considered that before now?

Why did it make her blood zing with excitement?

Her shocked silence must have been too stressful for him because he carefully moved to the edge of the bed and peered at her through his shaggy bangs. His fists were clasped tight, and shoulders hunched. He looked smaller in that position. Uncertain.

Cute.

She quickly moved to alleviate his worries. "It's not bad, Brovdir. I don't mind."

His shoulders sagged with clear relief.

"I've taken a couple of men to bed before, so I know the way of things. I can guide you through." She squirmed a little at the thought.

His brows pinched into a scowl. He bowed his head to hide it and his balled fists tightened.

Trinia moved to sit at the edge of the bed with him. "What? What's wrong?"

"Nothing."

"Obviously something," she muttered only to think. "Oh, biscuits. Sorry. I know orcs can be possessive. I'm not with those men anymore. They were just a one-time thing."

He shifted. "Tobbis?"

"What? Oh, *no*. Fades, no. Not him." She waved her hands to shove the idea right off.

"Who?"

Her eyes narrowed. "I think it's probably best I don't tell you."

He let out a hard sigh, but nodded.

"Let's not talk about other people right now." Especially since it was putting a stall on things. "What do *you* like, Brovdir? Is there anything you want to try?"

He opened his mouth and then closed it as his cheeks and neck turned a much darker shade of green. His eyes snapped quickly down her body and then away.

Oh Fades, being with an embarrassed virgin hadn't at all been what she'd thought this night would be like. "Would you like to touch my breasts again?"

His expression was flooded with confusion as he met her eyes. "You don't like it."

"It's not my *favorite* thing, but I certainly don't mind. We really just need to get *you* ready. You're the main event here. It's your son you're putting inside me."

For some reason, this forced a low, threatening growl to escape the orc's throat and Trinia could do nothing but stare into the face of his anger with wide eyes. *"No."*

"No . . .? You . . . don't want to put your son inside me?"

"No, I am not the '*main event*.'"

Trinia blinked.

"What do *you* like, Trinia?"

The question was spoken so low it quivered in her guts and forced her to respond quietly, "I . . . don't really know."

His brows shot up.

"I've been with men before, but it was always rather quick."

"You enjoyed that?"

She swallowed hard. "Well . . . yes, I suppose." She *had* taken some enjoyment from it.

"You don't know what you like, either."

Trinia snapped her gaze back to the brooding orc, who was leaning in closer now. She could feel the heat of him on her damp skin. The heady woodsmoke and spice scent of him curled up in her mind and her tension melted.

"They only touched you here." Brovdir reached out and grazed his fingertips along the side of her right breast and her skin broke out into goosebumps. "You don't know what else you like."

"I . . . suppose I don't," Trinia said carefully. She'd explored on her own, but only between her legs, and it had never produced much more than efficient satisfaction.

Brovdir's eyes smoldered as he moved back toward her. Back onto the bed. The intensity of his expression stole her breath. She leaned down onto her back and he kept coming until he was right over the top of her.

He was huge. And warm. And his woody scent mingled with something hotter. Like spicy cinnamon. Her muscles relaxed, and she breathed in the delicious scent.

He must have seen her ease in her expression because a grin split his face so wide she could see the sharp points of his fangs. His huge tusks appeared even more massive as they jutted up to his nose.

She should be terrified, right? Why wasn't she terrified?

Why did she want him so badly that she was nearly trembling?

"I'm going to touch you now, Trinia of Oakwall." Brovdir's voice vibrated through her whole body and made her shiver.

"W-where?"

His dark green eyes hooked deep, right into her soul.

"Everywhere."

Delicious goosebumps broke out all over her body. Her thighs clenched together as a pulse of deep pleasure bloomed between her legs.

Brovdir leaned in closer, watching carefully. His knees braced on either side of her calves and his hands rested next to her head. She was completely surrounded by his heat and scent and everything about this felt so *good.* It shouldn't feel this good to be caged by him.

She shouldn't be indulging this. Lingering wasn't going to get her pregnant. It was just making this whole thing take longer than it needed to.

And yet . . . Fades help her.

His eyes caught her up, never leaving her face as he dipped low, so close she could feel his breath against her collarbone. He adjusted his weight and snaked a hand around to brush her still damp hair away from her neck.

Then he placed a kiss right under her ear.

Jolting pleasure snapped her to attention and heated her blood in an instant. The tender kiss was hard enough she could feel his tusk digging into her jaw, but his lips were so soft they felt like the pass of butterfly wings. It made her toes curl and her legs quiver.

Just from a single kiss on her neck. *One kiss*.

What did that mean for the rest of this?

Brovdir moved to look her over and then let out a pleased hum. Her cheeks heated, but there was no way she could hide how squirmy that kiss had made her. He leaned back in. His tusks dug gently into her neck as his lips grazed the sensitive flesh. Her toes curled as his hot breath warmed her neck.

"W-what are you doing?" She was breathless as he continued to trail kisses down her shoulder and to her right arm. Each one sent sparks like lightning through her. She dug her heels into the bed and pointed her toes as she resisted the urge to wriggle.

His tusks poked gently into the sensitive underside of her elbow, and a flash of heat washed over her. Her pussy pulsed with the beat of her heart and she could feel herself grow slick. Why did being pricked by his teeth feel so *good*?

She swallowed thickly. This wasn't supposed to be about pleasure. This was a one-time thing. She really should get him back to the task at hand. She should convince him to simply rut her with the efficiency of a hand plow and be done with it.

She edged away from his touch and he looked at her with wide-eyed confusion. Fades help her he was *cute.* Too cute. "You don't have to go further. I'm . . . ready for you."

He rose an eyebrow before inhaling long and deep. Then he shook his head. "Not ready."

Irritation flashed behind her eyes. "I think I know my body better than you do."

He growled in a way that made her stomach turn into jelly. "Not ready. I want you *ready*."

Ooh, fuck. Her pussy throbbed with that promise and more wetness pooled between her quivering thighs.

Brovdir took a deep, long inhale, closing his eyes as if

relishing the scent of her. Because he *was*. She knew orcs had a sense of smell unlike any other, but she hadn't realized it was good enough to smell a woman's *arousal*!

He made a low, happy noise in his throat. "That's better. But not enough."

He dipped close to her ear again. With his chest pressed close to hers and his heat radiating into her skin. Her pussy pulsed as he whispered. "You liked this best."

His tusks pressed into her neck as he kissed her. Coiling hot pleasure curled up in the pit of her stomach and rolled over her in waves. A whimper broke from her lips as he licked her pulse. She could barely catch her breath.

He moved up, slowly, carefully. Her breath hitched as he exhaled right around her ear.

His lips closed around her earlobe.

Deep, unfettered *need* flashed throughout her. Her arms broke out in goosebumps, her stomach quivered, her pussy clamped hard as if desperate to be filled.

The reaction caught her so off guard that she sucked in a breath and froze. The sensation rolled over her, caught her in its grip. She couldn't escape and didn't want to.

The tip of his tongue grazed around the edge of her ear, and it made her eyes cross. She clenched her thighs together and squirmed against the bedding.

"Hmm. That's it."

She could hardly fathom what he was saying because the words seemed to course directly into her brain. They flashed hot and quick and blissful in her mind and churned her up to the point of bursting. Her clit throbbed almost painfully as he nibbled at her earlobe again.

His hand moved to the opposite side of her face and pushed

her hair back, grazing at the tip of her ear before moving lower to the other earlobe.

It was too much. On a shuddering gasp, she pressed his chest and forced him back. He got up without hesitation, lowering his hands and backing off until she could see his lightly surprised expression. His brows were raised but his eyes were warm, and his mouth was curled into a little smile.

Fades, help her. Her body was still reacting. Her clit was aching with need, and her pussy clenched hard. Her limbs felt like they were vibrating.

Brovdir sucked a hard breath in through his nose and her stomach flipped over as a triumphant grin spread across his face. The teasing expression hooked right into her heart and threatened to tug her back into his arms.

She was getting too attached to him, wasn't she? This was supposed to be a *business* transaction. Nothing more.

Her stomach twisted up at that thought, but she pushed away the pain, fought against her aching basal needs, and gripped his arm tight.

They had a job to do. They needed to stay focused on that.

Brovdir's eyes flashed with surprise as she forced him to stand.

"Get undressed. I'm ready."

CHAPTER TWENTY

BROVDIR

She didn't have to tell him twice.

Brovdir rose to his full height and pulled off his damp pants without preamble. Perhaps he should have taken things slower. Perhaps he was shocking her, but he couldn't help it. She'd made a demand of him, and he was going to follow her orders.

He would follow every one of them for all eternity.

The imprint in his chest was thrumming and he couldn't fight down the desire for her. The memory of her squirming and bucking with pleasure drenched moans. He wanted that while he was buried deep inside her. He wanted her to be groaning as he plunged his cock and spilled his seed and made her *his*.

He tensed at that, caught off guard. He was creating a *son* with her, not keeping her.

The thought made his chest tighten with dismay. He could feel the imprint burning.

"Oh."

The exclamation made his back straighten and he turned his attention to the woman seated on the bed before him. She was curled, with her knees up and her back bowed. The position hid her rounded stomach and thighs.

His heart clenched with dismay.

"Huh." Trinia tapped her chin as if in thought. Her expression was not one of concern or disgust, and he counted himself lucky for that. And then she said. "You're . . . very big."

He searched her face. He'd been told everything he needed to know about rutting humans and knew the scent of one who was ready to be taken. She was ready. And yet her comment made his gut twist with worry. "Hurt you?"

She blinked and her gaze shot away from his cock, back to his face. "No. I don't think so. Lay down here. On . . . your back."

He got on the bed and lay directly where she'd pointed, with his head on the pillow. He watched fixedly as she crawled to his side, sat next to his hip. Her eyes were back on his jutting cock. It twitched with want under her heady gaze, so hard and tight it was pulsing with every beat of his heart.

He'd never been so desperate in all twenty-six years of his life.

"Can I touch you?"

He wanted absolutely nothing more. His nod was too fast and eager.

She reached without hesitation. Grazed the head of his cock with the tips of her fingers.

All his breath left him in a rush.

Fuck, he understood now why she'd stopped him from

playing with her ear. He'd touched himself before, but it was nothing like this. Every caress from her sent a cascade of pleasure through his body. The tips of her fingers grazed around the head of his cock, and he helplessly thrust his hips upward. Her index finger and thumb enclosed around him, just under the head, and he hissed with need.

The palm of her hand stroked down gently, and then she gripped him hard in her fist.

That was *too much.* And *not enough.* His mind quailed with desperate need so hot and tight he was trembling.

Then she let him go. "I'll need more preparation, I think. Just a little."

His mouth went dry as he searched her lovely face. "Preparation?"

"I'm . . . fairly wet already." Her cheeks turned a perfect pink, and her eyes darted away. His heart swelled and his limbs ached to pull her into his arms. "I'll just need to . . . stretch myself."

Stretch herself?

His expression must have mirrored his confusion because she held up her fingers and then indicated between her legs.

"Can . . . I?"

She hesitated, squirmed, her cheeks turned even darker in color.

She nodded.

He wasted no time. He trailed his fingers over the perfect swell over stomach and down between her lovely thick thighs. Her soft, dark curls tickled his fingers as he stroked lower, deeper. Pressed up.

Fades, she was so hot here. So wet. The scent of her was maddening. Like dewdrops at daybreak. So delicious it made his mouth water. Everything was slick and soft. His body quaked with excitement, but the need to be gentle was paramount in his mind.

Trinia let out a hissing breath and his eyes shot to her face. She'd gone down on all fours next to him with her fists gripping the sheets and her eyes closed tight.

"Hurt you?" he asked breathlessly. Though the scent of her told him she was experiencing the opposite, he wanted to be certain.

"N-no . . ."

The confirmation made him bold, and he took time exploring. He'd been told many things about human women, so he knew there was a little soft nub near the top. He found it and gently stroked over it.

She bucked, breath hitching as her thighs trembled around his hand. He stroked again, watching her face for any sign of distress.

She groaned and quivered in pleasure and triumph burst through his entire frame, but her hand shot out to stop him. "L-lower."

Lower? He let her guide his hand. Her entrance was slick, and he easily dipped a finger into her.

"Oooh." The moan she gave took his breath away, but then she bit her lip as if embarrassed. Little noises still emitted from the back of her throat, but she wouldn't let them out.

She didn't stop him, so he pushed deeper. Inside was so slick and hot and *tight*. The idea of her walls trembling around his cock like they were around his finger made him nearly daft.

Her groans were louder as he delved deep into her channel, pumping softly. His thumb found the little nub in her folds again and gently stroked it at the same time.

She lit up like a beacon. Her body quaked and her eyes

flashed open, and her hips dropped to take him deeper. He doubled his efforts, and she moaned, still thrusting her hips. Her grip on the bed sheets tightened.

"I think . . . I think I should do it after all."

Her voice was breathless and rich, and she made no move to stop him. He couldn't bring himself to obey her and, instead, quickened his thrusts. He sought to increase her pleasure and make her forget ever wanting to take this away from him.

He was rewarded as she groaned, and her hands moved from the bed to grip his shoulders as if she wanted to be nearer to him. To use him as an anchor.

Pleasure like he'd never known thundered through his veins and flooded his mind like the purest light of the Fades. He carefully delved a second finger into her. Her pussy gave easily. She was so *slick*.

"Ohh, *Brovdir*."

Fades help him, her *voice!* It shivered through him, rich and pleasure drunk. His control slipped, and he curled his fingers up, moving deeper. The scent of her was like a dream, so rich and sweet and he could hardly stand it.

His mouth watered.

"Want to taste you." He *needed* it. To feel her slick, hot flesh on his tongue.

"You . . . what?" Her words were clipped and breathless.

He pushed his finger deeper, curled it up until she let out a groan and bucked against him. "Here. Taste you here."

She made an odd hiccuping noise in the back of her throat that spiked deep longing in his bones. Was there anything about this woman he didn't adore?

He slipped his finger between her warm, slick pussy and curled it around her clit, gently stroking until he felt her body start to shiver. The rich, heady scent of her intensified. He swallowed so hard it made his throat burn and ache. He longed for her as if she were the balm that could heal him.

"*Please*, Trinia." He would get on his knees and beg if he had to.

But she didn't make him. With wide eyes and a hard swallow, she nodded, "Yes, Brovdir. You can."

CHAPTER
TWENTY-ONE

TRINIA

Fades, have mercy. She couldn't deny him.

Her cheeks were flushed with embarrassment and anticipation as he hooked his arms around her thighs and dragged her toward his face.

"B-but how will you breathe?" she squeaked.

Brovdir shot her a darkly amused look and her reservations fell away. He lifted her right under the ass and picked her up like she weighed no more than a feather pillow.

She yipped in surprise as he dropped her down. Right onto his face. His *mouth*.

His tongue snaked into her pussy, hot and slick and *long*.

Her cry turned into a long groan as pleasure skittered up her spine. Her thighs trembled around his head and she felt like she was vibrating.

His tongue went deep, licking from right above her entrance before it curled around her clit. The tip flicked gently, swirled in a circle. Her head muddled up and her vision blurred.

She'd never imagined that anything could feel like this. "Oh, *Brovdir*."

He groaned loudly as she called his name, and the sound of it rumbled through her gut. Oh *Fades*, that felt so good! Too good! Her hips bucked helplessly, and she sank down further.

She was going to suffocate him. She could feel his nose pressing right above her pussy. She tried to move away.

Only to have his grip on her ass tighten and hold her steady. His tongue snaked over her slit again, flattening over her clit before he flicked it with the tip of his tongue.

Pleasure scorched through her. Her hips bounced and her mind blanked. Her need for more built to a tremendous peak.

Brovdir groaned again. The vibration of it made her eyes cross. It was *exquisite*. Rippling pleasure danced all the way up her spine.

He withdrew his tongue, and his lips formed a tight circle around her clit. His tusks dug deliciously into her thighs, spreading her open for him.

And then he sucked.

Spikes of aching bliss so strong she saw stars raked through her. She bounced, clenched tight. Her body was aching and needy and desperate. And *right on the edge*.

"Oh, *yes*, Brovdir!" She ground herself against him and he rumbled out another mind-altering growl. Everything in her quaked for release. There was a quick stretching sensation as he pushed another finger into her. The slight burn was incredible. Her skin felt hot and shivery. Her scalp tingled.

Brovdir sucked her clit hard.

Her body exploded with a blinding orgasm that raked through her. It bloomed in her stomach and raced up her back.

She let out a long, babbling cry that had her hips shivering and bucking as waves of pleasure crashed over her. She needed *more*.

She wanted more than his tongue. She wanted *him. Now*.

With a quick motion, she moved her heels back and pushed up off him. There was a light pop as his mouth broke free from her pussy. The chill of the air made her shudder as she scooched back and away.

Brovdir let out a little whimper that tore at her heart. His brows were pinched, and his wet mouth was set in a frown like he'd just gotten his favorite treat ripped away.

Fades, help her. Why did he have to be so *cute?* The longing in his face made her want to derail her plans. But she knew he'd be just as bliss wrecked the moment she got where she wanted to go.

She moved down his body until she felt the hard length of his cock, pulsing and hot, against her ass.

His eyes popped wide, and the pleading expression evaporated. "Trinia?"

"I want you." She adjusted her legs so she could press more firmly into his cock. "Are you ready?"

"Y-yesss." His voice sounded more like a rumble than words, but his eager nod left no room for misinterpretation.

She moved back further, pushing down until his cock was stroked between their bodies. The thick, hard length of him raked between her legs, wetted by her pussy, sliding effortlessly.

Brovdir's eyes crossed, and he let out another of those amazing low groans that left her breathless and trembling. Her clit pulsed again from the sound of his whimpers of pleasure.

She bounced her hips a little to get his cock lined up properly. It was huge, with a dark green head and a wide base.

She could feel it pulsing, bobbing and desperate. One of his hands clenched and unclenched in the bedsheets, curling with need. The other gripped her thigh.

Still, she hesitated to let him in and instead continued to stroke his cock against herself. Teasing him was cruel, but it had its purpose. She was trying to judge for size, trying to see if the three damp fingers Brovdir was clutching her leg with had stretched her enough to fit his massive cock.

It would have to be good enough, because she no longer had the stamina to wait.

She slid his cock to her entrance.

"T-Trinia." Brovdir's groan caught her up in the most delicious way. Fades, was he already close?

She needed him to be inside her before he came.

She rose up on her heels, positioned the thick, dark head of his cock and pushed hard.

It popped in so smoothly it was like they were made for each other. Her body swallowed him up. Ecstasy burst through her gut. She'd *never* been so full before. *Never*.

And she never wanted to feel empty again.

CHAPTER TWENTY-TWO

BROVDIR

Sweet, searing tightness clenched around the tip of his cock as it pushed deep into Trinia's body.

His mind winked out from the bliss, true rapture flooded through his veins. He barely had time to catch a breath as she sank down further, taking his member almost to the hilt.

Her body swallowed him up like a dream. The smooth glide was incredible. Her channel was so tight light burst behind his eyes.

Her hips twitched, and her pussy clenched tight around his cock. Squeezing.

He arched up against her and roared. Ecstasy mounted deep in his bones; pleasure trembled. He couldn't hold it.

Trinia braced her hands on his chest and put her face close to his. Her hips curled to thrust him deeper, and he bucked upward helplessly.

"Brovdir."

Her channel began to clench and flutter around him and her dewdrop scent washed over him as she *came*.

The ecstasy was so great that his orgasm was instant. Deep, raw pleasure that made his hips jerk and his mind fracture into shards of bliss. It was unlike anything he'd ever experienced. It gripped him, hooked in his gut, in his *soul*, connecting him to this woman in a way he could not fathom. The imprint soared and bloomed brighter, building up the exquisite ecstasy until he felt choked on it.

His hand gripped her hips as he bounced her on him, filling her up, soaking her. He could feel it gush from her channel as her body flooded.

Her head flung back and her breast pushed out and he trembled again, rippling pleasure dancing in his veins as her body came down from the peak. She was flush, her skin glistened, her brows were set tight with exquisite pleasure.

He'd never seen anything more beautiful in his life.

"Oh, *Brovdir*." She collapsed on top of him, and he wrapped her up in his arms.

Her name on his lips was exquisite. His chest felt full, and the imprint hummed out a tune so sweet and low it almost made him feel like he was buzzing. A deep-seated contentment he'd never known before mingled with the final pulses of his release. He wanted to bury his face in her neck and breathe her scent and soothe her until she was boneless, until she forgot time and decided to stay with him.

Forever.

Fuck, he wanted her so badly.

For a few blissful moments, they lay there as their shared pleasure went from intense to sated, and he got to live his dream.

And then Trinia adjusted, sat up and away so she could look him in the eyes. “That was . . .”

He grinned, waiting for her praise.

“I’m looking forward to the next round.”

Her statement hit him like the crack of a whip. He’d felt so connected to her, so *tethered* to her by the imprint that was blooming in his chest and mind, and now he was reminded . . .

She only wanted to be his conquest. Not his mate.

His stomach twisted up, and he carefully gripped her torso and pulled her back down onto him. She came willingly, though her brows rose with surprise. Especially when he adjusted her to the side and his cock popped out of her pussy. The cold air hit him like the swing of a fist, but the sensation was short-lived as he concentrated on nestling his woman into the crook of his arm.

Her beautiful brown eyes were so big he could see little flecks of green in them he’d never noticed before. Her cheeks were flush bright pink, and her lips were swollen from his attention.

She felt like a dream made real.

“Ooh,” she murmured as she curled even tighter into him. One of her legs went up to rest atop his own, her cheek pressed into his shoulder, using his body as a pillow. Her lips gently grazed his chest, and his heart clenched. “This is nice.”

She relaxed into him, happy, content.

He was never going to give her up.

“We fit pretty good together, don’t we?” Her warm breath tickled.

“Like my favorite boots.”

There was a breath of silence where he realized what he’d said, and his throat constricted painfully from embarrassment before Trinia finally made a sound.

Laughter.

The full, rich sound was like the warmth of the sun after a bitterly cold night. He basked in it, jaw slacked slightly, eyes stuck on her face as he tried to memorize her joyful expression.

"Fades, I never thought I'd be compared to a pair of boots." Trinia pushed her curly hair back and all the breath in his lungs expelled in a rush, leaving him dizzy and disoriented. "Though I suppose it's not the most insulting thing I've been compared to."

Brovdir's delight extinguished and simmering rage took its place. "Who?"

She rose her brows at him. "I'm not sure it would be a good idea to tell you."

He growled low, and she didn't even flinch.

"Besides, I've already taken care of it."

Unless their noses were crooked, or they walked with a limp, he couldn't imagine they'd been adequately brought to justice.

She smirked as if she read his mind. "No, I didn't injure them. I did something *far* worse. I refuse to trade with them."

His brows pinched in confusion.

She curled into him, willingly snuggling up. His imprint was a blissful, thumping mess of gratitude. He felt like he was floating.

She stroked her fingers over one of the scars on his chest. "I'm the only decent baker in Oakwall. People can make their own bread, of course, but it's a lot of work to mill the grain and I'm the only one with a crank turned grinder to make that task easy. I have a handful people or so that are blacklisted."

Her eyes took on a haunted quality that sucked out his breath. "Or . . . I guess I *was* the only decent baker. I suppose no one will be getting my bread now, enemy or not."

Fuck, her sadness felt like a spear through his heart. He stroked back her still damp hair. “You are a strong, beautiful woman. Must have many enemies. Many jealous competitors.”

Her cheeks went flush with embarrassment. “N-not really.”

He didn’t want her bashful. “I’d help you vanquish them if you’d let me.”

She snorted, amusement chasing away the sadness in her eyes. “You gonna cut them down with your claws and ruin the peace between our communities?”

“I don’t want peace with anyone stupid enough to make you their enemy.”

Trinia lifted her head to blink at him and then burst out laughing again, and he felt like he was drowning with contentment. He could hardly breathe.

She examined his face, and her expression softened. She tapped his nose gently. “Don’t look at me like that, Brovdir. It’s too cute.”

He blinked rapidly as shock snapped at him. Cute? Had she just called him *cute*?

She leaned up and kissed his nose then, further baffling him. Then she kissed both his cheeks and his forehead and finally his lips.

It was so soft this time. So, bone achingly *right*. These little teasing kisses that muddled up his mind and forced the imprint to do the thinking for him.

“I suppose . . . we need to get back to business now?”

He blinked his eyes open rapidly and, Fades, rutting her a second time and begetting her with child should be the first thing on his mind.

So why did his whole body shiver in dismay at the thought?

He reached up and rubbed at his throat. The easing of the tension in his muscles there helped to clear his mind a little.

"Oh, raisin rum . . . I'm so sorry. I didn't even think."

He snapped his attention back to Trinia as her face flooded with guilt. "I completely forgot about how badly your throat hurt. And I'm sure all that . . . it made it worse, didn't it?"

Honestly, his throat wasn't any worse than it would be after any other day.

Trinia reached out her hand, stroked her fingertips along the scar, and his body all but melted into her.

"I'll make you some tea. You have tea, don't you?"

She wanted to make him what?

"Don't look at me like that." She narrowed her eyes, but her voice held no real irritation. "It will be good for you. Just wait here."

Wait here? What?

Suddenly, she was slipping away from him.

He snatched her back in an instant.

She blinked her beautiful brown eyes at him, brows raised. "Brovdir, *what* are you doing?"

"Keeping," he said without hesitation.

She let out a trail of laughter that lit up the room. He was going to melt into a puddle of happiness.

"I'm in your house, Brovdir." She shifted away from him, and he was forced to let her go. He didn't want to harm her. "I'm about to spend the night in your bed. That's about as *kept* as one can get."

She was going to spend the night! He'd almost forgotten.

He wanted her to stay the night forever.

"One night." She obviously read his expression. "I'll stay with a friend in Oakwall after this. What would people think of me staying with Rove Wood Clan's new chief?"

They'd think she was his mate and he would be *ecstatic*.

His heart clenched. That's what he wanted, wasn't it? He wanted to keep her.

She left him then. Out of his grasp and into the cold. She was so determined, so strong. She'd had a major setback this night and yet all traces of the sorrow she must feel inside had been wiped from her face.

No, not entirely. There was a tension in her jaw and a tightness in her movements. He wished he could drag her into his arms and stroke her hair and back until she finally relented her sadness.

She disappeared into the bathroom. "Biscuits and jam, this room is a *disaster*! I promise I'll help you clean it in the morning."

Like the depths, she would. He'd slip out of bed after she was asleep and get it done.

She came out of the bathroom dressed in *his* shirt, and *Fades, have mercy*. The blasted thing was short enough to show generous glimpses of her thighs every time she walked. It draped perfectly over her breasts and rounded stomach. The white cloth was so thin he could see her dark nipples poking through it.

This was torture. She looked more erotic than she had when she was fully naked. His fingers twitched with the need to yank it off her and cast it into the fire.

"Oh, no you don't," she said warningly. "I know that look. You stay right over there."

She . . . knew his look? Most of the Rove Wood orcs couldn't read his expressions yet and he'd lived in their company for half a season.

The grin fell away as she pulled back her curly hair and tied it up. Her neck was long and the scent of her, like vanilla and dew at dawn, was the best thing he'd ever smelled in all his years. He took a long, deep inhale, letting the scent fill him up. The imprint he held for her was pulsing contentment in his veins.

"Where's your tea and honey? And cups."

She'd ordered him not to get up, so he simply pointed to the cabinet nearest the oven. The few kitchen items he had were in there.

Trinia walked over without preamble and pulled out the cup. Her nose curled in clear disgust. "Brovdir, what *is* this?"

"Mug."

"No, it isn't. This is broken shards kept together with nothing but spit and sheer force of will. How do you even drink out of this?"

It had worked fine for him so far.

"Are you being serious? Brovdir, you are the chief of Rove Wood Clan! I'm sure you could get a better cup than this." She went to the spigot and turned on the tap. She looked more at home here than he did. "I cannot believe this holds water. The Fades themselves must have blessed it with their mighty endurance."

He laughed. The deep sound filled his gut and burned his throat, but his mirth couldn't be contained.

To his delight, he found Trinia was grinning back at him, her cheeks flushed a pretty pink, and then she slipped over to where the kettle was and popped off the lid.

"Brovdir, there is *dust* in this." Her chiding tone made his smile widen. She rinsed the kettle, filled it, and set it up on the stovetop with practiced efficiency. She even knew how to light and adjust the fire in the oven to heat the burner. It had taken him a half a day to figure out how to properly use the magical kindling and shift the temperatures without extinguishing the flame.

He could learn much from her.

"Now, where is the honey?" She went back to the cabinet and got up on her toes to reach the highest shelf. His shirt rode high on her thighs, almost to the swell of her bum, and his blood heated. Her thighs were dimpled and lovely. Her skin looked so soft it made his fingers twitch. His mouth watered just from the memory of her taste.

She dropped down onto her heels and quickly pulled the shirt down around her legs. He tried to snap his gaze to her face before she'd turned around, but he wasn't fast enough.

To his alarm, she snorted. "I guess I look a bit strange wearing nothing but your shirt, right?" She set down the honey and tugged at the hem. "It's a decent fit, though."

"Breathtaking."

The words slipped out before he could think better of it, and she let out a wry laugh. "You don't have to flatter me."

His brow furrowed. "Not flattery. Fact."

"Fact, huh?" Her tone indicated she did not believe him. The way she covered her stomach with her arm and turned her body away made a spike of alarm go down his spine.

He got up and crossed the room to her. Her eyes widened as he loomed over her, but she didn't order him to go sit back down, nor did she seem alarmed. She did not even flinch.

"Here is *fact*, Trinia of Oakwall. You are the most beautiful woman I have ever seen. So beautiful that I believe the Fades must have been inspired when they rendered you. To deny that fact is to deny our gods themselves. I suggest you do not do so again."

CHAPTER
TWENTY-THREE

TRINIA

Those were the most words she had ever heard him speak, and they made her stomach do flips and her heart fluttered like it had grown wings.

"W-well." She couldn't break eye contact. Blast, what was happening to her? Her head felt all muddled. "Thank you. That's really sweet of you to say."

A satisfied look flooded his features, and all her breath left her in a rush.

The teapot on the stove began to squeal.

Brovdir backed away from her in an instant, looking almost as if he was unnerved by his show of confidence. She was far *less* unsettled. In fact, she felt like she was soaring. Excitement bubbled up in her chest and heated her through.

The second round together was going to be fun.

Her gut twisted up as she adjusted the teapot. It wasn't supposed to be *fun*. This was an agreement. A business deal.

She couldn't let herself get attached. Not to him. Or to the baby.

She could do this.

She ignored her reservations about the cracked cup and its ability to hold anything heftier than air as she poured the tea and added the honey.

Brovdir had sat down at the table, and she walked over with the mug. "Here." His brows furrowed with confusion as she placed it in front of him. "Drink up."

He picked up the cup and downed a large gulp.

"Biscuits and jam, not that fast! You'll burn your tongue." She rushed to the tap to get cold water on a cloth and went back to him. "Stick out your tongue."

He did so without any hesitation, displaying the large, dark green tongue that had given her so much pleasure just a few moments ago.

She flushed so much she could feel it in her neck and shoulders, then tried to distract from it by patting his tongue with the cloth. Brovdir sat stock-still with wide eyes and simply let her.

After a moment that was *far* too long, it dawned on her how absolutely ridiculous this was. Why had Brovdir not taken the cloth from her? Why had he just *let* her pat down his tongue like this?

"Is . . . is that better?" she asked. Fades almighty, *please* say yes.

"N-oh bhur-nh."

She was a complete ninny. She took the cloth away from his mouth. "What was that?"

"No burn."

"What?" Her voice was too shrill, and it made Brovdir

blink. “You aren’t burned? Then why did you let me put a cool cloth on your tongue?”

“You . . . ordered it.”

“I did not order it! I was trying to help you.”

His face fell. “I apologize.”

Blast it all. She didn’t want to make him feel *bad*. “You don’t need to apologize. I should apologize to you! I’m the one who forced myself on you.”

He quirked an amused brow at her.

“You know what I mean.” She was going to burn to cinders from embarrassment. “You don’t have to be so obedient all the time.”

He tipped his head at her in that way that made her heart swell. “Don’t want me obedient?”

Oh *fuck*, why did that make her stomach go all quivery? “W-well, I don’t—I mean—”

He took a deep inhale. Too deep. His brows rose.

“No, I don’t want you obedient!” she spouted out only to have his lips quirk. “Stop it! You don’t have to follow my orders.”

“Like following orders,” he rumbled. A tremble flooded her as one of his hands curled around the base of her spine. “I’d follow any you gave.”

She couldn’t get out words.

“Trinia . . . what would you like me to do?”

Oh, *rolls and rum*, his voice was like something tangible. Alive. It nestled deep in her mind and made her whole body thrum with desire.

“My tongue does hurt.”

What? It did? She searched his face for any sign of pain and saw nothing but hot desire. His eyes were smoldering and his smile lit something deep inside her. Some wonderful spark that had been dormant and cold for so long.

She wanted him.

"Does hurt," he repeated as his hand continued up her back. Shivers of delight quaked through her as he pulled her a little closer. "Will you help?"

Oh, *Fades*.

She leaned down and pressed her lips to his.

He tensed up, as if in shock. Blast it all! Had she read him wrong? Had he meant something else?

Too late now. She'd already fitted her lips between his tusks. He tasted as sweet as the honey he'd drank. He was so soft and smooth. The spicy smell of him was flooding her senses and making her a little dizzy.

She used her tongue to probe at the seam of his lips and he opened his mouth.

Only after she'd delved her tongue inside did she realize he'd opened up to *gasp.* Too late now.

She pushed a little harder into him, and used the pad of her thumb to push on his chin, wanting deeper. He'd clearly never been kissed by anyone else before and had *no* idea what to do, but a deep groan as she stroked his tongue with hers betrayed his delight.

He tasted like *bliss*.

He made a little choked sound in the back of his throat.

"Breathe, Brovdir," she said against his lips. "Through your nose."

He sucked in a hard breath and then exhaled it on a growl that made her pussy clench with want. Feeling his tongue against hers, it was hard to forget how it had felt flicking her clit, pushing into her.

She clenched her thighs together at the memory. She'd gotten so slick!

He inhaled so sharp and quick it made her eyes pop open. His pupils had dilated to pinpricks, and he jerked away from her.

"Taste you again?"

She nodded before she'd even fully processed his request, and the grin of delight that flooded his features made her a little giddy.

At least until he swung her up and plopped her down on the table. Then burning need swallowed up every other emotion.

She spread her legs for him. "Yes, Brovdir. I want it."

He let out a low growl that rumbled all the way from the tips of her toes to the top of her head and made her clit throb.

And then he pushed her legs further apart.

CHAPTER
TWENTY-FOUR

BROVDIR

He could not wait to taste her even a moment longer.

He spread her legs wide, and lapped the sweet, wetness from her entrance all the way to the little nub at the top.

She let out a groan that barreled through him, gripping his throat like a vice. That hardened his cock to the point of pain.

He licked again, drinking her up. Her hips trembled as if she were resisting the urge to thrust into him.

Fuck, he wanted her to. He wanted her to grab his hair and pull him in deep and grind herself on him. He wanted her to use his tongue for her pleasure.

Her feet flexed, heels dug into his back. He licked her again, swirled the tip of his tongue around her nub, and she twisted against him.

He doubled his efforts, licking, swirling, sucking.

He slipped his hands under her bum. It felt so fucking good in his palms, plump and soft. He pulled her up, bracing her weight in his hands as he flattened his tongue and raked it up her slit.

Her heels pushed into his shoulder blades as she thrust up into him.

"Brovdir, *yes*," she groaned and the sound of his name on her lips was so sweet it nearly did him in. His cock was throbbing and weeping.

He tightened his hold, firmed his lips around her nub, and sucked hard.

She instantly fell to pieces. Her cry was deafening. Her hips bounced, her thighs clenched.

Her hands reached down to clench his hair, and she ground herself against his mouth, just like he'd longed for. *Fades help him!* It felt too good. It was too much. His cock swelled, and he teetered right on the edge.

He couldn't. The next spill *had* to be inside her or she would not be rendered with child.

His heart pitched and his muscles bunched.

Why was his body rebelling against that thought? Didn't he *want* to render her with child? Wasn't that the point of this?

Confused and dismayed, Brovdir tried to distract himself from the oddity by lapping at her again.

"H-hold on." Her voice was a sigh of deep satisfaction. It felt wonderful in his ears. "I need a break. Just . . . for a moment."

Yes. That's exactly what he needed to. A break.

He sat back, placing her bum back down on the table, and his sight was filled with her gorgeous form. Her chest was heaving, her body was shaking, and her brows were pinched with ecstasy. He'd never seen anything more beautiful in all his years.

He moved up and away from her pussy, allowing her legs

to come down off his shoulders so he could curl into her side. He just wanted to be close to her. To feel her warmth against him. To breathe with her tempo until their heart beats matched.

But just as he'd settled in next to her on the table, she said. "T-the couch?"

His heart felt like it fell right out of his chest.

He shouldn't be so disappointed. She'd *just* asked for space.

He got up to let her have it, and a tightness firmed around his arm. He blinked down to find Trinia scooting off the table. She pushed off and got to her feet.

Only to have her knees buckle.

He caught her instantly, lifting her up with ease.

"Thank you," she squeaked. "I . . . I just need a moment. Can we go to the couch?"

She wanted to join him on the couch!

He walked them both over without preamble and flopped down with her snugly in his lap. Right where his cock was trying to tear free of his pants.

Trinia sounded breathless, but she didn't try to escape him. Instead, she snuggled in a little. Placed her small hands against his chest, right over his heart, like she was cradling it with her palms.

She leaned her head against his shoulder, and her body went lax.

Oh, *Fades be praised!* That felt good. So good. He couldn't resist snuggling into her too, resting his cheek on her hair. Nothing had ever felt this full and light and comfortable.

She let out a contended hum that made his bones melt. Her voice was sleep rich as she murmured. "We . . . we should keep going right? We need to finish."

Fuck no. "It can wait till morn."

"Really?" she asked softly. "But I can tell how queued up you are."

She wiggled her bum against his erection, and he gritted his teeth. "*Break*."

Her sigh of relief felt magical. "Thank you, Brovdir. I know . . . I know I'm making this difficult on you."

She was. She absolutely was. But not for the reasons he knew she meant. He held her a little tighter. "I like this. Want a break too."

"All right." She paused a moment and then brought her hand up to his face. Passed his tusk. Over his ear.

Her hand grazed through his hair. The tips of her nails scratched along his scalp.

He moaned and a delighted shiver swept over him.

She continued to comb his hair with her fingers and his body progressively became more and more relaxed. Every muscle loosened, even ones he had not realized were tight. His eyes drooped, and his mind succumbed to a deep, unwavering contentment. A kind of ease that had been so incredibly rare in his life of fighting and fear.

It felt like home.

Fades, he'd never truly known the meaning of that word until this moment.

Home.

A slight murmur met his ears, and he somehow found the strength to open his eyes.

Trinia's eyes were closed. Her body had gone boneless. Her lips were parted as she sighed in her sleep.

And she was still gently caressing his hair. Just slightly. Even in her slumber, she tried to comfort him.

His chest swelled with an emotion he couldn't name. One

that made the world brighten and go quiet at the same time. One that felt so rich and wonderful he could hardly fathom it.

He picked Trinia up from the couch—very carefully. Her hand fell away from his head and down into her lap, but she did not wake.

With quick and quiet steps, he carried her to the bed, laid her down on the farthest side, and crawled in next to her.

She rolled toward him, back into his chest. She used his arm as a pillow and his body heat as her blanket. The contentment he felt in this moment was unreal. Like a gift from the Fades themselves.

He did not deserve her.

And he would never let her go.

CHAPTER TWENTY-FIVE

TRINIA

She awoke warm, satisfied, and without a single stiff muscle.

Stretching slightly, Trinia mused on the last time she'd woken up without being in pain. After sleeping on flour sacks in her dusty bakery for nearly a full season, she'd forgotten just how wonderful being in a bed was.

Even if two-thirds of that bed was taken up by a huge, *naked* orc.

He looked even more like a puppy when he was sleeping, with his shaggy hair covering his eyes and his face relaxed. The powerful, pleasure wrecked male who'd rutted her into oblivion was gone and a docile, sleepy pup remained. She resisted the urge to rustle his hair, knowing it would wake him.

He didn't snore, which she found a bit surprising. In fact, she almost couldn't hear him breathing. She could feel it though, because his arm was draped heavily over her hip and his warm stomach was so close she could feel it expanding against her with each breath.

The rhythm made her cheeks heat. Fades! They still needed to go another round before she was pregnant. She filled her lungs and resisted the urge to squirm.

Brovdir sucked in his breath then and was instantly awake. He went from completely asleep to alert so fast Trinia jolted backward.

Off the bed.

She didn't even have time to yip before a hand gripped her around the middle and saved her from the fall. She was flush back up against Brovdir again. He adjusted, flipping onto his back and taking her with him.

She ended up half on top of him, resting in the crook of his arm. His hot skin felt so good against her bare legs. Her thighs were widely parted around his stomach and her breasts were tucked right up against his chest.

Brovdir wrapped an arm around her middle. Not tight enough to hold her captive, but he made it clear he didn't want her to go.

She gave up refusing. He was too warm, felt too good.

His eyes were still closed. He had little creases around them that told her he smiled often. He had scars *everywhere*—forehead, eyebrows, one right next to his jaw, on his lips . . . across his neck.

There was no denying his neck scar was the worst. She reached out to gently touch it. He tensed and sucked in a breath as his eyes cracked open.

"Sorry." She pulled her hand back. "Does it hurt?"

"Not on the outside." His voice was sleep drenched, but clearer than she'd heard it before.

"How did it happen? Were you in battle?" she asked. "You don't have to tell me if it's uncomfortable."

His brows pinched for a moment, and his fingers drummed at the small of her back before he sucked in a hard breath. "I . . . have a habit of taking unwilling conquests."

She jolted. *"What?"*

He quickly amended. "Not in that way, I swear. Out there, many are desperate. They trade women for boons whether she consents or not."

Trinia's stomach twisted up. "That's horrible."

Brovdir nodded. "I take them. I do not touch. Then I return them with the boons promised."

Her chest warmed. "Goodness. That's so decent of you, but why would you give them the boons if they didn't hold up their end of the bargain?"

He rose a brow as if confused by her question. "Most are desperate. Starving. Have starving children. Or an abusive man who forced their hand. No boons means she will suffer more than the terror she already endured."

She melted for the male even as she flinched with shame. "You're right . . . I didn't think about that."

He reached up to touch her cheek. His warm skin was gentle as he stroked the edge of her jaw. "Glad you didn't."

She blinked rapidly. "You're glad I was an insensitive ass?"

He snorted with amusement. "You're not. And *yes.* You did not consider it because you have never endured it. I'm glad for that."

She wondered just how much hardship this kind male had suffered outside the Rove Woods.

Her eyes went back to the scar. She tapped it with her fingertips. "So then . . . one of them gave you this? Did she not realize you were trying to help?"

He shook his head. "Was walking her home. Her brothers came to her aid. Twins. Smelled like just one when it was two. Caught me by surprise and . . . Karthoc found me in time."

"That's horrible. You were only trying to help." Trinia's chest went tight.

But Brovdir just shrugged. "Brothers didn't know. Just wanted to save their kin. Only one to blame is father who sold her, and brothers took care of him. Heard them talking as they escaped."

"She didn't even try to help you?"

"She did. She screamed Karthoc's name for me. He'd never have found me in time if she hadn't."

Her brows furrowed. "And let me guess, they took the boons with them too?"

His eyes went wide, and his brows went up, and his head did an adorable tilt that made his shaggy hair fall over his forehead. "Of course. It was a misunderstanding. I did not wish for them to starve for that."

The gracious words combined with the adorable, wide-eyed, puppy-like expression made Trinia's heart swell. Warmth bloomed from the top of her head all the way to the tips of her toes, and the urge to cling to this orc was almost overwhelming.

"I'm . . ." She couldn't think of the right words, so she leaned down and kissed him.

That seemed better for him than words anyway. She could feel his smile under her lips. His body relaxed and the hold on her waist tightened, and he didn't hesitate to open his mouth to deepen the kiss.

Fades, she felt like she was drowning. Her head was all muddled up, and she didn't want to stop. She moved up to straddle his torso while still dueling with his tongue and he let out a low, pleased groan that rumbled through her until her pussy clenched.

He broke off first by cupping her face in his huge, warm hands and pulling her back slightly. His eyes searched hers and his lips parted like he was in disbelief.

She adjusted until she could feel the swell of his cock against her ass. He hissed out a breath as she squirmed against it. "We . . . we should finish things up."

They should. She'd lost her bakery. None of her friends could take her in indefinitely, and she had no other resources by which she could trade for a new home.

He reached up to pull her close again. Back into his strength and warmth. Her breath left her as his touch eased away the pain of her loss and thrumming anticipation took its place. Just one look from his dark eyes and her toes were curling.

He pulled her head down and kissed the world out of her. Surrounded her in heat. His tongue smacked, licked, and swirled around hers until she was almost boneless.

But her mind flashed back to the night before and how generous he'd been. How good he'd made her feel. She wanted to reward him, let him concentrate on his own pleasure and not think about pleasing her. She pulled back to look into his eyes. "Grip the sheets, Brovdir."

His eyes shot wide, and his hands moved away from her waist, down to the bedding without preamble. He tipped his head adorably again, and she grinned. He was so obedient.

"You really do like taking orders, don't you?"

His cheeks flushed a brighter green and being embarrassed was the last thing she wanted him to feel.

"I like it." She leaned in to kiss the bridge of his nose. "You know you can say 'no,' don't you?"

"Yes," he breathed.

"I know . . . I know that this is just business." Her throat constricted around the words, and she hid her tension by trailing more kisses down his throat. Right over the scar. "But it might be fun to play a bit, if you're willing?"

He hissed. The sound was laced with deep pleasure, and he murmured, "Yes, anything you desire."

A tingle of sheer delight coursed down her spine, and heat pulsed between her legs. Three little words and she was already so *hot*.

"In that case," she said slowly as she crawled down his body. His head lifted to watch her, but his hands never left the bedding.

She could feel how huge and hard his cock was as she adjusted, but nothing prepared her for the sight of it.

Fades help her. He really was massive. She got on her knees next to him and wondered how she'd been able to take him so easily. He was larger than she could fit her fingers around. The tip was a much darker green than the shaft. She reached out and stroked him with her thumb, starting from the top, teasing under the head, and tracing the veins down his shaft. They pulsed with the frantic beat of his heart.

"*Trinia*," Brovdir gasped.

"Want me to stop?" She searched his face, but all she saw there was pleasure.

He swallowed hard and shook his head.

"I know the next spill has to be inside me. You can hold out for me, right, Brovdir? You can be strong for me?"

He let out an exhale hard enough to rustle her hair and nodded.

She wasted no time stroking his cock with her hand. "Did you fit the full length inside me?"

"No," he panted.

"Hmm," she mused, stroking back to the top. "Do you think you could?"

He swallowed hard. "No. I won't."

That was a quick refusal. "Why?"

"Don't . . . want to hurt you."

"What if I controlled it?" Trinia said, stroking down again. It probably wasn't fair to use petting his cock as a distraction, but she didn't care. "What if I was in complete control?"

His eyes flashed wide in an instant and his expression took on a slacked, wonderstruck look that made her stomach flutter and her thighs squirm. His nod was quick, focused.

Ooh, so he wanted her to be in control? She supposed she should have guessed that since he liked to take orders. To test it, she said, "You're going to follow every direction I say, Brovdir."

His eyes shot wide and his jaw slacked a little.

"I'm going to tell you when to thrust, how hard, how deep . . . I'm going to tell you when you have to be still and when you can touch me."

A groan flooded out of him as she stroked his shaft again. He was shivering like he had a fever.

"You can still say no if you don't like something." She felt the need to ensure him. "But if you don't say no, I'm going to do what I want. *Everything* that I want. What do you say to that?"

His nod was so eager it would have been adorable had her blood not been set to boiling. The thought of controlling this powerful, massive male made her pussy pulse with desire.

"In that case, I want to get you nice and wet so you slide inside me better." His eyes flashed as if he was trying to work out what that meant.

There was no better explanation than by example. She gripped his cock tight in her hand and slowly dipped her head. She saw the realization flash in his eyes as he sucked in a sharp breath.

He didn't tell her no.

She leaned down and licked from the throbbing base all the way to the twitching tip.

"*Fuck!*" Brovdir's grip on the sheets tightened until she heard them ripping. "Trinia, I—"

She gave him no time to process and instead swirled her tongue around the head until he groaned and arched his back.

It was so easy to pleasure him. She'd barely started, and he looked spent already.

"Trinia." His groan was vibrant and made her quiver as she continued to lap at the head of his cock. He gasped between quivering jolts. *"I'll spill."*

"Not yet." She lapped gently at the head, and he groaned piteously. His fists tightened in the bedding, but he didn't let go. "Be a good boy and hold it."

He sucked in a hard breath and his eyes shot open.

Ooh, so he liked that. "You can, right? You can be a good boy . . . *my* good boy and hold on for me?"

He let out that breath in quivering gulps and nodded his shaggy head so eagerly it left no room for doubt in her mind.

"That's it." She dipped low again, right at the base of his cock, and flattened her tongue against it so hard she could feel his heartbeat pulsing against her lips. She cupped her hand around the opposite side and crawled toward the head.

He let out a strangled groan that shot bliss all the way through her. She was trembling almost as badly as he was. Her pussy ached. Her clit throbbed.

She got to the top and swirled her tongue around the tip of

his cock, teasing the underside and taking it into her mouth. It barely fit.

He let out a roar that may have shaken the leaves off this tree house had there been any.

"Trinia." Brovdir's moan raked up her spine and blasted her with a deep need the likes of which she'd never felt before.

The burning desire to mount him grew too high for her to take.

CHAPTER TWENTY-SIX

BROVDIR

He had not known such ecstasy was even possible.

Trinia's orders felt like the flash of lightning in his mind. They brightened his world and shot bliss down every limb. The hold on his control was maddening, but every moment he obeyed her brought intense pleasure. He knew his restraint was pleasing her. His willpower, despite the shuddering, aching *need* she teased him with, was making her hot. The scent of her arousal flooded his senses, churned up his mind. It was harder to fight that than her touch.

"You've been a *good boy*, Brovdir. You've earned your reward."

Her voice was husky, sweet *madness* and his mind rippled with pleasure as she mounted him. She drew up on her knees, bent his cock forward, and lined up her hot, wet pussy.

And his flesh went ice cold.

Shuddering fear raked over him. His mind quailed. His tongue went dry and his erection . . . softened.

This wasn't right.

He . . . didn't want this.

He didn't want a son.

He wanted *her*.

"Stop."

Trinia did in an instant. Her eyes flew wide, and her breath caught. "Did I hurt you?"

"N-no. No." He shook his head and carefully pulled her off him. Her eyes snapped from his face to his now softening cock and realization flooded her features.

The dismay that furrowed her brow was so intense it choked him.

"You . . ." Her voice was so quiet. "What did I do?"

"Nothing," he said. "Nothing at all."

This had been the best thing he'd ever experienced, and he never wanted it to end. He didn't want to stop.

"So then . . . why did you stop me?" She sat back a little further and his fists balled to prevent himself from grabbing her. "We'll need to finish soon, right? Otherwise . . ." She touched her lower stomach. Right where his babe might grow.

Fades blast him to the depths. He didn't know what to do! He didn't know what he wanted. His mind scrambled over itself, trying to find a solution.

If he got her pregnant . . . she'd go back to Oakwall. He'd build her a home behind those walls. Deep inside a village where he could not visit. He'd raise the son on his own. Without her.

The idea of it made his mind quail and his instincts roar.

It felt wrong. Too wrong. He couldn't do it.

"I—" Fuck, what to say, what to say . . .

I want to be with you.

I want to keep you.

I want you to be my mate.

Her stomach grumbled slightly, and he clung to that sound like it was his lifeline.

"I want to get you some food."

"Some . . . food." Her brows scrunched up in obvious confusion.

"Yes," he said desperately. If he could just get a few moments to *think*, he would come up with a different exchange between them. Something that would keep her at his side. Keep her coming *back*.

He just needed more *time* with her. That was all. Just time.

"Yes," he said more firmly. "Your body needs to be well nourished to carry an orc babe."

She blinked wide, and then a wry laugh left her lips. "Brovdir, I think I have *more* than enough *nourishment* to carry a babe." She patted her stomach slightly and his irritation swelled to painfully constrict his throat.

He dipped close to her, until his nose was nearly brushing hers, but she didn't flinch, only widened her skeptical eyes. "Trinia of Oakwall, your beautiful curves hold no bearing on whether you deserve *breakfast*. I intend to see to your every need while you are in my care. And after last night, you are in desperate need of replenishing. Do you deny it?"

Her cheeks were colored so brightly he could almost feel heat radiating from them. "O-oh . . . I mean, no. I don't. I just—"

"Do not argue with me on this, Trinia," he said firmly as the imprint raged instinctual drive through his veins. "I am an orc and you are my conquest. It is my honor to serve you and keep you hale."

There was no fear in her beautiful face, no hesitation or upset. Instead, her eyes blinked in surprise, and she shifted in her seat and held his gaze with a confidence that bloomed delight in his chest. "Then . . . then thank you. Breakfast does sound nice."

He grinned as relief flooded him. He dipped in close to her ear.

"Good girl. Wait here. I will go to the hall and be back soon."

CHAPTER TWENTY-SEVEN

TRINIA

Apparently, Brovdir *was* able to take command of a situation when he wanted to.

That fierce determination combined with the rumbled "good girl" had cued her up so hot she was both regretting his departure and relieved by it. She needed a few moments to catch her breath.

Her stomach clenched with dismay as she tried to convince herself that he *really* just wanted to get her food before begetting her with child. That's all this was.

He hadn't changed his mind.

And . . . she hadn't changed hers either.

She shook her head to push away the anxiety. The deal had been struck. She would not back out now. She needed to stop overthinking everything and *relax.*

Brovdir's grinning face flashed in her mind's eye. His big eyes and his calm demeanor and his rumbly perfect voice.

"Good girl."

She sucked in a breath and pushed herself off the bed. She was being ridiculous.

She looked around the room to distract herself from her anxiety.

Her eyes landed on her dress hanging on the back of one of the table chairs next to the still crackling fire. It had been cleaned and appeared to now be dry.

Brovdir had gotten up and done that while she was sleeping?

Her heart tugged at the thought, and she crossed the room to finger the blue wool gown. It was only a little damp, and most of the mud stains had been scrubbed out. So much work.

His words spiraled through her mind again.

"It is my honor to serve you and keep you hale."

A little shiver coursed up her back, and it had nothing to do with being naked.

When was the last time she'd relied on someone to take care of her? Not since her mother had died, surely. Even longer. Her mother had gotten sick, and Trinia had gone from child to caretaker.

She shook her head, unhappy with these thoughts. Usually, she had her baking or sketching to keep her distracted from unpleasant memories.

There certainly wasn't any baking to be done *here*. It wouldn't even be possible. The kitchen area, if one could even call it that, was tiny, and the stove was only large enough to fit the kettle. All orcs ate together in the hall, so there was no need for anything more.

She moved around the room, taking time to examine everything as she went. He had very few personal effects. It made sense he wouldn't, since he'd been on the move for war campaigns all his life, but it was disappointing. She would have liked to see more of his interests.

She shook the thought from her head. His interests didn't matter. She was playing conquest for him, not forming a relationship.

Her heart squeezed at that, and she ignored it. She moved off to the only cluttered place here, a rolltop desk at the corner of the room. The craftsmanship was excellent, and she was certain it had been made by Savili's father. It was cluttered with parchment and black coal pencil marks. It took her a moment to realize that the beautiful swooping handwriting was *Brovdir's*.

She supposed it made sense. He couldn't talk much, so he'd have to write to communicate often. But still, the image of that huge, scarred male writing so beautifully . . .

Would he write to her if she asked?

Her cheeks warmed as she smiled.

She quickly wiped it off her face and muttered, "He's not going to write to you, you dolt. What would he write for?" They only needed to talk about the building and perhaps pregnancy updates from here on. They probably wouldn't see each other much.

She sighed, but it did nothing to ease the heaviness that had settled over her.

Her eyes scanned the large, open room again. There were very few furnishings and a lot of empty space. The bed was also right across from the door, which left little to no privacy.

A few walls would help. Maybe a built-in bookshelf so he could organize some of these papers. And if she did that, there could be a little nook area near the fire that would be quite cozy.

Her fingers twitched to sketch it the way she'd done so

many times before. Daydreaming about how her own home might look had been her favorite pastime, but redoing Brovdir's was an interesting challenge.

She glanced at the desk with its papers and pencils.

He wouldn't mind if she used some, right?

"It is my honor to serve you."

She picked up a paper and charcoal pencil and quickly sketched the outline of the tree with the furniture. She spent time figuring out what could and couldn't be moved. The table was attached to the floor and so was the couch, but the bedframe was adjustable.

Before long, she'd sat down on the chair and had used up three pieces of paper. She reimagined the space into a dwelling with two smaller bedrooms and an open living space.

Perhaps if things didn't work out with having her own house in Oakwall, she could ask to move in here.

Oh, biscuits. She needed to *stop* thinking about this.

She reached for another paper and accidentally knocked a whole stack. They flew off the desk and scattered all over the floor.

"Blast," she muttered, getting down on her knees to clean up. The little slips were clearly bird missives.

She shouldn't snoop.

She really shouldn't.

But she couldn't help herself.

She picked up the first slip.

Toclad Clan and Welvio Clan are both preparing to travel. Suspected arrival, late winter. Estimated 430 adult orcs, 90 sons, 12 mates. Needs at least 200 new homes in Rove Wood to accommodate.

Trinia read the parchment again. And then a third time. Still, she couldn't quite understand what she was reading.

They'd been told that warrior orcs were coming to settle in the Rove Woods, but only a few hands' worth. Perhaps fifty at the most.

Four hundred and thirty adult orcs. Two hundred new homes.

That . . . didn't make sense.

She shouldn't snoop anymore. This wasn't her business.

She *really* shouldn't.

But she did anyway.

She picked up the stack of parchment and began to read.

Arrival at Toclad. Told of prophecy. Refusing to leave. Want to wait till spring. -Karthoc

Trinia's hand was shaking as she picked up another.

Toclad relented after Seer showed Earth vision to Chief. Will leave after preparations are made. Suspected late winter arrival. 203 males, 52 sons, 8 mates. -Karthoc

Earth vision? What did that mean?

Why were the warrior orcs from outside Rove Wood come *here*?

She scoured over every letter, parchment, and note on the desk, searching for answers. Hands shaking. Blood hot. Her breathing grew heavy.

She didn't find any details she wanted. Nothing about the prophecy or the seer's vision. But one thing was certain.

The orcs of Rove Wood, including Brovdir, were keeping far more secrets than she could ever have fathomed.

CHAPTER TWENTY-EIGHT

BROVDIR

Brovdir stepped out of his home, into the crisp, chilly morning feeling lighter and fuller than he'd ever been in all his years.

The sun was bright, birds chirped in the trees despite the winter cold, and the clan members he passed were both lively and pleasant.

He could not wait to get back to Trinia.

But he needed to find a way to *keep* her first.

"Brovdir, hold a moment!"

He would have groaned had he not been in such a good mood. He turned to find Plog rushing over to him as fast as his elderly legs could carry. The male certainly was spry for his old age.

"Brovdir, you look fit. I suppose last night perked you right up."

Irritation flashed behind his eyes, but his spirits were too high to censure the male. "What do you need, Elder?"

"I just came to let you know that we've gathered some of the males and sons and are going to start digging."

Brovdir's stomach dropped.

"Don't worry." The male held his hands up with a smile. "I've got all the right tools in all the right places. If you know what I mean. Women can be a good motivator to our males, and I've got a few on my side already. Hilva in particular has been ripe with worry over the boar, so she's convinced her mate to help. Not sure his hearing will recover, but he won't need that for digging, anyway."

"No," Brovdir said quickly.

"Don't look so aghast. I was just jesting. I don't think Hilva did any real damage that a quick healing tincture can't undo."

"No! No *digging*."

"No digging? But how will we make the trap?"

"No need for a trap." Brovdir groaned. "There are no boars!"

"Well, not yet, but there will be. I can feel it."

Brovdir blinked in bewilderment. "You can feel *what*?"

"The need to dig! I feel it right deep in my bones. Right where the Fades themselves speak. I've got the truth deep inside me just wriggling to get out and the only way out is through digging! Don't worry, all three of us elders have it under control and are communing as often as we need to make sure the Fades will is done."

Brovdir's mind reeled from all this random information. "*Fades* will?"

"I'm sure that you're worried because of the sinkholes. I understand. But we're taking every precaution."

"No. That isn't . . . I don't mean—"

The elder turned away. "You come by later to have a

gander. We're on the westernmost point near the butchery. I'm certain once you see it, you'll just be delighted."

Before Brovdir could argue any more, the male walked away and disappeared down another wooded path.

He took a few deep breaths and pinched the bridge of his nose.

Imagined how Trinia would laugh when he told her about this.

His irritation faded to a brief chuckle as he envisioned her lovely, smiling face.

He continued on to the hall, making quick work of the walk, blessedly thankful that he didn't get stopped again.

Inside, many orcs and a few human mates had settled in to eat, though not as many as usual. The smell of the breakfast stew was more pungent than usual, and the combination of dandelion greens, lavender, and fish being boiled in the three main cauldrons made his stomach twist.

Most of the orcs he passed were eating fruit.

And listening in as Sythcol censured Gegvi.

"I just don't understand how you could mess up the entire meal *this* often." Sythcol raked a dirt covered hand through his white hair and left streaks of grime. His eyes had deep, dark green bags beneath them. His skin had lost its luster.

"I was just telling you it's not finished yet."

"I don't want to hear it. Breakfast is to be served at dawn. It's well past dawn." Sythcol's voice was rising. "What is even in here? Dandelions and *lavender*? What possessed you to make such a grotesque combination?"

Brovdir was about to intervene when Ogvick approached him from the left. He stopped, glad to see a friendly face, though his relief dimmed when he noted that the usually jovial young warrior's expression was a mask of concern.

"Chief," Ogvick's voice was a low whisper. "Have you spoken with Caivid yet?"

"No. He's looking for me?" Since taking up with one of Oakwall's shepherdesses, Caivid spent very little time in the clan. Brovdir was glad that one of his oldest friends was happy, but would be lying if he said he didn't miss him.

"He was supposed to . . . maybe he got caught up with Susara and . . ." Ogvick glanced nervously toward Sythcol.

"What's wrong?" Brovdir demanded. It was unlike his young friend to be so uneasy around the conjurers.

"Last night, we . . ." Ogvick lowered his voice. "Last night Sythcol was—"

"Ogvick! What are you saying to Brovdir?" Sythcol's shout caused Brovdir's spine to straighten.

"Nothing, Chief." Ogvick's voice was strong and firm, but Brovdir had known him nearly his entire life and could sense unease in the way Ogvick held his arms and balled his fists. "Just informing him what was made for breakfast."

Sythcol narrowed his eyes. "I'm certain he could smell it. Just like the rest of us." Sythcol waved an arm to indicate the fifty or so orcs and women who were all looking about as uncomfortable as Brovdir felt. Then he turned on Gegvi again, and the male shrank in on himself like a small child about to get a wallop. "I've had *no* sleep last night and now no food either, and that's thanks to your abysmal skills, Gegvi. Now get out of my sight! You're completely useless to me."

The small male jerked as if cracked with a whip and darted for the door. Brovdir's chest felt like a hallow pit as he watched the cook scurry from the room. Sythcol straightened his clothes, the same ones he'd been wearing the day before and approached. "Ogvick. Get to work on the cooking."

The young male's eyes widened, and he looked to Brovdir as if he wanted to confirm the order.

Before Brovdir could respond, Sythcol snapped, "*Now*," and the male swallowed hard before heading off toward the storage room near the back of the hall where extra provisions were kept.

Brovdir couldn't recall the male *ever* cooking *anything* besides roasting meat on a stick. He couldn't imagine it being any better than Gegvi's work.

"Where's Trinia?" Sythcol started and then he inhaled sharply. His eyes widened. His face paled. "You *smell* of her."

Irritation bloomed in Brovdir's chest. "That is none of your concern."

"Come with me. Now." Sythcol turned toward the doorway which led to the spiral staircase.

Brovdir followed without a word, though he longed to argue.

The moment they were within the privacy of the tiny room at the base of the stair, Sythcol rounded on him. "You *rutted* her? What were you *thinking*?"

"My personal life is none of your concern." Brovdir worked to keep the snarl from his tone.

"It *is* my concern when it keeps you from your duties and forces them all onto my already overfull plate." Sythcol's snap echoed off the trunk of the Great Rove Tree and surrounded Brovdir in a spiral of fury and indignation. "It took you *far* too long to call the conjurers and warriors to my side last night. And I know that is because Trinia was distracting you."

Brovdir gritted his teeth. He couldn't deny that.

"Why can you not just do as I say, exactly when I tell you to do it?" Sythcol raged.

Trinia's words from the night before flashed in his mind.

"You're a chief too, Brovdir."

"Why must I follow your every order? Am I not your equal in this?" Brovdir's throat felt like acid as he forced the words.

"Oh, Fades, *don't* try to make excuses. You've never once complained about following my lead. Not *once*."

Brovdir went silent. Sythcol was right. He *hadn't* ever complained. In fact, he'd *welcomed* Sythcol's judgment this entire time.

He swallowed so hard that he could feel the pain of his scar ricochet down into his chest.

He looked into the eyes of the powerful conjurer before him, with his knotted hair and disheveled clothes.

Brovdir took a breath. "We should discuss later. You need *sleep*. And *food*."

Sythcol gritted his teeth but finally relaxed. He raked a filthy hand through his white hair again and grimaced. "Fuck, you're right. My mind isn't what it should be."

Brovdir nodded. "Later. After rest. I will deal with the clan for now."

"Thank you." Sythcol's shoulders sagged. "Just make sure you don't change anything without getting my approval first. And don't let your warriors lapse in their duties. And . . . and make sure Trinia doesn't leave before I've spoken with her. I need to make sure she doesn't tell her headman about the sinkholes."

Brovdir exhaled hard, but nodded.

"Good," Sythcol said. "Now I'll go sleep first, I think."

With that, they both exited back out into the hall. Sythcol did not pause and headed right out the intricately carved double doors. Brovdir headed for the fruit table and began to fill a bowl for Trinia.

"Chief."

Ogvick stood behind him, his bushy brows were furrowed with worry and his square jaw was clenched tight. “I need to speak with you.”

Brovdir had already spent far too long away from Trinia, but could see this was important. “About Sythcol?”

Ogvick nodded. “About . . . last night.”

His stomach twisted. “Are things not well?”

“I . . . I can’t really say. He’s just acting . . . odd.” Ogvick looked around the room and Brovdir took note that most were paying them little mind. “Caivid and Hendr think so, too. Perhaps if we discussed as a group, we could figure him out.”

Brovdir sighed heavily. He did not want to make Trinia wait for her food another moment. “Sythcol is resting. He’ll be gone a while. Can this wait until the eve?”

Ogvick’s brow furrowed up even more, but he said, “I . . . suppose.”

“Work the soup,” Brovdir said with a nod toward the bubbling pot that smelled more like a bathtub than a stew. “When done, go find Caivid and Hendr. I’ll be back shortly.”

The warrior’s expression shifted to one of dismay as he looked toward the cauldrons, but he nodded and said, “Yes, Chief.”

Brovdir exhaled with relief and walked toward the exit. As he did so, his eyes scanned the room, focusing on one particular area.

The table where the families sat together.

Govek was seated nearest, with his arm around Miranda and the three boys they’d adopted, chattering happily as they scarfed down their meal. Next to them sat Iytier who bounced his infant son on his lap while his mate laughed at something Miranda said.

They looked happy. Full.

He wanted that.

His chest tightened around the sharp truth. He'd always wanted that, hadn't he? Maybe that was why he'd only ever taken women who he knew would refuse to play conquest.

He didn't want Trinia as his conquest. He wanted her as his mate.

He wanted *her*.

And he'd thought of the perfect way to win her.

He quickly carried the bowls of fruit out of the hall and pretended not to hear whenever any of the orcs called after him, demanding his attention.

His mind was centered on convincing Trinia to meet with him regularly and advise him about the clan.

That was how he would get her to see him often.

She'd been born and raised here. She knew every orc and male personally. She could give him valuable information. Perhaps every day. In return, he'd build her a home. Slowly. *Very* slowly. So slowly that she would have to stay with him here in the meantime.

And if he was lucky, perhaps, by the end, she might decide that the home he'd built for her at Oakwall wasn't as good as the one they shared here in Rove Wood Clan.

Fades, please, let her choose to stay.

He all but kicked down the door when he finally arrived home.

Only to find she was standing at his desk. A cold chill raced over him.

He'd forgotten to close the roll top.

"Trinia?" His heart was up in his throat.

She turned, and he saw the letters held tight in her hands. Correspondence from Karthoc about the prophecy.

Fuck.

"What is this, Brovdir?" Her expression was flat, unreadable, tense. "Brovdir, tell me what these are."

"Letters. From Karthoc."

Her eyes flashed with fury, and he couldn't catch his breath. "That isn't what I'm talking about, and you know it. According to these, over thirty clans and communities of orcs from outside Rove Wood are going to settle here within the next few seasons. Is that true?"

He couldn't lie to her. He forced a nod.

She covered her mouth with her hand, and her eyes turned glossy with tears. He felt like his heart was being trampled on. What could he do? What could he say to make this right?

Then she blinked away her tears and her voice came out sharper than his finest blade. "You must be jesting! You told us it would only be fifty warriors at most!"

He swallowed and averted his eyes. They landed on a sketch on the floor under his desk that he didn't recognize. A floor plan of a house.

His house. She'd drawn his home?

"These numbers—it's going to be *thousands* of orcs. How can you think that Rove could even hold that many? Our resources might be plentiful for the few *hundred* we have, but *thousands*? And so soon? It's not possible!"

He looked back to her face, unable to find words.

"And what's this about a prophecy and Earth? Does Miranda have something to do with this? Why? *How*? I've spoken to her at nearly every trade since her arrival and never *once* has she mentioned this."

"Sythcol ordered silence." Brovdir felt guilty for pushing the blame off, even as the words left his lips.

"Oh, did he? Why am I not surprised?" Trinia snapped, throwing down the papers. Then she went still, eyes widened on the stack before they snapped to him. The ice in them sent a shiver down his spine. "He's told Headman Gerald at least?"

Brovdir gulped so thickly his throat began to throb.

He shook his head

"*Brovdir*." Hearing his name spoken so harshly by her hurt more than the crack of a whip across his back. "You cannot be serious! Tell me you're lying."

"Not lying."

"*Why*?" She threw out her arms. "What justification does he have to keep something so vital from us?"

"Did not want to threaten the peace. Was afraid you would leave."

Even as he said it, he could see how wrong it was.

Trinia's face contorted. "Brovdir, *keeping* this from us is what will ruin the peace. The sinkholes are already bad enough, but this? This is inexcusable. This isn't just about the wellbeing of a few villagers who like to walk in the woods, this will affect our *entire* community. It will affect our relationships, our trade, our *resources*. Explain how you think keeping this from us is justified. Look me in the eye and tell me you agree with Sythcol's decision."

He couldn't. He truly couldn't think of any justification for keeping the prophecy from them.

But that is what Sythcol had demanded, so that is what they'd decided to do.

Trinia shook her head in disbelief, clearly reading him. "*Brovdir*. If you thought that keeping this secret from us was a bad idea, then *why* did you *do it*?"

The pain in his throat was an inferno that spread through

his whole body. The imprint was thundering agony, and he worried his chest might explode.

"Sythcol . . . ordered me not to."

Trinia dropped her arms and her jaw went slack. Tears welled in her eyes and, once again, she blinked them away.

Her voice was deadly quiet as she said, "You've followed orders your whole life, Brovdir, so I understand how difficult it must be to change. But you are a *chief* now. There's absolutely *no* excuse for allowing something like this to be kept secret when even *you* can see how wrong it is."

She moved around him and went to the door. The need to cage his arms around her and force her to remain at his side was blinding.

But so too was the fear of what forcing her to stay would do.

She turned back only once to look him in the eyes. Her tears had broken free and were creating tracks down her cheeks.

"I think we need to part ways here, Brovdir. Please, don't follow me."

With that, she was out the door, and only the sound of it slamming behind her remained.

His muscles bunched with the need to chase her down. He paced the room to fight his instincts. Forcing her would ruin *everything.*

She'd ordered him not to follow her. *She'd ordered him.*

His eyes shifted to her drawing on the floor, and he crossed the room to scoop it up.

She'd drawn a floor plan of his house with two bedrooms.

Had she been considering living here with him?

His chest filled with emotions he had no name for. The

imprint thrummed in his veins. His longing to be with her, to keep her, outweighed all logic.

Outweighed all orders.

He shoved her sketch into his waistband and followed after her.

CHAPTER TWENTY-NINE

TRINIA

Her eyes prickled harshly as she stormed along the paths through the clan. The air was brisk and thick patches of frost lined every branch and leaf. The sting of the icy breeze on her cheeks only hastened her steps and solidified her determination to get away from Brovdir as soon as possible. She'd go . . .

Go where?

She stopped dead in her tracks and barely managed to resist the shout of fury that welled in her throat.

Two hundred orcs. Two *hundred* would be arriving to *live* here in half a moon. *Half a moon*. Less than fifteen days.

She needed to tell the headman what was coming. He needed to know.

She couldn't.

She pressed her palm to her head. She knew there was no possible way for her to tell Headman Gerald about what she'd learned and not threaten the peace. He'd be *livid* when he discovered the orcs had been keeping this from him and had no intention of telling him anytime soon. He'd view it as a betrayal, and rightly so.

And Headman Gerald's reaction would be *nothing* compared to how her fellow villagers would react. Brovdir was right to worry about them leaving. Folks had made glum threats about resettling outside these woods since the warriors had arrived. Most of those threats were empty, but if they found out *thousands* of orcs were coming to stay instead of a few dozen?

She pressed her palms into her eyes so hard she saw stars.

Maybe . . . just maybe, if she brought someone from Rove Wood Clan with her when she broke the news, the headman wouldn't be so mad. If the villagers heard it from the lips of one of their own, they might receive it better.

She turned on her heel to head back toward the center of the clan. Toward Savili's house. She remembered the way well enough although she'd only visited a handful of times.

After only a few missed turns, Trinia arrived at her destination and wrapped hard at the door.

There was no answer.

Had she gotten the wrong house? Or were they just not in? It dawned on her that most of the orcs ate their meals at the hall and it was about time for the first meal.

Blast it all, what should she do now? Should she try to go find them?

She could find herself a new orc to play conquest to while she was at it. Any one of them had the skills to build her a home.

But the thought of that made her whole body shiver with dismay. What was wrong with her? Her reaction wasn't *practical.* She needed a home. She couldn't get one from Brovdir. She had to find someone else.

Her vision blurred from her tears.

"Trinia?"

She dashed the tears away with her palms and quickly got up from the stoop as Savili approached, blonde hair caught up in a tight bun, clean cotton dress swaying as she hurried up the path.

"What are you doing here? What's going on?" Savili quickly took her hand. "You're freezing! Let's get you inside."

"Thank you," Trinia said past the lump in her throat. She looked toward Iytier, Savili's mate, who followed close behind with their toddler in his arms. "I'm sorry about intruding."

"You're family to me, Trinia," Savili chided. "You are never intruding. Yerina on the other hand . . ."

Trinia snorted and good humor lightened her chest as Savili ushered her into the tree home.

The downstairs was cozy and open, with a large kitchen table and two couches flanking a fireplace that crackled merrily. Their kitchen was only a little bigger than Brovdir's had been, but had quite a few storage cupboards lining the wall all the way to the staircase.

Iytier headed for it, pausing long enough to let Savili pluck a kiss to her son's forehead. "I'll put Haysik down for his nap. Make yourself at home, Trinia."

"Thank you," Trinia said as he made his way up the steps. She looked at Savili when she said. "I really am sorry for intruding like this."

"Stop saying that and come sit at the table. Would you like some tea?" Savili went into the kitchen and filled the kettle from the sink.

Trinia shook her head. She wasn't sure she could stomach

anything right now. She couldn't hold her words in either. "I know about the prophecy."

Savili dropped the kettle with a loud clang. Water splashed across the counter and dripped onto the floor.

Trinia rung her hands. "So, it's really true that thousands of orcs are going to be settling in these woods, all around us, in just a few seasons. *Thousands*, not fifty."

"Trinia . . . I . . ." Savili got a cloth from a hook on the wall and busied herself drying the counter. She wouldn't look her in the eye.

"Why haven't you convinced them to tell Headman Gerald?" Trinia stepped closer to her friend. "I know the orcs have loyalty to their clan, but you have loyalty to Oakwall. They deserve to know and prepare."

"It's . . . it's not that simple." Savili still wouldn't look at her and instead turned away to scrub at another spot in the kitchen.

"Savili. I need you to stop for a moment and talk to me."

"There isn't anything to talk about."

"What do you mean? Of *course* there is. We need to think of a way to tell Oakwall about what's coming. We especially need to tell them about the sinkholes. Yes, I know about them too now. I almost *died* falling into one last night."

"You fell in? Are you all right? Are you hurt?" Savili took a few steps forward, looking her over.

"I'm fine. Sythcol and Brovdir arrived in time to save me. But someone else might not be so lucky. We need to go to the clan together and tell the headman about *everything*."

Savili stepped back then, looked away.

"Savili, you can't possibly think it's a good idea to keep all of this from Oakwall!"

Savili sighed. "Trinia, we need to leave this to our leaders."

"Leave it to *your* leaders, you mean. Headman Gerald knows nothing about it!"

"It doesn't matter anyway," Savili said. "Soon the winter storms will be too bad, and they won't be able to leave."

Trinia felt her blood still in her veins. "Savili, you must be *jesting*."

Her cold expression told Trinia everything.

"You intend to *trap* the villagers here." Suddenly, the room around her felt too small. "To force us to stay in these woods."

"No! It's not like that. You just have to stay until spring. By then, they'll be used to the warriors and won't want to leave anymore."

"Savili, that's *deceit*. Lying to them by omission. Can't you see how wrong that is?"

"My mother already wants to leave, Trinia."

Trinia stilled at her words. Her eyes went so wide she could feel a chill on them.

Savili's eyes were shimmery as tears filled them. "She wrote to me just a few days ago. Said she's almost convinced father and wants me to go with them."

Trinia shook her head. "She . . . she *wouldn't*. These woods are our home. They're all we've ever known."

"Yes, they are, but that isn't stopping her, and many of her friends, from wanting to leave."

"It makes no sense," Trinia said breathlessly.

"Doesn't it?" Savili asked. "We talked about leaving while we were growing up, don't you remember?"

"Those were just childish fantasies," Trinia said with a shake of her head. "Daydreams."

"They weren't just daydreams to many. My mother often talked about wanting to see the world. To travel. To leave

Oakwall behind and set out to make a new life for herself in a new place."

"But . . . but what about our traditions? Our values? The businesses and legacies our ancestors left behind?"

Savili's eyes softened but her words were firm. "Trinia, I know your family's traditions mean a lot to you, but there are many in Oakwall who didn't inherit their families' businesses."

Trinia's throat closed.

"Many have started to think that if the warrior orcs can settle *here*, then humans could easily settle out there. They've come with their new stories and their new ways and tales of all the amazing things they've seen—the mountains, the rivers, the new plants and animals." Savili looked her in the eyes. "Human settlements ten times larger than Oakwall with new opportunities to match."

She couldn't speak. She couldn't do anything but wring her hands.

"They want to leave already, Trinia, and if they found out about the sinkholes, about the *prophecy*, that would push them over the edge they are already teetering on."

Trinia took a deep breath as her mind rebelled against the truth she already knew. Most of the villagers worked under business owners. Most had siblings they shared their inheritance with, or they didn't inherit anything at all.

She was one of them now.

She was going to have to start all over.

Iytier came down the stairs and had obviously heard their conversation. "I'll contact Sythcol and let him know you're here."

Trinia's back straightened. "There's no need. I'm going back to Oakwall now. If you won't help me tell Headman Gerald about this, I'll do it on my own."

Iytier's eyes were cold. "We can't let you do that, Trinia."

Goosebumps broke out along her arms. "I'd like to see you try to stop me."

She got up and went to the door. Yanked the doorhandle.

But it didn't budge.

"Are you serious?" She whirled on her former friends. "You locked me in here?"

"Just until you talk to Sythcol. He'll help you understand why it's so important not to get Headman Gerald involved," Savili said. "Just wait for him. *Please*."

Trinia's anger felt like magma burning the back of her throat. "What the *fuck* is wrong with everyone locking me up and forcing their will down my throat? You're no better than my sister! I thought you were my friends, but friends would never do something as heinous as this."

"Trinia, that's *not* what we're trying to do." Savili's face was pale.

"We're just asking you to wait for a moment," Iytier said. "I'll send a bird now and Sythcol will be here faster than you can finish your cup of tea."

But there could be *no* waiting in this. Her blood boiled. Every quaking bit of her rebelled. She may as well have been back in Oakwall, locked in her former home, with her sister screeching and Ronhold leering and his son whining.

With her father passed out drunk in the corner.

With her mother coughing wretchedly in the bedroom.

With the walls closing in all around her and no way out.

"Let. Me. Out!" Trinia slapped her hand to the door so hard it stung. *"Ouch!"*

The front door exploded off its hinges and flew into the room with a deafening crash.

Brovdir stormed inside. His footfalls sounded like thunder

and the fire in his eyes burned right through her. She had no time to back up before he was suddenly upon her. He swung her up from the ground, cradling her to his chest. Her breath caught in her throat.

"Put me down right now!" she demanded as he carried her across the room. "Right. Now! Brovdir, I mean it!"

He plunked her down on the ground outside of Iytier and Savili's home.

She blinked in surprise. He'd faced her right toward the path out of the clan.

"Go," he said. "I will escort."

"Brovdir, you can't!"

Iytier barreled out of their home and Savili was close on his heels until Haysik's cry sounded above them. She shot Trinia one last worried look before disappearing back into the tree.

"She has to talk to Sythcol first, Brovdir! You know that!"

Brovdir pushed her behind him and growled low. "No."

"Brovdir, he'll be furious."

"I will *not* hold her prisoner."

"So instead, you'll let her tell her village without any preparation and risk them *leaving*? If they leave these woods, they'll *die*."

Trinia's breath caught in her throat as she searched Iytier's face. "What do you mean *die*? Are you talking about the war? Or the winter storms?"

Iytier's expression went stricken. "I shouldn't have said that. We need to wait for Sythcol. He'll tell you what he thinks you should know."

"And by that, you mean he'll tell me *nothing*," Trinia snapped and Iytier looked away. "How can you tell me all this and expect me *not* to tell Headman Gerald about it?"

"We've been friends a long time, Trinia." Iytier looked into her eyes and her throat closed up at the pleading she saw in his expression. "My mate and you have been close since you were babes. *Please*, just trust us."

Trinia's hands began to shake. She felt like she was being ripped in two. Torn between lifelong friendship and a desperate need to do what felt right in her soul.

"I will tell you."

Trinia blinked rapidly and snapped her gaze to Brovdir. He regarded her with a level, calm expression that eased her tension in an instant. "I will tell you all, Trinia."

It was a wonder she didn't collapse with relief.

"Brovdir, you can't just tell her. You know Chief Sythcol's orders—"

"Chief."

The venom in the word almost made Trinia flinch and Iytier blinked.

"I am *chief*," Brovdir said firmly. Iytier instantly bowed his head in a nod. "I am chief as much as Sythcol, I have the right to speak these truths. And I have decided I will."

With that, Brovdir whistled and a messenger bird flew down from the trees and landed on his shoulder. Then he reached into his waistband and produced a paper.

Her sketch of his home.

She blinked at the two-bedroom layout she'd drawn. "Why do you have that?"

Brovdir glanced at her and his cheeks went dark, but instead of answering he shoved the sketch back into his waistband and turned to Iytier. "Fetch a pen and parchment."

Iytier hesitated. "You . . . are you really going to send a message to the headman?"

Brovdir stood tall. "You wish to challenge me over it?"

Iytier paused a moment, he glanced back over his shoulder

toward the door where Trinia realized Savili was lingering. Her cheeks were wet as she bounced her baby on her hip.

"No," Iytier said as Savili's lip trembled. "No. I won't fight you, *Chief* Brovdir. But I hope that you know what you're doing."

With those quiet words, Iytier went into the house and fetched the paper Brovdir needed to send the message. Brovdir took it from Iytier gently and began to write before the male had returned to Savili's side.

She watched him, with his brow set tight and his posture hunched, as he scribbled a message on a tiny note in his palm. He tucked the remaining paper into his waist band and called a messenger bird.

Her chest swelled with emotion she could hardly put a name to. One that made her feel like she was floating. Like she could finally breathe again. Like she was warming up after a hard freeze.

But as she watched the bird fly off, the weight of what was coming settled firmly on her shoulders.

Everything was about to change.

CHAPTER
THIRTY

BROVDIR

The message was sent to Headman Gerald. A call for a meeting with him the next morn. A confession that secrets had been kept from him and that they would be coming to light.

And he felt nothing but an ease of tension in his chest. Nothing but steadfast *relief.*

This had been the right thing to do.

"What . . . are we going to tell Sythcol?" Iytier pulled his woman into his side. His shoulders were tight, and his mouth was held in a firm line.

"You say nothing," Brovdir said. "I am chief. It is my duty. I will not mention your part."

Iytier sagged with relief even as he said, "It would be easier with his fury divided between us."

Brovdir snorted. "You think I cannot stand against his fury?"

Iytier broke a smile.

"Sorry about your back door," Brovdir said, "I'll come by later to fix it."

"No need, I can mend it." Iytier tightened his hold around Savili, "I'd do the same for my woman."

Brovdir's chest swelled, "Go inside. Cherish your woman and babe. Rest easy in the knowledge that these secrets will be done by the morn."

"Thank you." Savili's voice was choked. "So much."

He nodded, and they quietly returned to their home.

And then he was alone with his woman.

And he was never going to lose her again.

"Brovdir, tell me *everything*. Right now."

Ah fuck, he couldn't put off that order. "Come off the path." He wanted a more private place to tell her.

"What exactly is this prophecy?" she demanded as he guided her into the woods. "Why are Savili and Iytier so determined? I understand not wanting to lose family, but it's madness to try to keep everyone captive."

Brovdir took her hand and shifted her to stand in front of him. Fades, she was small. Her head barely came up to the middle of his chest.

He wrapped his hands around her waist and boosted her up onto the boulder so she could meet his eyes without straining her neck. She murmured thanks and quickly adjusted into a more comfortable position. Her squirming drew him to distraction.

"Brovdir? The prophecy? Please?"

He puffed out a breath and forced his mind to the task. "The Fades are remaking the world."

"Re . . . make. What does that mean?"

"Don't know for certain."

"But you have theories. Out with it. I want to know." Her expression was steady and her eyes bore into him.

"The world will be destroyed."

Her face went pale and he quickly gripped her arm to keep her steady. "Destroyed. Destroyed *how*?"

"Not sure. The Fade storms may have something to do with it."

"You mean those wind spiral storms some of the warriors talk about?"

He nodded.

"And . . . and what happens after that?"

He shrugged and shook his head. "Only know that the Fades want us to gather here before the reckoning."

"So, the Rove Woods are the only place that *won't* be destroyed?"

"Think so." He nodded.

"Think so? You don't know?" Trinia was going paler by the moment.

He shook his head again and stroked her arm tenderly, wishing he knew how to offer comfort. He'd seen how the orc mates in Rove Wood Clan had taken the news. Many were still riddled with fear over what was to come.

"That's why you can't let anyone from Oakwall *leave*," Trinia breathed. She looked off in thought, but brought her hand down to grip his tightly. "Because if they go, they'll . . ."

He stared at their clasped hands. Chest warming and fluttering as delight overshadowed his discomfort. He hoped she felt as comforted by this touch as he was by hers.

"Do you have proof?" Trinia asked quietly.

He let out a huff that made his throat burn. "No. Not here. Seer had a vision. Was shown to the clan."

"But he's gone now."

He nodded.

"So, there isn't any proof you can show the villagers of Oakwall." Trinia began to stroke his hand in thought. Her fingers were so soft and gentle as they caressed his knuckles. He never wanted this touch to end.

"No proof. Only words."

Her eyes took on a haunted look, and he turned her hand so he could rub her knuckles the same way she had done for him. She blinked down at their clasped hands; cheeks colored a pretty pink that he knew wasn't just from the cold.

But she didn't pull away as her eyes squeezed shut. "This is just *too much.* I thought losing my mother's bakery was bad enough, but now the whole *world*? Brovdir, I don't . . . I don't know if I can . . ."

"Just breathe," he said firmly, pressing a hand to her chest. "Breathe, and know I will be with you. At your side."

She let out a sound that he thought was meant to be a snort but came out suspiciously like a sob. Her eyes were misty, and her lips were trembling. "You have the whole *clan* to worry about. Not just me."

"You are all that matters."

Her eyes went a little wide and her jaw went slack, and he could feel the imprint thrumming deep in his bones as delight twinkled in her eyes.

And then her brows furrowed into a dark glare, and his back straightened. "Brovdir, I am *not* the only thing that matters. The clan matters and so does Oakwall." She took another deep breath and placed her hand over his where it still rested on her stomach. "How are they going to react to this? This is just . . ."

She looked off into the woods, eyes haunted, as if she were

imagining what it might look like to have the world swallowed up by a terrible wind and raging water.

He used his knuckle to gently tip her face toward him. “I know not what the future holds, Trinia. But I *do* know this. I will be by your side through it all.”

Her eyes blinked wide.

“You can rest assure that I will keep you hale for as long as you allow me to be near you. All I ask is for your trust. And I also swear to do whatever is necessary to keep both of our communities whole.”

She never looked away from his eyes, not even once. Not even to blink. He felt that he was being pulled into her, being consumed by the intensity of her gaze.

“All right, Brovdir,” she said slowly, carefully. “I’ll trust you.”

And in an instant his whole world grew brighter.

CHAPTER
THIRTY-ONE

TRINIA

She was in *trouble.*

Brovdir walked next to her slowly. The clip he set was easy for her to keep. The paths they walked were clean and free of ice. There were no homes here, just large fir trees that made a thick canopy around them, offering seclusion. Something she desperately needed right now.

Because her mind was lit up like the first dawn of summer.

"I will ensure no harm comes to you."

It was big talk considering their world was about to be redesigned. And yet she knew he could. She trusted this male to the very core of herself.

She shouldn't.

He was basically a stranger!

She shouldn't trust him, should she? Not after everything . . .

And yet . . .

"You are all that matters."

Her stomach flipped and her heart fluttered and her body was hot with longing.

"Are you well, Trinia?"

She snapped up. "Hmm? Oh! Yes, I'm fine. Just fine."

She was not fine.

He tipped his shaggy head, and her heart started skipping all over itself. "You're going to wring your skirt until it rips."

"Oh." She dropped the fabric, but the wrinkles remained. Biscuits and jam, she hadn't even realized she was holding it.

A green hand appeared before her, and she blinked rapidly. "Why not hold this instead?"

She shot her orc a hard look. "You want me to rip the skin off your hand instead of my dress?"

He snorted. "Not possible. Skin's too tough." Then his voice lowered as he said. "And pain would be worth it if it brought you comfort."

Her heart jumped up into her throat all over again. The things he said . . . the way he acted . . .

One might think he was imprinted on her.

But that couldn't be right. Orcs took *years* to form imprints. They came from *loving* someone, and love took time to grow.

But what if he was? How was she going to grapple with that in addition to everything else? Her mother's bakery had been lost to Ronhold. Her woods were being lost to sinkholes.

Her entire world might soon be lost to the Fades themselves.

"Trinia, breathe."

She sucked in a breath and her head cleared. She hadn't even realized she'd stopped breathing.

"Here." He held out his hand to her again, and she took it without thought. His fingers engulfed hers almost completely.

His warmth flooded every part of her and made her stable despite how uneasy she'd felt a few moments prior.

"All will be well, Trinia," Brovdir said again, and like before, his vow calmed her, soothed her. She wanted to lean into his chest, shut her eyes, and let him protect her until every calamity that was about to befall them had passed.

She wanted to stay at his side through *every* hardship from here on.

"W-where are we going?" She stroked her thumb along his knuckles.

He let out an adorably content huff and her heart tripped over itself. "To Elder Plog."

Her brows arched. "Why?"

"Need to check." Then he paused to consider before saying, "Rather go back to tree? Wait for me there?"

"Oh no." She huffed out a dry laugh. "Absolutely not. The last thing I want is to be alone right now."

His expression softened. "I vow never to let you feel alone again."

Her lips parted in shock at his words and the intensity of the contentment they made her feel. Like finally catching her breath after a hard sprint or warming up after getting caught in a blizzard.

She hadn't felt like this since . . . since before her mother had gotten sick.

And then Brovdir slowly lifted her hand up. His grip was loose, tender. She could have pulled away.

She didn't.

He pressed his lips to her palm and her whole body shivered as lightning struck through her. His tusks felt cool against her fingers, but his lips were so hot she felt like he might be branding her. Marking her as his own.

Still, she didn't pull away.

He lowered her hand again, his expression relaxed with pleasure, and then he looked into her face and his eyes went wide with surprise. She knew her expression must have been telling.

She didn't care. She reached up, stroked her fingers through his shaggy hair, gripped hard. Pulled him down to her.

He came with a low rumble of pleasure that made her toes curl. Their mouths collided.

He tasted so good. Husky with spice. His lips were so soft, and the contrast against his hard tusks was incredible. She opened her mouth, wanting more. To taste him. To drink him up.

He let her delve her tongue into his mouth to duel with his, and she lost herself, drowned in him. She didn't want it to end even as her body grew hot, her thighs clenched, and her core began to pulse with need.

He broke off the kiss, and she blinked up at him in shock.

"I . . . want you." His voice was a bare growl. "Want you badly. We must stop."

"W-why?" She could hardly keep track of what he was saying. It felt like her thoughts were thickly coated in sugar. "Why can't we?"

"Because I will render you with child."

Her breath hitched. She'd almost forgotten about that. About their deal. About the house he was supposed to build for her. About the *business* transaction.

But then she blinked rapidly as she comprehended his words. "Wait, you . . . you don't want me to play conquest for you?"

His beautiful green eyes went wide, and his complexion

went a little pale, but then he sucked in a hard, determined breath.

"Trinia of Oakwall." His eyes held her captive. "I don't want a son. I want *you.*"

She lost all the air in her lungs.

"I will . . . build your house for you, and in exchange, I will host you until it is ready. You will keep me company during lonely nights."

She exhaled, shivering at what he might have meant by "lonely nights." "A—a whole house for advice and companionship. That doesn't seem like enough."

"It's more than enough," he said firmly.

She forced a laugh. "Oh Brovdir . . . you . . . you're still really bad at making trades. I'm getting a much better deal."

He gave her a lopsided grin that melted her heart. "Is that a yes?"

Was it?

"Brovdir, I—" Her mind grappled with this decision. It was too soon, wasn't it? They barely knew each other!

He must have read her face because he pulled a paper out of his waistband.

The sketch she'd done of his house. The one that turned it into two bedrooms.

"We can do this," he said. "Can build it in a day. You stay with me, but also have space until I have finished building your home."

She couldn't believe this. This was insane. She shouldn't even consider staying with him.

She watched his hand as he held the parchment. His thumb brushed it almost tenderly. His grip was careful, like he didn't want to risk creasing it.

He was trembling a little.

"Forgive me."

Her eyes snapped right back to his face and her heart squeezed. His eyes were downcast, and his lips trembled, and she'd never seen anyone look more earnest in all her years.

"Forgive me for lying, Trinia. I vow never to keep secrets again."

"Never again," she repeated softly, unable to look away from him. Her whole body was drumming with longing. She'd lost *everything*.

But . . . gained so much just from *him*.

She exhaled shakily. "You . . . you can really work up this floor plan in a day?"

His eyes lit up with hope, and he nodded eagerly.

Biscuits and jam. She *shouldn't*.

Staying with a friend would be far more logical.

She didn't want to stay with a friend.

She wanted *him*.

She swallowed thickly and licked her lips. She could still taste him on them.

"Yes, Brovdir. I'll stay with you."

CHAPTER THIRTY-TWO

BROVDIR

She'd said yes. Yes! He could hardly believe it.

His steps felt light, and his mind was clear. His veins pulsed with pleasure. He should at least *try* not to look so pleased. He'd just told her about the prophecy, and she was still recovering from the shock.

"How . . . long will it take you to build my house?"

Forever. "How long are you willing to wait?"

Her brows arched in surprise, and then she looked away from him. Her steps crunched in the ice at their feet and her fingers felt cold in his hand. He should have brought her a cloak. In the distance, he could hear the orc sons chattering. Elder Plog was with them. Maybe one of them would have an extra cloak for her to wear.

"Would it be all right to wait until spring or maybe . . ." She worried her lower lip, reminding him of how good she tasted.

"Would love to host you for spring. Summer too." Every spring and summer for the rest of her life.

"It's just that I was thinking of how busy you're going to be with the warriors settling here and the sinkholes. You'll need to put your duties as chief first."

His heart swelled so much he lost his breath. She'd make a wonderful matriarch.

She picked up the pace. "And I'll want to draw up some proper design plans for you to work from. It will make your task much easier. What are those voices?"

"Orc sons. Going to check," he explained as he guided her off the path and into the dense woods.

"Right. They probably shouldn't be playing out in the woods with the sinkholes opening up . . . but I suppose the clan isn't necessarily safer, is it?"

He supposed not.

She hugged herself. "Nowhere is really safe now, is it? Everything is . . ."

He placed a hand on her shoulder and gave a reassuring squeeze. "All will be well. I vow it."

She looked up at him with such trust his heart felt like it might burst. She edged in closer, nearly to his side. "I suppose I know for sure of one place that is safe."

She said this so quietly he nearly didn't catch it. With his head tipped in confusion, he asked, "Where?"

Trinia looked up into his eyes. Her smile was soft and her gaze was filled with such warmth he wondered if he was melting.

"With you."

Was it possible to suffocate from delight? Because he could have sworn that was what was about to happen.

Trinia's eyes drifted back to their path and then widened. "What . . . exactly are they doing?"

Brovdir stopped abruptly, suddenly realizing that they had

reached their destination. Through the trees, he could see Elder Plog surveying a clearing and the sons were all around him working on . . . on . . .

On digging up the frozen ground.

"Hello there!" Elder Plog hobbled over with his same wide grin and his fresh demeanor, but the mischievous glint in his eye had Brovdir wishing he could turn tail and run back to his home. With Trinia.

One glance at his woman, however, had him rethinking his quick exit. Her expression was bright with curiosity, and a light smile played at her lips.

He would stop at nothing to keep her happy.

So, in the madness, they would stay.

"Well, don't you both look about as pruned as a plum," the elder said. "Little baker, you seem a little more prune than usual. Is something haunting you?"

Trinia's face fell and Brovdir wanted to smack the male for reminding her of her troubles.

"All's well. What is going on here?" Brovdir said decisively. Trinia squeezed his hand and gifted him with a grateful smile.

"Come to see our progress, did you?" the elder said with a beaming smile. "They're doing well, aren't they?"

"What *are* they doing?" Trinia's eyes widened as a young male who could not have been more than seven lifted a rock the size of his abdomen out of the hole and chucked it onto the frost laden ground.

"Digging boar traps, of course!"

"Foolishness," Brovdir muttered nearly at the same time. The elder shot him an amused look, which he ignored. "Stop this."

"How will we prepare for the boar then?" the elder asked

almost flippantly. "And besides, the boys are enjoying themselves. They need to practice their magic, you know. Otherwise, it will get as rusty as my old paring knife. They'll be good for nothing but washing and flaking off rust in chunks."

"Are you talking about the knife or the children?" The mirth in Trinia's voice was clear and Brovdir's irritation lessened.

"Both, I suppose. One and the same, aren't they?"

"The children and your paring knife are one and the same?" Trinia asked.

The old male laughed heartily in response to Trinia's question and then turned to Brovdir. "So! What brings you here? Have you got the skewers?"

"No," Brovdir growled low. "Here to *stop you.*"

The statement had the children all popping their heads out of the massive hole, which was much deeper than he'd thought.

"What? We're stopping?"

"I don't want to stop!"

"We've almost got it deep enough."

The chorus continued as the near *thirty* boys all began complaining at once. They were covered head to toe in mud. Many had pickaxes and shovels, but a few were working the ground with their *bare claws.*

Brovdir felt like his head might explode.

Warmth clasped around his fingers, and he shot his gaze back to Trinia. She rubbed her thumb over the back of his knuckles, quirked an enchanting smile, and murmured, "They look like they're having fun."

His brows pinched, but when he looked back toward the boys, he suddenly saw them in a different light. They were exhausted and filthy and performing a futile task.

But also grinning from ear to ear.

"Look at this one!" Vaiteg, Estoc's eldest son, who'd been oblivious to Brovdir's presence, popped up out of the furthest side of the trench. "Come help me! We have to get it!"

More than half the boys raced to Vaiteg and jumped into the hole. The others watched from the edge, clamoring and boisterously proclaiming their excitement.

And a moment later, Brovdir saw why.

The boulder these boys were lifting out of the ground was *enormous*. At least one and a half of his lengths around and nearly as tall.

How they were able to move it with just fifteen of them was beyond him, but move it they did. They heaved and hollered and hoisted the rock out onto the stable ledge.

"Good show, boys! Good show!" the elder exclaimed, quickly hobbling over. Trinia went too and Brovdir instantly followed. He kept a keen eye on her and the littlest sons, making sure they stayed clear of the boulder's path.

They rolled it up onto the frozen grass with a final cry and then cheered so loudly Brovdir thought his ears would burst.

"Amazing!" the elder yelled above the celebration. "You did it! This one is as big as a boar's behind, for sure!"

Brovdir was overwhelmed by the desire to smack himself in the face until he saw stars.

At least until he heard Trinia laughing. Then his whole body lit with delight. The sound was melodic and soothing.

"Let's get back to it!" Vaiteg announced and the other boys whooped with vigor and jumped back into the hole.

"You see! They're doing marvelous!" the elder said with a laugh as he returned to them.

"Sythcol says the ground isn't stable," Brovdir said.

"This ground is perfectly stable," the elder said. "I

communed with the Fades just a few moments ago. They want us right here."

"The . . . Fades want you to dig a hole here?" Trinia asked carefully.

"They do, indeed!" The elder nodded. "Sneaky things trying to trick me into using my magic to blast the ground myself, but *I* know better. I know the success needed to be shared."

"Not worth the risk," Brovdir said. "The sinkholes—"

"The sinkholes all give warning before they rattle open. We're keeping a close eye out and are prepared to leap into trees the moment we notice the ground shaking," the elder said with more lucidity than Brovdir had ever seen. "I know you're worried, Brovdir, as any good leader should be, but have faith. It's good for them to have something to take their mind off the chaos and change. And besides, they are no less safe *here* than they are playing together in the clan or forest. The sinkholes could open *anywhere*, but at least here we are being diligent and I'm keeping a close eye."

Brovdir couldn't fight that logic. These sons were *always* together. Usually without their fathers, since the Rove Woods were so safe.

Or at least they used to be.

But . . . "I should seek advice from Sythcol." Brovdir felt a hollowness in his chest as he spoke.

The elder's face fell because they both knew what Sythcol would want.

Trinia tapped his arm. "Can I speak with you a moment?"

He nodded immediately and followed her to the edge of the tree line. The elder went back to watching the children, as diligent as he promised he would be.

Once they were a good distance, Trinia turned to face him.

She fidgeted with discomfort, but she was so Fades blasted beautiful, he couldn't take his eyes from her.

"I understand this isn't my place . . ."

"Please speak," he assured her, desperate to hear anything she wanted to tell him.

"I don't think you should stop them."

He let out a long sigh that expelled much of his tension.

"The elder might act two apples short of a pie at times but he *loves* those boys, and he'd never put them in danger."

Brovdir nodded, eager to hear her input on the dynamics of the clan.

Trinia continued with more confidence. "I also know that you warrior orcs don't commune with the Fades much."

Brovdir couldn't remember the last time he'd done so.

"Communing isn't the silly nonsense that some of your brethren say it is. I've seen miracles come from simple communions. The orcs of Rove Wood really do communicate directly with the Fades will through it. Or . . . at least they get messages from them."

"Who?"

Trinia blinked. "Who?"

"Who disparaged against communion?"

"Oh . . . uh . . ." She fidgeted. "I don't want to get anyone in trouble."

"Not trouble. Correction."

She blinked, and then nodded. "It was Ugeth and Ovig mostly."

"I will speak with them."

He watched her sag with relief as a grin flooded her lovely features. He wanted to burst with happiness over how easy it was to please her.

"So," he said, determined to solve this issue and please his woman at the same time. "You think I should leave this?"

"This is the first time I've seen the boys truly happy since what happened with Ergoth."

He considered this, mind working over the logic and always going back to one stark fact. His title.

Chief Brovdir.

"Then I will let them dig."

CHAPTER THIRTY-THREE

TRINIA

Trinia watched from the sidelines as Brovdir spoke to the elder. She couldn't hear what was being said over the whooping and chatter of the orc sons, but judging from their expressions, they were both relaxed. Elder Plog was smiling and Brovdir's posture was loose.

He was really going to take her advice? Just like that?

The elder's grin widened, and he gave a nod to Brovdir before waving to her. "You can have your orc back now, little baker. Thanks for sharing."

Her stomach and heart flipped over at the same time.

Brovdir returned to her side and held out his hand to her expectantly. "Told him he could keep digging. Told him to keep *teaching*."

"Teaching?" She laced her fingers with his and began through the woods, back to the path.

"He's teaching old magic," Brovdir said with a shrug.

"Know nothing of it, but they enjoy it and that's important, yes?"

"I think so." She gave his hand a squeeze. She glanced up at the burly, scarred orc and her heart skipped a beat. He looked so confident. So strong and assured.

He looked like an orc chief.

Who would have thought something as simple as watching this male step into his role would make her light up like a candle in fog? She was just so *proud* of him.

"To the hall," Brovdir said. She turned to look at him just as a large, blue and white bird swooped out of the trees and landed right on top of his head. It flapped its wings so hard he had to squint, but he didn't look surprised.

She chuckled. "Do birds always land on your head?"

His grin softened his features. "It's a message. From Oakwall."

Her heart was hammering as he reached up and plucked a piece of cream-colored paper out of the bird's taloned grasp.

"Headman Gerald has confirmed the meeting time," he said.

Her stomach clenched with anxiety and anticipation. "Really? So, tomorrow morning, then?"

"Yes."

She wrung her hands. What new changes would tomorrow bring? What upheaval would come next? She could hardly fathom it. Her stomach tied itself in knots all over again.

The bird on top of Brovdir's head began to flap and spin around, distracting her in an instant. It tussled up his hair every which way, pecking and fluffing and spinning until his head was one big mat.

A mat that the bird promptly plunked itself down in.

Trinia slapped a hand over her mouth to keep from

laughing as Brovdir scowled and waved his hand to get the bird to fly away. The silly thing *pecked* at him and stayed put.

Trinia lost her composure then. She burst into laughter and had to clutch her stomach.

The sudden noise, thankfully, startled the bird into taking flight, but what remained was a bird nest made from Brovdir's hair that gave him the ridiculous wild look of someone who'd been out in a windstorm. Chunks of hair were jutting out every which way, some even straight up. There were even a few feathers.

Tears flooded her eyes. She couldn't get enough air into her lungs. She'd *never* laughed so hard.

"I'm sorry," She managed, wiping her cheeks. "I'm so sorry. I don't mean to laugh."

But when she looked at Brovdir, his expression was so soft, so gentle, that all her laughter died away, and in an instant, the fluttering in her gut took her breath all over again.

"L-let me fix you up," she stammered, looking away from the tenderness of his gaze.

"No need." His voice was low and warm.

"Of course there is," she insisted with a gulp. "Sit down somewhere."

There was a *fwump* sound, and she spun around to find that he'd instantly gone to his knees.

"I-I didn't mean on the *ground*." He looked up at her with huge puppy dog eyes.

Blast it all! He was just so *obedient*. It made her blood heat up, her thighs clench, and her body go all squirmy with longing. But there was something else too. Something warm and tender. Something she wanted to lean into despite the fact that this massive, battle-scarred orc was nearly a stranger.

"Thank you. I can reach easily now." Being on his knees

would make it easier for her to reach his head. She went around to the back of him, mostly to hide her blush. She combed her fingers through the strands, and it was surprisingly soft and clean and smelled slightly of lavender.

It took little time to get the knots out, and then she slicked it back. Brovdir sat stock-still through the process and made not a single sound.

She came back around to examine her handiwork.

And burst into uncontrollable laughter for the third time.

With his hair slicked back and parted right down the middle, he looked completely and utterly *ridiculous*. Like one of the village children whose mother had gotten fed up with her boy looking like he was a miscreant and taken drastic measures to make him look presentable for school.

"I'm sorry! I'm so sorry! I shouldn't laugh."

Brovdir let out an irritated rumble, but the anger didn't meet his eyes.

She reached up and tousled his hair back into its natural place. "Well, I guess we won't be doing *that* again. The shaggy puppy look is much better."

"Shaggy . . . puppy?"

Her stomach dropped.

Brovdir's brows rose. "You . . . think I look like a dog."

"No—er . . . I mean, a little, but not in a bad way." She found she simply couldn't lie to him. "It's cute. I've always thought puppies were adorable."

"I'm . . . adorable?"

Ah shit, she'd really messed this up, hadn't she?

But before she could pull herself out of the hole she'd buried herself in, Brovdir had placed a hand on the small of her back. Her breath left her in a rush, and she quickly moved her hand down off his head, only to have him tip his face, so she cupped his cheek briefly. His eyes closed as if he relished her touch.

So, she didn't pull away.

"Trinia?"

"Y-yes."

"You are adorable too."

Her cheeks heated up almost to the point of pain, but in a flash, her embarrassment was forgotten. The look in Brovdir's eyes made her whole body light up like an inferno.

She dipped in to kiss him.

"Chief Brovdir?"

Trinia moved away from Brovdir so quickly she almost fell over. His arm came around her back to steady her as he got to his feet. She quickly regained her footing before she looked over and saw Estoc, a hunter orc with a surly disposition, coming up the path.

On a gasp, she stepped back out of Brovdir's embrace, even as her heart tugged at his rejected expression.

"Sorry for interrupting," Estoc said with a grin that made his sharp white teeth seem to glow against his dark skin. It was obvious he wasn't the least bit sorry. "I've just come to check on my sons. They're here digging under your orders, right?"

"Not mine," Brovdir growled low.

"Oh? The elders said it was your idea." Estoc shrugged. "No matter. Got them off me, at least. But it's nearly time for the midday meal. Are you aware of what your warrior is cooking up in the hall?"

Trinia's brows rose and she looked at Brovdir. He had one of his warriors *cooking*? Which one? She hoped it wasn't the one she'd seen eating a fish raw at the last trade.

"Yes. My orders."

Estoc nodded slowly. "You *might* want to go check on that.

As it stands, I'll be keeping my boys to the fruit and dried meat for this meal. And I think most of the clan would agree with my choice."

Brovdir's groan was laced with frustration, and Trinia's stomach tightened with sympathy. "I'll take care of it."

Estoc shrugged and, as he passed, he patted Brovdir on the shoulder. "Worry not. There's plenty of food. We can use the stew as fertilizer."

Trinia couldn't tell if that was supposed to be an honest suggestion, or an insult.

Brovdir let out a ragged sigh that seemed to take all his tension with it. Then he turned to her and held out his hand. "To the hall?"

She nodded instantly and put her hand in his. His skin was warm, and his hold was tender and all traces of his anger vanished the moment she willingly followed him through the icy forest.

CHAPTER
THIRTY-FOUR

BROVDIR

He was going to slaughter that male.

Trinia walked next to him with a brisk but relaxed clip. Her dark curly hair bounced, and her lush hips swayed, and her eyes flitted to his more than once.

Her hands in his hair had felt so blasted *good* and reminded him of how it had felt the night before to have her stroking him in such a way. Awash with contentment. Warm to the core with a sense of belonging. Of safety.

Like home.

She felt like *home.*

He wanted to tell her that. But *how*?

They arrived at the hall far too soon and found that there were a few males lingering within. They sat at the table furthest away from the still bubbling cauldrons.

Bubbling cauldrons that stank like the foulest brew imaginable.

"Oh, Fades." Trinia gasped as she covered her nose with her hand. "What is that?"

Brovdir screwed up his nose as the distinct scent of burned grass mixed with old fish permeated his senses. The smell was so potent it made his eyes water, and his throat constricted.

"Wait outside?" he offered, gesturing back toward the massive entry doors.

"No, it's fine. I'll get used to it," Trinia said with a little cough. "But what was the cook trying to make? It smells horrible."

Blast it, he'd made a mistake. "Ogvick. A warrior. Not much experience cooking."

"Fades, help us." Trinia's nose wrinkled in disgust even as Brovdir fought a grin at their similar reaction. "It's almost time for the midday meal. Won't the whole clan be here for food soon?"

"Perhaps." He honestly thought it unlikely. Certainly, most in the clan had smelled what was being boiled here a while ago and decided to eat in their homes instead.

"Where is Ogvick?" Trinia looked around. "I don't see any warriors here. Did he make a run for it?"

"No . . ." Brovdir recalled that he'd asked Ogvick to find Caivid and Hendr once he was done with the soup. "Likely he's just . . . done with it."

Trinia chewed her lower lip. "Oh. I see. Should we try to fix it for him?"

Brovdir had no idea where to start with that, but Trinia was a baker, so cooking must have been second nature to her.

Still, he hated forcing his woman to work.

Before he could shake his head, she snorted and said, "I *want* to help, Brovdir. It would be a fun challenge."

She'd have fun with it?

"We should probably find something else to serve and dump those. I think they're beyond repair." She looked to where the group of males was sitting. "Hey, Tovid! Do you think you could empty these pots?"

"Fades, *yes*," the conjurer said in a rush as he got up. He was a scrawny thing. Barely enough muscle to heave his own soup bowl. His friends, of equal stature, followed suit. "Any longer, and the tree's going to soak the stench into the bark and never let it go."

Trinia let out a laugh at the male's joke that made Brovdir instantly on edge. "Thank you."

"Anything for Oakwall's prettiest baker," the male said, and Brovdir's skin prickled. His fists balled with the urge to punch the grin off his face. To crack his jaw so he could never speak another word to his mate.

Fuck.

She wasn't even his.

"We're going to need to make something else. Do you have a storeroom for food here?" Trinia turned her attention back to him. She paused and blinked as he tried to wipe the irritation from his features. It was clear he'd not done a good job of it when she said, "Don't fight them, Brovdir. They're just being nice."

"They're too puny to lift that cauldron," Brovdir muttered despite himself.

Trinia rose her brows, and one of the four males glanced over with a scowl. Blast, orc hearing was far too good. Especially the ones that were magically infused. The conjurer orcs had senses that were ten times more potent than those of his warriors if they put their skills into the task.

"Let's cool it down first," one of the four said, and they all lifted their hands to work the Fades gifts and cool down the boiling muck before handling it.

Had he been asked to put someone to this job, these males would have been the last on his list. A hollowness pitted in his chest as he watched them effortlessly fulfill their given task.

He didn't know this clan at all, did he? He barely knew the orcs' names, let alone their skills. It was no wonder they didn't follow his commands.

He took a deep breath and pinched the bridge of his nose.

"Hey."

He blinked rapidly, suddenly remembering that Trinia was next to him.

"Apologies."

"No need." She waved off his remorse before stroking his arm. The touch was so warm and soothing he lost his breath. The desire to hoist her over his shoulder and carry her back to their home was so strong he almost trembled from it. "Which way is the storeroom?"

He pointed to a door at the far back of the hall and they made their way to it. The door led into a hallway and the moment it closed behind them, all sound from the hall was dimmed and the scent of herbs and vegetables was so strong it drowned out the vile scent of the stew completely.

"It must be through there." Trinia walked to the end of the hall and opened a second door, revealing a large storage room with shelves lining the walls all the way to the ceiling. She waved him inside as comfortably as if she'd lived in the clan her whole life. She looked so self-assured.

Confidence looked good on her.

She shut the door behind him and then turned to face him with a fierce expression. He blinked in surprise as she crossed her arms, leveling him with an intense look. "All right. Out with it. What's wrong?"

He rose his brows.

"Don't give me that. It's written all over your face that you're worried about something. Are you worried about me being friendly with Tovid? Because you shouldn't be. I've known him my whole life. If I'd wanted to start something with him, I would have."

The idea of her being intimate with another male made his blood boil. It made his flesh feel like it was crawling.

But he swallowed the sensation down, because that wasn't what she was asking, and he'd vowed not to lie to her or keep things from her ever again.

He shook his head. "I . . . am not a fit leader."

Trinia snorted. "Brovdir, *all* the orcs are possessive over the women their interested in. Even the conjurers. No one thinks you're a bad leader for that."

He shook his head. "No. Not that. I . . ."

"Go on." Her voice was so gentle, and he lapped it up.

"Sinkholes, digging, elders, even this simple stew . . ." He sighed raggedly. "Nothing goes right. I order, but it doesn't get done. I plan, but it always fails. I . . . should not have been made chief of this clan. Sythcol should have sole control."

Trinia's lips parted and her eyes softened, but the pity in her expression made him want to rip out his own hair.

And then it fell away, and anger took its place. "That's boarshit."

He blinked rapidly in shock.

"Brovdir, you've been here for *less than a season* and now you're comparing your leadership skills to someone who worked directly under the former chief his entire life. Ergoth might have turned out to be a bad leader, but he was well loved until the end and Sythcol has spent a lifetime learning from him."

"I was the warlord's second," he countered.

"Yes, you were. But, yet again, leading a band of warriors who see *battle* every day is not the same as being chief of Rove Wood. We don't fight here. We barely bicker. And we've all known each other for our *entire* lives."

"All the more reason I should step back. My ways are too different."

"No. That's not true. You bring a fresh perspective that no one else could. Your insight is invaluable *because* it is different. Not only that, but having you as chief when the warrior orcs arrive here is vital to things running smoothly. You'll bridge the gap between their ways and ours." She blinked in thought, as if she'd just realized this herself. "It . . . will be a disaster if you aren't there to help bring our communities together."

He'd never really considered that. He'd always assumed that the warriors would live separately from the Rove Wood Clan. They'd maintain a respectful distance from each other, despite the close proximity. Sythcol had said as much many times, even when they'd discussed putting some of the families into empty tree homes within the borders of the clan.

It was foolish to assume staying separate like that would ever work.

"Like you said, I don't know this clan. There's so little time to learn them." How could he bridge a gap when this community was such a mystery to him?

"That's why you have me here to help you."

His heart soared as he looked into her determined eyes.

"I'm staying with you already, so it will be easy for me to give you advice when you need it. I'll tell you who in this clan to put tasks to and who to keep *far* away from your projects. I'll tell you who is sure to follow through on your orders on their own and who will need you to hover over their shoulder. I can even tell you what orcs do well working together and which ones would bicker until the Fades struck them down."

He swallowed thickly. "Thank you. I would be honored to have your advice."

Trinia shrugged as if she'd just offered him a strip of dried meat and not a solution to his most dreaded fear. "Of course."

Brovdir stared at her like he was seeing her for the first time. *Really* seeing her.

She was so quick-witted and made everything seem so *simple*. She looked proud, confident, and powerful. These were attributes he fought for every single day, but she wielded them so *effortlessly*.

He felt like he was melting and sinking at the same time. He lost all the breath in his chest and yet he was also warm. Comfortable. Her vanilla sweetness curled in his nose and his fingers grazed her wrist gently.

She blinked down at his touch, and he quickly pulled back, only to have her reach out and clasp his hand. She held firm and looked back into his eyes. "You've been doing this alone for quite a while, haven't you, Brovdir? You have Sythcol, but he isn't *really* on your side, is he?"

He lost his breath.

"But I'll be on your side. I'll help you figure things out. And I'll try not to influence you too much."

He wanted this to last *forever*.

Fades, he was in love with her.

What was he going to do?

CHAPTER
THIRTY-FIVE

TRINIA

The expression he'd made when she'd promised to help him turned all her insides to mush and she wasn't sure she was going to be able to get them solid again.

"We . . . we should find something to cook." Her voice sounded strained and breathless as she looked around the room. It was a fairly small storage space with shelving stacked up to twice her height and a long, clean countertop for prep work on the far side. There were no windows and only the one solid door, which could easily be blocked by the barrel of fish sitting beside it.

Biscuits and jam, *what* was she thinking? She was in here to figure out how to feed three hundred hungry orcs, not make a new one.

"L-let's look over . . . um . . . maybe we could cook this fish? We just need to find spices." She went to the drawers and opened the bottom one.

Inside was filled with spice jars, clearly labeled, organized by flavor. Spicy, savory, sweet . . . the next drawer was similarly categorized. Above that were bundles of fresh herbs preserved by magic and then—

"Perhaps this?"

She went over to where Brovdir was standing next to the countertop. On top was a cookbook that looked as old as the Fades themselves. Its pages were tattered and worn. Some were almost translucent from age. Had magic not been at play it would have disintegrated.

And next to it was a much newer volume with the recipes from the older book copied on one side and a *new* version on the other. The new version outlined different flavor combinations, various methods of preparation, and alternative cooking options.

"This is so detailed," she said, flipping to the front of the newer book. "It puts my family's recipe book to shame. The cooks must have been working on this for years."

"Cook," Brovdir corrected. "Only Gegvi's scent is on this book."

She blinked up at him in shock. "Are you serious? But there are *hundreds* of recipes copied down already. This is so much work!"

Brovdir flipped through page by page of both volumes. "Looks like he's going one at a time."

"It's . . . incredible. He's so dedicated." She spotted a smaller scroll near the wall and unrolled it. She read, "'*Fish and lavender soup notes. This one is going to be disgusting if I don't fix it. Going to be hard without the elite conjuror's magic, but I'm certain I can get it done.*'" She glanced up at Brovdir, "Why can't he use magic? I thought all the conjurors could."

"They can. To varying degrees. But Sythcol's elite are more advanced. Most Rove orcs use the elite tinctures and magic imbued objects for basic tasks like cleaning and lighting fires. Can't now. The elite are busy holding back the sinkholes."

"I see." She turned back to the book and skimmed over the list of variations on the recipe Gegvi had attempted. She had to flip the page twice. "Incredible, he's gone through at least a dozen different methods trying to fix this soup."

"Fuck."

Trinia jerked to attention. "What? What's wrong?"

Brovdir's expression twisted with remorse. "Shouldn't have let Sythcol demote him."

"Sythcol got rid of him? Why?"

"Thought his cooking was bad. It *has* been bad." Brovdir heaved a heavy sigh. "But only because he's been *trying*." He waved at the notes.

"You couldn't have known that, Brovdir. Gegvi didn't tell you."

"But I am *chief*." He pinched the bridge of his nose and squeezed his eyes shut as if he were trying to hold back a headache. "I should have looked further. I should not have allowed Gegvi to be dismissed."

She pulled his hand away. "Brovdir, this isn't your fault."

He shot her an incredulous look and her stomach twisted with guilt.

"Not *entirely* your fault. I know I've been pushing you, but that was only to get you to see how leaving everything to Sythcol was causing strife." She gave his hand a squeeze. "You've realized that now. You're making amends. You're fixing things."

His expression shifted to one of exhaustion, and she knew in an instant what he was thinking.

If he had realized this sooner, he would have far less to fix.

"Oh, Brovdir." She reached up to stroke his forehead,

brushing his soft, shaggy hair away from his eyes. He was so tall she could hardly reach, but he leaned down into her touch. "I have many things in my life I wish I could change too. Many mistakes and regrets. Everyone does. What's most important is to *move forward*. To learn from our mistakes and keep going."

His brows pinched together in confusion.

"I understand. It's hard to know where to go when the destination isn't clear. You and Sythcol are still trying to figure out how to work together. Having two chiefs is a completely new thing for both of you *and* the clan."

He looked deep into her eyes, hanging on her every word. Her chest swelled with warmth.

"I had to figure out the same when my mother passed away. I had to find my place managing her bakery all on my own." She stroked his hair again, and he melted into her touch. "I made so many mistakes, but if I hadn't, I wouldn't be half the baker I am today. I'd never have been able to manage my mother's bakery on my own for as long as I have. It's overcoming adversity that makes us *strong*. If everything was easy, we'd never learn any lessons."

She looked him right in the eyes. "You are going to do *great*, Brovdir. I can feel it. I'll help you whenever you need it, but I've seen you . . . talking to Iytier, to Elder Plog, I know you have it in you to be a good leader. You just need more practice and to *stop* worrying about making mistakes. You're going to make them, accept them, learn from them, and keep moving forward."

He closed his eyes then and exhaled hard, and it seemed to expel all his anxiety with it. When he opened them again, he looked steadfast. Strong. Determined. It made her breath catch in her throat and her heart quiver with longing.

"Thank you, Trinia." The words were tinged with warmth

and sweetness and *gratitude*. She felt her knees buckle from the weight of it.

Brovdir caught her swiftly around her back and brought her up, boosting her until she was sitting up on the high countertop. Her cheeks went flush at the heat in his eyes.

And then he kissed her. His lips slanted tenderly into her, while his hard tusks surrounded her cheeks, holding her captive. His hands came around her back gently as he held her still.

It felt like she was *melting*. Melting *into* him. She balled her fists against his chest and met his kiss with equal gusto.

A clatter from the hall reminded her of where they were, and she broke off the kiss. Brovdir let out a little huff of frustration, but she pushed him back.

"Put the barrel in front of the door," she ordered, and his eyes flashed with heat before he went to do her bidding. He lifted it like it weighed nothing, but the *thunk* she heard when he dropped it told her it was quite heavy.

He turned back to her. "What else?"

What else?

He was looking at her with expectant, heated eyes and her toes curled in her shoes.

"Trinia." The sound of her name rumbled low and sweet and threatened to turn her into a literal puddle. She took a deep breath and snapped her gaze back to the orc's face.

Not just any orc. Brovdir.

Her orc.

He regarded her with a raised brow, a quirked smile, and a relaxed posture that instantly put her at ease. So what if he was huge and deadly strong and had claws and teeth that could rip her to shreds . . .

Her pussy clenched at that thought and *what* in all burned biscuits did *that* mean?

"What next?"

"Hmm?" She snapped back to attention and found Brovdir looking amused by her shock.

"What next, Trinia?" He tipped his head slightly.

He wanted orders. Of course he did. Goosebumps broke out over her arms, and she couldn't decide if she was more excited or nervous.

"Go sit down on that box so I can reach you more easily."

A zing of delight shot through her as he obeyed her commands without question. He settled down on the wooden crate against the wall, underneath multiple shelves holding baskets of berries and cooking tools.

In this lighting, from this angle, his scars looked so much more prominent. His body was literally covered with them. Harsh jagged lines, some with pockmarks on the side. She came up and traced the one along his pectoral muscle, and he let out an exhale that rustled her hair.

"It looks like this was stitched."

"It was."

Her brow pinched. "But don't you have healing tinctures?"

He shook his head. "Not enough."

Her heart clenched. "So many of these could have killed you."

"Didn't." He rose his chin as if in triumph.

"You're right. They didn't. But you still suffered."

His expression wavered a bit.

She reached up and stroked her fingers through his hair. Using her nail to scratch gently from his forehead, all the way down the back of his scalp.

He produced a full-body shiver and his eyes shuttered closed. A low grown left his lips.

Just this little touch was enough to melt him.

"You've never known a moment of tenderness in your whole life, have you?" she asked quietly.

His only response was to swallow hard.

She gripped the hair at the back of his head and gently pulled until his neck was extended. With eyes wide, he blinked. He didn't fight her, but he wasn't wholly comfortable either.

The horrible, jagged scar at his neck was so prominent. The one that stole his ability to talk and caused him constant pain.

She wanted him to forget that pain for a while.

She dipped down low and kissed the scar.

His whole body tensed under her, but he didn't jerk away. She knew he could easily escape her if he wanted.

She traced the edge of the scar with the tip of her tongue. Following the deadly path someone had left behind. Where they had tried to kill him, she soothed.

She was rewarded with a groan, and his body shuddered again. *"Trinia."*

Oh Fades, why did her name on his lips sound so *good*? She doubled her efforts, licking and nibbling and treating the long-healed wound as tenderly as she was able.

She moved away from his neck and down to his chest. The scar here went right across his pec, right next to his beaded nipple. She kissed along the scar until she got down to it and then lapped at the hard nub with the flat of her tongue.

Brovdir let out a sharp growl as his body shivered. He squirmed as she licked again and brought a hand up to clutch at her hair.

"Don't," she ordered, and he let go of her in an instant. She looked up into his wide eyes. "I'm in control right now."

His jaw slacked, displaying his sharp rows of teeth. He was a predator. A fierce, vicious warrior.

And he melted at her demands. His whole body was relaxed as he nodded in agreement.

Oh *fuck*, his submission made her pussy clench with need. She felt empty and achy and wanton.

And she was going to drive him just as insane as she felt before she let him take her.

CHAPTER THIRTY-SIX

BROVDIR

Fades have mercy! He wasn't going to be able to take much more of this.

"Hold still, Brovdir."

But he would have to.

Trinia's little mouth moved down, licking each of his scars. Nibbling gently. She bathed the old wounds at his chest and flicked at his nipple again and sparks of desire shocked his system. His muscles bunched and his teeth gnashed and the basal need to have her was a real thing in his mind. It gripped so hard around his head that he saw stars.

She moved downward, tracing each puckered scar with her perfect tongue. She paid careful attention to where she was touching. And where she was *not* touching. His cock was so hard it was aching. It twitched at every touch. Pulsed with every wicked flick of her tongue. It threatened to rip through his leather pants.

Finally, her eyes flickered to it, and he could *feel* her stare. *Fuck!* He wasn't going to last!

"Let's take these off." She traced the edge of his waistband.

His hands were shaking as he undid the ties and shimmied them off his hips.

Trinia's breath caught and her eyes went impossibly wide as she examined his cock. Should he have gone slower? Was she going to change her mind?

But then her eyes drifted slightly to a thin scar on his right thigh that was dangerously close to his groin. He'd had many grizzly, deep and life-threatening injuries, but that one was one of the worst. That one haunted him with how close it had come to destroying any chance of bearing a son. Sometimes he could still feel the sharp pain of it, like it had been slashed all over again.

His breath caught in his throat as Trinia dipped.

He felt the heat of her breath first, soothing and hot. Then the press of her lips.

Sweet Fades her *tongue*.

He let out a quiet groan as pleasure raged through him. His blood caught fire as tingling bliss radiated from his thigh to his groin. His cock pulsed hard with every beat of his frantic heart, and his mind reeled.

He would not be able to hold out. He couldn't do it! The urge to plunge deep into her and fill her with his cum was *overpowering*.

Her lips brushed away from his thigh and she said low, "Good boy."

Oh, Fades be *fucked*.

That praise felt like a *lifeline*.

"Hold out for me."

Blast him back to the depths! His muscles clenched and his skin tingled and his very veins pounded with aching *need.*

But he would *hold.* He had to! His woman had given him a command, and he would die before disobeying her.

She wasn't making it easy. She kissed a path to his lower stomach, licked right under his belly button. His muscles contracted and he let out a hiss.

"Hmm . . . you look so desperate."

Ah *fuck*, he was. He wanted her so badly he could taste it on the back of his tongue. His mind felt muddled and raw. His flesh was shivery and damp from the exertion of holding out against her wicked little tongue.

"I think you can handle a little more."

No, he couldn't! *He couldn't—*

She positioned herself on her knees, with her mouth right next to his cock. Her cheeks were rosy, eyes were twinkling, and her smile was a gift from the Fades themselves. She was so blasted gorgeous. He lost all his breath.

Oh, sweet mercy, he absolutely *would* handle more.

"Don't come, Brovdir. That's an order."

He *would not*. He'd die first!

She dipped in low, mouth open, damp tongue extending. The blood in his veins stopped.

She lapped at his cock. Her hot, wet tongue starting from the base of his shaft and going all the way up, up, *up!*

Jolting waves of pleasure burst from his cock as her tongue flattened over the top, but he *did not come*! He *couldn't*! She'd told him no, *no*, *NO.*

"Such a good boy." Her voice was teasing and low and husky and *fuck*! He wanted to bottle up that sound and drink it. To make it a part of him. "You're holding out so well. I can feel your body convulsing. It's hard, isn't it? Hard to stop yourself from coming?"

"*Ye-es*." His voice didn't sound like his own.

"Just a little more." She dipped low and lapped at him again.

The sound he made in the back of his throat didn't sound *real*. Like pure desperation and pleasure twisted into a basal *plea*. He dug his nails into the box he was seated on and could feel it splintering in his palms.

And then she was gone. Moving away from him. Panic gripped his chest, and he reached out to snatch her arms. He would never let her leave. *Never*.

Fuck! He was being too rough.

A chuckle met his ears, and he snapped his gaze to search her face. She was absolutely the most breathtaking sight he'd ever seen. Beaming, flush, lips parted as she panted.

"You are such a good boy, Brovdir." She settled in his lap, crawling close. He tightened his grip on her. "You've held out long enough."

Fuck yes! *Yes!*

But what about her? Was she ready? He hadn't even touched her yet.

"I know this is going to be hard for you." She leaned in close to his ear and he took a sharp inhale through his nose.

She smelled exquisite. She was just as needy as he was. Her sweet, dewdrop scented arousal was so strong it surrounded him.

He needed to prepare her. *Now*.

"Be careful not to let your cock go inside me."

What?

His confusion must have shown because she met his eyes. "I'm . . . not your conquest, Brovdir."

Oh fuck. He'd almost forgotten. His throat closed.

She hiked up her skirts high, stretched her legs around his thighs. He could feel the heat of her core warming his cock.

He could not fathom what she was doing.

"I'm not your conquest." She cupped his face with both of her hands, stroked back his hair. "I'm *yours*."

Yours.

Yes!

The word rippled through him and then she spread herself further and plunked right down in his lap.

The lips of her pussy instantly enveloped his cock. Wet and hot.

His rational mind winked out.

And then she thrust her hips, gliding his cock along her pussy. It slipped through her damp core, raking over the hot flesh. He could feel every twitch and twist as she rode him.

The thrill was unbelievable. The temptation to thrust inside her was maddening. The fierce need to *control* himself only made his desire and pleasure greater.

"Oh *Brovdir*," she groaned, and his hips bucked helplessly at the sound. It was too good. Too much! He couldn't stop himself.

As if she sensed his control slipping, she reached down to grip his cock, making sure the head never found her entrance. She bucked and rocked and ground her clit against him. She was so wet the motion was effortless and she began to pant in his ear, moan against his neck.

It was too sweet. Too *good.* The pleasure was vibrant and overwhelming and *raw*. He reached between their bodies, placed a hand over hers, helped her grind the head of his cock against her clit.

This was far more than just rutting her. Far greater than

simply plunging into her body and finishing the job. They worked in tandem, focused on each other. He met her eyes, and she held his gaze.

In her eyes, he could see *everything.*

Their *future*.

He hissed out a breath as his jaw threatened to unhinge.

Fuck, he wanted to *bite her*.

"Oh *Brovdir*," she groaned, eyebrows pinched. She was getting close. He could feel her clit hardening against his cock.

Fades help him. His instinct to bite was absolutely *screaming*, overwhelming his brain. He tried to clench his teeth together to stop himself.

And then her head lulled to the side and her neck extended and words slipped from his lips. "I need to *bite!*"

Her eyes shot open. Her body trembled and bucked.

He panted. "Don't show your neck. I want to *bite you*. Too hard to control."

Her lips parted in shock and he felt her pussy clench around his cock. He hissed with pleasure.

And then she spoke words he never thought he would hear.

"Yes, Brovdir. I want you to!"

CHAPTER THIRTY-SEVEN

TRINIA

Her pussy clenched and her thighs trembled. Pleasure like she'd never known was coursing through her veins as Brovdir ground his cock against her clit.

And the idea of his fangs at her neck, his mouth holding her *captive*.

It only made the desire *stronger*.

"*Would mark you*," he gasped. "Mark *forever.*"

Forever.

Forever marked by *him*.

"*Yes!*" She couldn't think of anything she wanted *more*. "Yes, I want it!"

His hips thrust and the head of his cock threatened to plunge inside her. She should be fighting it. She wasn't in her right *mind*. The pulsing, aching bliss was too great to fight!

"Sh-shouldn't," Brovdir gasped out. The hand at his cock quickly pushed it upward, out of the danger zone and *right* into her aching, needy clit. She groaned loud and tipped her head again, elongating her neck. She heard him hiss out a desperate curse.

"*Please!*" She needed it. To feel his mouth around her neck, the sting of his fangs. She wanted to feel him everywhere, taking her in the only way he could.

Proving that she was *his*.

She wanted to belong to him the way he belonged to her!

"I'm *yours*, Brovdir!" He went still at her declaration, totally unmoving as he soaked in her words. "I'm yours completely. *Mark me!*"

His groan sounded first.

Then she felt his breath all along her shoulder, her neck. The prick of his fangs.

The sting as he *bit down*.

It should have hurt! She'd seen his fangs; they were *huge* and *ruthless* and sunk so deep! Sunk deep in a way only he could!

Pleasure roared through her body as the sensation of him holding her captive rippled over her skin. He gripped her ass, claws stinging her sensitive flesh as he ground her pussy on his cock. Her desperate, pulsing clit raked over the rim where his shaft met the head over and *over*. Flicked back and forth.

She bucked wildly with his grip as the bliss built high. Up into her throat.

Brovdir roared into the bite! She felt the sound shuddering from the top of her head to the tips of her toes. She went shivery cold and blistering as he came against her. His cum blasted right into her clit.

Ecstasy exploded behind her eyes as she came too. She couldn't get enough air to scream. Couldn't do anything but *feel* as pleasure pulsed in waves through her. It rippled from the sting of his bite. Roared down her back and limbs. She trembled and writhed, and through it all Brovdir held her, kept her safe, helped her to ride out the storm.

She collapsed into his panting frame. The feel of his hot, heavy breath over her stinging shoulder felt *so good*. Her body was sated and relaxed and her frantic heartbeat subsided into a content, pulsing rhythm. She felt each beat in the bite.

Brovdir carefully released her, only to start lapping at the injury with his tongue. She squirmed under his attention, and he instantly stopped.

"Hurts?"

The worry in his tone made her melt. "No. Feels good." It did. She could see the deep ring of teeth marks from the corner of her eye, feel the blood that trickled down her back, and yet it didn't hurt. It simply tingled slightly and pulsed with her heartbeat.

"Can . . . I lick?"

"Yes."

He instantly went back to the task of cleaning the wound with his tongue. Each lap was slow and methodical. His warm tongue soothed the sting away.

"Thank you," he said between long licks. "Thank you, Trinia."

She chuckled at the warmth in his voice. "You've earned it." She dipped close to his neck, pressed her lips to his ear. "You're such a good boy."

He fell forward, buried his mouth against the bite wound and *groaned*. The only reason that the whole hall didn't hear it was because it was muffled by her shoulder and instead, she felt that sound soak into the mark he'd given her and tremble all the way through her body.

She could feel *him* in every piece of her. Like a real thing curling inside her chest. Comforting, warm, supportive . . .

"You're . . . mine now," he whispered against her skin so low she almost couldn't hear it.

"Yes," she affirmed. "I am yours, Brovdir."

She yipped as he picked her up, swung her around, and plunked her down on the box he'd been on. Her thighs clenched together, still sopping wet. Her pussy pulsed at the sudden loss of his cock.

But she didn't have time to brood on that for long. Brovdir knelt before her, eyes fiery with intention.

"Fades, look at you." His voice was husky and raw. "The most gorgeous woman I've ever seen. I adore every bit of you."

He pushed up her skirts and kissed her damp thighs.

"What are you doing?" she squeaked, but he didn't linger, instead he kept trailing his lips upward to her rounded stomach, kissing tenderly as he went.

"You're mine now. And I want to bask in my treasure." His words made her shiver with pleasure. "I adore how soft you are. How smooth. How your body gives as I press into it."

She lost all her breath as his lips caressed the folds of her skin, the bulges and creases and curves. He treated them with *reverence*.

He met her eyes. "I adore your fierceness. Your strength. Your intelligence. Your determination to do what is right and bravery to tell me what needs to be done without faltering."

Tears pricked her eyes, and her heart swelled.

He cupped her face and pressed kisses to her forehead, her cheeks, her flooding eyes. "Everything, Trinia. Everything about you feels . . ."

She waited, breath caught.

His gaze was so soft. "You are home to me, Trinia of Oakwall. That is what you feel like. You smell like it, taste like it, and *look* like it. Everything about you draws me in and makes me more comfortable."

She felt so warm and fluttery that for a moment, the world around her didn't seem real. Everything blurred except for *him*.

And in his eyes, she could see the truth. "You . . . really are imprinted on me, aren't you?"

Brovdir tensed and sat back slightly. "I . . . do not intend to pressure you."

She grabbed his hands before he could go any further. "No, that's not what I—so you really are? You've imprinted? On me?"

He nodded hesitantly.

"For how long?"

He averted his gaze, but she cupped his cheek and forced him to look at her. His hard swallow made him wince, and she stroked his temple until he relaxed.

Finally, he mumbled. "First kiss. Didn't realize at the time, though."

"The first kiss." She cupped his face with the other hand and searched his worried eyes. "You've felt this way from the *first kiss*. But how is that possible? It's supposed to take time."

"Don't know," he said carefully. "Same happened to Govek."

"Oh, right. I heard about that," Trinia said, thinking back to when her sister had come back from that first trade with the warriors ranting and raving, threatening to bring down the bakery with her fury over losing Govek.

And Trinia had barely minded because she'd just shared a kiss with the male kneeling right in front of her.

"But you avoided me for *so long*. You were fighting the imprint this whole time? Even when you were avoiding me?"

"Yes." He held her gaze. "Regret it now. Won't make this

mistake again. I will never run from your side again, Trinia of Oakwall."

Despite everything that had happened, *because* of everything that had happened, she believed him. To the depths of her soul, she knew that from this moment forward, she would never feel alone again.

Her body went lax and her mind calmed, and her tension eased away. Tension that had been lingering since her mother had gotten sick so many years ago.

Tears flooded her eyes.

Poor Brovdir's blurry face instantly fell into panic. "Wha— I apologize. Trinia, I—"

She dashed at the tears. "No, it's not. It's not you, it's just . . ." She moved her hands down from his face and gripped his shoulders. "I've been on my own for so long. I had friends, of course, but it's just . . . it's not the same as . . . as . . ."

He cupped her neck and drew her forward, pressed her forehead to his. She could feel his steady breath on her face, helping her to breathe. His pulse was strong under her fingertips.

"You will not be alone again." His voice was so solid and certain, and she helplessly leaned into him. "I vow this, Trinia. You are *mine*."

She felt that down to the pit of herself. To her core. She was *his*, and in this moment, nothing else mattered. Not the bakery, not the sinkholes, not the prophecy. It was just her and him anchored in to ride out the storm.

They sat like that for a long time, just holding each other, allowing a moment of stillness which was so rare of late. She relished it. Relished the steady feeling of being cared for, of being given the space to breathe.

"I feel like I've been sprinting for years," she murmured,

eyes still shut, but she could feel Brovdir all around her. His warmth, his spicy scent . . . "Since I took over mother's bakery, I've never had a chance to slow down." She opened her eyes and found him staring back at her. "Thank you, Brovdir, for giving me a moment of peace in the chaos."

His hand came up and brushed at the back of her head.

"Always."

He truly meant that.

And she believed him.

She leaned in and kissed him tenderly. Sweetly. She poured her gratitude into the kiss, nibbling gently at his lips, scratching at the nape of his neck. He let out a huff of pure contentment and pleasure.

She tipped her head to deepen the kiss.

And a sharp pain radiated from her neck. From the bite wound. She'd almost forgotten.

Brovdir instantly released her. "I'll find bandages."

He got up and her hands fell back down into her lap, as disappointment flattened her. She would have him back the moment her neck had been fixed up.

Brovdir searched the storeroom shelves. His posture was easy, and his expression was calm but for a light furrow of concentration.

He was so stable.

And she was so lucky to have him for support.

"You always call it your mother's bakery."

She blinked, her thoughts derailed instantly.

"Oh . . . uh. Yes, because it is hers." Or at least it *was*. It was Ronhold's now.

"Shouldn't it be yours?"

What?

"It was your grandmother's. Then your mother's. Now yours."

Oh. That's what he meant. "Well, that's only because . . . because . . ."

Because why?

Her throat tightened with confusion. Her heart quailed against a truth that she did not want to name. She wasn't ready. She'd lost so much already. She didn't want to give up yet.

Brovdir came back and settled back down at her feet. He had a healing tincture in one hand and held it out to her. "Found this. Drink."

His voice sounded rough. She reached out and gently touched the scar at his throat. "Is it hurting?"

His lips quirked in a half smile. "Too much groaning."

Her cheeks heated. They had been loud. She wondered if everyone in the hall heard them. "You should drink it then."

He shook his head. "Won't help."

"Why?"

"Too old. Nothing left to heal." He pushed the tincture into her hand. "Drink, and the bite will be gone. Like it never happened."

Like it never happened. Her heart squeezed in her chest. "No."

He tipped his head, eyes wide. "No?"

Biscuits, he was so cute. "I want to keep it. I don't want to forget this. Being with you. Not that I ever *would*, I just . . . I've lost so much in the last few days but gained much too. This included."

His face lit up with delight, so vibrant it lit up the whole room. It bloomed her own happiness so high she felt like she was floating. She leaned forward to kiss him.

"BROVDIR!"

The rage-laced shout cracked like a whip around them, and Trinia jumped. Brovdir gripped her shoulder and looked toward the door with narrowed eyes.

"What was that?" Trinia asked.

"Sythcol," Brovdir said.

"Where the *fuck* is he? I can scent him here!"

Footsteps stormed toward the storeroom and the door would have burst off its hinges had the barrel not been in the way.

"Brovdir! I can scent you in there! Come out now!"

Brovdir flinched but said, "One moment." He began to dress while she straightened her clothes.

Then they exited the room and every scrap of tenderness disappeared.

"What the fuck were you thinking?" Sythcol's booming voice thundered off the walls of the tree, vibrating all around them like a storm of fury. He charged toward them, eyes wild, vibrant purple robes billowing in his haste.

Brovdir gripped her tight around the middle and pulled her behind his back.

"How dare you!" Sythcol's bellow dripped with venom. Behind him, she could see the other orcs watching with wide, shocked eyes. "How *dare* you schedule to meet with the human headman without discussing it with me first! Don't think I don't know what you're going to speak on! You're going to tell him I'm not fit to lead, aren't you?"

Not fit to lead? What?

"No." Brovdir's voice was tinged with confusion. "I will tell him about the sinkholes."

"The sinkholes?" Sythcol blinked his damp eyes and shook his head as if trying to clear it. "That's not . . . You aren't allowed to do that *either*."

"I must." Brovdir's voice was solid, but his posture was slightly hunched. "Things have changed."

"Changed so fast you couldn't even *bother* to tell me? Changed so fast you couldn't consult me at all? Changed so fast you forgot that I am your *partner* in this? How dare you treat me like I'm beneath you!"

"Meant no disrespect." Brovdir bowed his head.

"You've done far worse than *disrespect* me! You've betrayed me!" Sythcol's eyes were wild and reflecting the flames from the cooking fires. "Now the humans will use this as leverage against us!"

"Leverage?" Trinia stepped around Brovdir so she could get a better look at Sythcol. "What do you mean?"

"For more boons! More services! More *magic*!" Sythcol roared into her face. His breath smelled of rot. His skin was a glassy grayish green, and his cheeks were hollow. "Magic I do not have the energy to provide—"

Boom!

Trinia jumped and the floor beneath her feet rumbled. It took a moment for her to realize that Brovdir had slammed his heel into the solid wood floor. It was a wonder it hadn't cracked the tree open.

"Are you going to *challenge* me, Brovdir?" Sythcol's posture was tight, and his arms came up as if poised to protect himself should Brovdir lunge.

Trinia gripped the back of Brovdir's shirt and tugged. "I'm all right, Brovdir. Please. Don't."

He snapped his gaze to her, and she could see the anger there. She wasn't too pleased that Sythcol had yelled at her either, but attacking him wasn't the answer. Especially because there was clearly something *wrong*.

"This isn't like him," Trinia whispered to Brovdir. "Sythcol isn't like this."

"Don't speak like I can't fucking hear you." Sythcol's voice was shrill. "There is *nothing wrong with me.*"

The inflection in his tone was so odd and unnerving that it made her blink.

"I'm going to tell Oakwall." Brovdir let the words echo in the hall, strong and certain. "Sinkholes, prophecy, warriors. *All* of it."

Her chest swelled with pride.

Sythcol looked ready to combust from the rage simmering behind his eyes. "You will not."

"I will," Brovdir insisted. "You can come or not, but I will."

Sythcol's face contorted. "You will obey my orders! I am the reason you thrive. This clan would be *nothing* without my rule."

A deadly quiet settled on everyone and everything in the hall. Even the fire hesitated to crackle as the venomous weight of Sythcol's words rocked every one of them to their core.

Including Sythcol.

His whole body went slack. His eyes widened. A fine sheen of sweat appeared on his forehead.

Brovdir exhaled slowly. "Orders do not suit between us, fellow chief. We work in tandem. Together. I am not yours to command."

She expected Sythcol to continue arguing. To clench his teeth. To shout. To whirl around in a dramatic huff and storm out of the room with a veiled threat.

Instead, the male's expression twisted as if he were about to weep. He shrank back, curled in on himself.

And then he fled the room.

Trinia was awash with confusion at the odd reaction. Brovdir's tension told her he was just as befuddled. Even the males on the opposite end of the hall seemed speechless. The tension was so tangible it was like breathing through stone.

A light touch fluttered at the small of her back and she looked up at Brovdir. His expression had fallen into one of exhaustion. "I need to speak with him."

"Take your time," Trinia assured. "I'll wait here for you."

CHAPTER
THIRTY-EIGHT

BROVDIR

Brovdir found Sythcol where he usually was, within Ergoth's study with scrolls surrounding him and dim candlelight casting deep shadows around his slender frame.

"Leave me." His voice wavered as he buried his head in his hands.

"No," Brovdir said. He could not. Should not have in the past either.

Sythcol looked up at him with a sneer. "You already *won* this, Brovdir. I've lost. I can't change your mind despite all logic, and I accept that."

"Don't want to win."

"Oh, you don't?" He sat up, crossed his arms over his chest.

"I want to be partners."

Sythcol's eyes widened and then he let out a dry laugh that did not meet his eyes. "Partners? You really think that's possible now?"

Brovdir's brows furrowed in confusion.

"Don't give me that. You *know* you've betrayed me in this," Sythcol snapped. "You know how hard I've been working. *Slaving.* And now you're going to undo it just like *that.*" He snapped his fingers. "All because some woman wants you to—"

"Don't speak of her." Brovdir growled so low it felt like embers sparking in his guts.

Sythcol gritted his teeth and straightened his back, but said nothing.

"You know it's not her." Brovdir worked around the agony in his throat to get the words out. "She showed me, but that's all. I've made my own mind."

"And with it, you've betrayed me. Your partner in this. The one person you are supposed to rely on in this clan. You think she knows the situation better than I do? You think her words hold more weight than mine? I've been the lead conjurer for this clan since I was a mere *sixteen summers*. I've been making the bulk of your healing tinctures since I was barely eighteen. You see your scars. Half of those were healed by *my magic.*"

Fades, had this male really been forced to toil for so long? Sythcol may not have gone to battle, but he had just as many scars as Brovdir and wore them in the blackness of his hands, the wrinkles in his brow, the resignment in his eyes.

All caused by the pressure Ergoth had forced upon him. Pressure that was still building now.

"I've worked *so hard* for my *whole life* to keep our kind safe. And now you want to just undo *all of it*?"

"Not undoing the *safety*," Brovdir said slowly. "Undoing Ergoth's *lies*."

Sythcol's jaw tightened.

"Undoing that vile male's *control*. He wanted the divide,"

Brovdir said. "*He* wanted you fearful. To control you. To keep you."

Sythcol's eyes went huge at that.

"We are the same, Sythcol. We've only ever lived in fear and taken orders. It's time to release that fear and do what is *right*."

Sythcol trembled, swallowed. His eyes went shimmery and wet as he whispered, "I don't know how."

And as if on cue, a bird swooped into the room and dropped onto Sythcol's shoulder. The conjurer snatched the note tied to its leg so fast that the bird squawked and a few feathers escaped as it darted away.

"What?" Brovdir grated as Sythcol's eyes widened in distress. The male was frozen to the spot. Unblinking and pale.

"What!" Brovdir demanded and Sythcol finally jerked his gaze up.

"It's a sinkhole at the edge of Oakwall."

CHAPTER THIRTY-NINE

TRINIA

"I'm coming with you!" Trinia sprinted after Brovdir as he rushed through the clan. She was sweaty, out of breath, and completely determined.

He'd just told her there was a sinkhole at Oakwall. *At her village*. Her stomach twisted so hard she was afraid she would vomit.

"No," Brovdir said over his shoulder. He didn't speed up, though she could see from his expression that he regretted telling her. He probably wished he could have snuck out of the hall unnoticed.

"I'm coming!" She gulped air, refusing to slow even as her lungs screamed and panic gripped tight in her throat. "I'm coming whether you want me to or not and I swear if you try to stop me, I'll—"

Brovdir whirled around so fast dust and rocks sprayed out around him. He took her shoulders in his huge hands as he stared into her face. "Trinia, it's not *safe*."

"I know it's not!" Tears flooded her eyes. "I *know* that. But I can't sit here wondering and hoping and . . . *please.* I need to come with you."

Brovdir swallowed, and then looked up at the path. Sythcol had already run ahead and disappeared into the forest. There were no other orcs around. Just empty homes and an icy wind.

He picked her up in his arms and began to sprint.

"Thank you," Trinia managed as she clung to him. "Thank you, Brovdir."

The trip took too long. It felt like a lifetime. The crisp scent of the forest mingled with Brovdir's spice as she buried her head in his shoulder. The roaring of the wind in her ears grew louder with every passing breath.

And then, they finally came upon the sinkhole and she realized it wasn't the wind that was roaring.

"Fades," Brovdir breathed as he held her a little tighter. She couldn't even get out words.

Before them was a massive, churning pool of muck and debris. It bubbled like it was boiling from beneath. The whole grange hall and yard could fit inside it and with every moment it chipped away at the edges, swallowing up bushes and ground.

On the opposite end, through only one layer of trees, she could see the massive wall of oaks that protected her village.

And the churning depths grew larger by the moment.

"Ogvick!" Sythcol called to a warrior orc Trinia had only just noticed. The warrior ran over, giving the roaring sinkhole a wide berth. "How fast is it growing?"

As if on cue, one of the pine trees at the edge groaned and tipped as the ground beneath it was swept away in the current. It disappeared beneath the water's surface, sucked into the unknown.

It was swallowing everything up!

Brovdir snatched her up by the waist and yanked her back, even though she was nowhere near the edge. "I'm fine!"

"Not safe!" he nearly roared. "Ogvick! Report!"

The male straightened. "It only started a few moments ago, but it's gotten *huge*."

"Send a message to my conjurers!" Sythcol demanded and the warrior pulled a paper from his leather pants. "Call them here *now*. We have to try to stop it!"

Was there even *time* for that? With every breath, the hole grew wider and closer to the wall. Toward *houses*! Toward—

Trinia's eyes locked on the wide, spiraling trunk of a huge willow tree on currently stable ground to the left of the sinkhole. Its branches stretched high all the way up and over the wall of oaks. It was a tree that every person in her village would instantly recognize.

"The schoolhouse is right on the other side! The willow!" She pointed to the tree. "That willow shades the schoolyard!"

"Fades mercy!" Sythcol bolted toward the sinkhole, getting so close that the edge around his feet began to crumble, but instead of backing off, he extended his hands toward it. "Ogvick, you need to get my conjurers here *now*."

"There isn't enough time!" Trinia yelled. The roots of the oaks jutted out into the water like bone stripped of its meat. The ground chipped away under the wall and toward the willow. She could hear the trees groaning as their support weakened. "We have to warn the villagers. We have to get the children out of the schoolhouse!"

"I'll send a message to Headman Gerald!" Ogvick cried.

Sythcol burst out of his concentration and rounded on the warrior. "*No*! I can fix this!"

"We have to!" The young warrior's eyes darted between

them and his hands trembled as they pulled a piece of parchment from his pants pocket. "There are *children*!"

"He's right!" Brovdir shouted. "We must!"

Sythcol scowled. "Do *not* disobey me! I *will* stop it!" He reached into the sleeve of his robe and pulled out a slender brown vial the length of his palm.

Ogvick's face went pale. "Chief Sythcol, *no*!"

"This doesn't concern you!" Sythcol snapped as he uncorked the top.

"Brovdir! He can't!" Ogvick said. "It's killing him!"

Brovdir sucked in a hard breath, and he advanced on Sythcol.

"It's only to increase my magic! Without it, there is no hope of stopping this sinkhole!" Sythcol uncorked the vial and downed its contents with one gulp.

"Fuck!" Ogvick stepped back, eyes wide and aghast. Brovdir's complexion had gone pale. Trinia could not see magic as they could, but she knew what they saw must have been a horror.

Sythcol turned to the sinkhole undaunted and thrust his arms down toward the crashing waves of water. It was shooting out of one side and spiraling into a hole on the other. The cavern sucked in everything it could: dirt, bushes, entire trees—

The *wall*—

Sythcol let out a cry so sharp it sounded over the roaring of the water. His back bowed, his fingers contorted. It was a wonder they didn't break.

And then he collapsed down to his hands and knees. He fisted the dirt, heaving for air. His eyes were huge, his face pale. He shook like he'd seen a ghost.

"I can't . . . I can't bend him," he breathed.

Him?

"Ogvick. Send the warning to Oakwall now!" Brovdir demanded, and Ogvick had a bird before Trinia could blink.

"I can't stop it!" The panic in Sythcol's voice was so shrill that Trinia shuddered from the top of her head down to her toes. "I can't! It's too powerful. It broke my—" Sythcol looked down at his shaking, blackened hands. His fingers were twitching and seemed to be out of his control.

"We could tie the willow to the wall!" Ogvick said as he released the bird. The robin darted off through the trees, taking Trinia's hope with it. "Hold it up that way!"

"No!" Brovdir said. "The willow is going to go too!"

And it was. The sinkhole was chipping away beneath it already.

"We must do *something*!" Trinia's throat was choked from her panic. "What if Headman Gerald doesn't get the message in time? What if they haven't noticed the wall is tipping yet?"

The thundering crash of the land being ripped away raged on. The roots of the wall were fully visible. The tops of the trees were shuddering, buckling.

Tipping toward the town.

"Ogvick, run down to a stable point, climb over the wall, and evacuate them!" Brovdir ordered.

Ogvick sprinted off into the trees.

There was another tremendous crash as more of the land was sucked away. The frothing brown water roared as it spiraled into the deep.

"I'll try again!" Sythcol said. "If I could just plug the tunnel."

Brovdir inhaled sharply and Trinia turned to find him

yanking a scrap of paper out of his waistband. He pricked his thumb with his claw and scrawled a note in blood.

"What are you doing? What are you writing?" Trinia said, craning her neck to see. "You . . . you're calling on *Elder Plog* for aid? What? Why?"

Brovdir whistled, and a bird swooped down, snatched the note from his outstretched palm and disappeared into the trees.

"I don't understand! What are you *doing*?"

Brovdir turned to her and gripped her shoulders tight in his hands. The warm, heavy weight grounded her and the steadfast determination in his face helped her breathe. He took a long inhale through his nose, and she copied him, filling her lungs, exhaling with him.

The panic eased.

A tremendous boom sounded, and they both jumped and spun around.

A huge stretch of ground beneath the wall had been swept away.

The wall rippled and leaned.

"I must tie the branches of the willow to the wall." Brovdir gripped her shoulders again. "I must."

She knew he did. She knew he had to try, even though it seemed impossible.

Her eyes flooded, and she wanted to start wailing and never stop.

"Stay here," Brovdir ordered. "Stay here . . . my love."

Her stomach flipped over, and her eyes widened. Her blood heated up in her veins.

"I love you *too*."

Joy flooded his features, and he pressed a hard, fast kiss to her lips.

"Come back to me!" she demanded as tears began to course down her cheeks. He paused only briefly to brush one with his thumb.

And then he was gone.

CHAPTER FORTY

BROVDIR

She loved him. *She loved him!*

He refused to lose her!

Brovdir barreled toward the willow and sprang halfway up the tree. His plan to call on Elder Plog for aid would work. It *had* to! There was no other choice!

The willow buckled and swayed with every one of his motions. Already a third of its roots had been washed out, but where the wall leaned toward the village, the willow leaned away. With any luck, tying them together would hold the oaks in place or even pull them away from Oakwall entirely.

The water was so loud he could barely hear anything else. The desperate need to turn back and look to ensure Trinia was still out of danger was overwhelming.

He couldn't. One wrong move and the tree would topple.

The tree buckled like it had been struck by lightning. The sound of the ground tearing out from under the tree was deafening.

The sinkhole was taking the willow.

"Brovdir!"

Trinia's scream made his teeth gnash, and he heaved his weight backward, hoping it could shift the tree away from the swirling death trap of water.

It leaned and *leaned.* The water was *right there.*

And then the tree *swung back.*

"You've got it! Keep going!"

Trinia's voice drew his attention, and he saw Sythcol at the edge of the sinkhole on his knees. The swirling tendrils of dark magic hooked into him like blades, tearing through his arms and carving jagged black patterns in his flesh. His face was screwed up tight and he let out a roar that chilled Brovdir right to his core.

But there was no time to fear for the conjurer. The willow was going down. He had to jump.

Brovdir took his chance and leaped from the willow's shuddering branches toward the leaning wall.

He hit the oaks hard. His hands scrambled, his feet kicked to find a foothold among the tightly twisted, twining branches.

He found a hand grip first. Then another.

There was a tremendous splash as the willow fell into the water. He watched in horror as it contorted, breaking up. It was sucked beneath.

And disappeared.

The water continued to rage, and the wall was wavering, threatening to fall.

A shriek pierced the air and made his blood run cold.

He turned to find Trinia panicked at the edge of the sinkhole, trying to drag Sythcol's unconscious body away as the water sucked the ground beneath her.

She wasn't going to make it.
He bellowed in terror.

CHAPTER
FORTY-ONE

TRINIA

Sythcol was dead weight and his feet were already dipping into the sinkhole.

He'd used the last of his energy to save Brovdir! She couldn't let him *die*!

But he was so heavy, and the sinkhole was *right there*.

"TRINIA!"

Brovdir's agonized cry tore through her and gave her the strength she needed.

She could not die here. She couldn't leave him now.

She hoisted Sythcol under the arms and used her full weight to pull him.

She slipped in the muck. Her leg sunk into the mud all the way to her knee. The water rose and she couldn't get out. The wall was still buckling and swaying with Brovdir clinging for dear life right above.

One wrong move and he would fall.

One wrong step and she would slip.

They would both be sucked in.

"It's here, Elder!"

Trinia gasped in shock as a group of young orc sons burst out of the tree line.

They ran right for the sinkhole.

"Wait!" Trinia cried as the children got far too close. "Stop! It's dangerous!"

Another group emerged, led by Elder Plog. "It's here! Bring the boar!"

The *what?*

More boys appeared ahead, clearing the path, ripping out bushes, moving aside debris.

"Over here! This is the best spot!" One of the younger sons cried from a precarious position on some rocks right at the edge of the sinkhole.

"Get away from there!" she cried.

"Nice work, boys, but she's right! Come on down!" the elder agreed and the boys instantly ran to safety. Plog looked around. "Niloc! Ulid! Get her and Sythcol away from that edge before they get sucked into the drink! The rest of you, hook onto the wall!"

Hook onto the—

"Don't get close! It's too dangerous!" she broke off, eyes wide, as the boys stopped a safe distance away. Their arms outstretched; their feet were braced.

They were going to hook into the wall with their *magic.*

Just then, another group appeared out of the trees. The older boys.

They carried the *massive* bolder.

"Good show, boys! Right up that way! Quickly, quickly!" The elder guided as the boys struggled to heft the enormous thing. It was only after looking closely that Trinia realized their hands weren't *touching* the rock. They were using magic too. The task was still arduous. Their jaws were tight with the exertion. Sweat covered their faces.

But they were grinning from ear to ear!

"W-what is going on?" Trinia gasped as the two boys that had been told to help her appeared at her side.

"Chief Brovdir called us to help," Ulid said. "We should get Chief Sythcol out of here first. He's out cold."

"That's what he gets for never sleeping. Catches up with you at the worst time."

They dragged the conjurer out of the frothing sinkhole, and Trinia breathed a great sigh of relief. Her arms ached and trembled from the effort of holding him for so long.

The boys lifted the unconscious conjurer by his arms and legs and carted him off toward the safety of the forest. They made it look so effortless.

"TRINIA!"

Brovdir's loud bellow reminded her she was a hair's breadth away from the edge of the sinkhole. It was churning and swirling and still eating away at the ground.

But she was still stuck. She couldn't pull her leg free.

"She's *fine*, Chief Brovdir!" Elder Plog said. "Now *relax*! Boys, this way! You've got it!"

Trinia watched with wide eyes as the young orcs positioned themselves right above the frothing whirlpool.

"Hold that boar butt steady!" the elder called. "Line it up proper!"

Boar butt? What was he—?

Her eyes went huge with realization.

"I think we've got it!"

"No, a little more this way!"

"Yes, that's better. There's the hole."

The elder had come up with this crazy plan all along. To plug up the holes with boar.

But not boar. *Boulders.*

"Is that a *tree* in there?"

"There is! Elder, there's a tree in it already!"

"That's fine! Less to plug for you. Do you have a good spot?"

"Yes, elder, we have it."

"Count of three then!" the elder cried. "One, two, *throw*!"

Her heart was in her throat as a tremendous splash broke. It fell beneath the surface of the churning water. She held her breath and waited. Waited.

A silence descended as everyone forgot to breathe.

And then the water stopped churning.

Cheering erupted all around her.

"It really worked!"

"I can't believe it!"

"We fixed it!"

They fixed it.

"Haha! I knew it!" the elder cried with a bellow of a laugh. "Thanks to the Fades!"

Trinia's throat went tight, her vision blurred, and her whole body sagged with *relief.*

He had, hadn't he? The elder had known this whole time through communing. The Fades had told him to dig. And they'd dug up exactly what they'd needed to fix this sinkhole.

The elder snapped his gaze to Brovdir who was still clinging on to the nearly toppled wall. "Come along, boys! We need to get that wall righted. Chief, you just stay put and look pretty. Not that it's so hard for you."

Brovdir's disgruntled huff had a smile stretching her lips despite everything.

"Trinia," he called, and her chest swelled with relief. "I'm coming."

"No, you are not!" the elder said. "Can't you see these boys struggling to hold the wall still? You can't be wiggling about all over like a spider in honey or they'll lose their hold and splat the village."

Trinia's stomach twisted at the harsh reminder that the schoolhouse was on the other side. "What about the evacuation? And Ogvick?"

"They're fine," Brovdir said. "I can hear them. Evacuation is ongoing."

Trinia exhaled again just as the two boys that had saved Sythcol reappeared from the woods and ran over to her. How far away did they take him?

"Fades have mercy, you really got this stuck in there!" Ulid, a slender nine-year-old with a cheery disposition, kneeled at her side. He started digging at the ground around her stuck leg with his slender pale green hands.

"Should we just chop it?" Niloc, a much larger boy of the same age, asked.

"No, you idiot! Humans like their legs attached!"

"You're the idiot! I meant chop with our *magic*! At the *ground*!"

"Just say that then!"

"Now, boys, don't bicker or our good chief might give you a wallop!" Elder Plog chided her wayward rescuers.

"Chief Brovdir wouldn't wallop a flea," Niloc muttered, and Trinia huffed out a shocked laugh.

Brovdir had led a life of brutal fighting and turmoil, only to enter Rove Wood Clan and become known as the chief who wouldn't wallop a flea.

The elder turned back to the group of nearly thirty orc sons who were now all braced to pull the wall back into place. "Remember what I taught you. Lean into the Fades light. Use their magic to fuel your intention."

The look of concentration on the boys' faces was adorable.

They'd done it.

They'd stopped the sinkhole.

And now they were going to right the wall.

Everything would be okay!

Niloc tugged at her leg, and she let out a hiss as pain bloomed sharply in her ankle.

"Trinia!"

She snapped her gaze to where Brovdir was now trying to edge his way down from the wall.

"Chief Brovdir, *stop moving!*" the elder demanded. "I told you to just sit still. You need to be patient and wait until we're completely done!"

"Then stop hurting her!"

"I'm *fine*, Brovdir," she insisted. Though, truly, the only thing she wanted was for Brovdir to come down and sweep her off her feet.

She really did love him, didn't she?

Brovdir grumbled with irritation but settled back down.

"Now, on my count, boys. One, two, *heave*!"

Trinia watched in awe as the group of boys, with beaded brows and trembling muscles, *heaved* the wall forward.

Way too hard.

The wall snapped upright in an instant and Brovdir was launched off it like a shot! He flew through the air and landed right in the sinkhole.

"Brovdir!" Trinia cried, but he burst up from the surface immediately.

"Well, that's one way to get off the wall!" the elder said

with a laugh. Most of the boys were laughing too. The mirth forced Trinia to relax, but she still wanted Brovdir out of that water as soon as possible. What if the boulder dislodged, and he was sucked inside?

He made it to the edge and came straight for her. He was back on solid ground and all right.

She wanted to cry with relief.

"Trinia." He kneeled next to her, pressed his soaking wet forehead to hers. "You are well?"

"Yes," she managed as tears of relief soaked her cheeks. "Yes, I'm fine."

His thumbs brushed them, only to leave more moisture behind than was already there. He looked down at himself as if he'd only realized he was soaked. She didn't care. She was just so glad he was with her.

But he stepped back again, moving off a fair distance.

And then he shook like a wet dog.

Trinia slapped a hand over her mouth, but it couldn't stop her laughter. Biscuits and jam, this male *was* just like a puppy.

Her puppy.

He came back to her side and turned his attention to her stuck foot. She cupped his face instead. "What am I going to do with you?"

"Stay with me." His voice was rough and quiet.

"And love you," she said breathlessly. "I love you, Brovdir."

His expression melted, and he leaned in to kiss her.

"What in all *blast* has happened here?"

Trinia's heart jumped right up into her throat.

Headman Gerald had arrived.

CHAPTER
FORTY-TWO

BROVDIR

"Don't you worry, Headman. These boys have got a fine hold on that wall. None of your villagers are going to splat today. And we've got a boar's butt all nice and plugged up under the water too so the sinkhole can't get any bigger."

"That— They . . . *what?*" the headman exclaimed. His face was pale. The group of five human men that had come with him were equally shocked and disheveled. "Where is Chief Sythcol?"

"Our conjurer chief is a little out of sorts now. Think he's unconscious in the woods over yonder there. Right, boys? Where'd you cart him off to?"

"He's on a rock somewhere."

"We draped him nicely. Like a tablecloth! Humans like those, right?" Ulid looked to Elder Plog expectantly.

"That they do, son. Very wise."

Brovdir would have groaned had he been able to produce sound out of his worthless throat.

Plog continued. "Sythcol might be underdressed, but our warrior chief is right over here with your baker. He's in much better shape, though a little damp from his catapult into the sinkhole."

"He was—you were—are you all right?"

"Fine," Brovdir coughed. He tried to get more volume, but it was no use. He'd bellowed too much and now he had no words left. At the absolute *worst* time.

"He's fine, Headman Gerald," Trinia said as he quickly went back to digging her leg out of the muck. It popped free, and he gave it a quick once over. She was no worse for wear. Thank the Fades.

Headman Gerald let out a sharp breath that seemed to give him courage, and he stepped in closer to the huge sinkhole. Little waves lapped gently at the muddy banks. It seemed the intake had slowed to nearly a halt now that the outtake was plugged.

"Careful, Headman!" Estoc's oldest son proclaimed. "It's undercut there, I think."

Headman Gerald backed off and examined the group with confusion before his eyes found the group of thirty or so boys with their arms outstretched toward the wall. The younger sons had their brows knitted with concentration, but the older ones looked almost relaxed.

"Are you boys all right?"

"Course we're all right! It's just a little bit of magic. Can't you see that?" one son said snidely.

"Humans can't see magic, you dolt!"

"You're doing well, boys. Keep it up while we call for help," Headman Gerald said in a much more powerful voice. He straightened his back and looked around with more purpose. "Everyone on the other side of the wall has been moved, but we need to brace it. You boys can't hold that magic all night."

"Bet you we could!"

"I'm not even breaking a sweat!"

Headman Gerald turned to Brovdir. "This is what you were meeting with me about tomorrow, isn't it?"

He nodded. "And . . . more . . ." His throat felt like open blisters were being grated with a metal file.

"Let's speak on it tomorrow," Headman Gerald said with a sure nod. "One task at a time. Could your warriors cut down and carry some larger trees? We could use those to brace the wall."

Brovdir rose his brows but nodded.

"You want to use the warriors?" Trinia asked. "Folks won't be put off by them?"

Headman Gerald shook his head and dug in his coat pocket for some paper. "It's high time we saw the benefit of having warrior orcs in these woods. The tension between our communities has gone on far too long."

With that, he held out the parchment to Brovdir expectantly.

Brovdir exhaled with relief and took it. Trinia gave his arm a squeeze as he began to write.

As the birds flew off, Elder Plog approached. "I suppose the conjurers can help cut down trees too, as long as they're willing to learn the magic from me."

Brovdir's brows rose at the elder and the male shrugged.

"Physical tasks have always been put to the wayside in our clan. It's not the kind of magic Ergoth liked to have taught, so nobody knows it. But I learned it long ago all on my own. Great fun to throw things at people too far away to know it was you!" Elder Plog said with a laugh.

"So, you taught it to the boys? Just now?" Trinia asked as Brovdir helped her to her feet. Her leg seemed to hold weight well.

"Earlier during the digging." The elder shrugged. "Too many big rocks, too many small hands. You know, it's not hard to learn it if you try. This kind of magic is what we're *meant* to do. Orcs are guardians of the land. We aren't supposed to use the Fades gifts to force growth. We're meant to work *with* Faeda, not try to change it. We forgot that along the way."

Brovdir's shoulders sagged as he thought of his brethren who had never even tried to commune with the Fades before.

A warm hand patted his shoulder, and he looked down at Elder Plog's kind face. "We've all lost our way, haven't we? All lost the purpose the Fades set us before they went into the great unknown."

"You mean when they went to sleep?" one of the sons asked.

The elder chuckled and shrugged and Brovdir could not fathom what Plog meant by any of this, but after today, he would never again think the male's odd words were entirely nonsense.

"Brovdir," Headman Gerald said, "if your orcs cut and place the trees, my men can build braces at the bottom."

Brovdir considered. "Set in holes?"

"Yes, that's a good idea. We'll need some for both sides. How many trees do you think it could take?"

The conversation continued until the orcs and men arrived to work. There was no time to linger on the devastation, and soon everyone had a task to do. Warriors alongside conjurers. Orcs alongside men. None noticed their differences as they pulled together to right the wall.

"It's unusual for you, isn't it?" Trinia asked him as she clasped his hand. "Having a mixed community like this."

He nodded. He'd never seen the like before, not in all his years.

"This is why the peace is so important," she said quietly. "Because in times like this, when hardship inevitably rears, it takes all of us to right things again."

That he could agree with wholeheartedly.

"Hold that steady!"

"Shit, it's too heavy!"

Brovdir jerked around to find two conjurer orcs trying to bring down a huge tree. It was cut partway through already but leaned dangerously toward the wall where others were working. They struggled against its weight as Brovdir ran over.

Hendr got there first and pushed the tree back toward the forest with one hand while slicing through the remaining bark with another. Toj caught it as it came down and hoisted the huge trunk on his shoulder as the conjurers stared in awe.

"They're . . . really strong." Trinia's voice was breathy with shock.

Brovdir blinked down at her, considering this level of strength was fairly typical for warrior orcs. He noted that most of the warriors had no trouble moving the trees on their own, while it took two or three conjurers to lift them.

As the work continued, the shock gave way to determination and the repetition of building the braces became routine enough for light conversation. Humans and orcs arrived with food, all of which was put in a central location and shared. The orc sons were relieved of their duties and ran off to play with a few of the human children who'd joined their parents to help. As he listened to their laughter and looked into their smiling faces, he could see that the brush with death had left no lasting mark.

The sun had begun to set when they finally got the last brace into position. It wasn't perfect, but it was stable, and the humans seemed content with it. Goodbyes were shared and thanks were given, and the relief was palpable.

"This is what we needed," Headman Gerald said quietly as he joined Brovdir at the edge of the sinkhole. Most everyone was already heading off into the woods. "There's been too much tension of late, too many unknowns. Pulling together like this is exactly what our peoples needed to get back the sense of community we had before."

"Apologies," Brovdir managed despite the pain the words brought him. "Was the warrior's arrival that brought tension."

But Headman Gerald shrugged his burly shoulders and shook his head. "It was, but the only constant in this life is change. There will always be new challenges, and it will always be up to us, as leaders, to pull our people together and see them through the hardships."

Headman Gerald looked to Brovdir, met his eyes expectantly.

He took a breath and nodded. "Yes. Agreed."

No longer would he stand aside and hope that another would step into the role given to him. No longer would he allow his judgment to be waylaid by the opinions of others.

He would be chief of these orcs, warrior and conjurer alike. From this point forward, he would put the peace of their communities first.

Headman Gerald smiled knowingly. The creases at his eyes became more pronounced and his age showed. This male was as wise as the elders themselves.

"Tomorrow," Brovdir said. "I will tell you all. Start fresh."

Gerald's smile widened, and he gave Brovdir a nod before heading off toward the group of humans that remained. "Let's head home."

Home. Brovdir looked up to search for Trinia and found that she was already coming over to him. Her clothes were a filthy mess, and her curly hair was disheveled, but her expression was nothing but warm.

She was breathtaking. He loved her with all he had in him.

Trinia held out her hand, and he took it in his, soaking up her warmth and infusing her with his own.

"Let's go home," she said, and he found himself smiling, because with her at his side, he already was.

CHAPTER
FORTY-THREE

TRINIA

"It's cold out. Take another cloak."

Brovdir held the thick leather garment out and Trinia could feel herself start to sweat already.

"Two is more than enough, Brovdir. It's not *that* cold."

His hand came up to brush at her cheek. "You still feel chilled from yesterday."

"I am not." She clasped his hand, but couldn't bring herself to push him away. Not after everything from the night before.

It had taken until dark to get the wall braced properly. Nearly every able-bodied man in the village and every orc conjurer had worked tirelessly at the task. Cutting trees, hammering limbs together, digging holes to set the logs.

Brovdir had lost his voice almost completely, but he'd still managed to organize the orcs. It was like the warriors could read his mind and the conjurers took lead from them. Watching Brovdir so effortlessly give orders by way of pointed looks and hand gestures was . . .

"You did really well yesterday." She reached up to stroke his forehead with her free hand, brushing away his shaggy hair. "You're a good chief."

He smiled in a way that made her heart flip over and touched his forehead to hers. "Because of you."

"You were always a good leader, Brovdir."

"And you helped me to see it."

She was flooded with warmth and went up on her toes to kiss him. She could feel every bit of his devotion to her in the way he kissed her. It rooted her to the spot. Rooted her to *him.*

"Must go," he said against her lips, even as she teased him further. Gave into her, dueling with her tongue before groaning. "Trinia, the headman."

With that reminder, she found the will to break off the kiss. "I suppose we shouldn't keep him waiting."

Brovdir nodded and then led her out of his tree, into the crisp dawn. The sun had barely started to rise, but the world was iced over. Glittering frost lined every leaf and twig. The path crunched under her feet. It smelled fresh and crisp.

It was so beautiful it was almost painful. She'd only spent two nights here, and it already felt like home.

"Thank you again." She gave his hand a squeeze. "For letting me live with you."

He plucked a kiss to her forehead, and they continued up the path, hand in hand. She looked up at the canopy of trees, at the blue sky poking through the barren branches. The orange of fall was gone and replaced with the crisp smell of incoming winter. "This really is the end, isn't it? My job as town baker is over."

Today was likely the last day she would ever step foot in the bakery. Her chest felt tight and she couldn't manage a full breath.

"Wish it was your choice," Brovdir said quietly. "Your choice to stay with me."

Trinia blinked up at him in shock. His expression was tense, telling her that while she'd been lost in her thoughts, he'd been lost in his too. "It is my choice. I could stay anywhere. I have many friends who would take me in. I'm *choosing* you, Brovdir." She wasn't certain of anything else, but staying with him she was certain of.

"What if the bakery was a choice?" Brovdir asked, holding her gaze. "Would you go back?"

Her stomach dropped. What good did it do to muse over things that could never be?

"Hello."

Trinia nearly jumped out of her skin and whirled around to find Sythcol with an amused smile on his face. One that didn't quite meet his tired eyes.

He looked far better than he had the day before though. Actually, he looked better than he had in *days*. His hair had been brushed out. The bags under his eyes were not so prominent.

But the blackness of his hands was darker than it had ever been. There was an odd, spiral pattern etched into them.

"Sorry." He tugged down the sleeves of his brown cloak. "Didn't mean to startle you."

Trinia waved him off and then gave Brovdir's hand a squeeze.

"How are you feeling? Any better?"

The lead conjurer took a long, deep breath and then said, "No. But I will after today." He looked to Brovdir. "I'd like to come with you to speak to the headman."

Brovdir nodded. "Good."

Sythcol sagged with relief, and they began walking again. "I heard you did well bridging the gap yesterday."

Trinia's brow furrowed and Brovdir looked just as confused. "You mean the sinkhole?" he asked.

"No," Sythcol said with a slight chuckle. "Though it is good you found a way to mend the wall. I mean the gap between the warriors and the conjurers of Rove Wood Clan. And the even wider chasm between the warriors and the *humans*."

Trinia couldn't help smiling at the memory. The villagers had been so stunned that the warrior orcs were helping mend the wall. They'd been especially shocked by Ogvick who had worked tirelessly to evacuate every child and teacher from the school.

"You make a good chief, Brovdir," Sythcol continued. "Far better than I'd given you credit for."

"Trinia helps." Brovdir took her hands, and her cheeks flushed at the praise.

"That she does," Sythcol said quietly. "Can I assume you will continue helping?"

Trinia nodded. "For as long as he wants my help."

"Forever." Brovdir's grip on her hand tightened. "I want your help forever."

A warm tingle shivered from the top of her head, all the way to her toes, and she smiled at him helplessly.

Sythcol cleared his throat. "That is good, then. With the two of you working together, I believe you will mend the bridge between our communities." He took a deep breath. "As long as I stay out of the way."

Trinia exchanged a shocked look with Brovdir. "Sythcol, you're stepping down?"

The male took a deep breath and then nodded swiftly.

Decisively. "Not . . . completely. I'll still aid you when you need it. I'll act as your second-in-command and help as much and as often as I am able. It's just that . . ." Sythcol sucked in a hard breath and closed his eyes as if trying to find the words. "I've been spending too much time in Ergoth's *head.*"

Trinia clutched Brovdir's hand tight. "What does that mean?"

Sythcol wouldn't meet either of their gazes. "I've been poring over his notes, his thoughts, his very essence. It's swirling around me faster than the sinkhole from yesterday, and I don't have the strength to shake it off."

He broke off and placed his palm to his forehead, wincing like a headache was blooming.

"Should you stop?" Brovdir asked.

"I can't . . . I must discover what is going on, what he was *hiding* or we'll . . ."

"We'll what?" Trinia asked, but Sythcol just shook his head.

"So, my plan, if you will agree"—Sythcol looked at Brovdir—"is to default to you the same way you've been defaulting to me."

She could feel Brovdir tensing against her.

"You're ready," Sythcol insisted. "You have what it takes to lead this clan well and I know you will put the wellbeing of our orcs first, both conjurers and warriors alike."

Brovdir swallowed hard. "Will still . . . need help."

"And I will still be around to give it. And I know Trinia will too. I know you will do well." Sythcol chuckled, but the mirth didn't meet his eyes as he looked up at the tree canopy and said quietly, "In many ways, you are a much better chief than I am."

"We are good in our own ways," Brovdir said. Then he stopped and held out his hand to Sythcol. "Leave it to me."

Sythcol hesitated for a moment before clasping Brovdir's hand and giving it a shake. "Thank you."

The rest of the walk was passed in companionable silence and Trinia found herself holding Brovdir's hand tight as the wall of oaks that gave her town its name came into view. Back when her town was founded before the wall was built, the orcs were considered fearsome enemies.

So much had changed since then. For the better.

Today she was making a change for the better too.

"Well, I'm off to pack then," she said as they crossed through the village gates. Smoke billowed from chimneys. The paths were empty and sparkled with frost. The smell of porridge and eggs wafted in on the breeze. So familiar it made her ache.

Brovdir tightened his grip on her hand.

"I have quite a bit to do, you know?" She patted his chest. "Lots to organize and pack up."

"You're really moving to the clan?" Sythcol asked.

"Is that so shocking?"

"Yes," he said without hesitation. "Your family has baked here for generations, and I know what those traditions mean to you."

They did mean a lot to her. They had been her *whole world.*

Until now.

Now her world was changing.

She looked up into Brovdir's worried eyes and went on her toes to kiss him. He leaned down so she could reach. He felt so good against her. Warm and sweet and *right.*

"You'll do great." Trinia gave him another squeeze. "I know you will."

"Thank you." He nuzzled the top of her head with his cheek, and she found the will to step away.

And then she turned up the path and started the familiar trail from the village gates back to her mother's bakery.

For the last time.

CHAPTER
FORTY-FOUR

BROVDIR

"But you are still investigating, right?" The headman asked with a tense, worried crease furrowing his brow. He balled his hands tight on the tabletop, and lack of sleep had caused bags under his eyes. "You will discover *why* the Fades are remaking our world and how to stop the sinkholes soon, won't you?"

The three of them sat at a round wooden table in a room that felt too small with a window that looked out onto a quiet street. The houses were packed together with barely enough room to walk between them. The cobblestone paths were slick with frost. The sun had only just started to melt them, and villagers would be waking soon.

He wanted to hurry this along and return to Trinia's side. He wanted to throw all her things into her hand cart and drag her back to their home in Rove Wood Clan before she took too hard a look at the bakery and decided she couldn't leave it behind.

Was she only choosing him because the bakery wasn't an option?

He shook his head, forcing himself to concentrate on the matter at hand.

Sythcol took a deep breath. "I am still investigating. The details of the prophecy are not mine to decipher. I am no seer, but I won't stop trying. As for the sinkholes, finding a way to stop them is going to take much longer than I previously hoped."

Sythcol looked up and met their eyes in equal turn before saying. "I've broken my peace. My magic is gone."

Brovdir went rapidly very cold.

"*What*?" Headman Gerald gasped. "How is that possible?"

Sythcol shut his eyes as if steeling himself. "I've discovered that Ergoth had been using his magic to hold back the sinkholes for years. Possibly decades."

"He was holding them back? All on his own?"

"Yes. It used a tremendous amount of magic." He looked away from them. "Likely that is why he chose me to perform most of his conjurings for him."

Brovdir's chest felt heavy with pity for the male.

Sythcol met his eyes again. "I've been searching for information on how he made them, or how to stop them, but so far, I've had no luck. I suspect Ergoth created them as a way to punish us should we ever betray him. A trap he released as revenge."

There was a long stretch of silence as the gravity of this sunk deep into his bones.

"Then how do we stop them?" the headman finally asked.

"I don't know. He must have gotten rid of his notes. All I could find were a few details on how he held them at bay, but the spell is complicated. *Very* complicated. And it uses a kind of magic that Ergoth never trained me in. One I did not know even *existed.* It doesn't pull from peace or rage or even any emotions at all. The source is . . . *fluid.* I've been trying to learn it by tapping into Ergoth's memories."

Sythcol bowed his head low. "But instead, his energy bled into my mind and . . ." He squeezed his eyes shut tight. "It broke my peace. My tranquility. And with it, my magic is gone too."

"Then what do we do now? How do we stop the sinkholes?"

Sythcol laid a map of the Rove Woods down on the table. "We can't stop them, but we can slow them using magic and by plugging them up. They make a spiral pattern. When they open isn't predictable, but *where* is. As long as your people stay clear of these areas, it will be fine."

"But . . . this runs through the western part of our village." The headman breathed, tracing the line on the map.

"Yes," Sythcol said quietly.

"Fades help us. My people are already on the brink of wanting to leave this place and now I must tell a few hundred folk they have to leave their homes? Their businesses? The schoolhouse is there." He pinched the bridge of his nose. "There isn't anywhere they can move *to.* At least . . . not within our village."

"They cannot leave." Sythcol's voice held a tinge of panic. "As I explained, the prophecy foretold the Fades will remake our world. We don't know what that means exactly, but we do know the Rove Woods is the only place that is safe."

"How can it be safe when we have sinkholes threatening to swallow us up?" The headman shook his head. "No matter what I do, when the truth comes out, my people *will* be unhappy. No matter what I say, I am certain that some, *many*, will choose to leave."

"We must make them see that the prophecy is *real,*" Sythcol insisted. "That leaving will spell their doom."

But the headman just heaved a weary sigh and murmured, "It will not be enough. Some will refuse to believe it, and I cannot blame them. It is . . . very difficult to believe."

Brovdir gripped his hands tight and looked out onto the street at the houses that were far too close. He watched a family of eight leave a home he would have assumed could fit no more than four. His thoughts drifted to Trinia and her house drawings. The spark of an idea brought out his voice. "What if the warriors expand your village?"

"Expand? How?" Headman Gerald asked.

Brovdir sat tall. "We will tear down and extend out the wall at this side of the village, where it is safe from the sinkholes." He pointed to the eastern part of the map.

Sythcol blinked in shock. "What?"

"Is that even possible? The wall is ancient and strong. It did not break even where the roots are now fully exposed," the headman said, leaning in.

"Possible with magic," Brovdir said.

Sythcol shook his head. "Brovdir, weren't you listening when I told you my magic is gone? My conjurers are going to be stretched incredibly thin, picking up my slack."

"Not your conjurers. The incoming warriors will do it."

There was a long silence that Sythcol broke with a light scoff. "Brovdir, that's not possible. They don't have magic."

"Not the same magic as you. But it *is* magic. They used it last night, when fixing the wall."

Sythcol sputtered, "They used magic to fix the wall? But

none of my conjurers reported anything like that to me. They would have seen."

"Theirs does not look the same as yours. It cannot be seen by our eyes. Their magic is in their strength. In their tenacity and drive. They draw from the Fades to slash, lift, and carry," Brovdir explained. "It is *inside* them. Not outside. They *can* rework the wall, Headman. I am certain. The act will bring our communities together as one and show that our warrior orcs are friends and comrades. Just as it did yesterday. The warriors can offer to build new homes for your humans in exchange for sharing their woods and allowing them to stay."

"That . . . that could work." The headman's expression relaxed and the tension in his shoulders eased.

"And you can manage all that yourself, Brovdir?" Sythcol asked quietly. "I . . . won't be able to help you. And there is bound to be much strife as the humans and warriors figure out how to work together."

"Going to be like boars fighting saber cats," the headman said, though his voice was lighter than before.

"I can," Brovdir vowed. "I *will* make this work."

Headman Gerald sat straight and gave Brovdir a broad smile. "Then it's agreed." He extended his hand out.

Brovdir took it without hesitation. "Agreed."

The conversation swelled and tapered as the three of them discussed the future of the Rove Woods and all who lived within them. The pieces of their plan were carefully forged and snapped into place. In the end, they had a clear vision of what was to come, though it would be an arduous task to get it there.

By the time they had finished, the noon meal was upon them and Sythcol looked rather done in.

"I'm going to head back. I need to check in with my

conjurers. I suppose you'll be busy helping Trinia move today?"

Brovdir nodded. His throat was aching from having spoken so much and he was eager to get to Trinia's side.

"Trinia is moving?" Headman Gerald's eyes were huge with shock and Brovdir winced.

Sythcol snorted at the blunder but waved. "I'm off then."

He looked down at the headman's alarmed face and knew that he could not put off this truth.

"Her father traded the bakery to Ronhold for mead before he died. Ronhold has finally come to claim it."

The headman's eyes went huge. "What? That's not possible."

"Ronhold holds the contracts," Brovdir explained.

"No— That's not— You're going to see her now, right?"

Brovdir nodded.

"Wait here. I'll come with you. I just need to grab something from town records."

From town records?

"It will only be a moment," Headman Gerald said as he disappeared back into the meeting hall.

CHAPTER FORTY-FIVE

TRINIA

Standing within her mother's bakery, with the fire extinguished and the candles blown out and the scent of stale bread stronger than the smell of it baking, she had such a hard time believing that her time here was over.

And yet . . .

She took a deep, hard breath and picked up another bag of clothes. She hadn't thought she would have much to pack. In her mind, it all fit into a single bag.

Now she had half of the hand wagon filled to bursting, and there was still more. Items that did not belong to the bakery. Personal things, sketchbooks, and knick-knacks. There was a book of tales her mother used to read her and an old mug that her grandfather had made himself. There was her grandmother's old shawl and the stools that Ulia had given her as a birthday present.

In the corner, at the bottom of a drawer, Trinia found her

mother's favorite pair of gloves. They still smelled like her. Lavender lotion and rose tea.

She tried to concentrate on these things as she packed them. She focused on what she *could* take with her and not on what she was leaving behind.

She focused on what she was *gaining* instead of what she was giving up.

Warmth bloomed in her as thoughts of Brovdir flooded her mind. His laugh, his rough voice, his shaggy hair.

The way he supported and stood by her through everything.

"There you are!"

The shriek echoed in the bakery and Trinia spun around to find Yerina barreling into the room with the same ferocity as an angry boar.

"*Where* have you been?" Yerina reached out to snatch her arm, but she stepped back, evading her grip. "You've nearly ruined *everything*. Do you know how hard I've worked to get Ronhold to agree to marry his son off to you? Do you *want* us to be destitute? Now come on! We need to go to Ronhold before it's too late."

"It's *already* too late, Yerina." Trinia looked around the room for any more belongings she wanted to take. "There's no way I'm marrying Tobbis."

"You *have* to."

"I don't *have* to do anything."

"So that's it? We lose the bakery because you are too stupid and stubborn to see reason? What would mama think if she were here to see you giving up?"

The roaring flame of guilt that exploded in Trinia's gut was tremendous. What would she think? "I . . . I'm not—"

"You *have* to marry Tobbis, Trinia," Yerina snapped. "We'll lose *everything*. What would mother even think of you? You've been away from the bakery for *two days*. Don't you have orders to fill? Where have you even *been*?"

Then Yerina's eyes snapped to the bandage on Trinia's shoulder. One she'd nearly forgotten was there.

Because the injury felt like a part of her already.

Yerina yanked the bandage back so fast it was a blur, and Trinia wasn't able to smack her hand away in time.

"No!" Yerina gasped out. "Are those *orc* teeth marks?"

"That's none of your concern."

"It's that warrior chief, isn't it? The one who was sniffing around you before! That beast has—"

"Do *not* talk about Brovdir like that," Trinia seethed with enough malice that Yerina went pale and snapped her trap shut.

"Glad to see we're all in fighting spirits this morning."

Trinia's breath seized in her throat as she turned to find Ronhold stepping into the bakery. His eyes were beady and confident. He had perfectly combed his white hair, his face looked fresh, and he wore some of the finest clothes Oakwall offered. His posture reeked of superiority. Everything about him made her want to bolt.

But she couldn't. She needed to face this.

Tobbis followed close behind his father. He was dressed just as fine, but looked so much more awkward.

"Are you playing conquest to one of our new orc chiefs?" Ronhold asked.

"That isn't any of your business." Trinia worked hard to keep her voice level.

A wide grin spread across Ronhold's face, and Trinia shivered with dismay. "What boons did he offer you in exchange? He's the chief to the clan, so I know he must have promised something good."

Trinia clenched her fists and refused to speak.

"I assume it's for the bakery, since I know how devoted you are. Out with it, girl."

Trinia glowered at him.

Ronhold smirked in a way that turned her stomach. "Fine, keep your secrets for now. We'll discover what boons he's giving you soon enough, since half of it will belong to my son."

"I am *not* marrying your son."

"I'm afraid you don't have much of a choice," Ronhold said. "If you don't marry him, then you will lose this bakery forever."

"Trinia, please, listen to *reason*." Yerina stepped forward with pretty, shimmering tears in her eyes. "We'll starve if you try to go against Ronhold."

Trinia was done letting guilt force her hand. "No, Yerina. I've made up my mind."

"Little girl, *don't* underestimate me." Ronhold's expression went so cold it nearly made her shiver. "I've been running things since before you were even a twinkle in your father's eye, and I *suggest* you get in line behind me, or you'll quickly discover just why no one else dares to compete with my affairs."

"I'm not meddling in *anything*, Ronhold," Trinia said with a snort. "I'm letting you win. Give me a moment and I'll be packed up and gone and you can do anything you like to this place. Run it or burn it. It's all the same to me."

With that, she carried a handful of candles and a stack of paper past Ronhold and Tobbis out to the awaiting cart.

"What are you doing?" Ronhold snapped, storming over as she continued to load up. "These things are *mine*."

"I assure you they are *not*," Trinia said coldly as she

continued to organize her blankets so they wouldn't fall. "I'm not taking anything that could be considered yours."

Which was honestly most of the bakery. All the pans and tools, the furniture, even the flour and sacks of grain, technically belonged to the bakery.

She ignored Ronhold's protests as she went back inside. Her chest tightened as she looked around. An entire lifetime of memories flooded her. She'd taken her first steps on these floorboards. She'd played here more than anywhere else in the village. She could count the days she hadn't stepped into the bakery on two hands.

This was the last day she would ever step foot inside these walls.

Her eyes prickled as she went to the cabinet in the back of the room where there was a large, leather-bound book with yellowed pages and faded writing.

It was a bit dusty. She hadn't needed to reference it for a very, *very* long time. Within, the recipes from four generations of her family were scrawled.

Unable to help herself, she flipped through the pages. The scent of old flour and parchment filled her nose as her eyes glanced over the handwriting of her great-grandmother, her grandmother, and then . . .

Her mother.

Her mother's handwriting was large and looped. In the beginning, her mother's recipes had flowers doodled in the margins. The explanations were flourished with details like "rosemary is so good in this one" and "try this with cinnamon. It's divine!"

The writing became much more subdued after she'd married Trinia's father, and then, at the back, there were little notes specifically to Trinia.

"Don't forget to add the onion again, Trinia!"

"These were your favorite when you were a baby."

"You should try these with nuts sometime."

"I'm sorry I couldn't be there to teach you this recipe myself."

"I wish we had more time."

Trinia's eyes welled with tears as she closed the book.

"What do you have there? Show me. Now," Ronhold demanded as he stormed over to her.

"It's my mother's private journal!" Trinia snapped, but she wasn't strong enough to stop Ronhold from snatching the book out of her hands. Behind him, she could see Yerina had averted her gaze, clearly unwilling to step in.

"This is *far more* than a journal," he said flipping roughly through the pages. "And considering its contents, I would say this belongs to the bakery, not to you."

"It's in the hand of my ancestors. It's a family heirloom." Trinia tried to take it back, but Ronhold simply held it above his head, out of her reach.

"This whole *bakery* could be considered a family heirloom, but it is mine nonetheless." Ronhold's grin made her stomach turn sour. "But if you want to keep it in the family, you know what you have to do."

Trinia's stomach twisted and her mind reeled, and her eyes stung as tears welled up.

And then Brovdir's voice rang in her mind.

"You always call it your mother's bakery. Shouldn't it be yours?"

It should be. But it had never felt like that.

Because she'd never really *wanted* it.

Trinia stopped fighting.

Ronhold blinked in shock as Trinia took a step away from him.

"No. I won't marry your son, Ronhold."

The man's brows furrowed into a tight scowl. "You'll lose *everything.*"

She would. She'd lose her livelihood. Her home. The place where she'd made so many memories.

Memories with a mother she loved so dearly. The feeling of safety and security. The feeling of home she'd once felt here . . . all of that was already gone.

It was gone the day her mother died.

"This bakery . . . hasn't ever really been mine," Trinia said quietly.

"What was that, girl?"

Trinia met his eyes. "I said it's never been mine. I worked it out of *duty*. Because my father and sister needed me to. Because this was where my mother was, and I only ever wanted to be with her. But she's gone. And she's not coming back, no matter how much I toil here."

"So, you're just going to give up her legacy?" Ronhold snapped, waving the book at her. "The legacy of your whole family will be lost because of you."

"I'm not *losing* anything, Ronhold," Trinia said calmly. "My father already did that. *He* is the one who lost it."

"And I'm giving you the opportunity to have it back!" Ronhold cried. "I'm being generous and you're spitting in my face!"

"Generosity?" Trinia chuckled. "Is that what forcing me into servitude is?" Ronhold's face was beet red as he sputtered. Trinia continued. "Even *if* some might consider your offer to be generous, I still wouldn't take it. I won't continue to labor at something I don't enjoy. That's not what my mother would have wanted for me."

"This is your last chance, girl!" Ronhold raged so loudly she could smell the sour stink on his breath. "If you don't agree, I will *never* let you set foot in this bakery again!"

That should have spiked fear in her. Fear and sorrow and grief.

And instead, her chest lightened with . . . *relief.*

"Then I'd better finish gathering my clothes." Trinia turned toward her cabinets. "Or will you try to say those belong to you too?"

But as she stepped away, Ronhold snatched up her arm and held it so tight she yelped in pain.

"You think you can make a fool of me, girl!" he bellowed in her face. "You've seen what I do to people who stand in my way."

"I have." Trinia tried to yank out of his grip, but it was too strong. "And it's shown me I'd rather be destitute than work with someone who could be so savage."

"You *will* obey me!" Ronhold raged. His eyes were bloodshot. "You will marry my son and bake my goods and you will be *glad for it*."

In a flash of green, a force pulled Ronhold back. Trinia was yanked and nearly toppled as her arm was wrenched out of the vile man's grip. A thunderous crash sounded as Ronhold was pinned to the wall.

By Brovdir.

Trinia blinked in shock at the sight of the man going deathly pale in the face of Brovdir's snarling countenance. Her recipe book fell out of his hands and hit the floor with a hard thud.

Her shoulder was gripped tight and Yerina appeared at her side, holding her. "Are you all right? Did he hurt you?"

The concern on Yerina's face was so startling Trinia almost couldn't process it.

"What is going on here?"

The headman's booming voice sounded loudly as a deadly quiet fell over the room. Only Ronhold's gasping could be heard. His face was going bright red as he scrambled against Brovdir's chokehold.

"Chief Brovdir." Gerald's voice was tight. "I understand you're distressed, but don't choke him to death or you'll ruin the peace."

Trinia hurried forward and placed a hand on Brovdir's arm, and he instantly released Ronhold, who collapsed to the floor gasping and sputtering.

"Ronhold, explain yourself," Gerald demanded. "Why are you here attacking Trinia?"

Ronhold coughed as he grated. "I was not *attacking* her. I was trying to make her see reason!"

"Explain." Gerald's tone was low and unyielding.

Ronhold gritted his teeth, clearly unwilling to lay out all his dastardly plans to the headman.

"He made a deal with their father."

They all looked to find Tobbis in the doorway. His head hung and his eyes darting to his father and away. "He made a deal. Drink in exchange for . . . the bakery."

"I've heard about that from Chief Brovdir," Headman Gerald said with a glower at Ronhold. "*Mead* in exchange for the *bakery*? A dastardly deal, even for *you*."

"It was a fair deal!" Ronhold rose to his full height but flinched as Brovdir growled low. Trinia gave Brovdir's arm a tug, and he backed off. "I have the contracts to prove it!"

"Bring them to me. Now," Gerald said firmly and Ronhold instantly dug in his inside jacket to produce the dreaded paper Trinia had been shown before. Gerald took it and examined it, his brow furrowed by the moment.

Trinia knew from his expression that the contract was grim.

Gerald looked between Trinia and Yerina. "Why did you not tell me of this contract before now?"

"I didn't know," Trinia said.

"Yerina?" Headman Gerald's voice left no room for dismissal.

Yerina looked at the ground. "There . . . there was no way out of it. And Ronhold offered to let us keep control of the bakery until his son came of age, as long as we paid a stipend every moon. After Tobbis came of age, Trinia could marry him and still keep half of the bakery."

Gerald glowered at Ronhold. "Is that true? Did you coerce her?"

"It was no coercion! It was a fair deal! I was very generous!"

"Generous, huh? Tell me, how *much* was this stipend?"

"I let them stay in the bakery! Control *all* the trades!"

It dawned on Trinia then. She turned to her sister. "Is that why you kept selling things off? Why you kept taking pans and supplies? To pay for Ronhold's stipend?"

"What else was I supposed to do?" Yerina sounded alarmingly close to tears.

"You could have come to me," Headman Gerald said firmly and Yerina shrunk like a scolded child. The headman sighed heavily. "Yerina, I know we've been at odds before, but I can't believe you wouldn't trust me to help you with something so vital."

"There's nothing you can do!" Ronhold spat. "You may be

headman, but you cannot override valid contracts. *You* know that."

"I do." Headman Gerald rose his head. "And that is true. I cannot override valid contracts, but this contract isn't valid. The bakery wasn't Jevin's to give."

"Of course it was!" Ronhold said. "Mirrani was dead! Jevin had full control of the bakery at that time."

"No. He had *no* control," Headman Gerald said. "Mirrani willed the bakery to Trinia."

There was a pregnant pause where even the air felt still. All of Trinia's breath left her.

And then Ronhold raged. "That's absurd! Trinia wasn't old enough to inherit anything! She was still a child!"

"Children can still inherit, Ronhold," Headman Gerald muttered. "Just because you do not trust your son with your business does not mean others don't trust their own."

"I never heard about Trinia inheriting! She clearly didn't even know."

"Yes, it's clear she didn't. And for that, I apologize." Gerald met Trinia's eyes again. "Your father said that you and your sister were too distraught to attend the reading of her will, so I approached you delicately after. Too delicately, it seems. Do you remember when I came to you and told you that the bakery was yours now?"

"Yes." Trinia clung to Brovdir's arm for support as she reeled from this new information. "I just thought you meant it was my *responsibility*."

Gerald exhaled, "I'm sorry. I should have been clearer. I should have known your mind would be clouded at the time. The bakery is yours, Trinia. Here is the will to prove it."

Trinia felt like her chest would burst and her voice warbled as she took the paper from Headman Gerald. Her mother's hand was obvious. "My mother . . . really left it to me."

Brovdir shifted to bring an arm around her middle and pull her into his side. She sagged against him.

Headman Gerald's eyes softened. "She did. She loved you dearly and trusted you above all others to run it." He sighed. "I am ashamed to admit that because you immediately took it over, I took that to mean you knew it was yours. I am truly sorry for all the hurt this has caused you."

Trinia's stomach twisted and she couldn't find words. Brovdir pulled her in closer and she leaned into his strength and warmth. His support seemed endless, and she soaked it up.

"They still owe me for my deal with Jevin!" Ronhold raged. "They owe me his debt!"

The headman scowled. "Stop spouting nonsense. Debts die with the person who made them. You know that better than anyone."

Ronhold went so red in the face that Trinia thought he might explode. "I'll overturn that law!"

Headman Gerald grinned slyly. "You likely could. You have enough friends to sway the vote. But if you do, then *all* debts from the past will be owed by the kin. Including *your fathers*. How much leather had he neglected to pay for before he died? I suppose I can just look in the town ledger. I've kept excellent records."

Ronhold huffed and heaved and then stormed out of the bakery, shouting. "This isn't the end!"

"Oh, I think it is," Headman Gerald said smugly.

Ronhold turned to glower at him before shouting. "Tobbis, come on!"

His son reluctantly followed his father, but not before

pausing to give Trinia a sorrowful look and stare longingly toward Yerina one more time.

"S-so . . ." Yerina said cautiously, "it's ours? The bakery is really . . . ours?"

Gerald gave her a flat look. "It is your *sister's* and no one else's."

Yerina went pale and wouldn't meet Trinia's eyes. "I'm . . . I'm sorry. Truly, Trinia, I thought I was doing the right thing."

Trinia didn't have words. She'd hardly begun to process that they'd won over Ronhold, let alone think about the part her sister played.

But one thing was clear. "It isn't entirely your fault, Yerina."

"So . . . so you forgive me?" Yerina's voice was tinged with hope. "You'll still help me, right? I'll starve without the bakery, Trinia. I have no way of supporting myself otherwise."

Trinia took a deep breath, chest tight, stomach twisting. She looked up at Brovdir, who looked equally tense as he waited for her response.

Her heart swelled, and she gave his hand a squeeze before letting him go.

She steeled herself and walked over to where the recipe book had been dropped to the floor. She picked it up, brushed off the dust and flour, hugged it tight to her chest.

"For a long time . . . I worked this bakery out of duty. And I didn't love it like mama and grandma, but I couldn't give it up either, because it's all I had." She met Brovdir's eyes. "But that's not true anymore."

She walked over to Yerina, who was watching her with wide, hopeful eyes, and placed the book in her hands.

"I give the bakery to you, Yerina."

"W-what?" Yerina fumbled with the heavy tome.

"It's hard work, but if you keep at it, you'll have more than enough to support yourself."

"You can't be serious!" Yerina gaped like a fish. "You can't expect me to—to *work*?"

Trinia smirked. "You've relied on me and others long enough, Yerina."

"I'll fail, Trinia!" Yerina said frantically as Trinia grabbed the last of her clothes from the cabinet. "I'll ruin it! All of mother's hard work will be destroyed and it will be your fault."

"Perhaps you will destroy it, Yerina. But that will be *your* fault. Not mine." Trinia walked over to Brovdir and took his hand. He beamed down at her and she could feel his happiness warming her up from the inside out.

"But this is your home!"

"I have a new home now," Trinia said, still looking into Brovdir's eyes. "One I chose for myself. And it might not be the bakery my ancestors built, but I think they would be happy to see me thrive just the same."

Brovdir's face crumbled, and he gathered her up in his arms, lifting her so effortlessly it made her burst into laughter.

"Are you sure?" he asked, searching her face.

"Yes." She cupped his cheek. "Yes, Brovdir. I choose you over *everything*. I want to stay with you."

He clasped the back of her neck and kissed her so deeply it curled her toes and turned her muscles to mush. She felt awash with relief and comfort and wonder.

She felt like she was home.

"I can't believe this!" Yerina cried.

Brovdir put her down, but the feel of his warmth remained all around her. She took him by the hand and guided him out of the bakery.

Headman Gerald gave them both a nod as they exited. "I'll note the change in ownership in the records."

"Thank you," Trinia said. "For everything."

"I'll see you again soon, Chief," Headman Gerald said with a nod. He turned and began making his way back to the meeting hall.

"Wait!" Yerina rushed out of the bakery as Brovdir helped Trinia put the last of her clothes on the cart. "You can't just *leave*!"

"The bakery is yours now, Yerina," Trinia said with a little laugh.

"I refuse to take it!" Yerina stomped her foot like a child. "I *refuse*."

Trinia snorted. "Well then, you'd better catch up to Headman Gerald and tell him not to write your name down when he takes mine off."

Yerina sputtered, went pale, clenched her fists.

And then dashed off toward the headman.

"Are you concerned?" Brovdir gave her hand a little squeeze.

"No," Trinia said with a hard breath. "She's a grown woman—older than me. She'll figure it out."

She walked over and stroked the bakery's doorframe. "I've made a lifetime of memories here. And I still have them."

Brovdir watched tensely as she came back to his side. She reached up to stroke his cheek, brushed her fingers over the scar at his throat.

"So much about our future is uncertain." She felt him swallow against her fingertips. "Everything is changing."

"Too much?" he asked.

She looked into the warmth of his eyes and took his hand. "No. Not too much. Not when we're together. The future the

Fades call forth could shake the foundation of our world, and it wouldn't matter. Because we'll stay stable, Brovdir. I know we will."

Delight flooded his features, and he lifted her off the ground. He kissed her with a passion she'd never known. And when they broke apart, she could still feel his strength deep in her chest. Thrumming and warm and as sure as the coming of spring.

"Let's go home and make new memories."

The End

AUTHOR NOTE

Thank you SO MUCH for reading Trinia and Brovdir's story! If you have a minute, please consider leaving a review. It means the world to me to have your support.

Looking for more from the Rove Woods?

Ready to read the love stories of Brovdir's warrior friends? Check out my novella offshoot series! These are cozy, steamy, stand-alones! Happy ever after guaranteed! Just Follow the QR code below.

Or maybe you want to read Iytier and Savili's story? Check out my FREE novella, The Orc Gardener's Strawberry! **Just sign up for my newsletter** and it's all yours. Follow the QR code below.

Or perhaps you want to see my characters *in action,* *wink wink* Follow the QR code below to go to my NSFW patreon! All the spiciest art is *free*!

Or possibly you'd like some swag or signed books? Follow the QR code below to check out my Etsy shop!

LET'S STAY IN TOUCH!

Use the QR code below to sign up for my newsletter on my website, www.AuroraWintersRomance.com and get monthly updates and exclusive art for my subscribers.

Or use the QR code below to follow me on Instagram @AuroraWinters.Romance. Where I post almost daily updates about my writing as well as character art and all kinds of other fun stuff.

About Aurora Winters

Growing up in the Pacific Northwest meant many rainy days spent on indoor activities and from a young age one of my favorites has been creative writing. I was penning monster romance stories in high school between classes before I even realized it was a genre and still have many of those original drafts. (Which will never, ever see the light of day again because they are truly cringe worthy!)

It was only recently that my writing grew from a personal hobby into a dream of publishing. When I'm not obsessing over my writing, I can be found wandering through the woods with my daughter and husband, taking pictures of pretty leaves, and throwing sticks for my little dog, Dash.

www.ingramcontent.com/pod-product-compliance
Lightning Source LLC
Chambersburg PA
CBHW020341310726
48979CB00015B/2459/J
* 9 7 8 1 9 6 3 5 5 2 1 6 4 *